Best Summer Ever

ALSO BY
JESSICA CUNSOLO

The With Me Series
She's With Me
Stay With Me
Still With Me
Be With Me
Belong With Me

Best Vacation Ever

Best Summer Ever

JESSICA CUNSOLO

wattpad books **w**

wattpad books **W**

An imprint of Wattpad WEBTOON Book Group

Copyright© 2025 Jessica Cunsolo

Published in Canada by Wattpad WEBTOON Book Group, a division of Wattpad WEBTOON Studios, Inc.

36 Wellington Street E., Suite 200, Toronto, ON M5E 1C7 Canada

www.wattpad.com

First Wattpad Books edition: June 2025

ISBN 978-1-99885-415-8 (Trade Paper original)
ISBN 978-1-99885-416-5 (eBook edition)

Library and Archives Canada Cataloguing in Publication information is available upon request.

Printed and bound in Canada

1 3 5 7 9 10 8 6 4 2

Cover design by Art of Nora
Typesetting by Delaney Anderson

To Nonno Mario

Tell them to go jump in the lake, is what you'd say when someone upset me, and I laughed every time I wrote that line, hearing it in your voice.

I love and miss you every day.

ONE

23 Days to Muskoka

Jenna

My best friend just announced that she hates me.

Okay, she didn't *actually* use those exact words, but she might as well have. She's sitting across from me, with her blond hair and big blue eyes that make her look like an angelic little doll; meanwhile, she's just torn my world in two.

"What do you *mean* you're moving to Newfoundland? That's like thirty hours away! In a completely different province. A completely different *time zone*!" The people at the tables next to us in the mall food court shoot us disapproving glares at my loud tone, so I pull myself together.

"I know. I'm sorry, Jenna," Elena says, fidgeting with her friendship bracelet, which matches the one on my wrist. "I know we were supposed to go to Western together in September, and I thought I'd take the safe route with their business degree, but right at the last minute I got the acceptance letter from Memorial University. For *marine biology*! Do you know how competitive that program is? I applied on a whim because my horoscope encouraged me to, and I got *in*."

And I'm proud of her. I know how hard she works and how much she studies; if anyone deserves to get into a competitive undergraduate program to be with the best of the best, it's Elena. But that means she'll be moving to practically the furthest point in Canada from me, and I'm not used to being separated from her.

We've been best friends for four years, since the very first day of ninth grade when our homeroom teacher called on her to read out loud in front of the class, and a girl named Faye snickered at the way Elena was stumbling over words. I threw an eraser at Faye's head, one of those hard pink rubber ones that rip up your paper instead of erasing anything. Elena gave me a grateful smile when I took over reading for her, and we've been inseparable ever since.

It's an effort to keep my tone conversational as I ask, "Why can't you just study marine biology at Western? Why do you have to go all the way to the other side of the country to do that?"

Elena's sigh is sad, like she knew that question was coming. "Western doesn't have a marine biology program, and even if they did, it would be *nothing* like what they offer at Memorial. Newfoundland is an *island*. I'll be getting real hands-on experience with fieldwork. I'll be on *boats*, Jenna! Out on the water! That's not possible here."

Fine. That's a valid point. But school starts in just over a month. "How long have you known about this? When did you accept?"

Her shoulders curl in. "April."

"April?" I shriek, practically jumping out of the chair before taking a deep breath and composing myself. When I speak again, it's low and controlled. "That was four months ago. You've known for four months that you aren't coming to school with me, and you're telling me *now*? The biggest reason I'm even going to Western is because we were going together."

"I know, I know, I'm sorry!" She holds her hands up, and I realize this is hard for her to confess, but it's getting increasingly hard for me to keep my emotions under control with every detail she discloses. We were supposed to go *together*. She inhales deeply before saying all in one breath, "Telling you made it real and I was putting it off until I couldn't anymore and you're throwing me this gorgeous birthday party tomorrow and I didn't want to think about how I'm ditching you but the guilt was eating at me and here we are."

So that explains why we woke up early and had a Jenna-and-Elena day. We got mani-pedis, then massages, then came to the mall for a shopping spree where she even bought me this adorable mini-dress because she said I just had to have it. She claimed the day was to prepare for her birthday tomorrow, but really she was buttering me up before punching me right in the chest.

"So you're really going to leave me?" I say, the words turning my stomach sour as they sink in.

"I'm not *leaving* you. I'm following my dream."

By leaving me, I repeat in my mind, but outwardly I keep my expression as neutral as I can. I've already let the surprise catch me off guard and make me more emotional than I should be. Even Elena is taken aback by how outwardly expressive I'm being, her wide eyes pinging every which way, unsure of what I'll say next.

"It's not like we won't talk every day." Elena rushes to smooth things over. "I'll be back for summers and breaks! Plus, we have all month to hang out and make the most of it while we can."

She bats her lashes at me, looking through them so hopefully, like I'll have an epiphany and suddenly realize this is the greatest thing to happen since the invention of brownies baked inside cookies. And because she looks so hopeful, and she's so excited about the program, and my abandonment issues aren't her problem, *and* I don't want to have an emotional breakdown in the middle of the food court, I contort my face into something that could pass for a smile.

"You're right. We'll always be friends. I'm happy for you."

She hears the tinge of harshness in my voice but smiles nonetheless. "We'll make this the best summer ever, you'll see. Me, you, and Martina will be so sick of each other by the end of the month you'll be glad we're leaving the province."

I don't argue with her, locking down all my emotions and ignoring the tension in my chest and the churning in my stomach. We're three best friends going to university in three different provinces in Canada. It was bad enough that Martina decided to go to Montreal for school, but being with Elena at Western softened the blow. Now I'll really be alone.

I can feel my mental shield go up, and with it the perfectly curated mask I always have in place. Instead of replying, I stuff the remains of my chicken wrap in the paper bag it came in, standing to collect the garbage. "I've got to go pick up the cake and some extra stuff for your party tomorrow. Ready to get going?"

She's not expecting anything more from me. Not a teary round of pleading or an intense round of questioning or a huge hugging makeup session. Visibly relieved that the composed Jenna she's used to is back, she hooks her arm through mine as we weave through the mall to the exit where we parked. I nod along as she excitedly chatters about how her daily horoscope said she'd reunite with old friends this weekend, which she surmises must be referring to her birthday party tomorrow, but I'm only half listening. Mentally, I'm thinking about all the changes that need to be made, all the shifting that needs to be done now that I'm going to university without my closest friend. I requested her as my roommate, but now they're going to put me with some random person. Maybe one of my other friends who's going to Western hasn't requested a roommate yet, and I can room with them.

The stab in my chest tells me that's a shit alternative. They're all just *kinda* friends, people I talk to and get along with but not people who make me feel the way I do when I'm with my inner circle. Maybe it's not too late to switch to U of T and be with my cousin Olivia. But she's already looking at places to rent with her boyfriend, and besides not wanting to be an awkward third wheel—and also the likelihood that a last-minute school transfer will be completely impossible—I hate Alessio.

The early August heat blasts us as soon as we leave the air-conditioned mall, and I slip on my sunglasses, searching for my car in the packed lot.

"Are the guys coming early tomorrow to help you set up the heavy backdrops?" Elena asks, releasing my arm to rummage through her purse for her keys. We had to take separate cars because I went to pick up these beautiful pink vintage serving trays I found on a pre-loved selling website, so I met her at the nail salon.

"Kyle and Fletcher are. Robbie's coming later to set up his equipment." Even with the sunglasses on, I can't meet her eyes, keeping my face forward and neutral.

"Perfect. I'll come with sushi for everyone before Martina starts on our makeup," Elena promises, finally grabbing her keys. "See you tomorrow!" She turns to walk backward away from me. "And have I told you lately how awesome you are? Because you are! *So* awesome. The *most* awesome. You won't even notice I'm not there with you at Western because everyone will be so blinded by your awesomeness, they won't leave you alone for even a second."

"Yeah, yeah. See you later." I wave her off, turning and stalking to my own car parked in the opposite direction from hers.

What she said isn't true. I let very few people in, and when I do, they have my complete trust, my complete loyalty. I spend more time with Elena, Martina, and the guys than I do with my own dad.

On those days where I'm surrounded by silence in my huge house because my dad is off networking or hard at work, my friends are the ones who bring me joy and laughter, who keep the darkness away.

I get to my car, slipping my hand behind the door handle and pulling, but it remains locked. I pull my hand away a bit then try again, waiting for the sensor to recognize my keys in my purse and automatically unlock. But it doesn't. I try again and again, but it remains stubborn, like it knows I'm already having a shit day and wants to contribute.

Pushing my sunglasses up on my head to keep my hair out of my face, I fish around in my purse for my keys, but I can't find them.

Shit. Did I lose my keys? Of course I lost my keys; why wouldn't this day keep getting worse?

I drop my shopping bags onto the asphalt to free up my hands then properly dig into my purse, pushing aside lip gloss and receipts and tampons, feeling the frustration and panic building with each passing second. My dad will kill me if I call him and say I'm stranded in the mall parking lot because I lost my keys. Dad's in Vancouver closing a huge sale and won't stop what he's doing to help, and that's *if* he even answers his phone. But when he finds out I've lost the keys to the BMW for the second time this summer, he *will* kill me. He may even take the car away, and I absolutely cannot have that. I need my car; it's my most important possession. Without it, I'm stuck at home, and if I'm stuck at home . . .

"Come on, you *stupid keys!*" I rage out loud, turning my purse and dumping its contents on the ground. Gum and change and pens and other useless things clatter to the ground, and I drop to my hands and knees to frantically search through the scattered pile. "You have to be hiding somewhere you motherfu—"

"Jenna?" asks a deep voice from behind me.

"What?" I yell, turning to whoever's unfortunate enough to

catch me in the middle of a meltdown. "Can't you see I'm in the middle of som—"

It's the coy smile I see first. Then the straight nose, the brown eyes, the dark eyebrows, the mess of deep-brown hair that has grown out past his ears. My heart beats hard in my chest at the instant recognition. Even though I haven't seen him in four years, I'd recognize him anywhere.

"Hari?" It's a question, but it comes out like an accusation. He pushes the hair out of his face with a masculine hand, and my eyes are drawn to it.

"Yeah." He smiles fully this time, amused, and I notice that the gap between his two front teeth that he always hated has been closed, leaving a perfect smile. "It's been a while. You look . . ." He trails off as he takes in the sight of me on my hands and knees, distraught and sweaty in front of a pile of tampons in the middle of a parking lot.

I take my time getting to my feet, dusting bits of rock and loose gravel from my hands and where they've dug into my bare knees, pretending I'm not checking him out during the process even though I totally am.

He's obviously older than the last time I saw him on the final day of eighth grade. Taller, with broader shoulders and a sharper jawline and large hands that have no business looking that hot—since when have I been attracted to *hands?*—and even though he's a man version of the boy I spent my preteen years hating, he's handsomer than I could've ever imagined. *Hotter* than I could've imagined. *All of the adjectives* more than I could've imagined. And that pisses me off to no end. How unfair is it that *Hari*, the horrible boy from grade school, gets to look like this?

I brace for the insult to come. *Stressed* or *disheveled* or *like a crazy lady yelling in the middle of the parking lot.*

He settles on finishing his statement with, "The same," which somehow still feels like an insult, and the way his lip tilts up at the corner is a dead giveaway that it totally was.

"Wish I could say the same for you," I reply, playing along with his *insult-them-by-not-outwardly-insulting-them* game. "You've . . . aged."

"Ah, yes. Aging. The thing that happens when you're no longer a scrawny prepubescent thirteen-year-old boy and are instead a high school graduate." The British accent is more prominent now that he's saying more than a few words. I forgot just how annoying it was.

That's a lie. It only makes him hotter, which makes me even more irritated.

"I think these were what you were scrambling for?" The hand I wasn't watching run through his hair holds out a set of keys with an oversized fluffy pink pompom dangling from them.

Relief washes over me, the panic at having to tell my dad dissipating into a distant nothingness.

Closing the distance between us, I pretend I don't notice how long and dark his eyelashes are, how smooth and clear his golden-brown skin is. "My keys! You've had them this whole time?"

When I reach for them, he lifts his hand to keep my keys just out of my reach. "No. I was parked over there when I saw someone who looked like the girl who once dumped her entire plate of spaghetti on me when I accidentally got gum in her hair." It wasn't an accident. He and his friends were snickering for weeks about how Hari had gone through with his dare, and I had to cut my hair to get the gum out. I spent the rest of seventh grade with a short bob I hated, which is ironic because now I wear my hair no longer than my shoulders. "Then I happened to see a giant, impractical pink pompom keychain land by that car over there. So in actuality, I *haven't* had your keys this whole time, just right now."

The agitation that arises every time I've talked to Hari is

back, and the fact that he's incredibly hot now doesn't soften it. "Give me my keys."

"Ah, good old Jenna. Still as bossy and demanding as ever."

I snatch my keys from his hand. "And you're still a know-it-all who goes out of his way to annoy people."

"Have you ever considered that maybe you're just easily annoyed?" he asks, still seeming incredibly amused and in no rush to leave me alone.

"By you? Yes." I cannot believe it's been four years since he's seen me, and *this* is the impression I'm leaving. I am always cool and put together—I never even have a chip in my nail polish—and now the boy I spent years arguing with saw me mid-meltdown. *Great fucking going, Jenna. Pull it together.*

As I slyly adjust my short sundress, I ask, "How long have you even been here?"

He crosses his arms and leans against my car, confirming my hunch that he's planning to stay a while. "In Canada? Since last week. Watching you curse out inanimate objects? Only a few minutes. Quite entertaining, actually."

If there were ever a time to be grateful for my ability to conceal my emotions, it's now. Getting me riled up was always a favorite pastime of Hari's, like a one-sided game that he treasured winning. So even though we're all grown up and Hari Virani doesn't matter anymore, I vow to keep my composure in front of him during any and all future interactions. I'm Jenna McAndrews, and I am *always* in control.

"*So* glad I could provide that entertainment for you," I say, and even though my words are laced with sarcasm, his grin still spreads.

"You're usually pretty entertaining, even when you're not trying. The way your face turns the most delightful shade of red when you're trying really hard not to yell at someone was always fascinating."

I will not yell at him. I will not yell at him. I will not—

"Ah, just like that! Still the exact same shade."

"My face does *not* turn *any* shade of red," I say, bending to gather my scattered belongings and chucking them back in my purse.

"Well, maybe not to the untrained eye. But I have an intimate history of testing Jenna McAndrews's patience. I know your 'about to lose my shit' face better than anyone, even if you're always trying so hard to be an emotionless robot."

His eyes are still as bright and attentive as always, accurately calling me out even though he hasn't been around in years. I need to change the subject immediately, especially before he notices the acne cream and extra-strength deodorant I'm trying to discreetly put back in my shopping bags. "So, you're back in Canada. Are you sticking around for a while?"

"Until the end of the summer, at least," he answers flippantly, like the indecision doesn't matter. "I'm not entirely sure what I'll do after that. I might go back to England; I might stay here."

Hari, *here*, where he can continue to run into me and get the upper hand in every encounter and make me lose my cool in the way only he can? "You should go back to England."

He huffs a surprised laugh, but a ringing phone cuts off his response.

Hari reaches into his back pocket. "I've got to take this."

"Don't worry about coming back," I reply as he turns to answer the call, giving me a moment to compose myself.

Hastily, I swipe under my lips to check for rogue lip gloss and stick my hands down the top of my dress to try to help my non-existent cleavage. He glances back at me, and I instantly drop my hands, smiling casually at him like I wasn't just trying to mash my boobs together. If I'm going to see my annoying grade school rival for the first time in years, I'm going to look hot, dammit!

He shoves the phone back in his pocket. "That was Kyle Barnes. Remember him from school? We remained in touch after I moved away. I'm on my way to meet him for lunch. He just let me know he was running late due to traffic."

I'm going to kill Kyle. How could he not tell me Hari was back, *and* he's been friends with him this whole time? But then again, Kyle's oblivious and never knew how often Hari and I butted heads, and it's not like I have any reason to need the heads-up. So I guess I can't kill Kyle even though an irrational part of me still wants to.

"Oh yeah, Kyle's great," I say, standing up with my purse and bags.

Hari's had a growth spurt sometime in the last four years, because I used to be taller than him, but now at 5'9", I have to look up a bit to meet his eyes. We're standing closer together than we were before.

"He's actually invited me to a party tomorrow. I thought it would be weird if I showed up since people might wonder who the strange Indian kid is, but he said hundreds of kids will be there. You going?"

Okay, now I *really* want to kill Kyle, but I keep my tone neutral when I answer, "Yes, I'll be there. It's my house and my party."

This information seems to delight Hari to no end, his face lighting up as he says, "How interesting. I guess I'll see you tomorrow then."

I can't tell him to stay home or he'll know how much he's affected me. He's waiting for it, *itching* for the outburst to come like when he'd finally cracked my perfectly practiced composure in elementary school. But I'm older now and have had a lot more experience pulling up my mental shield. So I paste on the fakest smile I can manage and say, "Can't wait."

TWO

22 Days to Muskoka

Olivia

I duck just before a full can of beer flies by my head and smashes through the kitchen window. The noise of the shattering glass is drowned out by the sounds of the party as well as by the huge speakers blasting an interesting remix of a metal song and a top 40 pop song.

"Oh shit!" shouts Fletcher, a giant seventeen-year-old with fiery red hair and freckles dotting his pale skin. He's a few feet away from me, staring in disbelief at the pair of boys in matching pink football jerseys responsible for the incident. The one with a pink baseball cap still has his arms raised as if he was supposed to catch the hurtling beer can that almost took my head off. Fletcher points at them. "You almost killed Olivia! This is why you weren't invited."

"And it's why he didn't make a single college football team," the one with the pink hat says.

"No way, you moved!" his friend exclaims, reaching into the large pink ice bucket on the second kitchen island and pulling out another can. "Let me try again."

Fletcher's eyes widen, but now that the shock has worn off, I snap into action. "No!" Stepping into the space between them, I hold my arms out like I can telepathically stop them from moving. "No throwing anything! You already broke the window. Go outside so I can clean up the mess."

"Better idea, you're out of here," Fletcher says, signaling to some other guys who step forward to help escort the drunk guys out.

"No, wait, we'll be good!" they protest, but the guys keep pushing them out of the kitchen. "We didn't mean to, Olivia, promise!" They don't know me, and I don't know them, so I don't respond, instead grabbing a broom and dustpan, ushering people away from the mess and into the yard where crowds are gathered in a sea of pink.

Jenna loves parties, but more than that, she loves *throwing* parties. She's good at it too. No matter where you look, everything is aesthetically pleasing, cohesive, on theme, and most importantly for everyone's social media, photographable. Today's party theme is Fifty Shades of Pink, specifically requested by Elena for her birthday, and the dress code is being enforced. How Jenna managed to get all two hundred and something kids at this party to show up wearing pink is anyone's guess, but when she wants something done, she gets it done.

I clean up the mess then direct the caterers to set up on the further kitchen island and the decorated folding tables Jenna has out for the finger foods. She left a very detailed graphic of where she wants everything, so I leave them alone and venture outside to look for my boyfriend. He hasn't answered my last few texts asking him where he is, so he must have let his phone die again or accidentally dropped it in the pool. It's annoying but so like him. If I didn't remind him to tie his shoes or that his car payments are due on the fifteenth, he'd be walking everywhere in socks.

Robbie has his DJ equipment set up on the far end of the patio, overlooking the backyard. He doesn't look up from his laptop when I step over abandoned cans and pink cups to join him. He's bobbing his head to the beat, his short dreadlocks flowing with the movement.

"Robbie?" I call, tapping him on the shoulder.

He pulls an oversized headphone away from one ear and scans me from head to toe. "Don't tell me . . . Olivia, right? Jenna's cousin? The one who's really smart?"

It's an effort not to huff. "Yes, that's right." We've met and hung out multiple times before, since he's one of Jenna's closest friends, but I don't say that part out loud in case it comes off as haughty. "Have you seen Alessio around? You've got the best vantage point."

"Hmm . . . I think he was by the pool earlier." He doesn't ask me to clarify who Alessio is, even though Alessio's a year older and therefore was never in any classes with him, *and* he's met him the same number of times he's met me. Apparently, I'm the only forgettable one.

"Great, thanks," I say as he gives me a thumbs-up and slips his headphones back on. I check my phone again for a text, but my notifications remain blank, and my patience begins to wear thin.

I've been here for a few hours, and he said he'd be here, yet I haven't even caught a glimpse of him.

It's been almost three weeks since I've seen Alessio. First, he went on a weeklong trip to Cuba with his friends. But he's been back for two weeks now, and he's always too busy to see me, or sick with the flu, or working overtime. In all the years we've been together, this is almost triple the amount of time we've gone without seeing each other.

I miss him. It feels like we've been talking less and less over text and the phone than we were before he left for his trip, and I can feel his absence in almost everything I do. I can't even turn on the television for fear of accidentally seeing a spoiler for one of the many shows we watch together. He promised me he'd be here tonight and we'd *finally* be able to reunite. I'm so excited, I even had my sister do some pink sparkly eyeshadow for me that she said makes my brown eyes go from plain to sultry. But the longer the night goes on without seeing him, the more the unease churns in my stomach.

Jenna's pool area usually looks like an oasis straight from a travel brochure advertising vacationing in Greece, but it's hard to tell today. People are everywhere, and I briefly wonder if Jenna, or even the birthday girl, knows them all. Maybe they do. Jenna was very popular in school, and for all I know this is her entire graduating class, enjoying their last few weeks of summer before starting college in the fall.

I swear I see a hint of Alessio's dirty-blond hair, but before I can get there, a girl in neon pink jeans stumbles into my path. She knocks over a potted plant, soil spilling everywhere, then grabs the one beside it before knocking it over as well. She grabs a third one, bends over, and pukes right inside it.

I can't in good conscience just *leave* her there, so I run over to her, pulling her long hair out of her face and helping her to stand. When I glance back to where I thought I saw Alessio, whoever it was is no longer there. *Shit.*

I get the girl, whose name I can't decipher through her mumbles and the noise of the fireworks that start going off, inside to the bathroom. As I help her start to get cleaned up, a group of her friends come rushing in, taking over for me.

By the time I run back to the pool, I don't see Alessio anywhere, and my heart sinks. I try texting him again, but it's just another in a chain of unanswered messages tonight.

My younger sisters, identical twins who are far closer to each other than they've ever been to me, are sitting with a group of people on a cluster of lounge chairs. I have to dodge a total of five different drunk but still coherent people staggering around before I finally make it to them. Bianca notices me first.

"Liv! I made a new drink! Come try." She holds a pink plastic cup out to me, and I give her a concerned frown. Her hazel eyes are glassy, and she's slurring just the tiniest bit, not noticeable to outsiders but enough that Maddalena elbows her and whispers, "Be cool."

"You're sixteen, Bianca. You're lucky Mom even let you come."

"Way to give us away, Bianca," Maddalena mutters under her breath at the same time Bianca says, "Come on, Liv, you're only a year older than us. Don't be such a party pooper. I bet you haven't had any fun all night. You've probably been so busy being 'party mom' you haven't had a single drop of alcohol or made any friends."

My sisters both look so disappointed in me, like I'm the one who's doing something wrong, and I can't stand the way they share a disapproving glance like they've discussed this before.

"I'm not a party pooper, see?" I grab the drink that Bianca offered and take a large gulp. It burns the whole way down, like gasoline mixed with cinnamon and the hottest peppers from our nonno's garden, and I choke on it. It takes everything in me not to immediately spit it out.

"What the hell is in that?" I sputter, wiping my mouth with the back of my hand.

Bianca smiles widely. "Four shots of Patrón, a shot of Fireball, and a splash of pineapple juice."

My throat still feels like it's on fire as I shake my head at her. "This is going to kill you, and I'm trying to find Alessio. I don't have time to take care of you when you die from alcohol poisoning."

"Hey!" she cries as I dump the murder juice in the bushes behind them, emptying every last drop from the cup.

"Go get some water," I order, and as she marches to a pink cooler, she mumbles, "This is why you don't have any friends."

Even though she's drunk and I know she doesn't mean it, her words sting. Trying not to let the hurt show on my face, I look at the sober twin. "Have you seen Alessio?"

Maddalena shrugs. "He was with Dylan a while ago over by the cabana." The cabana that's currently filled with people who *aren't* my boyfriend and his best friend. With a grumble, she adds, "He didn't even say hi to us. The jerk."

"He must not have seen you. He needs glasses, and his appointment is in a few weeks. That reminds me, I have to remind him a few days before." Another mental item in the never-ending list of things I need to keep track of for Alessio. Sometimes I feel like I'm his secretary or his mother rather than his girlfriend, and it causes irritation to burn through me before I push the feeling down and remind myself that he does things for me too.

Maddalena raises an eyebrow and gives me a patronizing, "Mm-hmm. Of course you do."

I check my phone again, the empty notification center making my heart sink a little more. "It's been three weeks since we've seen each other in person. FaceTime just isn't the same. Why is it so hard to find him?" Granted, Jenna lives in a sprawling mansion with more acreage than five football fields, and there are tons of partygoers here all wearing the same color, but still. He should be trying to find *me* just as hard as I'm trying to find him.

Maddalena huffs like she does when she's run out of patience and is trying really hard not to snap. "You're smart, Liv. So smart you skipped fourth grade—could've skipped more if Mom and Dad weren't worried about it stunting your social development. You started university at sixteen and just finished your first year while everyone else your age is graduating high school. You do research for fun, and you spend every spare second tinkering away on that app you're creating. So I *know* you're not actually ignorant about what's going on here."

Heaviness surges through my chest, the same feeling that settles there in the late hours of the night while I'm lying in bed, staring at my phone with its unanswered voice mails and proof of canceled plans.

I'm not ignorant about what's going on. But we've been together for five years, ever since we started dating in the ninth grade. Sometimes Alessio knows me better than I know myself, like knowing when I'm going to give myself a headache from eating too much chocolate or that I left my study notes in the refrigerator when I'm running around panicking that I've misplaced them. We may have had some small disagreements before he went on his trip, but our relationship is solid, so much so that we're going to live together for our second year at school—which reminds me, I have to email our landlady about our deposits. All these facts help push out any doubts, reminding me that I can't go jumping to conclusions without even seeing him.

To my pessimistic sister, I say, "I won't know anything until I talk to him, and neither can you."

I glance back at the cabana, and like saying his name earlier summoned him, there's Dylan, playing beer pong against his friend Ray.

"Take care of Bianca!" I shout over my shoulder before rushing over to Dylan. It feels like Alessio and I have been missing each other all night, and this is my first solid lead.

"Dylan!" I call, and he turns suddenly, the pink plastic cup balancing on his head for Ray's trick shot falling, soaking him in beer. Dylan jumps at getting drenched unexpectedly, but he doesn't yell at me for distracting him; instead, he laughs, shaking the liquid from his arms.

"Livy! Hey! I haven't seen you in forever." I haven't seen Alessio or *any* of his friends since they all went to Cuba. I didn't realize how lonely that made me feel until just now, when Dylan holds out his arms and threatens to pull me into a soaking wet hug.

I squeal, laughing as I dodge him. "You reek of cheap beer."

"I'm covered in cheap beer." He smiles in that easygoing way that's so natural for him, the way that makes it almost impossible for girls in loving relationships to ignore how hot he is. The soaked pink T-shirt stretched over his broad shoulders and sculpted biceps isn't helping, either, and I force my eyes to his face.

"I got one for you," Dylan starts, trying to be serious. "How many bones do sharks have?"

I pretend to think for a second, only to make him feel better about not being able to stump me with this trivia question. "Zero."

"Damn, you're right," he says, not looking upset in the slightest. "I thought I'd finally get you with that one."

"You'll have to try harder than using a classic beginner trivia question then."

He laughs, throwing a slick arm over my shoulder. "Well, I was shocked when I heard that. I mean, they're *sharks*! How do they not have any bones?" He releases me when I push his arm off me with a laugh, and his dark eyes shine. "Be my beer pong partner? Ray's losing anyway."

"Am not!" Ray protests from the other side of the table, but we both ignore him.

"Maybe another time. I'm looking for Alessio. Have you seen him?"

A look crosses Dylan's face, almost like he sobers up for a brief second before recovering. "Alessio?" He casually takes a step away from me and picks up his beer can from the table, though he doesn't make a move to drink from it. "Yeah, he's, uh, somewhere, though I haven't seen him recently."

I frown at him. Didn't Maddalena just say he and Alessio were here at the cabana together only a short while ago?

I glance back at my sisters. Bianca's pouting at a water bottle in her hands, but Maddalena's watching me. She raises a perfectly arched eyebrow, and I can practically hear her cynicism from here.

Dylan tells someone to take over for him at beer pong, and his hand presses against the small of my back as he guides me out of the way. "You okay, Livy?" he asks as he drops his hand.

I study Dylan, considering my options. He's always been a good friend to me. He's known me since the fifth grade when I started at a new school as the weird younger kid who raised her hand for every question. I've seen him grow through the awkward, gangly-limbed stage to the tall, confident man he is today. Watched as the one small tattoo he got to pay homage to his French-Canadian and Jamaican heritages transformed into the full sleeve he now wears with pride. He may now be Alessio's friend before he's mine, but Alessio met him through me, and if I ask Dylan a question, I trust him to be honest with me.

"What's going on with Alessio?" I ask him directly instead of dancing around it. "He's been avoiding me for weeks. Does he . . . does he not want to be with me anymore?"

It's hard to get out the last words, and Dylan's eyes soften.

"What? Olivia, don't be ridiculous. Alessio is *crazy* about you. The man literally couldn't even tie his shoes without you."

"Well then, did something happen while you guys were in Cuba?"

Something dark and unreadable passes through his eyes. "If it did, then he'd be the biggest fucking idiot in the world."

That only gives me the tiniest bit of relief, but it's not enough to squash the building worry. "But *did* something happen?"

His jaw tightens for the briefest of moments before that carefree Dylan smile is back. "Alessio's being a dick to everyone because of his new internship. I told him if he can't handle a summer internship, paid or not, there's no way he's going to make it in the real world.

He'll pull his head out of his ass eventually. You didn't do anything wrong."

Those words help lift the weight from my chest, but just to put my worries at rest, I ask, "You swear?"

"Would I ever lie to you?"

I blow out a breath, and with it, all my reservations. "You're right, I'm just overreacting and missing him. Thanks, Dyl."

He looks like he wants to say something more, but before he can, Jenna appears out of nowhere. She's wobbling a bit and looks slightly disheveled but still manages to look model gorgeous like always.

She grabs my arm and says, "Sorry, Dylan, I need to steal my cousin."

She doesn't wait for his response before pulling me away to a more private section of her yard, farthest away from the speakers.

"What's going on?" I ask. "I haven't seen you all night." Not that that's unusual at one of her parties. She's always off running around having fun. Earlier, she was one of the people dancing on a table when it broke, and I moved all the debris so no one got hurt while she went inside to serve guests edible pink glitter Jell-O shots.

"You'll never believe who's here!" she says, her icy blue eyes hazy, and I realize that she's drunk.

"Are you dr—"

"Hari is here!" she exclaims in a half whisper, eyes darting around conspiratorially like it's some big secret.

"Hari?"

"Hari *Virani*," she emphasizes, like it will help me read her mind.

At my blank look, she sighs dramatically. "Come on, Liv. You have to remember Hari. We had every class with him until you transferred. The guy with the sexy British accent." She slaps her hands against her mouth like she said something she wasn't supposed to. "I mean *annoying*. His annoying British accent. The alcohol has got me mixing up words."

That detail triggers my memory. "Ohh. *That* Hari." Most of our summer nights at twelve and thirteen years old were spent bundled up in sleeping bags and tents at Jenna's cottage, where she'd rant for *hours* about how awful Hari was. "Actually, saying it's a *British accent* is technically imprecise. He wouldn't have a *British* accent; he'd have a cockney accent or a Yorkshire accent or—"

"He has whatever British accent the hot guys who play princes in those steamy historical romance movies you force me to watch have," she cuts me off, annoyed, this time not catching her implication that the accent is hot. "But that's not important right now. What's important is that he's here at my house, walking around, most likely talking shit about me to all these people and just waiting for the opportunity to corner me and make me feel stupid and weak." She glares at the open expanse of partygoers as if directing her rage at the boy she can't even see. "Maybe I should hook up with Cooper. He beat out Hari for the eighth-grade soccer captain, and I *know* it still kills Hari inside. If Hari sees that, he'll definitely leave me alone all night, and Cooper is hot, he'd be a good distraction. I could use a good distraction."

"You need the distraction, huh?" I ask, and she nods, her short hair bobbing at the movement. I pull the strands that got caught in her shiny lip gloss away from her face. "Maybe you should sober up before making a decision like that? Especially since it's only been a couple months since you broke up with Adam."

Adam, who's one of Alessio and Dylan's best friends. Adam, whom Dylan and I grew up with. Adam, who introduced me to Alessio once we started high school. Adam, who dated Jenna for two years before they broke up at her high school graduation.

"Psh, that was, like, forever ago." Jenna waves me off.

"But still—"

"Olivia," she interrupts me for the umpteenth time. She puts a hand on my shoulder, and since she's practically a runway model, height and all, she has to duck her head to look in my eyes. "This may be hard for you to understand, because these days you seem to hate all forms of fun unless your boyfriend specifically instructs you to *have* fun, but people are actually allowed to do whatever they want. I don't need permission from anyone. You know I hate giving up control, unlike you."

My stomach churns at her tone. "What's that supposed to mean?"

She drops her hand and steps back. "It means Alessio says *jump* and you say off which cliff? Your life doesn't have to revolve around him, Liv. I bet you've spent all night doing whatever he wants and getting him food and making sure he's comfortable, while I just saw him playing strip poker in the living room and having a grand old time." Her words are a punch in the gut, but she doesn't notice. She sticks out her other hand, which is holding a sweating can. "Now, take this vodka cooler—it's mango, your favorite—and try to have some fun at my party."

She shoves the open drink into my chest, and I'm forced to take it. There's a ring of her pink lip gloss on the lip of the can, but it's mostly full.

"I'm going to flirt with Cooper and try to pretend the annoying British guy isn't here. Go have fun," she commands, then she's gone. I stare after her for a few seconds before I head inside.

Jenna is a lot of things, unrelenting, dominating, loyal to a fault, and sometimes intimidating to people who don't know her, but she never says things just to hurt people. Is that what people think of me? That I'm Alessio's pathetic, overly doting girlfriend? That can't be true. That's just drunk Jenna saying things she doesn't *entirely* mean.

She's always been so independent, so used to locking down her emotions, so of course to her, a relationship like mine and Alessio's doesn't make sense. Even when she was dating Adam, they acted like two individuals instead of a couple.

In the living room, there *is* a game of strip poker going on, and I have to commend the players for sticking with the pink theme all the way down to their undergarments, but Alessio isn't here. Annoyed, I head back into the kitchen. Everyone at this party has seen my boyfriend except me. He's *here*, and his first thought wasn't, *Hey, let me find my girlfriend who I haven't seen in weeks?* I shouldn't have to run around and beg my own boyfriend to see me instead of playing beer pong or strip poker or whatever else he's doing.

My stomach growls, and I dump Jenna's drink down the sink before throwing the can in the recycling bin and grabbing a pink plastic plate. I didn't realize how late it's gotten and that I haven't had anything to eat all night. Most of the food has been ravaged already, but there are two slices of pizza left. *And* they happen to be my favorite: Hawaiian. Maybe my luck is turning around.

Just as I grab a napkin, Kyle bounds into the kitchen, practically shaking the floor.

"Good, more pizza!" Kyle exclaims, grabbing both slices in one large hand. He sees me standing there and pauses. "Oh, Olivia. You didn't want these, right?"

My stomach growls in protest as I say, "No, they're all yours."

"Awesome. It's so good, this is like my twentieth slice," he says before shoving them both in his mouth practically in one go as I set my sad, empty plate back down.

I should just go home and call it a night. It's well past midnight, but it's not too late to crawl into bed with a pack of mini chocolate cupcakes and finish my book about coding and programming. I'd much rather be doing that than be here, annoyed, alone, and hungry. If Alessio doesn't want to see me, fine. I tried all night, and he couldn't bother to seek me out or answer his phone, so I'm not going to waste more time trying to chase him down.

I text my sisters to let them know I'm ordering an Uber in case they want to come home with me, but before I order it, my phone pings with a text.

It's Alessio. *Finally.*

> Got to Jenna's late and got wayyyyy too drunk trying to make up time. Took an Uber home. Didn't want you to see me like this. I'm sorry.

Pissed, I exit out of the conversation without replying and confirm my own Uber to take me home.

THREE

21 Days to Muskoka

Jenna

Elena, Martina, and I wake up equally hung over. At least I had the good sense to wash my makeup off before collapsing in bed. The pillow Elena used in the spare room across the hall has an exact imprint of her face made of makeup, and Martina woke up in the bed next to her with pink sparkles all the way up her face and into her hairline.

I'm not exactly sure what time the party was over, but I do know that by the time Robbie, Fletcher, and Kyle did a final sweep of the property and house to kick out all the stragglers, the sun was practically peeking over the horizon.

The three boys sleep well past noon in the other spare rooms, only waking when they smell the food we ordered, thundering down the stairs like starved men who've never tasted a hamburger before.

Martina sinks into her seat at the patio table, putting her hand against the side of her face like she can block the sight of them. "Oh great, I forgot *Fletcher* slept over."

"Don't be so dramatic," Elena says, swirling her fry in ketchup.

"So what? You got drunk and made out with him last night. It doesn't mean you have to marry the guy."

"Tell him that," Martina mumbles as the guys join us, pulling up chairs and making the table feel infinitely smaller than it did before.

"Martina Perez, good morning, or I guess, good afternoon." Fletcher grins as he drops into the seat beside her. He's huge, easily towering over her with his knees practically hitting the underside of the table. "*Muy hermosa hoy vez tu.*"

Martina rolls her eyes. "That was terrible Spanish. And I look beautiful *every* day."

He's undeterred by her chilly exterior, his grin growing wider. "Don't I know it!"

They grab their takeout and dig in, and it's a good thing Martina ordered more than we thought we needed, because the bags are practically licked clean and not a crumb remains. We chat about the party in the mid-afternoon sun, and when it's time for them to leave, I wave at them from the front door before heading back inside.

Despite my drunken proclamation to my cousin, I didn't, in fact, end up making out with Cooper to get a rise out of Hari. I realized doing so would make me admit that I *care* about what Hari thinks and that he holds some kind of power over me, and since I both don't care and he *doesn't* hold any power over me, I decided to have fun as if he wasn't there at all and enjoy my party. So that's what I did; dancing on tables with Martina; setting off fireworks with Kyle; pressing buttons on Robbie's turntable, not caring that I had no idea what they did, all the while pretending I couldn't hear Hari's obnoxious laugh or the way people clamored for his attention, all enamored by his stupid accent and stupid stories and stupid, annoyingly handsome face.

—

I'm spreading some peanut butter on toast for dinner when my dad crosses the kitchen threshold, still in his perfectly fitting designer suit.

"Hey, when did you get in?" I ask. I didn't hear anyone in the house from my room.

He pulls a mineral water from the fridge, taking a sip. "Not long ago. I've been in my office getting some last-minute paperwork done or I would've come to find you earlier."

"Have you eaten? We could order some food, and you can tell me how your trip went. Let me grab some takeout menus. I stashed some over here for wh—"

"Jenna, sweetheart," Dad cuts me off, and I realize his black hair, just as dark and shiny as mine, has been freshly styled back. "I'm going for drinks with some colleagues in a few hours to celebrate closing on both the penthouse and the lake house. But I'll leave you my card, just order whatever you want for yourself."

I instantly deflate. "Yeah, sure, okay."

He gestures with his bottle to the window behind me that's been boarded up until the company can come to fix it. "Looks like it was a fun party. Is that the only damage?" The cleaners he hired came shortly after my friends left, and by the time they finished, minus the window, you'd never know there was even a party here.

"The wooden table in the back broke too. Some kids"—*and* I—"were dancing on it."

"Anyone hurt?"

I shake my head, and he hums his approval. "I guess Elena had a good birthday then. But you know you can't be throwing these kinds of parties in your dorm."

"Elena's actually . . ." I shift, trying not to think too hard about it. "She's not coming to Western anymore. She's going to Memorial in Newfoundland, so we won't be roommates."

"Newfoundland, huh? That's, uh . . . far away." He scratches his chin and clears his throat a few times, doing that uncomfortable Dad thing he does when he doesn't know how to handle an important life moment, like when I got my period for the first time, or when I broke up with my boyfriend of two years. Both times he shoved his credit card at me and told me to buy whatever I wanted, then ran to hide in his office. "At least you'll get your own room now, and maybe you'll be more focused on your grades. You'll need good ones to get into law school. You know your mom went to Western's law school, and if you stay there, you'll be in the same lecture halls she was in, maybe even have the same professors she did."

I'll never forget that Mom did law school at Western, especially since Dad brings it up every time the university's name is mentioned.

"I don't think I'll get the room to myself. The university will probably put me with someone else." Someone who's *not* my best friend. They could be the worst person in existence, someone who clips their toenails on my bed or cuts my hair while I sleep, and I'd be trapped in a tiny room with them all year.

"That means new friends, new beginnings." He smiles easily, then grows serious. "Speaking of new beginnings, I have some news. I didn't want to share until everything was finalized, and it looks like now is the time. Let's sit."

He points to the kitchen table, and I follow, incredibly confused.

We never *ever* sit at this kitchen table together. It's a beautiful custom-made walnut table that Dad's interior designer picked, and it's more for show than anything else. We usually eat at different times: I eat alone at the kitchen island while he eats in his office when he doesn't go out or eat at work.

Dad sits on one side of the table, and I drop into the seat across from him. My mind reels, wondering what he has to say that's so important that we need to sit here, and suddenly I remember the last time he told me to sit in order to share news. It was a snowy day, I was eleven years old, and he told me Mom had died. It was the first and last time I ever saw him cry, though for months, every time her name was brought up he would teeter on the edge of a breakdown. I was always better than him at putting on a brave face, taking the casseroles from well-meaning neighbors, giving the speech at the funeral, and thanking people for their condolences, even though it felt like my heart had been stabbed and I couldn't take a full breath.

With this in mind, I ask, "Did someone die?"

Dad's eyebrows shoot up. "What? No one died. I have good news."

Relief replaces the worry squeezing my chest. "Tell me."

"So bossy," he says with a laugh. "I'm opening up a second real estate firm."

That explains all the late nights, the phone calls, the unplanned trips—or at least, it explains why all those things have been more frequent than usual this past year. "Wow, that's great. Congratulations. When does it open?"

"Next month," Dad admits, waiting a moment before adding, "in Vancouver."

"Vancouver?" I repeat. It makes sense. Dad deals with a lot of high-profile clients and properties, and a lot of them are in Vancouver anyway. It's a logical step.

"It's all ready to go. I've signed all the paperwork, have the office space, and already got all my clients set up," he explains, giving me that charming realtor smile that gets people to buy multimillion-dollar properties. "And Vancouver is beautiful. I'm closing a deal on my own house right now. The room you'll stay in when you visit has a perfect view of the mountains."

What does he mean the room I'll stay in when I visit?

When I stare at him with a blank look on my face, he adds, "I've already sold this house, and the new owners take possession August twenty-third, so we'll have to start packing up. Three weeks will fly before we know it."

Wait, wait, wait. He *sold the house*? When? How did I not know this? There was no sign on the front lawn, no house tours or showings that I know of. I didn't see anyone poking around my room or underwear drawer.

I wait for him to tell me that he's joking, that this is just an elaborate prank to teach me a lesson about throwing parties or something, but no such relief comes.

"You sold the house?" I ask, trying my very hardest to ignore the ball of anxiety that forms in my chest. "And we're moving to Vancouver?"

Dad's eyebrows draw together. "I'm moving to Vancouver. You're going to Western."

This is the second time I've been ambushed at a table in the last two days, and like the first time with Elena, I feel like I'm going to be sick.

I must let the mask drop for a second, because Dad rushes to add, "I know you love this house, sweetheart, but there's no point in keeping it." I have no attachments to this house. I couldn't care *less* about this huge show house we've only lived in for a few years; in fact, if he's not here, I crash with Olivia or Martina or Elena, but I don't correct him. "You're going to be living on campus for four years, and then law school, and I'll be in Vancouver. Carlos is going to take care of the firm here, so I can focus all my attention on growing the new one." So he's letting his business partner stay here, but he's got to move? "Plus, I needed the money from this house to help with the costs that come with my new venture. Selling it was for the best."

This is *not good*. Not good. This is too big of a problem for me to ignore, too big to fit in the handy box of problems that I keep tucked in the darkest corner of my mind. He's leaving me, and now instead of being a few hours away, he'll be *several provinces* away, and I'll be stuck on campus all by myself without a real home. And sure, my friends are moving away anyway, but they'll be back here on holidays and during the summers, and I won't. I'm going to be stuck in *London, Ontario* for a minimum of four years. I won't even get to see my cousins.

My body breaks out in a cold sweat, and my chest tightens so much it's almost painful, but still, I keep it together.

My throat is dry when I ask, "When do we have to be out again?"

"August 23, and I'm catching my flight that night," Dad says, pulling out his phone when it pings with a text. "So you'll need to move into your dorm a week earlier than planned."

I force myself to breathe, to be calm, to pretend like none of this is a big deal, like I'm still in control.

"But my birthday is the twenty-fourth. I was supposed to throw my big birthday bash."

"You'll have plenty of other birthdays, sweetheart," Dad responds, but he's not really paying attention; instead, he's reading something on his phone.

No birthday bash, I'll lose my last week with my friends before we all go our separate ways, and I'll have to move into a new place all by myself. That is not going to work for me, not at all.

"How about the cottage?" I ask, grateful for the sudden epiphany. "I can stay there instead of moving in earlier, throw my party there too." It's a brilliant solution, so brilliant I wish I had thought of it originally. A whole week with my friends, a week so great they can't possibly forget about me, can't fathom not keeping in touch with me when they meet their cool new college friends.

Dad looks up from his phone, his forehead creasing as he frowns.

"I'm moving to Vancouver, Jenna. That means I'm selling *everything*. Including the cottage. I've already listed it."

We're selling the cottage? *My* cottage? The place where I've spent every summer since I can remember? The cottage that Mom fell in love with the second we pulled up to tour it and just had to have? We've had it longer than we've lived in any of our other houses, this one included, and it's the one property of ours where I actually enjoy spending time. I was there last weekend with Olivia, Bianca, Maddalena, and Aunt Eloise. We ate Maddalena's horrible tofu burgers and laughed at the ridiculous sunburn lines Bianca got on her back. And three weeks before that, I was there with Elena and Martina for Canada Day weekend, where we huddled in thick blankets on the dock to watch the fireworks. I even go there in the winter when the roads aren't too bad, and the guys will light a bonfire while the rest of us run, freezing and squealing, to the hot tub. This is all too much too fast. Everything is changing, and there's nothing I can do about it. Everyone is leaving me like it's the easiest thing in the world to do and I don't matter at all.

The anger and frustration finally break free, and I don't bother reining it in. "You can't sell the *cottage!*" I jump up, so upset I'm practically shaking. "It's the cottage! You can't just do that! Especially not without telling me!"

Dad's completely taken aback. "Get a hold of yourself, Jenna. Throwing a tantrum at news you don't like isn't any way to conduct yourself, and it's especially not behavior befitting a future lawyer. You think your mother would've gotten anything done in court if she reacted like that?"

Mom would *never* have let Dad sell the cottage in the first place. But he's right, and I take a deep breath, locking down my emotions as I sink back into my chair.

"I'm sorry, I was just caught off guard." Like I was at the food court with Elena's news. What is with the people closest to me ambushing me with life-changing news lately? Calmer, I ask, "Can't we keep the cottage? Don't you need a place to stay when you come back here?"

"If I ever need to come back, I'll get a hotel, or maybe your aunt and uncle will let me stay with them. But let's face it, neither of us will have time to enjoy the cottage anymore, and I could use the money. University and law school aren't cheap, and that's extra money I can use toward my loans and lines of credit and your trust fund. Selling the cottage makes sense."

He's really going to sell the cottage. He's selling everything that's tying him to Ontario—to me—and never looking back.

"Then let me throw one last cottage week with my friends. It's the last time we'll be together before we go away to school. It'll be an end-of-high-school party, my birthday, a farewell to our teenage years before officially becoming adults, and a goodbye to the cottage all in one."

Dad shakes his head. "Absolutely not, Jenna. The property is valued at fourteen million dollars right now, and I've got buyers interested, so it needs to be in pristine condition at all times for last-minute viewings."

"It can just be a week—"

He stands, cutting me off before I can even make my case. "You're not having people at the cottage, never mind a weeklong party. Look at what happens when you throw a party." He gestures to the window, and I can't even argue with him because he has a point. But it's never been an issue before—he's never cared, and everything has always been fixed right away. "I've already had all our personal belongings at the cottage packed up and stored in the garage, so there's no reason for us to go at all. Besides, school should be your priority right now." He pulls out his wallet, plucking out a credit card and placing it on the table in front of me. "I'm going to be late for my dinner. Why don't you order something for yourself, maybe even start on your back-to-school shopping?" He doesn't wait for a reply, tucking in his chair and heading to the front door. "Don't wait up."

His phone rings as he walks to the door, and he laughs and turns on the charm with whoever he's talking to. If I were to guess, judging by the warm tone and the confident lilt in his voice, it's a client, or more specifically a client selling a seven-figure property.

The front door closes, then he's gone, and I'm left sitting at the table in shock, staring at the no-limit credit card that he always gives me when he wants to run away from a conversation. But the longer I sit there, the faster the shock turns to betrayal, then betrayal turns to anger, and soon I'm so pissed a fingernail snaps off where I'm gripping the table.

He's picking up and leaving me behind like it's no big deal, like it doesn't matter that he may not see me for approximately seven years while I'm in school. He doesn't even seem to *care*. He said it was good news. *It's a good thing I'm leaving Jenna behind. It's a good thing I don't have to deal with her anymore.*

Everyone is moving on, moving away from me: my friends, my dad, even Olivia spends every spare second with Alessio, so I barely see her. They're all abandoning me, and I didn't even get a proper heads-up! I had no time to prepare, no time to pivot or adjust my own plans as needed.

I'm going to be alone a week earlier than expected in a tiny dorm room, where I'll pop a bottle of champagne on my eighteenth birthday for the world's most depressing party. *Welcome to adulthood, Jenna, hope you're used to disappointment!*

I force myself up from the table to save my fingernails from any more trauma. If I'm going to sit and stew, I might as well do it in my room where I can start forming a plan about what to do next.

As I storm down the hall, I pass a picture of me and Mom, ironically taken at the cottage, and I stop to pick it up. We're on the dock in matching green swimsuits, hair soaked from swimming and skin tinged red from a day in the sun. She's glowing, with a naturally elegant, polished type of beauty I'll never achieve. I got my looks from Dad—the straight black hair, the icy blue eyes, the sharp cheekbones—but I got none of his charisma or outgoing personality. Dad could meet a statue and get it to fall in love with him and sign whatever he wanted, whereas I'll glare a stranger into submission if they try approaching me while I'm in a bad mood, something Dad lovingly jokes is all Mom.

I trace Mom's smiling face, remembering how she laughed that day when I accidentally dropped a whole tray of hot dogs in the lake, how she let me eat so many s'mores that night I couldn't look at a giant marshmallow for weeks.

The heaviness I try so hard to suppress weighs on my chest, and I gently put the photo back. Mom loved going up to the cottage, and we went every single weekend, even if it meant she was inside on her laptop for most of the day if she needed to get work done. I thought going up that first summer after she passed would be hard, that I would see Mom's ghost everywhere, but it was the opposite. As soon as we pulled up to the Muskoka property, a sense of peace washed over me. Mom loved that place, and so do I, and I'm not going to give it up without so much as a goodbye. I'm not going to sit in my dorm room, alone and sad on my birthday, when I have a perfectly good cottage for the perfect last-week-of-summer celebration.

Before I can change my mind, I open the group chat on my phone and type out a quick message.

Cottage trip for the last week of summer. Everyone meet bright and early at my house at 9am on Friday the 24th.

I've barely just pressed Send when the responses come flying in.

Robbie: Hell yeah! I'll pack my DJ equipment.

Elena: Woo! This is going to be the best cottage week ever! And the most memorable 18th birthday for you, Jenna!

Kyle: I'm going to make a shopping list so we don't forget any food, because you know I need to eat at least 3,000 calories a day for my bulk. Plus, I just really love food.

Martina: I call the blue room with the lake view!

Fletcher: I call the bed beside Martina!

He punctuates his statement with three winky face emojis, which I know has Martina gagging and rolling her eyes.

The texts continue flying in, and each one lifts the heaviness in my heart a little more. So what if Dad told me not to host this trip? He won't even be in the province; how will he know? My friends won't see him and accidentally tell him, and I won't invite Olivia until the day before. There are so many memories at that cottage, ones that will become a distant recollection of people we used to know once we go our separate ways and the years pass. But if I go through with this, I'll make the last week with my friends one worth remembering forever, truly making it the best summer ever.

If I have to lie to Dad and cover the trip up, then that's what I'll do.

FOUR

4 Hours to Muskoka

Olivia

It's a beautiful, wonderful, warm day, and I tip my face up to the sun as I lounge on my front steps. My luggage is packed and ready to go, and I'm waiting to *finally* reunite with my boyfriend. It's been over a month since I've seen him—six weeks, to be exact—and today is the day I get to jump into his arms and hold him close and kiss him so hard we're both breathless and lust-crazed by the time we pull away, even if I'm still upset with him.

After Jenna's party, the company Alessio's interning with sent him fifteen hours away to Thunder Bay for three weeks. I secretly wanted him to turn down the offer, like most other people at the company did when asked, but like Alessio explained, it was good money, a good opportunity for growth, and a chance to impress his bosses with his ability to be a team player. I understand the need to excel, and I know how badly he wants to continue working there after he graduates, so I supported him, even though that meant being apart for so long again.

But now he's finally back, and yesterday Jenna invited us to her cottage for the week, so Alessio and I will be together without any outside interference. All the missed calls, unanswered texts, and FaceTime tag will be in the past. He's picking me up soon, and we'll be in the car for three whole uninterrupted hours. I can't wait to finally ease the nerves that sit tight in my stomach every time I think about Alessio, to finally confirm that we're still in a good place. We can talk about all the things we've been missing, and I can't wait to show him what I bought for our new apartment only a few blocks from campus. I had to tour it myself while he was away, which was disappointing since I thought it would be something he'd at least try to care about instead of palming it off on me like so many other things in our relationship. I'm annoyed when I think about it, but I force myself to remember that it's not his fault he's working out of town and that it doesn't matter where we live as long as we're together. I was so excited when he suggested we move in together, especially since it was hard for me to connect with my roommate last year. And now that we'll be living together, I won't feel as left out when he goes out to the bars with his friends and I'm forced to stay alone in my dorm since I'm not of legal drinking age. I mean, I *still* won't be legal drinking age since I have a late birthday and I'm a year younger, but at least I'll be with him all the time, so it's not like his going out will take away from our time together.

A car pulls into the driveway, and I jump up so fast I almost trip on the interlocked steps, but I'm too excited to care. My body is practically vibrating with anticipation, my heart beating so fast I'm breathless.

The birds are singing, the sun is shining, and my boyfriend is *finally* here!

I wave at him and skip down the driveway to meet him while he parks the car. He's always been handsome, so handsome that I was shocked when he asked me out way back in the ninth grade because he could've gotten any girl he wanted. His blond undercut has grown out a bit, with the sides needing to be shaved down again, and his eyes look tired when he smiles at me, but he's the most perfect man I've ever seen.

I bounce in place beside his door, and when he emerges from the car, I throw myself at him so hard he's knocked off balance before catching himself.

"I missed you so much!" I exclaim, squeezing him to me with as much force as possible. He's warm and familiar and smells like my favorite fresh laundry detergent.

"Hey, Liv."

I stand on my tiptoes to kiss him, but he dodges, putting his hands on my shoulders and holding me at arm's length.

Alarm bells go off in my head, and all the doubts that creep into my mind late at night come rushing back. "Alessio? What's wrong?"

"Nothing, babe, I'm just . . ." His eyes search mine, and they look troubled. "I have to tell you . . ."

He doesn't say anything for a moment, like he's searching for the proper words, and my stomach twists. "Tell me what?"

He steps back, his arms dropping from my shoulders. "I . . . I think I got the flu from traveling. I don't think I should come to the cottage with you. I know you've been looking forward to going with me, and I don't want to let you down, but I don't think I can go."

Another excuse to avoid hanging out with me? "What? Don't be ridiculous, you're not letting me down. We don't have to go to the cottage. I'll make your favorite soup, and we can watch the entirety of that drag racing movie franchise you love."

"No, you should go to the cottage. Don't let me ruin your trip."

"I don't care about the trip; I care about you." I try to reach for him, but he takes a step back.

"You need to go. You know how Jenna is. Someone has to be there to make sure the house is still standing at the end of the week."

"I'm sure she'll be okay." I try to reach for him again, but again he steps back. A ball forms in my stomach. It's been six weeks of *I'm busy* or *I'm working* or *I'm sick*. Something is going on.

"Honestly, Liv, I just need to sleep it off. Go have fun. Dylan hasn't left yet, so I'll ask him to drive you up," he says as he pulls out his phone and sends a text.

His words only deepen the hurt and confusion swirling through me. Alessio's a huge baby when he gets sick. He likes being doted on and taken care of. Last time he had a cold, I had to make him ten different kinds of soup until he found the one he liked best. I had to pick up medicine and sit beside him in bed and stroke his hair. He loves the attention. So why is he pushing me away now? Something is wrong here.

"Do you have a fever? I have a thermometer in the house, and some medicine and orange juice. Come inside and I'll get you set up on the couch."

"God*damnit*, Oliva!" he exclaims. "Can you stop being so fuck-ing *good* and *perfect* for one second?"

The words are like an arrow through my chest. Hurt and con-fused, I stammer, looking for whatever I can say that will make him happy. "I—I'm sorry?"

He scrubs his hands over his face and pulls at his hair. "Just . . . just *stop* for a second, okay? This is hard enough without you being so . . . *you*."

Suddenly, the sun feels too hot on my skin, the air too dry, the birds too loud in the silence that stretches between us. Something *has* been wrong all these weeks, and I've been trying to ignore it despite everyone else warning me, despite my own internal alarms.

The anger I've been holding back finally emerges. "What the

hell is going on, Alessio? You've been avoiding me for weeks. For *six weeks*, to be exact. Avoiding calls, taking all day for a lousy text back, going to Jenna's party and not even bothering to see me! It's like I'm single given how much contact we've actually had. And now that we actually get to spend time together, you're standing there telling me you *can't go*? What's going o—"

"I cheated on you!" he blurts out, and I freeze, my arms dropping to my sides like they've turned into heavy lead weights. He blinks at me like he can't believe he admitted it out loud, his face drawn and tortured.

My throat is sore and dry when I croak out, "What?" I had suspicions that something was wrong, but I never suspected *that*.

He takes a deep breath, hesitant, like he can't bear the thought of having to say it out loud again. I almost wish he wouldn't, wish he'd stuff the words back in his mouth so we could return to a reality where those four words were never spoken, but he forges on, forcing out a life-shattering confession.

"I cheated on you in Cuba. I slept with someone. More than once."

The blood drains from my face as I stare at him, processing his words. The trip he went on with his friends, six weeks ago to the day, was spent having sex with a girl who wasn't me. All this time I've been trying to see him, missing him, wishing more than anything that we were together, and he's been sitting with the knowledge of how he hurt me.

"I was stupid. So fucking stupid," he says, reaching for me, but this time I'm the one who steps back. He looks like the action kills him. "I've been avoiding you like a coward, trying to put off having to tell you. I was going to at Jenna's party, but I chickened out. And every time your name pops up on my screen, I'm wracked with so much guilt and fear I can't even function. I don't want to lose you,

Liv. I *can't* lose you. You're the best thing to ever happen to me, and I was an idiot for jeopardizing that."

There are so many questions running through my head I can't even fathom beginning to make sense of them all. But the biggest one is the question I'm too scared to ask. Nevertheless, when I open my mouth, it comes out. "Why did you do it?"

"I don't know, Liv. We were at a resort and drinking, and she was there, and you and I have been together since I was fourteen, and . . . I don't know. There's no justifiable reason. But I'm so sorry. I'm so fucking sorry. If I could take it back, I would."

He tries to take my hand, but I sidestep. Moments ago, all I wanted to do was hold him, touch him, be with him, and put all the weird behavior behind us, but now the thought of taking his hand, the hand he used to touch another woman, makes me want to puke up my breakfast.

"You slept with someone else," I say, almost to myself, like I need to hear it out loud for it to sink in. "You had *sex* with someone else."

His voice breaks when he whispers, "It was an accident."

"An accident? An *accident*?" I repeat, anger breaking through the shock. "An accident is when you get a bit too close to the garage wall when parking and scrape your mirror. An accident is when you forget to set an alarm and sleep through class. An accident is *not* sticking your dick in someone who's not your girlfriend. *Multiple times!*"

As my voice gets louder and louder with each point, he shrinks into himself, looking like he's going to keel over from the guilt alone. But I don't care. This is not the boyfriend I've been with for five years, the one who's my best friend, my soulmate, the only person in the world who makes me feel whole. My Alessio would never have hurt me like this, never have even *looked* at another girl, never mind slept with her the second I wasn't around. I don't recognize the person standing in front of me, and it breaks my heart.

My voice cracks when I say, "You were getting your grandmother's ring resized."

"And I'm still going to propose to you with it when we're done with school!" he rushes out as I dodge his grasp. He lets his arms awkwardly fall to his sides. "You're the only girl for me, Liv. I'll do anything I can to make this right. I love you. Please give me a chance to make it up to you."

The part of me that's been in love with Alessio since I was thirteen, doing everything I could to make him happy, wants to tell him it's okay, to say and do whatever I can to take that pained look off his face. But the logical part of me knows I can't do that, *refuses* to do that, even though it's my first instinct.

"Please, Olivia," he pleads, and I have to look away from him. My eyes sting, but I don't want to cry in front of him.

"I need you to leave."

"Babe—"

"I'm serious," I say, my voice coming out stronger than I feel. I take a few healthy steps away to stop him from advancing any farther. "I can't even look at you right now. Leave."

He releases a broken breath, and I want to kick the part of me that actually feels *sorry* for causing him pain.

"You need time, I get that. I'll give you whatever time and space you need. But I love you, Olivia. You're the only person for me, and I'll regret what I did every single day of my life, but I know we can work through this. Together."

His words are like knives through my heart, and my mind spins as I try to process my thoughts. I can't make sense of anything while he's still standing there, looking like the guy I thought I knew better than anyone in the world. He's proving that maybe I didn't know him at all.

"Go," I say, crossing my arms against my chest like I can hold myself together.

He holds up his hands, palms facing outward, and backs toward his car. "Okay, right. I'll give you some time to cool off, and we can talk after you've processed. I love you, Olivia. Forever. You're my person. Never forget that."

I don't say the words back. I physically can't. How can he love me if he's capable of betraying me so deeply? How can I be his person if he slept with another girl? He wasn't thinking about me when he was having a blast in Cuba, meanwhile I've been at home, doing almost nothing *but* thinking about him.

He gives up waiting for a response, getting into his car dejectedly and backing out of the driveway.

I watch until he's out of view, sinking onto the porch steps once I can no longer see his silver Acura. I don't realize I'm shaking until I try unzipping my light sweater, suddenly feeling too hot and stuffy, claustrophobic even though I'm outside in the summer breeze. My fingers fumble with the metal zipper, and I eventually tug the sweater over my head and toss it haphazardly behind me.

Alessio and I have been solid ever since he first asked me out all those years ago. We were supposed to finish our degrees and get married. He was going to get a job in finance, and I'd be a neurosurgeon. We'd buy a cute house by the water because we both love it so much, and we'd teach our kids how to swim.

The plan has always been *him*. But with that one action—multiple actions, apparently—everything I've ever known has been shattered.

There are so many things I never even got to ask him, things plaguing me now. Has he cheated on me before? Has he thought about it before? Did anything happen when he turned nineteen and started going to bars and clubs while I waited at home for him? Does he still talk to that girl? But the most pressing, even though I asked it already, is *why*? His answer wasn't satisfying. There's no logic in it, nothing that can be used to rationalize it. Did I do something wrong? Wasn't I good enough for him? Was he bored of me? I did everything I could to be perfect for him, to be the perfect girlfriend, and it still wasn't good enough. I thought he loved me, I thought he'd never hurt me, and yet I'm sitting here with tears streaming down my face, my heart in shambles.

A car pulls into my driveway, and I quickly swipe at my wet cheeks. Dylan hops out, looking carefree and summer-ready in a loose tank top and flip-flops.

"Hey, Livy! I've got another one for you! What's the fattest organ in the human . . ." He trails off when he notices me. His face pales as he scans me, and instantly, I *know*.

"You knew." It's a statement and an accusation, one he doesn't bother refuting. "Did you know, Dylan? Did everyone know?"

Dylan doesn't ask for clarification, just presses his lips together and shifts on his feet, looking like he's been punched in the stomach.

"Oh my god!" I exclaim, jumping up to round on him. All this time, everyone knew Alessio cheated on me. Adam, Kellan, Dylan, people I thought were my friends—people I've known forever—all knew what happened, and no one told me. I guess they've always been *Alessio's* friends, not mine, and the realization stings.

"I asked you straight up at Elena's birthday if something happened in Cuba, and you *swore* to me that everything was fine. You lied to my face, Dylan!"

"I wanted to tell you, I swear, but it wasn't my place, Liv. *He* needed to tell you, not me or Kellan or Adam or Ray or Freddie or Eli."

"Ray, Freddie, and Eli didn't even *go* to Cuba, and they knew too?"

Dylan snaps his mouth shut, eyes wide and guilty like he's only just realized he admitted something he shouldn't have. I feel like I'm being betrayed all over again. It wasn't just Alessio who hurt me, it was all of them. "What? So everyone knew? Were you guys all laughing at me behind my back? Poor, stupid, clueless Olivia."

"What? No, Livy. Never." He rushes to close the distance and puts his hands on my shoulders, but I push him away. I don't want his pity, don't want his sympathy, not when he knew what happened and lied to me about it, especially not when it's obvious his loyalty lies with Alessio, not me, even though I've known him longer.

"Everyone knew but me. I feel so stupid. I've got a 4.0 GPA, take astrophysics courses for fun, and I'm launching a whole app, but I couldn't figure out my boyfriend cheated on me despite him blowing me off for six weeks."

The anger drains from me, and I sink onto the steps, my legs suddenly too tired to support me. If he didn't blurt it out, would I ever have figured it out? Would I have brushed off his strange behavior and pretended everything was normal despite all the signs and my own sense that something was wrong?

I can't stop my tears, and I angrily swipe at them. Dylan hesitates for a moment before sitting beside me. He opens his arms like he's going to wrap them around me, but I glare at him, and he quickly retracts them. I don't know why he's here, why he feels like he needs to be the one to comfort me. The last person I want watching me melt down over Alessio's actions is his best friend.

"You can leave now. There's no reason for you to stay," I tell him, but he doesn't make a move to leave. In fact, he looks like he's settling in, sighing sadly and planting his elbows on his bent knees, watching the occasional car drive by. He doesn't say anything as I quietly sob beside him, unable to stop the tears this time and not caring that he's chosen to stay and witness them.

It feels like my whole life has blown up. Alessio and I did everything together. He was more than my boyfriend. He was my partner, my best friend, the person I've loved and grown with since I was thirteen. If I'm not with him, what does that mean for me? Who am I supposed to be without him? So much of my life has revolved around him, around *us*, and if we break up, there's going to be a huge chunk of me missing. But how can I move past this, even if that's what Alessio hopes will happen? How can I possibly feel okay again? How can I look at him and not imagine him kissing, touching, doing *things* with some other girl?

"Olivia, I—" Dylan cuts himself off with an angry huff, like he can't find the words to say what he really wants to say. "I'm sorry."

I'm mad at him, but *he's* not my boyfriend. *He's* not the one who ruined a perfect relationship for a few moments of fun.

"It's not your fault he couldn't keep it in his pants," I say, wiping my nose with the back of my hand, not caring that it's gross. I just don't have it in me to care.

Dylan's jaw ticks, and the muscle in his neck tenses with the movement. "But still. I—"

A ringing sound cuts him off, and I'm confused for a moment before I feel the vibration in my pocket. I fish my phone out of my jean shorts, and my caller ID informs me that it's Jenna.

Wiping the last of my tears and clearing my throat, I answer the call. I barely get the whole greeting out before Jenna starts.

"Where are you? It's noon and you're still not here, is everything all right? Fletcher and Kyle have almost finished the entire container of gummy worms, and I know those are your favorite." There's talking in the background, then rustling like she's pulled the phone away from her ear as she shouts, "No, I don't know where the keys to the Sea-Doos are! Can you relax, we literally just got here!"

I glance at Dylan, and he's staring intently at me. On my quiet street, I know he can hear every word Jenna's saying, even without her being on Speaker.

Her voice returns to normal on the phone again. "Are you on your way or what?"

I don't want to tell her what happened, especially not over the phone, and doubly not with Dylan sitting beside me. I don't want to give him a play-by-play recap, because Jenna will definitely want details. Plus, I've finally managed to calm down, and I don't want to relive it.

"I'm not sure I'm coming."

Jenna's quiet for a moment, uncharacteristically so. I can even hear faint background music and what sounds like people loading up the fridge and freezer.

"What the hell do you mean you're not coming? You have to come!"

"I don't know, I'm not feeling the greatest right now." I shift uncomfortably, refusing to look at Dylan. I can feel his gaze on the side of my face, and I'm not sure what emotion I'll see reflected back at me. I don't want his pity; I already feel pathetic enough.

"There's nothing some sun, the open lake, and a few bottles of tequila can't fix," she says, only partially joking. "This is nonnegotiable; you're coming."

I don't want to go to Muskoka and be around everyone for a week pretending everything's okay. All I want to do is crawl into bed, wrap myself in my blankets like a little burrito, and cry into my pillow.

"Maybe I'll skip this one, Jenna. You have fun with your friends."

She huffs, annoyed. "*You're* my friend, too, Liv. Come on. It's the last week of summer."

"You and I can go up for the weekend in a few weeks once we're settled into school. Maddalena and Bianca will be back from camp by then, too, so they'll be able to come with us. I'll even bake you your favorite cookie brownies—"

"No!" she blurts out quickly. "No. You need to come up *this* week."

"Jenna, I don't see the differ—"

"You need to come up, Olivia!" There's something frantic in her tone, a deeper meaning that I'm too distracted to figure out. I don't know why I need to come up for this particular week, especially when she's already got so many other people there and we go to the cottage together all the time, but I don't want to disappoint her. I hate letting other people down.

There's a nudge at my shoulder, and when I look at Dylan, there's something in his eyes that makes me pause. To Jenna, I say, "Let me call you back."

"It better be to tell me you're on your way!" she exclaims before I hang up.

I set the phone on the porch beside me, and Dylan seems to be choosing his words carefully before he says, "I can't even begin to imagine what you're going through right now, and I know you probably want to hide away from everyone and everything, but I think you should go to Muskoka."

Why would he think that? He literally admitted to knowing what I wanted to do then suggested the opposite.

"You go without me," I tell him, standing and rolling out my neck. I feel like I've been hit by a truck.

Dylan gives me a funny look as he stands. "I'm not going to Adam's ex-girlfriend's cottage alone. I was only invited because of you and Alessio. But that's beside the point. You should go up, get away from all this for a while."

"I don't want to go and be surrounded by people and parties and music and crowds right now, Dylan. I want to be alone."

I grab my phone from the ground and head to the door to do exactly what I said I wanted, but he runs around me, stopping me in my tracks.

"Okay, I get that. But really think about it, Liv. What will being alone, lonely and depressed, surrounded by pictures and memories of Alessio, really accomplish?"

I pause, and like he knows he's got my attention now, he forges on, more confident this time.

"You've spent the last five years doing everything Alessio wants, always putting him first, always catering to his needs. This is the first time since the ninth grade that you can pull back and think about what *you* want. Sort out your thoughts and feelings and figure out what it is that makes you happy. You can't do that in a dark room surrounded by all his things and his pictures. And it's the last week of summer. You're not going to spend it moping in bed and eating an entire carton of chocolate fudge brownie ice cream until your head hurts."

I'm taken aback by the fact he knows exactly what I would do, right down to the chocolate-induced headache.

"So, let me take you to the cottage. You can think about Alessio or don't think about him at all. If nothing else, it'll be a good distraction from the pain you're going through right now."

He's making some valid points. If I stay here, I'm going to be surrounded by Alessio's clothes and pictures and gifts. I'm going to make myself sick crying over him, especially if Jenna and my sisters aren't here to give me a reason to leave the house. I thought I wanted to sit and mope, but maybe Dylan's right; maybe I should take this week to get my mind off Alessio and my shattered trust, use it to figure out what to do next.

I run my hands through my hair, trying to compose myself as best I can. "All right. Yeah. Let's go."

Dylan smiles at me, not his bright, carefree smile but a softer one, and for some reason his sadness on my behalf makes my stomach ache.

"I guess we can head out," I say, since the door's already locked and my luggage is ready to go on the porch.

Dylan approaches me cautiously, like a hunter approaching a skittish deer. Slowly, as if giving me time to push him away, he raises his arms. When the distance is closed between us and I haven't shoved him away, he wraps his arms around me and pulls me close. Drained of energy, I let him, resting my forehead against his sturdy chest. He's warm and solid, and his weight is comforting in a way I never expected. Maybe it's because I'm feeling particularly fragile right now, and he's almost a foot taller than me, but I feel safe wrapped in his arms, and I let myself enjoy the feeling for a few moments longer than I probably should.

"I'm really fucking sorry, Liv," he whispers, and I know he means it. Whether it's about him not telling me or Alessio cheating on me or both, I know he means it.

I pull away, sniffling and wiping away any last remnants of tears. My hand comes back black, and I realize I probably look like a raccoon—a super disheveled raccoon that fell face-first into garbage. I put makeup on since I wanted to look good for Alessio after not seeing him for so long, but now it's definitely smudged all over my face. I can't show up at the cottage looking like this, especially if I don't want everyone harassing me with questions and wanting details and sending me pitying looks all week.

"Actually, let me get cleaned up really quickly, then we can go." I collect the sweater I threw off and dig my key out of the pocket.

Just as I unlock the door, I look back at Dylan. He's leaning against a beam, looking out at the street, the muscles in his back flexed as his arms cross against his chest. There's always been something so grounding and reassuring about Dylan, and for a moment, I'm glad it was him Alessio asked to drive me up over anyone else.

"Hey, Dylan?"

He turns to me, and the genuine concern in his face makes me pause. I'm not used to this Dylan, the one who's sweet and kind and treats me like I'm fragile. I'm used to the Dylan who's carefree and teasing and playful, whose laugh is infectious, and who is a beacon of fun for everyone he interacts with. Sure, he's always been sweet and kind and considerate, but the way he's acting right now serves as a reminder that Alessio smashed my heart into pieces. I don't want Dylan to treat me like I'm a pathetic, mopey girlfriend. I don't want to be reminded about how my life has imploded. I want my friend.

I straighten my spine and harden my resolve. "If we're going to do this, I don't want to talk about Alessio this week. In fact, I want to pretend like I've never met Alessio, like he never cheated on me. I don't want you to walk on eggshells with me. Also, stop giving me those eyes."

He pushes off the beam. "What eyes?"

I gesture vaguely at his face, which is still handsome even when confused. "Those eyes. I don't know how to describe it."

"All right, I'll just grab a rusty spoon and pop them out real quick so you don't have to look at them anymore."

His joke pulls an unexpected laugh from me, and my throat is so sore from crying it almost hurts.

His smile turns light again, the usual Dylan one, and a slight weight lifts off my chest.

"Don't do that, I need you to see on the highway *and* watch for deer on the side roads."

"Well, make up your mind then! I can't not have eyes and watch for deer."

I shake my head at his antics, glad for the shift to a lighter mood between us, and pull my door open with a slight smile. A quick glance in the hallway mirror reveals my mascara *is* smudged all over the place, and I look ridiculous. It's a wonder Dylan didn't burst out laughing at the sight of me.

I don't want to walk through my room and see the pictures of Alessio tacked up on the walls, or his sweater hanging on the post of my bed, or the six-foot giant teddy bear with the pink bow he got me for our first Valentine's Day resting in the corner of my room, so I use the twins' bathroom, digging through their cabinets for makeup remover and face wash. Thank goodness they're working as counselors at a sleepaway camp this week or they'd kill me for being in here then launch an interrogation as to why I'm crying, in that exact order.

By the time I'm done drying my face, my phone vibrates for the hundredth time in a row. It's a string of texts from Jenna, demanding I come to the cottage no matter what. I send a quick text back that I'm leaving now and will see her soon, but I don't mention Alessio. I don't know what I'll say about why he's not coming, but like Dylan and I agreed, I'm not supposed to be thinking about him.

Dylan's sitting on the steps when I get back, and he stands as I lock the door.

"Okay?" he asks, and I want to tell him to stop looking at me with those eyes again, but I don't want to have to explain what I mean. I don't even know what I mean. Instead, I just nod my head as he grabs my luggage, and I follow him to his car.

"Hey, uh . . ." I start, stopping him as he effortlessly lifts my luggage into the trunk. I don't want to ruin the delicate, lighter mood, but it still has to be said. "Do you mind not telling anyone at the cottage about what happened? Between me and Alessio . . ."

He blinks at me before he smoothly recovers. "Yeah. For sure. Whatever you need, Livy."

I blow out a relieved breath. "Thanks."

As we get into the car and buckle up, my phone vibrates. I think it's Jenna, messaging me yet again, but it's not. It's Alessio, and the three red heart emojis I saved beside his name in his contact profile are a cruel taunt.

I love you. Please forgive me. We can work through this.

I exit out of the conversation without answering, and Dylan doesn't seem to mind that I'm not exactly in a conversational mood as he pulls out of my driveway and heads to the highway. I stare out the window, trying and failing to push Alessio out of my mind before I burst into tears again. I'm done crying, at least for the day. My eyes are red and puffy, my temples are pounding, and my throat is all scratchy like I've been screaming for hours.

My phone vibrates again just as Dylan pulls onto the 400, and I can't stop myself from opening it, even when I notice the three red hearts.

Please don't break up with me.

I feel like tossing my phone out the window, but instead I shove it into the small purse I brought and drop it at my feet. I don't want to think about Alessio anymore. Every time his face pops into my mind, my heart feels like it's breaking all over again. I need to push him out of my thoughts, snap my hair elastic against my wrist every time I feel like talking about him, do *something* to banish him from my brain. From this moment on, I'm not bringing up his name.

"How many girls did Alessio sleep with in Cuba?" *Dammit.*

Dylan glances at me warily. "I thought you didn't want to talk about him?"

I don't. I really, really don't. But I need to know. "Please, Dylan. Just tell me. Don't lie to me anymore."

"I've never lied to you, Liv," he says softly.

I don't want to rehash how he lied to me when I asked him if something happened in Cuba at Elena's birthday party, so instead I say, "Please tell me. I want to know."

He runs his hand through his hair before placing it back on the wheel, relenting. "It was just the one girl."

I'm not sure if that makes me feel better or worse. I don't think any of this information even matters, but I continue asking anyway. "How many times did he sleep with her?"

"I don't know. A few, I think."

Again, information that doesn't make a difference in the grand scheme of things. "Was he planning on telling me, or was he thinking *what happens in Cuba stays in Cuba*?"

"Livy . . ." He hesitates, and his tone gives it away.

"Tell me!"

He doesn't want to, it's obvious in the way his jaw works and his knuckles turn white on the steering wheel, but he still tells me. "The girl had an on-again, off-again boyfriend who found out and confronted them in front of everyone. I didn't know until that moment either. If the boyfriend hadn't done that . . ."

My inhalation is sharp, and I have to blink back fresh tears. He wouldn't have told me. I know it in my gut. He blew me off for six weeks because he was so scared of telling me, and the only reason he did was because everyone found out about it.

Dylan's voice is rough when he says, "He's an asshole, Olivia. Don't cry over someone stupid enough to get the most amazing girl to himself and then throw it all away."

I stare at my purse on the floor, as if I can see my phone and his messages from here. "He asked me to forgive him and not break up with him. What would you do?"

"You know he's my best friend, right?"

He glances at me, and I nod.

"If I were you, I'd dump his ass. Hard."

I don't know what I was expecting Dylan to say. Maybe defend his friend, tell me everyone makes mistakes, that Alessio has learned and will never do anything like that again. But telling me straight up to break up with him, even though realistically Dylan should be on Alessio's side, helps cut through my muddled brain and give me some clarity.

"Even though I love him?"

Dylan's jaw clenches. "If he loved you, he wouldn't have jumped into bed with the first girl that blinked at him the second your back was turned."

My flinch is involuntary, and he catches it.

"I'm sorry. I shouldn't have said that."

"No, you're right. It's the truth." And that truth is a real kick to the chest.

Dylan doesn't say anything when I turn up the volume on the radio, effectively sending the signal that I want a moment to myself. I can't get to the cottage and spend the whole week replaying my conversation with Alessio while my future hangs over my head. I know what I should do, but I can't imagine life without him. Forgiving him scares me, but so does letting him go. In either scenario, I'll end up more hurt than I've ever been before.

Dylan and I spend the drive quietly, and I appreciate that he doesn't push me. I need to sort out my thoughts, and I need to decide before we start the week.

By the time we pull onto the cottage's road, I know what I have to do. I fish my phone out of my bag, scanning the slew of other messages Alessio's sent, all along the same lines of what he said before. That he's sorry. That he'll never do something like that again. That he'll spend forever making it up to me. But none of that changes my mind. I've analyzed the facts and made my decision.

So, I send him the words I never thought I'd say to him, never even fathomed I'd need to.

I need to think, and I can't do that while we're together. We're breaking up. Please give me my space and don't contact me again.

Little bubbles pop up immediately, so I know he's texting me back, but I don't want to see what he's going to say in return. I stuff the phone back in my bag before I feel guilty for breaking up with him, because I *shouldn't* feel guilty. But just because my mind logically knows that I have nothing to be guilty about doesn't mean my heart does.

Dylan turns down the cottage's long drive, and we're surrounded by the trees and natural rock formations that follow the winding driveway. And then the area opens, and the cottage comes into view.

Calling it a cottage is an incredibly unfitting name. It's like calling a giant *tiny* or a castle a hut. Jenna's cottage is almost as big as her mansion back at home. It's a classic, elegant lakefront property nestled in five acres of forest, with exposed wooden beams and huge glass windows letting in lots of natural light and stunning views. With four massive bedrooms, it sleeps ten people, and there's a separate two-story boathouse on the water that stores the boat and Sea-Doos and other water toys. And yet, even though it's massive, there's always been a warm, welcoming feeling to Jenna's cottage, very different from the cold museum vibe I get at her house.

There are already a few cars parked, so Dylan pulls into a spot beside a black Honda I don't recognize and turns the engine off.

With the air-conditioning off, the mid-afternoon heat starts sneaking its way into the car, but neither Dylan nor I make a move to leave. He shifts in his seat to look at me, gently asking, "Okay?"

My voice sounds small after almost three hours of disuse when I choke out, "I told Alessio we're not together anymore and to leave me alone."

Dylan inhales sharply. He considers his words carefully before landing on, "You did what you thought was best for you, Livy."

I nod absently. I know it's the best thing for me, but it doesn't feel like it. It still feels like my heart is being torn in two.

The front door of the cottage opens to reveal Jenna in a blue bikini, holding a bottle of what looks like rum and waving at us.

I clear my throat and check myself in the visor mirror. My eyes are still slightly puffy, but at least it's not obvious I was bawling my eyes out only a short while ago.

We click off our seat belts, and I take a deep, cleansing breath. Dylan waits for me. There's something deeper in his eyes when he asks, "You ready?"

I'm unsure if he means am I ready to exit the car and start our trip or am I ready to live without Alessio.

Either way, my answer remains the same. "I'm going to have to be."

FIVE

Day I of Muskoka

Jenna

The second I get out of my car and inhale the deep, woodsy scent of Muskoka's fresh air, it's like I can breathe again for the first time in forever. The cottage itself is huge, but it's surrounded by acres of forest and the quiet serenity of nature. There's no traffic or light pollution or crowds of people. You can actually hear the calls of the loons on the lake directly behind the cottage, the chirping of birds, the buzzing of cicadas, the occasional boat engine slicing through the water.

Everyone but Dylan, Alessio, and Olivia drove up in a convoy of cars together, so when I unlock the door, my friends race in, either to claim beds or take first dibs on the bathroom. Normally, I'm right there with them, but today a sense of nostalgia washes over me as I step into the spacious, open-concept living room and kitchen, the wall of windows providing a perfect view of the lake I practically grew up on. Mom taught me to tread water in that lake. It's where my grandfather, Mom's dad, taught me to catch my first fish, and

Olivia, the twins, and I all squealed when he tried to make us hook the slimy fish bait. The wide dock floating over it is where Elena, Martina, and I made each other friendship bracelets that we still wear, even though we were fourteen and probably too old for that activity. The fire pit circled by red Muskoka chairs is where Robbie, surrounded by the peaceful night and fireflies, first told us he was gay. It's where the group of us would sit well past midnight, sharing stories so scary we'd all jump at the first snap of a twig in the woods, and one of the guys would purposefully try to sneak up on us to scare us.

There are so many memories here, and this is the last time I'll ever step foot on this property, ever get to enjoy it for what it is.

"Kyle told me this was a cottage, but he probably should've called it a lake house. *Cottage* doesn't seem grand enough to accurately represent this place," a guy with a posh accent says, and I spin at the sudden intrusion but am immediately distracted by my surroundings.

Now that I'm not staring at the lake, I'm shocked at what Dad meant by getting the place ready to sell. All our personal touches are gone, replaced instead by his interior designer's staging tactics. The framed photographs of me with Mom or Grandpa or Olivia and the twins are all gone, replaced with generic, fancy-looking landscapes. The terrible boat-shaped key holder I painted at a pottery place in third grade has been replaced with a chic, expensive-looking bowl, and the clear vase that holds the special pebbles from the lake I picked out with Mom at the end of every cottage weekend has completely disappeared from the bookshelf it normally sits on.

"Well, don't you look happy to see me?" Hari asks, and I finally notice him standing in front of the shelf that used to hold my vase of pebbles. Now I'm scowling for a different reason.

He runs a hand through his hair as he leisurely scans me from head to toe, seemingly amused that I'm most definitely *not* happy to see him here. This is supposed to be a week with my *friends* where we have the best time ever, not a week with the most inconsiderate, annoying jerkface with unreasonably attractive hands.

"What are you doing here?" It's a question that sounds like an accusation, especially as I eye the large duffel bag by his feet, as if, for some unfathomable reason, he's planning on staying.

"Kyle invited me for the week. What are you doing here?"

I thought I wanted to kill Kyle for inviting Hari to Elena's party, but now I *really* want to kill him. Hari once spilled an entire gallon of paint on my head in an action I'd bet my college tuition was deliberate, and I'm expected to host him here with all my friends and still have a great end-of-summer trip?

"It's my cottage," I say, maintaining my composure. Hari loves nothing more than to see me completely lose my shit, and he almost caught a glimpse of it as I scanned the changes Dad made. I'll have to keep it together no matter how intense the burning in my chest becomes from holding it all in.

The smirk on his face grows slowly, as if processing in real time. "Interesting. Looks like we've got the whole week to get reacquainted."

"Fantastic." My smile is so tight it's a wonder I can even spit out the word. "Why don't you go up and pick a bed?"

"That sounds great. Maybe I'll even get the bed next to yours," he says then pauses for a beat, watching me intently, as if waiting to see if I'll snap and tell him to get the hell out of my cottage or if my face will turn that *delightful shade of red* that it apparently becomes when I'm trying not to yell at him. But when I only keep my tight smile plastered on my face and wait expectantly for him to head upstairs, his anticipatory excitement seems to deflate, and he picks up his bag before going down the hall.

Score one for Jenna.

My phone pings, and it's a text from Dad, the first of the day, asking if there are any issues with my dorm room. A pit opens in my stomach. He flew out to Vancouver yesterday to settle things with his new home, one that I haven't even seen because it doesn't involve me in any way. Yet I still feel guilty for going behind his back and telling him I moved into the dorms yesterday like I was supposed to instead of sleeping at Elena's and then coming here. He's reminded me a few more times not to come to the cottage since dropping the news, especially on really beautiful days that would've been perfect lake weather. He'll freak when he eventually finds out I'm here, but I kick that thought into the mental box of things to deal with later.

"You okay, birthday girl?" Elena asks, sneaking up on me, or maybe I was just too lost in my thoughts to notice her there. She sets her third piece of luggage on the floor, and I fix my face into its normal, confident, everything-is-fine expression.

"Yes. It's so beautiful," I say, gesturing to the view of the lake. Muskoka is mostly an interconnecting series of lakes with small islands, but this part of the lake is private with very few boats passing by unless someone is trying to get to their own cottage.

"It really is," she says, eyes focused out the window. "Maybe if I'm not taking summer courses I can come back and we can do this again next year. Maybe it can be a new tradition? Like a last-week-of-summer thing."

The reminder of her leaving and probably never coming back instantly sours my mood. Since breaking the news to me, she's been busy getting everything ready to start her new life. Martina's been in group chats with her new friends from her program, practicing her French for life in Montreal, Olivia's been holed up in her room preparing for her app's launch, and Dad's been busy selling everything linking him to Ontario. I've been lonely these last few weeks, and no one's even left yet.

"Yeah, maybe," I answer.

Before she can say anything, I notice Kyle in the hallway. *"Don't!"* I yell, and he freezes just before poking at the abstract glass sculpture propped up on a thick marble stand. Everyone who's not upstairs turns to look at me like I just declared that I enjoy sucking peanut butter off people's toes. "I, um . . ." I march over to the delicate art piece and grab it off the stand. It's smooth and heavy in my hands. "I'm still on probation with my dad after Elena's birthday party, so we have to be careful during this trip, okay? No breaking things."

Everyone's still looking at me weird. I've never specifically asked them not to touch anything or be careful before. My house is their house, and as long as we had fun, it didn't matter. But now the house is filled with fragile things to make it look more expensive, and I can't exactly expect Dad to hand me his credit card when things inevitably break if I'm not even supposed to be here.

No one says anything, so I awkwardly back away. "I'm just going to . . . put this away." I turn and hustle down the hall before anyone can ask me what my deal is. On my scurry to the garage, I pass a few more damage-prone decorations that I make a mental note to come back for. I never realized how many breakable things Dad's interior designer uses to stage these places to keep the modern yet cozy look, but I swear that vase with the tall white pampas grass is in every single house she does. She'd know if something was broken, and we need to leave no evidence that we were here for as long as I can get away with keeping it secret.

In the garage, I set the sculpture on a shelf, scrubbing my hand against my face. This is going to be a lot harder than I thought it would be.

"Hey." A voice startles me, and I turn to see Hari holding the vase with the pampas and a large wooden model sailboat that was the centerpiece of the hall sideboard cabinet. He sets the vase down, curiously handling the delicate boat that probably cost a few thousand dollars. "Figured you probably didn't want these to break either."

He says it casually, like it's no big deal, but his eyes are studying me, making me squirm. I don't know what it is about him that he keeps catching me *not* being calm and collected like I am with everyone else, how he somehow seems to know exactly what's going on in my head despite me wanting everyone to think everything is fine. I didn't even know that he was back downstairs to witness me freaking out at Kyle.

"You didn't need to do that," I say like it doesn't matter to me either way. And because the stubborn part of my brain refuses to accept help from Hari, the boy who used to pull my chair out from under me just as I was about to sit and send me sprawling to the floor in front of the whole class, I add, "They were fine where they were. I don't care if they break."

"Well then, I guess I'll just—whoops!" The boat slips from his hands, and my heart sinks into my stomach as I lunge for it before it smashes to pieces on the cement garage floor, but strong hands grab it before it's anywhere near the ground. Hari smirks at me from behind the little replica sails, and I glare at him when I realize what he's done.

"Guess you *do* care if it breaks," Hari says smugly, setting it down on the shelf beside the vase and the glass sculpture. "Could've just been honest about your feelings, you know."

"Oh, I'll tell you *exactly* how I'm feeling right now—" I start, anger rising in my chest, but I stop when his lip twitches up the tiniest amount, and I'm reminded of the little game we play, of my dad telling me you get nothing done by being overly emotional, of the therapists telling me to compartmentalize my emotions after Mom's passing. I'm not going to keep letting Hari rile me up, letting him see me crack like he enjoys so much. I'm taking a stand and setting the record straight right now.

The pitch of my voice returns to its normal tone when I continue. "Nothing. I feel absolutely nothing for you, Hari. You are an inconsequential blip in the monumental journey that is my life. You were a nobody to me before this week, you'll continue being a nobody to me during this week, and you'll go back to being a nobody to me after this week when you fuck off back to England or wherever it is you choose to go. So whatever you think you're doing here, whatever game you think we're playing, quit now, because nothing you do or say will ever matter to me in the way it seems to matter to you. You are *nothing* to me, Hari."

He huffs a laugh, like none of what I said hurt him at all. "Wow, tell me how you really feel." He lowers his voice, growing more serious as his eyes peer knowingly into mine. "No, really. Tell me how you really feel."

For some ridiculous reason, my heart hammers as we lock eyes in a staring contest.

Before I can reiterate that I have been honest about my feelings, Martina's voice travels to the garage from upstairs. "Elena and I have already called dibs on this room! I will fight anyone who tries to take it from me. I'm serious, I'm not afraid to break a nail for the cause. Get out, Fletcher!"

I push past Hari to investigate, grateful for an excuse to escape his searing gaze, but he follows behind me, laughing as he says, "She sounds like she's not afraid to throw him off the balcony, which is hilarious because Fletcher's got about two feet and at least a hundred and fifty pounds on Martina."

Clearly whatever moment was happening between us has passed, and he's going to act as if it never happened, so I do too. "She could do it. You've never seen Martina when she gets really pissed off."

"Then remind me to never piss off Martina." He's joking, but when we enter the room, it's clear Fletcher didn't get the memo. He and Martina are having a standoff in front of one of the two queen-sized beds in this room, Martina with her face flushed and Fletcher with a goofy smile. I think he thinks they're flirting.

"You have three seconds to get out of *my* room, Fletcher," Martina declares, and he reacts by running a lazy finger over the white duvet cover on Martina's claimed bed.

We cannot start off the best end-of-summer trip ever with Martina stabbing Fletcher with the curling iron she's trying to unpack, so I quickly jump in. "As the birthday girl, I get final say in sleeping arrangements, and this room is Martina and Elena's. They called it in the group chat. Sorry, Fletcher."

He pouts but doesn't seem too upset about it. It was never about the room, anyway. "All right, but if you get lonely in that bed all by yourself, *ven a buscarme.*"

"I will not *come find you!*" Martina calls after him, mumbling about how speaking bad Spanish isn't going to win her over. I give her a consoling pat on the back and leave her to her grumbling, looking for the room where Kyle put my bags.

When we're all up here like this, I normally take the primary bedroom with Adam. But since we've broken up and this will be my last time here, I don't want to be isolated and lonely in the huge room and king bed all by myself, so I save that room for Olivia and Alessio. Realistically, we could fit four people in Martina and Elena's room, but no one wants to share a bed with either of them. Elena talks in her sleep, and Martina is a kicker.

I pass by the smallest room, which has two twin-sized beds for Robbie and Fletcher, their belongings already scattered all over the floor. The generic paintings of landscapes or canoes hanging on the hallway walls make my stomach hurt, and I avoid looking at them as I pass. I know it's one of Dad's tactics to remove all family photos from houses he's staging, as he says people want to envision their *own* families there, not someone else's, but seeing our photos replaced makes my throat burn. No one else comments on the change, or maybe they just don't notice.

The largest room after the primary bedroom has three twin-sized beds separated by a generous amount of space and large windows with a beautiful view of the forest and the lake. That's where I find my luggage propped on the middle bed, with Kyle's many tubs of protein and creatine on the bed closest to the door and Hari dropping his bag on the one by the windows.

Hari notices me standing there, his eyes darting from me to the dark pink luggage Elena bought me to match hers, then back to me. "Looks like I *did* get the bed next to yours."

I can do nothing but stare silently at him as I mentally run through the sleeping arrangements to see if there's a way out of this.

"Come on, Jenna," Hari says in his annoyingly deep voice. "Are you really thinking of ways to escape being roommates?"

I scowl at him, pissed he read my thoughts so easily when I'm sure my face gave nothing away. He moves closer to me in that easy, confident way of his, a stupid gloating smirk on his face as he says, "What is it that you said? I'm a nobody—an *inconsequential blip*? If that were true, us staying in the same room wouldn't affect you in the slightest. After all, you do feel *nothing* for me, isn't that right?"

Shit. I'm trapped by my own damn words, and he knows it. If I demand to switch rooms or make sleeping in beds next to each other a big deal, he's going to know just how *not* unaffected I am by him, know how tense my entire body gets just looking at him, both from pure annoyance and something else I refuse to acknowledge. He'll win, *again*, and I refuse to turn with my tail tucked between my legs and give him more ammunition to hold over me for the rest of the week. So no. I'm going to sleep in this middle bed between Kyle the snorer and Hari the annoying and show him just how much I *don't* care about his presence, and nothing and no one can stop me.

"That is correct," I reply breezily, moving past him to pull some dresses out of my luggage that need to be hung up in order to punctuate my point. He rests his shoulder against the wall, watching me. "I don't care if you sleep there, outside, or in England, as long as you don't try crawling into my bed."

He smiles knowingly at me, his warm eyes trailing leisurely up my body, and it's only out of pure stubbornness that I don't break out into goose bumps. Pushing off the wall, he strides to the door. "You never know, Jenna. I *am* irresistibly handsome and charming. By the end of this week, your bed may be the very place you're begging me to be."

He's done it. He's actually managed to leave me speechless. I struggle to think of a comeback before he leaves and gets the last word, but Kyle inadvertently saves me by entering the room and blocking Hari's exit.

"Oh good, you're here, Jenna. I need your help. I have two shirt options for your birthday party tonight, help me choose?" Hari freezes, and Kyle reaches for two shirts that are lying on his bed beside all the protein powder. "I'm so psyched, we've never done an eighties theme before. Robbie's mix is going to be awesome; that decade had some bangers. Super appropriate for the cottage vibe."

Martina and Elena, who were walking by the room, skid to a halt in front of it.

I look between the four of them. "Birthday party? What birthday party?"

The blood drains from Kyle's face. "Shit. Pretend the last two minutes never happened."

Elena marches over to us. "Kyle, you idiot. This is why I voted against telling you."

He raises his hands. "I'm sorry, really. Jenna, don't listen to me; I *don't* know what I'm talking about. Just ol' Kyle Barnes, spouting nonsense, as usual." He grimaces, his eyes darting back and forth like he's searching for an escape. "Oh, Hari, I have to show you . . . that thing . . . let's go do that now." He grabs Hari before he can protest and races out of the room before Martina throws him through the window, which, judging from her facial expression, she's seriously considering.

"What the hell is he talking about? What party?" I ask again, discreetly rubbing my chest to alleviate the sudden tightness.

Elena approaches me slowly, like she's confronting a skittish deer. "Okay, so I know you canceled your birthday party so we could all come here, and you said you didn't want one—"

"I don't want one," I reaffirm. There's no way I need this cottage, the one we're not even supposed to *be at*, to look the way my house does after a party.

Elena continues gently. "Yes, but you worked so hard on all the backdrops and even got that custom neon sign and the disco balls and the light machines, and it's your eighteenth! You have to celebrate your eighteenth!"

I stare at her, mentally oscillating between confusion and panic, but on the surface, I remain completely neutral.

Martina jumps in. "We picked up all the stuff you were planning on using for your party and brought it up here. We also invited a bunch of people who are either renting smaller cottages nearby or have a designated driver, and they're all excited to come to your party. Which is here. Tonight."

Elena holds her arms out and awkwardly exclaims, "Surprise?"

I'm still too shocked to speak. I can't throw a *party* here! The house is currently spotless thanks to the cleaners my dad sent in last week, and it needs to stay that way or he'll murder me.

"We're not throwing a party," I declare, putting as much force behind my words as I can. "I'm on probation, remember? We need to be careful with the property."

"And we will!" Elena rushes to add. "Come on, Jenna. You threw me the most extraordinary birthday party on the face of the Earth, and it's not fair that you don't get to have one of your own because you organized this amazing trip for us."

Martina picks up where Elena finished. "And you already had everything organized, and it's perfect, as usual for a Jenna party. There's no way we could let your hard work go to waste."

"And it'll be our last party before university, and who knows when we'll all be together like this again . . ." Elena's voice drifts off, speaking into reality the fears I've been plagued with since she told me she's going to Newfoundland.

Apparently, I'm not the only one thinking about the low odds of us all being able to do this once we start school, about how unlikely it will be that we'll make time for one another once everything gears up. But Elena, Martina, and the guys are social. They'll make new friends no problem. Olivia's already in university since she skipped a grade, and she has her boyfriend. I'm the only one who will be alone. I'm the only one who will truly feel how heavy their absence is. As they both look at me, so hopeful, wanting to give me a good birthday and enjoy the dwindling time we'll get to spend together, I can't say no. I *should*, but I can't.

My smile is tight, but I convincingly force out, "Fine. We'll have fun, and it'll be the best birthday party ever."

They cheer, rushing to explain what they brought up and how

they even grabbed the dress I was planning on wearing, and all the while I'm smiling and nodding, pretending not to hear the millions of alarm bells going off in my head, telling me that this is a terrible idea.

But the truth is, this whole *week* was probably a terrible idea. What's another one to add to the list?

SIX

Day 1 of Muskoka

Olivia

"Hey, birthday girl," Dylan says as we meet Jenna at the door, lugging his oversized duffel and my luggage up the stairs. "Thanks for putting this all together."

"Glad you could finally make it," Jenna says, then directs a glare at me. "I can't believe you weren't going to come. And on my *birthday*."

"I'm here, aren't I?" I say, pasting on a smile I don't feel and wrapping her in my arms. She's normally not a touchy-feely person, but it's her birthday, so she allows the extended embrace. "Happy birthday again." I called her first thing in the morning, before my heart was smashed to pieces, so my excitement was more genuine then.

"Where's Alessio?" she asks when we break away, scanning the driveway behind us like Alessio is hiding somewhere.

I readjust the little purse over my shoulder. "He's, uh . . . not coming."

"Not coming?" she repeats. To avoid her questioning stare, I move past her inside the house. It doesn't deter her, though, as she catches up, Dylan trailing along behind us with the luggage. She pulls me to a stop in the kitchen. "What happened? You're normally attached at the hip. I thought this was your big romantic week after he got back from working in Thunder Bay?"

Her words sting, but I force myself not to let it show. "He doesn't feel good, so he stayed home."

"So that's, what? Six weeks in a row he's blown you off? God, Liv, grab the turtle."

"Grab the turtle?" Dylan asks.

Years ago, before we were even legally old enough to drive a Sea-Doo, Jenna and I took them out, and as we were passing one of the islands, we saw a turtle. It was on its back and flailing, and I know they can flip themselves, but it seemed to be injured or something, because it couldn't do it. We stopped the Sea-Doos and floated nearby, watching the turtle struggle forever, until we finally had enough. I jumped in the water and swam to shore, and Jenna stayed back to hold onto my Sea-Doo so it wouldn't float away. But then I crawled up onto the island, and, like most tiny, deserted islands in Muskoka, discovered it was overrun by snakes. The turtle was still there, writhing legs and arms and making these desperate little noises, and though my heart couldn't take it, I was frozen in fear. I shouted to Jenna about the snakes, and she yelled, *Just grab the turtle, Liv! Grab the turtle!* It took all the courage I had, but eventually, with Jenna's urging, I did it, gently grabbing the turtle and leaving it right side up by the shore as I swam back to Jenna, my heart racing and body shaking with adrenaline.

"It's cousin speak for *grow some balls*," I inform him. Even at that young age, Jenna declared the phrase sexist, so we've replaced it with *grab the turtle* for times we need to step up and be brave.

Dylan's confused, but he doesn't ask for clarification. "All right. Why does Olivia need to grow some balls?"

Jenna's icy blue eyes look so much more intimidating when she narrows them at us. "So she can tell your shitty best friend that he's a pathetic excuse for a boyfriend and she deserves better."

I flinch, because she doesn't know just how accurate she is even though she's unaware of Alessio's infidelity. Dylan gives nothing away, just looks at me with an uncharacteristically serious expression that makes my heartbeat double as he says, "You're right. She does deserve better."

Jenna doesn't catch the deeper meaning to his words; how could she? Instead, she brushes past the intense moment and walks down the hall, sure we'll follow. "Glad we're on the same page. But now that Alessio isn't here, this is kind of awkward, since I saved you two the primary bedroom."

We follow her up the stairs, where she pushes open the door to the room I was supposed to be sharing with Alessio, and Dylan and I follow her in. It's a breathtaking, spacious room, one that you'd stay in during an expensive honeymoon. The decor is modern and elegant, and there's a king-sized bed facing the floor-to-ceiling wall of windows, which showcases a clear view of the lake and forest. There's a stylish couch against the wall that I doubt anyone has ever sat on, with a coffee table in front of it. The balcony doors are pushed open so there's a breeze coming in, and the fresh air helps calm my racing thoughts, because *this* is where I was supposed to reconnect with Alessio, and instead, I'm standing here with a broken heart and his best friend.

"Also awkward," Jenna continues, turning to face us, "is that Kyle invited Hari, so we're short a bed for you, Dylan. Maybe I can talk the girls into switching with Robbie and Fletcher so Dylan can share a queen-sized bed with a guy, but I have a feeling Martina will double down after the standoff with Fletcher, so there's no way in hell that will go down without a fight and a half. I guess I could give up my bed and sleep here with Olivia, since I'd rather sleep outside on the hammock than share with Elena or Martina, but I kind of had this whole thing with Hari . . . God, his stupid gloating when I move after I said I wouldn't is going to be *so* self-righteous." She says that last part more to herself than to us, glaring at the wall behind us like she's envisioning the scene playing out.

I don't want to make everyone move around because of me, especially since I know they've already unpacked, but I also don't want to share a room with anyone. I need a space for myself, a place where I don't have to pretend everything is fine and that Alessio just has the flu. I can't come here to escape if I'm sharing it with Jenna, and I can't hide anything with Elena and Martina coming in and out of the room on a whim. I'm friendly enough with them, but they're *Jenna's* friends, not mine. It will already be awkward sharing a bed with one of them, never mind trying to hold it together the entire time we're sharing, especially late at night when there's nothing to distract me from the anger and hurt and pain.

"No!" I protest a bit too loudly, and they both look at me, confused. I correct my tone to be less desperate-sounding. "No, it's, uh . . . it's all right. Don't move everyone around because of us, especially since there's clearly some . . . politics going on." I add that last part for Dylan's benefit to not give Jenna away, but I know my cousin, and I know she's probably being stubborn and trying to prove some kind of point to Hari, especially since she's apparently willingly sharing a room with him when she once told me that she'd rather rip her toenails off than be his partner for their upcoming science project. "Dylan and I can share this room, right, Dyl?"

It's not the same as being alone, but sharing with Dylan is the only way I can stay free of another roommate. Plus, Dylan knows everything already; I won't need to pretend with him like I would with everyone else.

Dylan studies me, hard, like he's trying and failing to read my mind. But like the selfless, kind man I know he is, he does exactly what I knew he would and says, "Yeah, we can, uh . . . we're good here."

Jenna's normally carefully composed face gives away every feeling of shock and bewilderment at my suggestion. She ignores Dylan as she clarifies, "You want to share a room with Dylan. A man who's not your boyfriend. The two of you. In a room together. With one bed. For a week. Knowing Alessio would lose his shit if he found out. You, my cousin, Olivia Rossi, are suggesting this?"

Dutiful, loyal, perfect girlfriend Olivia would never even dream of making that suggestion. But I'm not her anymore. I'm single. I'm just . . . Olivia. The thought is like a kick in the stomach, but I play it off, shrugging for Jenna. "It's not a big deal. It's a king-sized bed, I won't even know he's there."

Jenna stares at me, and it's an effort not to shrink under her intense scrutiny. I don't know how long I'll be able to keep this secret from her, but I'm not ready to share yet. It's only been a few hours, and not only am I still processing, but admitting it to her almost seems like it would make it too real, like I'd be declaring out loud how stupid I am to not have called Alessio out on his bullshit earlier like she demanded I do. Once Jenna knows, there's no going back.

Dylan drops his duffel bag on the floor, drawing our attention. He jumps on the couch and lies back, settling in. "It's all right, I'll take the couch. It's nice and big and comfy. Besides, I've heard Olivia likes to sleep starfish anyway, so she can keep the bed."

The couch is nice, but it's neither big nor seemingly comfy. Dylan's knees are bent to keep his whole body on the couch, and if he stretched them out, they'd hang right over the decorative edge. It's clear it was meant as a showpiece, not a replacement bed, so I highly doubt it's as comfortable as he's trying to make it seem, though his smile is lazy and his body relaxed.

Jenna's eyes flit between us. "Did something hap—"

"Hey, Jenna!" Fletcher's voice calls up to us from somewhere downstairs. "We're trying to take the Sea-Doos out, but the garage door on the boathouse isn't opening."

Panic fills Jenna's face. "Wait! I said not to touch anything without me!" she calls, sprinting out of the room without a backward glance. With her gone and an interrogation seemingly avoided, I blow out a breath, my shoulders dropping as the tenseness leaves my body.

Dylan sits up, rolling out his neck. I knew it. Despite the good job he did pretending otherwise, it's clear that the couch is little more than hard wood and cloth.

"For real, are you okay with sharing a room?" he asks. "I can sleep on the couch in the living room."

"No, it's fine. You wouldn't get any sleep out there, considering how some people stay up playing drinking games until five in the morning and others wake up at six to make smoothies. I *don't* care if we share." I realize it as I say it out loud. I don't care if we share the room, but I'm unsure if it's because I feel comfortable with Dylan or I'm just numb to the whole situation.

"Are you positive? I can get someone to switch with me."

"No!" I protest, again just a bit too loud, too desperate. Dylan freezes where he is, and my voice is small when I admit, "I don't have to . . . pretend . . . with you."

Understanding dawns on Dylan, and I look away before he hits me with those eyes again, the look that makes me feel like my ribs are too tight in my chest.

I still can't look at him when I say, "I, um . . . I think I'm going to take a shower. Wash away the day, you know?"

"Sure, all right." He hefts my suitcase on the white cushioned bench at the end of the bed, turning it so the zipper side faces outward for easy access. "If you need anything, let me know."

My eyebrows draw together. "If I need anything in the shower?"

He straightens up so fast he almost trips over the plush rug around the bed. "What? No, it's like—I mean—if you need anything in general."

He looks away and rubs a hand over the back of his neck, and I'm too drained to figure out why he's being weird.

"I'll be fine. Thanks, Dyl." I unzip my luggage to grab my toiletry bag, and he backs away to the door.

"I'll be downstairs if you need me."

"Again, I'm sure I'll be fine, but thank you."

Dylan curses under his breath, but I still hear it. "Right, okay. Have fun." His eyes widen, then he turns around, muttering to himself, though this time I can't make it out as he all but sprints down the hall.

The blood drains from my face as I consider his behavior. Maybe *he* didn't want to share the room with *me. So stupid, Olivia.* I can't believe I didn't consider Dylan's opinion before announcing we'd take the primary room. Now I feel even worse than I did before. Dylan's fun. People are naturally drawn to his charm, his charisma. He can walk into any room and make everyone there feel comfortable, get everyone to have a great time. And now I've forcibly shackled him to me, the sad girl whose heart was just broken. *That's* why he was acting weird: he doesn't want to spend the last week of summer dealing with me.

Grabbing my toiletry bag and, at the last minute, my phone, I slip into the private en suite bathroom, locking the door and leaning against it, sliding down until I'm sitting on the marble floor.

I was selfish for a moment, making Dylan room with me, and

now I've pushed him away. This is why I always try to consider other people before making my decisions. But then again, I did that with Alessio, and look at how well that turned out.

My phone in my hand lights up, and the background picture of me and Alessio stares back at me. It's from when we went apple picking around this time last year, on a double date with his friend Adam and Jenna. Alessio's carrying me on his back, and we're smiling at each other—no fears, no worries, just love—not even noticing when Jenna snapped the picture.

It's a cruel reminder of what I've lost, of how sour our relationship turned, and I set the phone face down on the floor so I don't have to look at it. A drop of water lands on it, and I angrily swipe at my face. I didn't even realize I started crying, and I hate myself for it. I can't spend this whole week crying over Alessio. I refuse to. That's why I'm here, surrounded by people, so I *can't* mope over him, and yet here I am, hiding away, crying.

I stand and yank the door open, ready to storm out and force myself to socialize, but stop just before bulldozing through a pretty blond. She's standing in front of the door, hand raised and poised like she was preparing to knock.

"Oh, hey, Elena," I say, hastily wiping away any remaining evidence of my breakdown. I should've looked in the mirror before marching out of the bathroom.

"Sorry, I didn't mean to intrude." She steps back and drops her hand. "But I really needed to use the bathroom, and the guys stunk up two of them and Martina is showering in the third one for some reason even though we don't have to get ready for tonight for a long time, and Jenna told me to use the one in here, but I heard you crying and I didn't know if you wanted to be interrupted and comforted or if you wanted to be left alone, so I was standing here debating whether or not to check on you and here we are."

She says the entire thing as one sentence, practically in the same breath too. I blink at her as she smiles innocently at me. She's taller than me and older than me by a few months, and yet it would be believable if I told people she was my younger sister.

I clear my throat, embarrassed at having been caught. "Yeah, sorry. I'm okay. The bathroom is all yours."

I step aside to let her pass, but she doesn't move, instead studying me with her huge blue eyes that only add to her beautiful, doll-like appearance.

"It's not your fault that you're crying, you know." She gestures to the drying tearstains on my cheeks. "Mercury's in retrograde. It's screwing with all our emotions. And you're a Scorpio, right? Yeah, makes sense. For Scorpios, when Mercury is in retrograde, emotions rule."

Mercury in retrograde? Scorpio? Is she talking about star signs and horoscopes? That has nothing to do with anything, but if she believes astrology is the reason I'm hiding in the bathroom crying instead of out at the lake with everyone else, I'm not going to contradict her.

She continues, nodding like this is a perfectly reasonable explanation, "Mercury in retrograde is going to make our lives as inconvenient as possible. Secrets come out, and we ignore common sense and lead with our hearts, but don't worry, it usually brings attention to situations that are unsettled and helps you leave the past behind and get closure."

"Right, for sure."

Elena may be the most approachable of Jenna's friends, but she and I are complete opposites. She's the kind of person who's content flitting from one relationship to another, who can talk to anyone about anything, who believes our behaviors and actions are determined by fate and the stars. But she's always been kind to me, she is being so right now, so I've never told her astrology is just pseudoscience.

I move from the threshold of the bathroom, throwing my toiletry bag and phone into my suitcase and zipping it back up. "I'll keep that in mind," I tell Elena before gesturing to the hallway. "I'll see you out there."

I leave the room—the one I was supposed to share with Alessio—and head down the stairs. The kitchen is empty, and I can see everyone outside in the distance. Fletcher and Kyle are on the two Sea-Doos, doing donuts around each other in the lake, and Jenna's at the edge of the dock, frantically flailing her arms and shouting something at them I'm too far away to hear. Dylan's there, too, with a beer in his hand, smiling as he talks to the other guys. My heart grows heavy as it sinks in who's missing.

Maybe Elena has it right after all. Maybe I don't have to look at the facts of my relationship with Alessio. I don't have to wonder why he cheated, what went wrong, how I'm supposed to go on without him, and who I'm supposed to be. Maybe I can blame it all on a bunch of planets rotating around us, influencing actions and behaviors, and pretend that it's all part of some predetermined greater plan.

SEVEN

Night 1 of Muskoka

Jenna

After a fun afternoon on the lake, I manage to convince everyone to put the water toys back into the boathouse for the day. Those are expensive, multi-thousand-dollar crafts, and I don't want anyone on them without me around. In a perfect world, we'd have just left them in the boathouse, but that wouldn't make this the best trip ever, and everyone would be bored all day on the lake. So they had to be taken out, and I'll just be extra careful making sure nothing happens to them. Now, it's nearly time for dinner, and since I don't want anyone out on the water while I'm getting ready for the party, I lie and ask for help.

I never need help setting up for my parties; in fact, I really enjoy doing it alone. I love taking any theme, any space, and transforming it into a perfect party environment. Not only does decorating set the vibe and energy of the party, but proper decorations create an *atmosphere*, an unforgettable one where you truly believe you're in a pink paradise or a winter wonderland or, in today's case, the 1980s.

And I've gotten really good at making backdrops that are perfect for photo ops, since I know people really want to show off in front of a great staged area for their Instagram. Watching it all come together seamlessly gives me a giddy feeling.

My friends somehow got into my garage before we cleared the house and brought all the boxes of stuff I prepared for this party. In another world, one where I wasn't worried about a party in this multimillion-dollar property, I'd be touched, but right now, I'm focused on setting up and getting through the night. I spend a lot of time delegating where each table should go and what prop should go where and *Fletcher for the third time that sign is upside down*, but it keeps them inside and away from the watercraft.

It's a last-minute "surprise" party, so it won't be as grand as Elena's, but I'm completely okay with that. I was prepared to have no birthday party, and I'm aware that I'd be alone in a dorm room right now if not for this impromptu trip. In fact, I wouldn't even have a cake if not for Elena surprising me with one, a three-tiered beauty that she has delivered to the cottage before dinner.

Seeing it makes my eyes water, and we are equally surprised when I pull her into a hug. I can't help it. My own dad didn't wish me a happy birthday today, not even a quick text, so it means a lot being here with friends who want to celebrate me. It makes me glad I orchestrated this trip even if I get grounded for eternity.

But that thought gets pushed to the back of my mind once it hits 11:00 p.m. and the party is in full swing. We're isolated up here, so you'd think fewer people would come than back home, where everyone lives, but as I run around my cottage, the crowd getting bigger and bigger seemingly by the minute, it's clear that's not true. Either a lot of people rented cottages this year because we've graduated or they've convinced designated drivers to make the trip up, because the cottage is livelier than ever.

Robbie set up his DJ equipment in the living room, the speakers scattered through the property carrying the sound of his 80s mix.

I'm currently on my hands and knees in the kitchen, soaking up a spill that was apparently an entire gallon of fruit juice. The red liquid is everywhere—puddled on the white granite of the kitchen island, dripping down the white cabinets to pool on the hardwood floor. I don't know much about cleaning, but I do know leaving a red liquid to sit on white surfaces doesn't bode well, and neither does leaving a puddle on hardwood floors.

Someone bumps into me, and I catch myself, soaking the sheer sleeve of my black dress in the juice. "Watch it!" I shout, ready to cuss someone out, but they're already gone. I growl out loud to myself, "This *sucks!*"

I was having fun earlier like I always do at my parties, but that was when there were fewer people so I was able to dance and drink and socialize without any worries. As the night went on, I started getting nervous about all the people who were showing up. The party is getting bigger than I'm comfortable with, and it doesn't help that it's raining outside, so besides the covered patio out back, everyone's inside. I've had to block off a section in the basement and stop multiple giggling couples from trying to jump over the barrier to the upstairs in search of a private bedroom. I'm so busy running around I haven't had so much as a drop to drink in hours.

I finally get the spill cleaned up, but I force myself not to look at the multiple other ones on the floor and go check on the basement. I can't follow everyone around with a mop, not when there are girls dancing on the glass side table and guys tossing a football around in the lounge area a bit too close to the flat-screen TV.

I confiscate the football and get the girls down, but I'm tired, and this is annoying. I want to have fun, and I want to make sure everyone else has fun, but it's hard managing this entire party by myself. Where the hell is Olivia? She's usually the one who controls the chaos a bit.

I run back up the stairs and spot her by her brown hair with the caramel highlights I made her get as a pick-me-up a few weeks back when Alessio went to Cuba without her. She's sitting on the couch in the living room, holding a drink and staring at the wall, surrounded by partiers but interacting with none of them.

I march over to her, and she doesn't even notice me standing in front of her until I flick her nose.

"Ow!"

"What the hell is wrong with you?"

Olivia rubs her nose then looks down at her drink without answering. Her shoulders are curled in on herself, and she looks like she'd rather be anywhere than here right now. Did Alessio call and give her shit for coming without him? He's such an ass, he doesn't even have to say those specific words to guilt her. When Adam and I were dating and he'd have us over, Alessio would stand with Adam's sister, Faye, the girl in my grade who's always hated my guts and gone out of her way to push my buttons since that first day of homeroom. She'd giggle and talk shit about me, even though I was standing right there, and Alessio would laugh with her and join in. It always grated on my nerves. But if Olivia wants to marry him, like her vision board implies, then I can't exactly force her to dump his ass.

"I'm sure Alessio will come up later. You're allowed to have fun without him."

She doesn't answer, just plays with the aluminum of her vodka cooler as her pout seems to deepen.

I study her face, daring her to lie to me. "Did something happen with Alessio?"

She opens her mouth, then closes it. As she opens it again, a glowing orange light catches my eye. On the other side of the house, where the fireplace and cozy sitting area is, a group of boys from our graduating class are lighting cigarettes. *In the house!*

"Hey!" I yell even though they can't hear me over the music, and I charge toward them. "You can't smoke in the house!"

Nicolas, a boy I took math class with for all four years of school, says, "It's raining outside."

"*And?* Smoke on the back porch where it's covered!"

He flicks his thumb against the cigarette, and ash falls to the floor. My blood pressure rises by at least 10 percent with the effort it takes not to grab the smelly little white stick and make him swallow it.

"Get the hell out!" I order, pointing to the screen door that leads to the back.

Boris, a boy who once broke his arm while jumping over the soccer nets on the school's field attempting to impress me and my friends, sends me a confused look. "But we smoke in your house all the time when it rains."

I stare at him, and he shrinks back a little, but the entire group of smokers are watching me as if waiting for me to remember.

People smoked in my house when it rained? I either never noticed or never cared before.

Someone else ashes on the floor, and my eye twitches. "New rules, no smoking in the house. Get out."

I stand there expectantly as the group trudges out, muttering something about it being windy out there, but I don't care.

"No smoking in the house," I say again as the last person passes me, then, as if anyone can hear me over the music, I yell, *"No smoking in the house!"*

The party continues, and I use a tissue to wipe up the ash and inspect the hardwood underneath it, breathing a sigh of relief when I verify that it's perfectly unaffected.

I barely stand up before I hear a commotion in the living room.

"God, what *now?*" I ask out loud. I swear I haven't gotten a second to breathe before having to run around playing party mom.

Two guys are in the living room, and their loud argument has escalated into a full-blown fistfight.

"Hey! Stop it!" I yell, running over to them.

Everyone except for Olivia has cleared the space, trying not to be collateral damage. She's still sitting in the exact spot I left her, unconcerned or unaware of the fight directly in front of her.

"That's enough!" I yell again, trying and failing to break them up without also getting a black eye. "Stop it! Stop fighting! You're going to break something! Hit each other outside where you're not going to go through my window!"

They keep fighting. The music keeps playing. Olivia keeps staring blankly at the drink in her hands.

"*Kyle! Fletcher!*" I call for my largest friends, but I have no idea where they are. I haven't seen any of my friends all night.

One of the fighters pushes the other away and uses the newly provided space to tackle him. They go straight into the wall, and my stomach drops when the drywall crumbles.

"*Noooooo!*" I screech. My knees almost give out as I stare at the torso-sized hole in the wall. There's mud and alcohol and crumbs all over the floor, empty cans and glass bottles and cups littered throughout the property, but none of that matters, not really, not compared to this. A hole in the wall is not something I can clean up, not something I can hide from my dad and whoever he gets to come view the house.

Fletcher, my 6'5" Scottish hero with slightly delayed timing and purple lipstick smudges on his chin and cheek, rushes in from wherever he was, taking each boy's bicep in his giant hands and ripping them away from each other.

"Get them out of my house!" I order, and Fletcher nods, struggling to keep them apart as they try to lunge at each other even with my large friend between them, yelling about how one of them did or didn't sleep with the other's girlfriend.

Hari appears and takes the alleged girlfriend stealer from Fletcher, but the fighters are drunk enough that they don't even realize they're being held back.

"You all right?" Hari asks me, catching me off guard.

There's no hint of his usual teasing tone or know-it-all smirk, and it ruffles me so much that my voice comes out earnestly when I ask, "Can you make sure they're not driving and have a safe way to get back to wherever they're going?"

"Of course," he says with no arguments or rebuttals or stupid comments, and the whole exchange unsettles me so much, I stand there and stare after his retreating form until a partygoer comments on the giant hole in the wall, and I'm brought back to the situation.

I can't fix the hole; in fact, I have no idea how to fix it. At home, the cleaning crew would make the calls to whoever could fix anything that was broken, but the only cleaning crew I have now is *me* and whatever emergency cash I have stashed in my luggage since I can't use my credit card and tip Dad off. That fight might have just drained every cent of that fund, plus more that I don't have.

I whirl around on Olivia, who's still sitting there on the couch, staring out the wall of windows now.

"Liv!" She's lost in her own thoughts and doesn't seem to hear me, so I get close and wave my hand in front of her face. *"O-liv-i-a!"*

She blinks and comes back to awareness, like she's just realized she's at a party, and it pisses me off.

"Who are you and what have you done with my cousin?" I ask her, pointing at the hole in the drywall. "The Olivia I know would have prevented that from happening! It's exhausting running around stopping people from ruining shit!" I'm having no fun, and the anxiety in my chest has grown so large it's threatening to overtake me. The only reason I haven't stopped breathing is because I'm too pissed to give in.

Olivia only shrugs. "Sorry."

I force myself to take a beat to calm down. It's not her fault those dickwads broke out in a fight, and she's clearly not herself right now.

"What aren't you telling me? Why do you look like someone kicked your dog?"

She blinks a few times then stands. "I don't want to talk about it." She pushes past me, and I stare after her, watching as she seemingly makes herself smaller in order to slip through the crowds of people.

All right, I'm going to have to add *hold intervention for Olivia* to my ever-growing list of things to do tonight. Something's wrong, and since this is the last time I'll see her in who knows how long, I can't have her being sad on this trip.

Glass breaks, and I let out a shriek. I'm tired, I'm frustrated, and I can't afford any more damage.

Before I can go investigate, Elena runs up to me, eyes alight and smile wide. "Jenna! I swear every time I catch sight of you, you disappear!"

Because I haven't stopped running around all night. "Yeah, it's been . . ." I don't want her to know how awful it's been, because I've never had a bad time at my parties, and I don't want that to be the memory she has of the only party she's ever thrown me. I finish with, ". . . a crazy night."

"Tell me about it!" she exclaims, but she says it like it's the best thing ever, not in the way I feel like pulling out all my hair. "*Everyone's* already been posting about how great this party is. You have a hashtag! It's trending!" She pulls out her phone, quickly scrolling through the pictures that people have posted from the party using the various 80s setups I put together.

There's nothing discernible in any of the pictures that could prove they were taken at the cottage; the photo backdrops with interactive props are the main stars, so I'm not worried about Dad seeing it. Dad doesn't use personal social media, and his assistant handles all his realtor posts, so he won't see it regardless.

She continues quickly showing me the various pictures, fawning over how great the sections that she helped set up ended up photographing.

This type of thing would have delighted me a few weeks ago. I would have been ecstatic about the success of the event, so proud that people were enjoying all the hard work I put in to make this theme come alive. And while I'm still proud of what I've put together, I'm so annoyed with all the things going wrong, all the people being so careless and disrespectful with my belongings and property. I never realized how inconsiderate partygoers are until now.

"That's really great," I tell her, even managing to sound like I mean it.

She tucks the phone in her bra and grabs my hand. "Come on, we need to do cake and get some photos in before I do that drunk squinty thing I always do in pictures after a few too many shots."

Someone knocks a bottle over on the counter, and half the beer pours out. *Seriously?* I start going to it, but Elena holds me back.

"Where are you going? I put the cake in front of the black backdrop with the neon JENNA'S 18TH BIRTHDAY sign. It looks so cute! Kyle is guarding it to make sure no one touches it, but we should go before some drunk guy dives through it on a dare."

I glance longingly at the mess on the kitchen island where more than just that one beer bottle has spilled. "Elena . . ."

She drops my hand and wraps her arms around herself, her big blue eyes watering. "Are you mad at me? You've been avoiding me all night. Did the party not turn out the way you wanted? Or is it something else? I'm sorry if I did something that upset you."

A ball forms in my stomach. Elena's going to school in Newfoundland, a whole province and plane ride away from here, and she's going to leave thinking I'm upset with her if I spend my whole time policing the party. All my friends will leave without even remembering their time with me this week, and that's the opposite of what I wanted.

"What? Of course I'm not mad at you!" A smile slides into place, and I physically feel the shift within myself as I shut off party-mom mode and slip back into no-stress-or-worries party Jenna. "You know how it is; everyone wants a piece of the birthday girl."

Relief crosses her face, and she links her arm through mine. "Well, come on, birthday girl! Time for your photoshoot with the cake!"

I follow her, waving to people and smiling and laughing the whole way to the cake, just like I would've done if the party had been at my house. And when I get to the cake, and my friends are there, smiling and laughing and trying to jump in the pictures or instruct me on the best cake-cutting technique, I promise myself that for the rest of the night, my problems are going to be ignored. I'm not even bothered by Hari's presence, not even when he boops me on the nose with a finger full of frosting and laughs in delight when my eyes cross trying to see the tip of my nose. I don't even say anything to Olivia when I notice her trudging through the house covered in mud way after 2:00 a.m., especially since she's smiling. For tonight, I'm regular Jenna with no worries or fears or abandonment issues and nothing on her mind but having a good time. And for the rest of the night, that's exactly what I do.

EIGHT

Night 1 of Muskoka

Olivia

After I leave Jenna in the living room, I slip through the crowd, trying to find some space, maybe some fresh air to help snap me out of whatever is going on in my brain. Jenna's right, I'm being a downer, and I promised myself I wouldn't do that this trip.

I pass Martina, who's using a framed mirror hanging on the hallway wall to reapply her smudged purple lipstick, and she winks at me as I pass. She's having fun, clearly, so why can't I? I should be there with her, giggling into the mirror and trading party gossip—that's what single girls do, and I'm single now.

Once I step outside, the cool air helps relieve the tension in my chest, and I take some deep breaths. It smells like wet grass and mud, and the pattering of the rain on the roof drowns out a fraction of the noise. The covered patio is large, almost as long and wide as the kitchen and living room inside. I cross it and lean against the railing, setting my untouched drink beside me, watching the rain hit the lake and create a beautiful mist on it. Other people are out here, but no one pays me any attention.

I'm not supposed to be thinking about Alessio, fretting about my future, or repeatedly running through a list of facts about why this break is for the best, but I can't seem to shut off my mind.

I was so lost in thought I didn't even notice those two guys going at it, not really. It registered, but it was like a leaf blowing in the wind, something I acknowledged in the back of my mind but ignored.

I was doing okay before the party started getting busy, then I saw happy couples everywhere, touching and kissing and laughing, and it got my mind spinning. That should've been me and Alessio, but he cheated on me, and I need to remember that. But he was my best friend. We did everything together. If I don't forgive him, who will I talk to? Share my secrets with? Laugh with? I don't even have any friends. I have people I'm *friendly* with, but no one is my *friend*, and not because a lack of trying.

It's always been hard for me to make friends. I couldn't even find study buddies for school, hence the creation of my app, which is out of beta testing and rolling out for real next week. My lack of friends didn't *truly* bother me because I had Alessio and *his* friends, like Dylan and Adam and Kellan, but they're his friends before they're mine, and if this breakup is permanent, I'll really have no one.

But is being lonely a reason to stay with someone who cheated on me? Did he really think he could just sleep around and not tell me? That's awful and irresponsible on so many levels. What if he got a sexually transmitted infection and gave it to me? He wasn't thinking about me at all, and I should be doing the same.

"Hey," a deep voice says from my left, and I startle. "How about this one: Among land animals, what species has the largest eyes?" Dylan asks, and I forget to pretend to take a few moments to think before I answer.

"Ostrich."

"I guess that was an easy one for you." Dylan's smile turns sad, and it looks all wrong on him. "You moved from staring blankly at the wall to staring blankly at the lake. Should I consider that progress? At least it's nicer scenery."

I blow out a breath. "I know, I'm sorry I'm a downer; Jenna already gave me the third degree. But cut me some slack here. I found out about Alessio *this morning*. Not even a full twenty-four hours ago. We were together for *five years*, Dylan."

"I know, I was there, Livy." He says it like the words weigh heavily on him, like there's another meaning behind them. He leans his forearms against the railing, settling in. "People change. You two started dating in ninth grade. You were both young, and even though you're smarter than most adults I know and you're not even eighteen yet, you're already a different person now than you were at thirteen, and you're going to be a different person again in another five years. So maybe you two were perfect five years ago, but when you think about it, even without the cheating, maybe you've outgrown each other. Maybe you're better off without Alessio holding you back."

"Alessio holds me back?"

He doesn't have to say *duh* out loud; it's written all over his face. "Come on, Liv. You're in the top one percent of students in the entirety of U of T, you created an awesome app that lets you find study groups and set up drop-ins by class and school that got amazing reviews from all across Canada during its beta testing, and yet you're still so oblivious when it comes to boys."

"I'm not oblivious, and Alessio isn't—wasn't—holding me back," I state, but a small voice in the back of my head disagrees, the seed of doubt growing.

"Really? Then what does he think about your app?" he asks,

raising an eyebrow like he already knows the answer but wants me to say it out loud anyway.

I think back to almost a year ago, when I was so excited because I'd already researched and created a rough prototype before telling anyone. He said he didn't see the appeal of an app that sets up study groups because normal people just make friends and study with them, they don't need an app for it. But I need an app for it, and so do other people like me, people who aren't like him, who can't just make everyone love them the second they meet. He's always been social enough for the both of us, so he's never understood the app.

It's filtered by school, and it can be filtered even further by course and section. Anyone can set a time for a study session, and people who added that course to their profile get a notification and can choose to join. You don't need to know the other person, and you don't need to have friends in the course. You just form study groups, and anyone is welcome to come.

Even after it rolled out for beta testing and was doing fairly well with the minimal marketing I was able to do by myself, Alessio still didn't understand why I was wasting so much time on research, design, development, marketing, and outreach when my goal was medical school followed by a residency and fellowship in neurosurgery. It made me want to give up, because maybe it *was* stupid, and I was blind to it. But a lot of the feedback was from people like me who said it helped them not only get the most out of studying but also make friends in an environment where they felt alone, and it pushed me to keep going. I stopped talking about it with Alessio.

"He just didn't understand it," I tell Dylan, but it sounds like a pathetic excuse even to me.

"Maybe, but if he loved you, he should've supported you to the fullest, asking you how he could help regardless of whether he understood it or not, because he wanted you to succeed." He straightens up from where he was leaning, giving me his full attention, and I'm hypnotized by his dark eyes, by the heat coming off his body, by the sensual yet smoky notes of his cologne. "If you were my girlfriend, I would've bragged to anyone who would listen about how amazing you are, about how they need to download the app when it launches next week, about how proud I am of you."

The way he's looking at me makes heat crawl up my spine, so like I did in the car, I deflect by pointing out, "You're his best friend, shouldn't you be defending him?"

"Friends or not, I'm not going to defend him if he's an idiot. He screwed up the best thing that's ever happened to him. You deserve better, Liv."

There's so much conviction in his words and ferocity in his eyes that my throat feels thick, and I have to turn back to the lake. He doesn't let me go far, though, because he gently takes my face in his hands, turning me to look at him again. He lowers himself to my eye level, and like he really wants it to sink in, he repeats, "You deserve better, Livy."

His voice and touch are so gentle, like he's being extra delicate with me, that I have to blink back tears. "I just hate feeling like this. Everyone's having fun, and I'm the annoying girl thinking about the boy who broke her heart."

His eyes search mine for a second before he drops his hands and straightens with a new resolve. "So let's go have fun."

Easier said than done. It's almost impossible when my mind keeps wandering back to Alessio.

"Come on," he says, grabbing my hand and leading me through the patio. People wave and call out to Dylan, but he's a man on a mission and ignores them all.

"Where are we going?"

He stops at the stairs and sits down. "Onto the grass."

"Why? We'll get soaked. And it's muddy."

"And? I like this song." He tugs me to sit with him, then he peels off his shoes and socks, tucking the socks into the shoes and setting them neatly to the side. I watch him, unconvinced.

"Come on, Livy. Do you want to keep staring at the wall aimlessly, or do you want to have fun?"

This sounds ridiculous, but he has a point. Screw it. What do I have to lose?

Beside him, I rip off my own sneakers and socks. He gives them the same treatment as he did his own and puts them together under a chair. Then he takes my hand and carefully helps me down the stairs. We're soaked instantly, my white 80s-themed crop top and jean shorts doing nothing to fend off the rain, but I follow Dylan as he leads us off the path and out of the landscaped area. There's tons of grass on the property—acres of grass and trees and nature—and he pulls us to a stop in what seems to be the muddiest, puddliest area not far from the lights and music.

"Now what?" I ask Dylan over the rain. His own white T-shirt is plastered to his chest, showing off every single line and curve of his sculpted chest and abs and shoulders and biceps. It's an effort not to stare.

He drops my hand, and I link my fingers together, as if that can replace the warmth and comfort his touch provided.

Dylan jumps in a puddle, and I shriek as the muddy water splashes all the way up my leg. "Dylan!"

"What? Have you never played in the mud?" He does it again, the mud splashing all over his 80s-style trousers and all the way up to my top. "Come on, Livy."

His smile is devilish, and I decide I like it more than the sad ones he gives me when he's comforting me. So I charge and jump into the same deep puddle, getting such a good splash his cheek gets a streak of mud on it.

"That's my girl," he encourages, then he scoops up a glob of mud and drops it on my head. It's cold and slimy and slides down the back of my neck, and all the while I'm staring up at him incredulously, he's looking down at me with this sparkle in his eye that makes me want to throw myself at him.

Instead, I pick up my own glob of mud. "Oh, you are *so* on."

His eyes light up as he turns to run, but he slips, his legs flailing as he lands in the watery mud. I show him no mercy as I cover his head with the pile I have in my hand, and he grabs my arm, pulling me down with him. I land on his chest, but he turns so I'm the one lying in the mud, and he uses the arm that's not propping himself up to scoop mud over me.

"No fair, you're cheating!" I exclaim, gripping a fistful of watery mud and smashing it on his head.

He's hovering over me, using his forearms to keep himself from crushing me. There's mud in his hair and all over his face, and as the rain continues beating down, it dilutes the mud, turning it into muddy water that streams onto my face. He realizes this and shakes his head, making me squeal as more falls over me.

"You are the worst!" I laugh, shoving at him and managing to flip him over, but at the last minute he wraps his arms around me, taking me with him.

I'm splayed out across his body, and the rain is pouring down on us, and Dylan's looking up at me through wet lashes with his arms wrapped around me, and my body melts into him of its own accord. Gone are his sad, pity-filled eyes, and in their place is classic carefree, fun Dylan, the boy everyone feels comfortable with, who's everyone's friend. My heart pounds extra hard, and it's not from the exertion.

"I am not the worst," he defends himself, and a sound from

beside us draws our attention. Other people from the party have followed us down, jumping and rolling around and throwing mud at each other.

"Look what you've started!" It's an accusation, but it's filled with way too much amusement to have any real effect on him. He shifts me off him then pulls us to our feet.

"I don't know what you're talking about. It looks like a bunch of people who know how to have fun."

Facing me, he hooks his arm through mine, and we skip and spin around to the song, kicking through the muddy water. We leap-frog over each other and lie on the ground to make mud angels, and he even pushes me on the old wooden tree swing that Grandpa made all those years ago.

I have fun. More fun than I've had on this trip yet, more fun than I had in the last six weeks, and maybe even more fun than I've had all year. My mind is free of all my worries and doubts and stresses, and I'm laughing so hard my stomach hurts. I never want the night to end.

And it's all because of Dylan.

—

Time flies, and by the time Dylan and I rinse ourselves off with the hose on the deck, it's 2:00 a.m. The party is still in full swing, and despite having an amazing time, the exhaustion from the day seems to hit me all at once. I can't stop yawning, and even my *bones* feel tired.

The few times I accompanied Alessio to a party, I wouldn't go to bed until he was ready, and that was usually *way* later than I would like. But I'm not with Alessio anymore, and I can go to bed whenever I want. I brace myself for a pang of hurt at the realization, but all I feel is relief.

"Hey." I tap Dylan on the shoulder, and he looks up from his plate of cake. Elena saved each of us a piece, hiding them in her blocked-off room. "I'm going to go shower and get in bed."

Some part of me expects him to tell me not to go to bed yet, that the night is still young and the party is still thriving, like Alessio would have, but he doesn't. "I'll give you the room to get ready."

Still wet, I tiptoe through the house, my shoes in my hand, and contort through the barrier to the second floor. Once I close the door to my room, the music is only slightly muffled and the floor seems to vibrate, but I'm so tired I doubt I'll have a problem sleeping through it.

I take an extra-long shower, the hot water making quick work of the dried clumps of mud in my hair and the tension knots in my neck. My mind briefly wanders to Alessio and how we would've been enjoying this huge marble walk-in shower with the rain showerhead and massage jets together, but then I force my thoughts from him to tonight—to Dylan. I think of the way he looked, smiling and hand-some even while covered head to toe in mud, how he felt against me as we wrestled, how he made me laugh. But then I feel weird thinking about my ex's best friend while in the shower, and instead I think about all the things I still need to do for my app.

I only blow-dry my hair halfway so it's not dripping anymore, then I moisturize from head to toe before wrapping myself in the fluffiest towel in the cabinet. As I slowly open the door, I peek out to make sure the room is still empty. It is, and I pad out, my toes sinking into the rug in front of the bed as I unzip my suitcase. The floor is still vibrating, and now that the rain has stopped, the music is even clearer.

As I mindlessly sift through my suitcase, my hands land on silk and lace, and my breath hitches.

Oh no. Oh no no no.

I didn't bring any pajamas—or at least, I *did* bring pajamas, but they're incredibly inappropriate to wear while sharing a room with Dylan. The only sleepwear I brought are scraps of lacy lingerie that don't actually cover anything or leave anything to the imagination.

I thought I'd be sharing this room with Alessio, and since I hadn't seen him in so long, I wanted to dress cute for him and make this week special. But standing here in nothing but a towel, alone in the primary bedroom while clutching a pile of straps and silk, I feel incredibly stupid. I knew something was wrong, and yet I was still trying so hard to make everything okay again. Maybe Dylan's right, maybe I am oblivious when it comes to boys.

A knock sounds at the door, and I stare at it, frozen in fear, willing it to stay shut. "Livy?" Dylan calls over the music. "Can I come in?"

"Just a second!" I yell back, frantically stuffing the lingerie back into my suitcase and rummaging through it for something to wear to bed.

Crap. I never thought to repack before coming on the trip. With everything going on, what I'd packed was the last thing on my mind. But now that I'm sorting through my clothes, I realize I *only* brought cute things I thought Alessio would appreciate. I didn't pack a single plain T-shirt or sweatpants or loungewear of any kind. All I have is swimwear or sundresses or jeans that aren't going to be comfortable for bed. I don't even have a single pair of proper underwear, only thongs or scraps of fabric they try to pass off as thongs.

"Can I come in yet?" Dylan asks from the other side of the door, and my panic doubles.

"Not yet!"

I dig through the pile of lingerie, hoping to find the most con-servative of the bunch, and find a tiny black lace cami that exposes my stomach and matching silk shorts with lace cutouts on the side that barely cover my ass. It's not ideal, and it's *still* lingerie, but at least all my goodies are covered.

I put on some underwear and the cami and shorts, then hang the towel in the bathroom. Slipping into the massive king-sized bed, I yank the sheets up to my neck, gripping them for dear life as if they'll fly off and expose me in my skimpy pajamas the moment Dylan opens the door.

"All right, you can come in," I call, and the door opens.

The only light is coming from the standing lamp in the corner of the room and the smaller lamp on the nightstand, yet I can see Dylan perfectly. He's shirtless, his wet shirt wrung out and hanging over a broad shoulder. His hair dried frizzy, and there's a streak of mud on his temple he must have missed when drying off.

He closes the door behind him, effectively shutting us in our own little bubble, the sounds of the party now somehow seeming far away.

"Everything okay?" he asks, but it's different than how he would've asked this morning. It's less . . . pitying, maybe, more just asking because he cares.

"Yup." I nod, my chin rubbing against the comforter. The action causes me to spot a lacy bra dangling out of the zipper of my suitcase, and I rip my eyes away from it in case I give myself away. My face heats up, and I know it's bright red.

Thankfully, he turns to sort through his duffel to pull out his toiletry bag. "All right, well, I'll be in the shower if you need me." He pauses, quickly adding, "Not that you'll need anything from me in the shower. Just that that's where I'll be, so you know my location if you do happen to need me, while I'm showering . . ." He shakes his head and strides to the bathroom, muttering something along the lines of, "Again with the shower stuff. Get it together, man."

The second the door clicks, I launch up, crawling over the bed to stuff my bra back into my suitcase before zipping it closed. From my position on top of the bed, I kneel forward to double-check that nothing else fell out when I hear the handle of the bathroom door turning.

"Hey, Livy, do you know where the—"

I've never moved so fast. I fling myself backward on the bed, grabbing the sheets on the way and throwing them right over my head. I hear Dylan step out of the bathroom.

"Actually, never mind," he says, returning to the bathroom and closing the door, and I blow out a frustrated breath, shoving the sheets off my face. I'm not sure if he got a good look at my ass while I was bent over with it sticking up in the air or not, but I want to die of mortification either way.

I'm too terrified to move in case he leaves the bathroom again, but as soon as I hear the shower running, I scramble to turn off my bedside lamp and use the remote to lower the blinds on the windows and balcony door before resuming my stiff position under the covers.

I lie there, heart racing, staring up at the ceiling while my ears strain to hear his movements. When he emerges, I contemplate faking being asleep, but the room is fairly dark save for the standing lamp beside the couch, so I don't. He's quiet as he crosses the room anyway, as if trying not to wake me despite the music from the party still blaring, and I don't bother telling him I'm awake—I don't think my voice would work right now anyway.

He settles in on the couch and turns off the lamp, and we're covered in darkness. I keep my gaze focused on the ceiling, watching as the light sneaking past the blinds from outside casts interesting shadows and shapes, trying to ignore how hyperaware I am of every move Dylan makes. Instead, I focus on evening out my breathing, trying to calm my racing heart and mind.

I started off the day with a boyfriend, and now I'm ending it in bed wearing lingerie with my ex's best friend, who's most likely shirtless, only a few feet away from me; the same ex's best friend who went out of his way to make sure this day didn't absolutely suck. If it wasn't for Dylan, I would've spent all day in my room crying and eating my body weight in chocolate fudge brownie ice cream. Not only was it Dylan who convinced me to come here and avoid that fate, he's the one who made me laugh and smile and forget all about why I was sad in the first place.

It's not fair for me to sit around feeling sorry for myself, not fair to *Dylan*. So, starting right now, I'm making a promise to myself to have fun this week, to make an effort, to do what I can to avoid Dylan looking at me with those eyes that make me feel like I'm a sad little girl he's taking pity on. I'm going to enjoy the cottage, and I'm going to do it not only for Dylan or to forget Alessio, but for myself. I'm going to keep chasing the feeling I had today while playing in the mud, a feeling that, if I'm honest with myself, I haven't felt in a very long time, not even with Alessio on our best days.

Because I'm still so hyperaware of Dylan's every movement, every breath, every readjustment of the blanket, I know he's not sleeping. So, staring at the ceiling in the dark, I say, "Dylan?"

"Yeah?"

"Thanks for today."

He's quiet for a moment, but then he replies, "Anytime, Livy."

NINE

Day 2 of Muskoka

Jenna

By 3:30 in the morning, I call it a night, making Robbie turn off the music so people will get the hint, then having the guys make sure everyone has either a designated driver or a safe way home. I spend another hour cleaning up the things that need immediate attention, like washing out the rugs—which I had to watch a few videos on the internet about first since I've never had to do it before—and vacuuming up broken glass. By the time my head hits the pillow, I'm so tired I don't even hear Kyle's snoring or *remember* that my elementary school archnemesis turned annoyingly hot guy is sleeping in the other bed next to me. But I'm too anxious to sleep, and a few hours later, at the first crack of dawn, I tiptoe out of bed without waking Kyle or Hari and head downstairs to finish the rest.

I vacuum, mop, scrub, disinfect, and organize until my arms are ready to fall off and my hands are burning. Lugging the equipment and chemicals from the garage was a workout in and of itself, never mind the actual cleaning. It sucks. I'm probably hungover if not still a little drunk, my nails are chipped and cracked, and I've never thought this was such a bad idea as I do now. But I did this to myself, so I can't complain. I wanted to come here to experience the best last week of summer ever, and this is the price I have to pay.

I finish the basement by the time the sun is mostly up, and I've never been so happy that I locked the door to the other half of the floor. Deciding I deserve a break, I pocket my headphones and push open the basement's walk-out doors, inhaling the sweet tang of wet grass and earth, a welcome relief from the cleaning chemical fumes. It's a beautiful, calm morning, with only the chirping birds and the churning of the lake, choppy from last night's storm, breaking up the silence. Before I realize it, I'm standing on the dock, staring out at the water and listening to the early-morning Muskoka sounds.

Mom used to wake up early and get work done right here on the dock. Sometimes the whirring of the coffee machine would wake me, and we'd come out together, content in silence as we watched the sunrise. She'd sit at the picnic table with files spread out, and I'd stand on the edge of the dock, counting the dragonflies that would skim across the top of the lake.

I do that now, taking the place where I'd usually stand, only realizing I'm barefoot when my toes curl over the edge of the dock. My body naturally adapts to the slight rocking as I focus on the surface of the lake, scanning for the inevitable dragonflies. A flash of bright blue draws my attention, and I count my first one skimming the lake, smiling as I think about how I'd call out the total to Mom. She'd sip her coffee and comment on whether the number was higher or lower than the last time, then fuss over tying her hair up off her neck. Or did she fuss about taking her hair down to block the wind from her neck? Up or down?

I frown as I stare out at the water, annoyed I can't remember that small detail. It's been years, but I should know. I should remember.

Dad's selling this place, and all I'll have are my memories, and they're already fading after a few years. Was she putting her hair up or taking it down?

"Jenna," a voice immediately behind me says, followed by a large hand on my shoulder that catches me so off guard I shriek. My foot slips as I turn at the sudden intrusion, and before I know it, my arms are cartwheeling and I'm falling through the air, piercing through the lake's surface with a harsh splash. The shock of the freezing water steals my breath, stunning me so completely that I only realize I'm underwater and should swim up to the surface when my lungs start burning.

My head pops up out of the water as warm hands land on me, pulling me toward a hard body. "Jenna! I've got you!"

I spit out the lake water I almost swallowed and try to tread water, but the water is choppy after last night's rain, and it's hard when someone is holding me against them and doing an incredibly terrible job of trying to swim me back to shore. I only end up getting more mouthfuls of lake water.

"Stop panicking, it's all right. I swear I've got you," a deep voice says, and I finally register whose hard body I'm pressed up against.

"Let go of me, Hari." I shove away from him, but his hands remain glued on my waist.

"Stop struggling!"

I finally manage a strong enough shove to escape Hari, putting a few feet between us and ignoring the feeling of missing his warmth.

Treading water on my own now, I turn to face him. "Did you seriously just push me off the dock?"

He's shocked into silence for a few moments before sputtering, "W-what? I didn't push you! You fell. Practically jumped in on your own!"

"Why would I jump in the water at 8:00 a.m.?"

"I didn't actually mean you—" He takes a breath and collects his thoughts, his tone becoming less defensive. "I was calling your name for a while, and you clearly didn't hear me. I didn't intend for you to fall in."

Pushing me in the lake while still in my pajamas before the water has a chance to warm up is *such* a Hari thing to do. But then again, he's in the lake, too, water droplets sliding down his face and goose bumps on his arms as he treads water. If he was trying to be an ass by pushing me in, it wouldn't have the full effect if he also jumped in. But he seems genuinely shaken at my being in the lake, not smug or amused like he would be if it was purposeful.

Like he's reading my thoughts, his eyes narrow at the way I effortlessly tread water. "I thought you couldn't swim."

"Why would you think I couldn't swim? This is my cottage. What do you think I do when I come up every weekend?"

"I don't know. You didn't get in the water yesterday, and I always thought you couldn't swim since the pool party for my birthday in eighth grade when you were the only one who refused to get in the pool. You perched in the shade with your nose turned up at everyone who tried to get you to come in. I figured it was because you were embarrassed about not being able to swim, or because you thought you were too good for us."

And that ended in him corralling every boy in attendance to assault me with water balloons until I was so soaked my fingers pruned. The memory makes my blood boil, prompting me to blurt, "I didn't go in the pool because I got my period for the first time and didn't know how to use tampons yet!" Wait, why the hell did I just admit that? It's none of his business that thirteen-year-old Jenna was wearing a pad to his birthday party and would've been mortified if it filled up with pool water and somehow floated to the surface in front of the entire eighth grade. As if Hari needed more fuel to tease me with.

"Oh," is all he says, his face free of any teasing or judgment. But then I start thinking about his words, playing back his initial reaction when I first broke the surface for air, how he grabbed me and wouldn't let go.

"Wait. Did you jump in to rescue me?"

He shrugs, and my heart rate picks up. He did. Hari, the person I'd put money on to laugh as I drowned, jumped in the lake after me because he thought I couldn't swim. He was really trying to help me, and the realization makes me uncomfortable for reasons I can't even begin to understand.

"No. Yes. I don't know. Do you feel like you need rescuing?"

"By you or from you?"

His lip twitches up in the corner. "By me, obviously. I'm very clearly the hot lifeguard in every teen beach movie. I can run in slow motion on the dock with a float if it will help paint you a picture."

"Oh God. Now I definitely need rescuing *from* you," I say, splashing him to punctuate my point, feeling better now that we're back in familiar bickering territory.

"Hey! No splashing the lifeguards!"

I splash him again. "Well, when you find one let me know and I won't splash him."

He pretends to be insulted but fails to hide his amusement. "I can splash you back bigger and better," he says, sending a wave of water at my face.

"Oh no, you can't. I grew up being a menace in this lake. I know how to make the biggest wave."

"I bet you can't—"

Floating on my back, I use my feet to kick up water at him, relentless in my task.

"That is so not fair!" he exclaims, trying to move out of the way to do the same to me. We continue kicking water at each other and maneuvering to evade the splash zone, and I laugh when he spits out a mouthful of water and a few reeds.

"All right, all right, I concede!" he exclaims, holding up his hands as he treads again. I break out laughing when he pulls a handful of lily pads from his shirt.

"That's right. Never challenge the champion again," I brag, not even caring that my gloating power weakens when I pull a reed out of my hair and throw it at him.

He throws it back at me. "Where'd you learn to do that? Or are you just a natural-born terror in the water?"

I can't help but glance at the spot where Mom would sit at the picnic table on the dock. "My mom loved the water, taught me everything I know. I've won every cannonball contest I've ever been challenged to, even against Fletcher."

Hari whistles, impressed. "That's a bold statement considering he's double your size."

"Bold and true."

"Well, maybe I can't compete with you in a cannonball contest, but I'd totally destroy you in a belly flop one."

"Why would I ever want to compete in a belly flop competition?"

"Oh, I don't know, maybe for a chance at glory, to hear the roaring of the crowd chanting your name, to feel the sting of success bruised across your stomach for the next few days."

I can't help but laugh at his exaggeration and the way he waggles his arms around to punctuate his point. "I highly doubt any of that happened except maybe the bruised stomach."

"It all happened, and I got it on video. I can show you. I've got my phone right here in my pocket."

He's telling the truth, and my stomach squeezes. "You jumped in with your phone in your pocket?"

"My shoes are on too."

I gape at him. He's completely serious, but he doesn't seem too bothered by any of it. He's still got this playful, nonchalant air about him.

"You really did think you were saving me, didn't you?"

His stare is intense, and my heart pounds, but the moment passes when he looks away and says, "I would've been lauded as a hero. There would be songs about my bravery and good looks for generations to come."

A laugh bursts out of me, and I don't even care that I'm laughing *with* him and not *at* him. "Always gotta throw in the good looks, don't you?"

"If you had a glow up as significant as I did once puberty hit, you'd be shouting it from the rooftops too. Hell, I'm tempted to print out little cards with my headshot and stats on them like a baseball card and pass them out on the streets."

"And what would they say? *I'm Hari Virani and I'm hot now. Call me if you want a terrible time.*"

His smile is victorious. "So you think I'm hot?"

My face burns, and I rub a wet hand over it. "You skipped over the second part where I said you're terrible."

"But still hot, right?"

I groan, but he pushes on. "I can deal with being terrible and hot. You're stubborn and hot. And demanding and hot. And have control issues and are hot. And bossy and—"

I splash him, telling myself I don't care that he's called me hot multiple times. "Yeah, yeah, I get it. I'm hot and have issues. Now quit stalling and check to see if your phone is destroyed." I'm changing the subject, but I do sort of feel bad that his phone may be ruined because he jumped in the lake without thought to save me, even if it's his fault I'm in here in the first place.

"It's supposed to be water-resistant, so it should be fine, right?"

"Water-resistant is not the same thing as waterproof. Check to make sure it's okay."

He pulls it from his pocket and clicks around on it as best as he can with wet hands. He makes a tsking sound. "Do you think it's normal for the screen to have rainbow static over it?"

I gasp, my hands flying to my mouth. "Tell me you're joking."

He shakes the phone like it will help get water out of it. "I'm not joking. I may be slightly exaggerating, though. Okay, a lot exaggerating. It looks fine."

"Hari!" I exclaim, automatically pushing water at him for making me feel guilty.

"Oh, that's it; that's the splash that pushed my phone's water-resistance right over the edge. It's ruined now."

I know he's joking, and he knows I know he's joking, and yet I find I'm not annoyed at him or this conversation. It's actually kind of fun bantering with him in the early-morning sun in the lake at my favorite place in the world. No thinking or picking my words carefully, just saying the first thing that comes to my head and not caring if it offends him.

"Then I did you a favor." I play along. "It was probably full of obnoxious shirtless pictures of yourself anyway."

"Only *some* of them were obnoxious. The rest were pretty tasteful."

My tone turns overly dramatic as I imitate his accent, and I throw in some hand gestures for good measure. "Oh my. How will society *ever* go on without Hari Virani's tasteful shirtless pictures? We must get you a bowl of rice to stick your phone in, stat, lest those pictures cease to exist. How can I possibly live with myself knowing those pictures will never grace my eyes."

He laughs, and it's a pretty sound. "I know you're being sarcastic, and yet I'm going to take you up on that offer anyway. And that was a terrible English accent, by the way. Even worse than Fletcher's attempts at Spanish."

I pile on the accent even heavier, throwing a leaf at him. "You wound me, good sir."

He throws it back at me with a laugh. "You know, you're actually kind of fun when you're not trying so hard to be an emotionless robot."

My smile immediately drops. "I'm not an emotionless robot."

"I didn't say you were. I said you try to be."

Leave it to him to ruin a nice moment. Not wanting to be under his scrutinizing gaze, I swim to the ladder on the dock and climb up. "Yeah, well, what do you know?"

"I know plenty of things," he says, following behind me and pulling himself onto the dock. "I know the square root of 841 is 29. I know how to turn a beautiful piece of oak into a dining table. I even know how to pat my head and rub my stomach while hopping on one foot and touching my nose with my tongue."

It's only from years of practice that I manage not to crack a smile at the silly mental image he conjured up. "That was a rhetorical question."

"I knew that too. I just chose not to treat it as such."

"You're so annoying."

His smile is cocky as he points at me. "I also know you don't really mean that."

I didn't, not really, not like I would've before, and the realization causes me to scowl. This is *Hari Virani*, not a *friend*. Who knows how many mental points he's giving himself for one-upping me in these few moments I've let my guard down?

"What are you doing out here anyway?" I ask, wringing out my hair and clothes as best I can without taking them off. There's still an early-morning chill in the air that causes me to shiver in my soaked pajama shorts and tee.

Hari shakes his head, sending drops of water flying from his hair. "I rolled over and saw your bed was empty, and I swore I heard the vacuum a while ago, so when I went downstairs and saw most of the mess already cleaned, I came to find you."

"I, uh . . ." *Get it together, Jenna.* "I couldn't sleep and wanted to get a head start on cleaning." It's technically not a lie, and I pull my shoulders back, allowing the mask to slide back on. But now I get a proper look at Hari, and my pulse quickens. He's hot first thing in the morning, even hotter dripping wet with his clothes plastered against him. Like, *way* hotter, as if that was even possible. His hair is all curled, and his sweatpants hang low on his hips. "I think your shirt is inside out."

He glances down at the soaked T-shirt that's plastered against him; it is, in fact, on inside out. He smiles sheepishly at me. "I rolled out of bed and got dressed in the dark. You'd think I'd have noticed when I brushed my teeth or washed my face."

And then he grabs the hem of his T-shirt and *pulls it over his head.* My eyes land on his abs, on his sculpted chest, but once the shirt is off his face, I rip my eyes away from his body and force them to focus on his brown ones. I can't stop myself from imagining the shirtless pictures that may be on his phone and begrudgingly admit they probably are magnificent, but I could never ever say that out loud.

He wrings the shirt out, and I ignore the flexing of his arms and the playful expression on his face. I almost forget what we're talking about, but because in-control Jenna has finally decided to take over, I keep the conversation—and my gaze—away from Hari's body. "So why don't you go back up to sleep?"

Hari slings his shirt over his shoulder, which blocks most of his body, and it helps clear my brain fog a bit. "Why don't you wait for everyone to get up to finish cleaning?"

He narrows his eyes at me, like he knows something is up, but I'm not going to crack. "It was my party, I'll clean up."

"We're all staying here, we all enjoyed the party, we can all help clean up."

I want my friends to enjoy their last week of the summer. I don't want to force them to clean, especially because not a single one of them, excluding my cousin, has ever cleaned anything in their life. This is probably the last memory they'll have of me, and I don't want to ruin it with this.

"It's all right, I can do it," I say, marching back to the house.

"You are so frustratingly stubborn." Hari falls in step beside me. "You can just *ask* for help, you know."

He caught me off guard while I was thinking about my mom and then jumped in to rescue me, and it made me vulnerable. But whatever fun moment happened between us is over, and my mask has slid firmly back in place. "Don't need it."

"Come on, Jenna. It's a huge house, and there's still lots to do. Just admit you need help."

I stop walking, rounding on him. "Help from who? You? Why are you even offering to help? So you can hold it over my head and gloat about how my asking you for help proves how superior you are to me?"

Something passes between us, and for a moment I think he's going to say something deep and reassuring, but then he opens his mouth and says, "Well, I'm *already* superior to you—"

I scoff and continue marching back to the house. "I'm joking!" he exclaims, jogging after me to catch up, tugging on my elbow to get me to stop. "I'm joking, swear."

"What are you even doing here, Hari? Why are you out here this early in the morning? Why are you offering to help me clean?"

He shifts nervously, running a hand through his hair. "I'd like to offer a truce."

"A truce?"

"Yes. It's going to be a long week if we're constantly at each other's throats. We'll have a lot more fun if we call a truce and try to get along, even if it's for this week only."

I eye him skeptically. Something is going on here, some trick or ulterior motive. But as far as I can tell, he seems genuine, and that makes me just as uneasy. "A weeklong, cottage-only truce?"

"Exactly. After that, we can go right back to how we were before. I can go back to being—in your words—nothing to you."

If he's being honest about this truce, and this isn't some kind of scheme to get under my skin in the way only he knows how, then maybe it can work. I'm supposed to be focused on creating lasting memories with my friends and making them want to come back to visit me, want to keep in touch and not forget about me, and I can't do that if I'm spending all my time worried about looking stupid in front of Hari.

"Fine," I say. "A truce then."

"Good," he says, and we continue to the cottage, walking in through the basement doors I left wide open. I reach for the spare towels we keep handy and hand one to Hari, drying myself off as best I can.

"Try not to get lake water everywhere, I just mopped these floors," I say to him, and he raises a brow at me as he towels off his hair.

"On that note, in the spirit of our truce," he says the word pointedly, as if insinuating we're already off to a bad start, "why don't you go shower, and I'll finish cleaning the main floor?"

"Why don't *you* go shower, and I'll finish the main floor?"

He towels off his torso. "You smell like lake water."

"*You* smell like lake water," I repeat childishly.

"Wow. You've gotten really mature and good at comebacks in the four years I've been away, haven't you?"

I'm tempted to stick my tongue out at him, but that would only prove him right. Instead, I roll out the stiffness in my shoulders and massage the pinch in my lower back. I *am* sore from doing most of the work, and if Hari wants to ruin his perfect nails and absurdly attractive hands, then I'll let him. But only because he's insisting, *not* because I need him.

"Fine. If you want to finish cleaning the main floor, be my guest, just try not to wake everyone up. All the stuff is over there." I point to the bucket of supplies sitting where I left it and head to the stairs. "I'll be upstairs rinsing lake water out of my hair, even though we're going back in later on anyway." Because I'll be more comfortable dry, and it's not warm enough to walk around wet, not because he said I smell like lake water.

"You're welcome!" he calls after me, and even though I hear the amusement in his tone, I don't turn around, because while we may be in a truce, the stubborn part of me refuses to let him see how easily he got me to smile.

The house is still quiet and calm when I get upstairs and into a shower, and I refuse to let myself think about the morning with Hari, and how it was . . . not awful. Okay, it was fun, and he isn't the worst thing to look at either. But it's almost scary how quickly I forgot to keep my guard up, how natural it was to fool around like we were friends. I can't just go letting everyone in all willy-nilly. That's another person to grow attached to, another person who'll be leaving at the end of the summer, another person to abandon me like it's nothing to them. We can have our truce, and then we'll go our separate ways.

By the time I exit the shower and pad to my room in a towel to grab a change of clothes, the house sounds alive. There are voices and banging and power tools and even the smell of coffee drifting through the air. I change in record time and race down the stairs, almost nauseous with worry that something has happened to the cottage. But I stop in my tracks at the bottom of the stairs as I take in the scene.

Everyone's awake and working together, practically done making the main floor sparkle. Hari's scrubbing a spot on the floor, Martina's wiping down counters, Dylan and Olivia are working on the bathroom, Elena's vacuuming, Fletcher and Kyle are disassembling the backdrops, and Robbie's carrying garbage bags outside.

I stare at them, stunned. Elena's been my best friend for years. We've had countless sleepovers, we've been to Costa Rica, California, and Aruba together, and one summer I stayed at her house for a full month straight when Dad went to Europe and I couldn't take the big empty house anymore, and in all that time, not once have I ever seen Elena clean anything or be voluntarily awake before 10:00 a.m., and here she is, doing both.

"Hey," I call. "What's going on here?"

"Nice of you to finally join us," Hari says, throwing a rag over his shoulder. "We're finishing cleaning up after the party. You're just in time to watch us."

Everyone looks like they're having a miserable time. Martina's pouting at a crack in her nail, and Fletcher is drenched in sweat. Is this what they're going to remember? *I'm never going to Jenna's again. She forces us to wake up at the crack of dawn to scrub the marble counters then doesn't even help.* "You all didn't have to do this; I was taking care of it. Why don't you get ready for the lake? It's going to be a great day; we can take the Sea-Doos out and race. Loser's on barbecue duty."

No one makes a move to leave.

"It's all right, we're almost done," Hari says. "Right, everyone?"

My friends nod in agreement, and I'm not sure if it's because they actually agree or they are being forced to agree. I'm going to have to make sure they have extra fun today to forget about how they started their morning.

"Just wish we could've started *after* we slept off the hangover," Kyle grumbles. "But *noooo*. Hari just had to burst into all our rooms and demand we start now—" A rag hits Kyle in the face, the very same one Hari was using.

I glare at Hari, and he shrugs innocently, not caring that I specifically told him not to wake anyone up.

"I'm sorry, I was going to do it on my own—"

"Don't apologize, Jenna," Martina interrupts. "We forgot there'd be no cleaning crew like usual. So here we are"—she spreads her arms with a smile—"the new cleaning crew."

"We're happy to help, Jenna," my cousin adds, and everyone nods in agreement.

Is it possible I underestimated my friends and their willingness to help? The grumbling seems to be in good fun, and with the house almost back to its perfect state, Dad will never know we were here, never mind that I threw a huge party that started trending on social media.

"All right. I'll help finish, and we can enjoy our day even faster," I say, picking up another rag.

Everyone gets back to work without any more grumbling, and the music playing in the background even gets a few of us singing along as we work. Before I know it, the house is sparkling. If I tilt my head at just the right angle so I can't see the wall in the living room, you'd never even know there was a party here. It helps loosen the ball of guilt in my chest for throwing a party when we're not even supposed to be here, and I'm even able to laugh my way through the pancake breakfast Olivia and Dylan make. They're giggling and hip-bumping each other out of the way at the stove, and I'm glad Olivia's out of whatever slump she was in last night.

For a moment out there with Hari, I forgot I'm supposed to be worried about my friends all leaving and forgetting about me, or worried about sneaking everyone here behind my dad's back, or worried about the hole in the drywall. I even forgot to keep my mask on—or as he said, be an emotionless robot—lest he catch me in a vulnerable state and exploit it. We were just two . . . friends . . . enjoying an early-morning swim, and it was . . . nice. It feels wrong to say spending time with Hari was *nice*, but it was. And then he got everyone to help clean and finish in a quarter of the time it would've taken me, giving us more time to enjoy the day together.

I take a seat beside Hari at the island, bumping his shoulder lightly with mine as a silent thank-you. He nods, receiving the message, then holds up a bowl filled with uncooked rice, his phone submerged in the middle, getting a laugh out of me before I remember to cover it up.

Maybe a truce with Hari won't be so bad after all.

TEN

Day 2 of Muskoka

Jenna

Breakfast is quick, and soon we're in our swimwear and out on the dock, enjoying all the sun and heat and nature Muskoka has to offer.

The dock isn't a regular skinny wooden dock; it's huge and can easily fit a circle of Muskoka chairs, tanning loungers, and a large picnic table with space to spare. Snacks are laid out on the picnic table, and there are multiple coolers filled with drinks to save us from warm liquid or running to the house every few minutes.

I'm lying with Martina and Elena in the tanning chairs by the end of the dock, the speaker playing a rock remix as we sip our virgin frozen strawberry daiquiris. It's the end of summer, so Martina's normally tan skin has already deepened, but Elena stays pretty fair no matter how long she lounges in the sun. I toss her a bottle of sunscreen as a reminder to reapply soon, otherwise she'll be bright red and in pain every time she moves all week.

"My phone has been blowing up all morning," Martina says, scrolling through her phone as it continues vibrating, proving her point. "People can't stop gushing about how much fun the party was last night. And now that I'm sober, I can appreciate all the pictures everyone posted on Instagram."

"Even that one of you kissing Fletcher?" Elena teases, and Martina glares at her.

"I did no such thing, so there's no photographic proof of that happening . . . Right? Please tell me you're joking. Oh God, someone has proof of me making out with the giant Scotsman."

"So it *did* happen!" Elena and I exclaim at the same time, bursting into laughter as Martina looks like she wants to jump in the lake.

When we calm down enough, Elena piles on with, "And I can't even blame Mercury being in retrograde, because you made out with him before that too. You're just *hot* for the *Scot.*"

We break out into more giggles while Martina frantically looks around to see if someone heard Elena's teasing rhyme. No one's around, and she relaxes.

"I don't know what comes over me when I get a few drinks in my system," Martina says, squinting at her drink as if to double-check there's no alcohol in it. "All it takes is two drinks and I want to climb that redheaded, six-foot-five tree and have him throw me around a bit."

My stomach hurts from laughing so hard, and Elena makes fake gagging noises as Martina scowls, shrinking lower in her chair.

"Yeah, yeah, laugh it up," Martina grumbles, looking out at where the man in question is driving around with Olivia on one of the Sea-Doos. "I'm going to stay away from him at tonight's party. Denzel said he's coming, so maybe I'll make out with him before Fletcher catches drunk Martina's eye."

I sit up straight, all humor gone. "Tonight's party? What party?"

The girls exchange a look, but Martina's the one who speaks. "The party you were telling everyone we're hosting tonight? To celebrate the last Saturday of the summer?"

"I did?" Shit. How drunk *was* I? I didn't feel that drunk, but I may vaguely remember getting lost in the heat of the party and saying something along those lines to a few people. But clearly another party is out of the question. I've already got the hole in the drywall and a questionable stain that won't come out of the living room rug to deal with; I don't think I can handle another party with more potential lasting damage.

Elena frowns at whatever expression I must be making. "Where has your head been lately? You barely even drank last night, and it was *your* birthday party. Did you even have fun? What's going on?"

I school my face into the mask I usually wear so well. "Nothing's going on. The party was just too big and messy, I wasn't expecting it."

Martina's eyebrows draw together. "Too big and messy? That wasn't even the biggest—or messiest—party you've thrown here. Last year, Fletcher walked through the mesh screen of your patio door, ripping it off entirely, Kyle dove down the stairs, breaking the railing off and giving the three cheerleaders he landed on concussions, and a guy from the soccer team tripped and sent his shoulder through the flat-screen television in the basement, and that was only in the first *hour*. This party was tame compared to the rest. Just a hole in the drywall, which isn't even the *biggest* hole we've seen after a party."

I barely remember any of those incidents, but I remember having a great time with my friends, feeling whole and happy at having a house full of people, grateful to see the theme I organized come to life after it had given me a goal and a purpose for all those weeks leading up to it.

But I never truly realized the cost of the damage, how ungrateful I was for what I had, how inconsiderate my "friends" are when it comes to my property, until last night, when I had to spend the whole night making sure no one broke or ruined anything. I've never had to worry about it before. The cleaning crew always came in and took care of everything, and Dad never cared about the price or the itemization of services and repairs on the invoice. *Did you have a good party? Great, here's some money, I'll be in Vancouver for the week.* That's how it would go when he returned the morning after a party, and it was no different after Elena's birthday, except his departure to Vancouver is *permanent* this time. Thinking about Dad, about the way he so easily brushes me off, makes the anxiety in my chest tighten so badly it hurts to breathe. But I'm here with my friends, people who *do* care about me, and I don't want to let them down. I'm losing everything, but I can't lose them. I'll finish giving them the best summer ever to remember me by, and I'll worry about the rest later.

"You're right, it's not the worst we've seen, but I think there'd be something cool about a smaller party. More intimate. Invite only." Less of a party, more of a small gathering where no one will break anything.

Elena considers it. "An invite-only party?"

"And *we* get to choose who makes the cut?" Martina sits up, an evil smile growing as she realizes the power she'll wield. "Oh yes, I like this a lot. Last night, Vinnie Reeves drunkenly told me he doesn't date fat chicks, but he'd make an exception for me. I kicked him in the balls—for the misogyny, I'm perfectly happy with my fat body—but we're still putting him and all his friends on the *no entry* list. But Denzel is definitely on the list; he's going to be my Fletcher distraction."

Elena's mischievous smile is almost out of place on her innocent face. "I feel like that's all the more reason I should conveniently forget to add Denzel to the list."

Martina points an accusing finger at her. "Don't you dare. I know where you sleep!"

She doesn't mean the threat, and we all know it. "Yeah, yeah.

That's just your fire sign hotheadedness coming out," Elena says, opening the Notes app on her phone. "Sagittarians tend to be commitment-phobes, but something keeps bringing you back to Fletcher. Maybe it means something."

"It means I'm drunk and bored," Martina deadpans, and Elena gives her a knowing smile but doesn't push it further.

"Let's start making a guest list. Say, a hundred people?"

"Seventy-five, max," I declare, since that's a manageable number. That's enough where I'll know everyone and I won't have to run around chasing after people, but it won't make it feel like three people sitting around awkwardly in a room. "And I get final say."

"Done," Elena says, clicking away on her phone. "Okay, so the first five people are Denzel and his friends . . ."

She and Martina start listing people they agree on and fighting about the ones they don't, and I tune them out, sipping my quickly defrosting drink and looking out at the water. Everyone else is out there, little moving specks in the distance. Robbie and Kyle are paddling in the canoe together, Fletcher is driving the red Sea-Doo with Olivia sitting behind him, Hari's on the blue one, and Dylan's on the third. Everyone seems to be having fun, and I'm glad, but I still can't shake loose the tension in my shoulders, no matter how hard I try to shove my drywall problem in my *to be ignored* mental box.

Elena and Martina argue back and forth about the list, and I mostly hum in agreement every once in a while, not really listening. Eventually, all three Sea-Doos come back to the dock, slowly stopping a short distance away from the spots where we tie them off when not stored in the boathouse. The guys turn the engines off, and the previously loud rumble is replaced with the gentle lapping of waves against the dock.

Hari's in the water closest to me, the Sea-Doo rocking in place with the waves, his dark hair soaked and curled at his neck, water droplets dripping down his shoulders and biceps. My breath hitches when I catch him checking me out, but he doesn't look away ashamed, only raises a defiant eyebrow as if to say *So what if I was checking you out?* It makes me think about this morning, how he called me hot. He also called me a bunch of other things, but *hot* was repeated and is the one I'm choosing to focus on.

Hari gestures to the handles. "Hey, Jenna, is being a terror in the water limited to swimming? Want to show me how it's done on this thing?"

I'd normally never voluntarily get so close to Hari, especially not on an isolated watercraft where he'll be tempted to throw me off in the middle of the lake and leave me there for fun. But we *are* having a truce, and I really do love being on the water, and he does look annoyingly handsome all windswept and wet, and I am sitting here being unproductive by worrying about the hole in the drywall. This will be a good distraction, *and* it will test this little truce of ours. If he pushes me off on purpose, then I know the truce is a hoax, and my guard is going up and staying up permanently.

"Make way for the queen." I stand, trading my sunglasses and flip-flops for a life jacket thrown over one of the Muskoka chairs.

"How about you girls? You want a turn?" Dylan asks my party-planning friends.

"I don't like driving them, but I'll play passenger," Elena says, setting her phone on the chair and joining me so I can help her get adjusted in a smaller life vest.

Fletcher only has eyes for Martina, who's doing everything in her power to pretend he doesn't exist. "How about you, *mi hermosa?* Care for a ride? You can forget the straps and wrap your arms around me. It would be . . ." He takes a second to think. *"Muy romántica."*

Martina grimaces. "It wouldn't be fair to kick Olivia off."

"It's all right, I don't mind switching," Olivia says softly, but the way she wistfully looks out at the water tells me otherwise.

Martina doubles down. "I'm not in the mood, and I've got invites to finish sending out. You guys go on without me."

"All right, Liv. Looks like it's your turn to drive. Let's switch," Fletcher says before looking at Martina, a flirty smile on his face that makes hers turn red. *"Beso en otro lugar podemos la próxima vez."*

"*Still* not proper Spanish, Fletcher." Martina rolls her eyes, sinking lower into her seat and mumbling, "Didn't even make sense. And there *won't* be a kiss next time."

Fletcher, as always, is undeterred by her coldness, his confident smile never wavering. To Olivia, he says, "We all took a mandated six years of French in school, but not one of us could confidently move to Quebec for school except Martina because she's great at everything. I've only been trying with Spanish for a few weeks, so I'll get there eventually."

Olivia pats his arm placatingly as he starts the Sea-Doo again to bring it into the dock so they can switch. "Of course you will."

"Some quality time with Martina on the swan floaty later will help," he says, then louder, so Martina can hear, he repeats, "When I come back, we can snuggle in the water on the swan floaty."

Martina shoves her headphones in, purposefully ignoring his suggestion as he switches seats with Olivia.

Dylan and Hari start their Sea-Doos as well, and when they come in, I help grab them so they don't float off or bang into the dock fenders. I help Elena get settled behind Dylan then take the key from Hari and secure it to my life jacket. "You're in for the ride of your life, pal," I tell him, not even caring about the flirty innuendo.

He laughs and slides back, making room for me to hop on in front. "Show me what you got."

As I settle into the seat, even though he's not touching me at all and we're both wearing life jackets, I feel his heat all down my back. I start the Sea-Doo and slowly ease away from the dock, clearing the rocks and shallower water. Everyone else has taken off already, and I turn to wave to Martina, who has already lain back down to suntan.

"You ready?" I ask Hari over my shoulder once we're farther out in the water.

Hari grips the straps on the seat and nods. "Let's do it."

I ignore the tingling from his proximity and the stress of my dad and worries about my future and launch the Sea-Doo into the open water. We fly across the lake, jumping on waves and twisting and turning through the water, leaning in tandem against the turns. Hari lets out a cheerful *Whoop!* and it spurs me on to take more risks and push it harder, faster.

We laugh as we ride, the wind flying through our hair and water spray soaking us. I've always loved being on the water like this, and it's just the distraction I needed.

We eventually cross paths with our friends, and we ride together, making circles and waves for each other to jump through. Elena's cheering and laughing behind Dylan, whose dazzling smile and handsome face are almost impossible to ignore, and Olivia's entire face is lit up, Fletcher behind her holding on for dear life. My cousin's always been a little daredevil on the Sea-Doo, so she's giving Fletcher an experience he'll never forget.

Eventually, we all separate, and I get itchy to push it, to feel the speed and power. "Hold on," I yell back at Hari, and when he tells me he's ready, I gun it in a straight shot down the lake, revving the Sea-Doo almost to its max. Hari's laughing and cheering and urging me on, and I get lost in the feeling of freedom.

I slow down before we hit the main area where most boats pass through, letting the Sea-Doo idle.

Still feeling the adrenaline rush from the ride, I twist back to look at Hari. "What did you think?"

His hair is wet and windblown, and there's an excited, wild look in his eyes that I'm sure mirrors mine. "You definitely delivered on your promise of giving me the ride of my life." He laughs, and I can't help my sly smile. He pushes his hair back and continues, "It was incredible, I've never felt so . . ." He struggles to find the right word, but I know exactly how to fill in the thought.

"Free?"

He nods slowly, like he's trying the word on for size. "Yeah. Free. It's addicting."

It is. For however long I'm out here, I forget about the crushing emotions I'm trying so hard to ignore.

"Want a turn?" I ask.

"Hell yes."

I turn off the Sea-Doo and remove the key, swinging my leg over to sit sideways in the seat and turning so I'm facing him. Hari blinks at our proximity, and I have to stop myself from glancing at his lips. We're basically alone out here, with only the occasional boat or other craft passing in the distance. Behind Hari is a small, lush green island with a house on it, but it doesn't look like anyone is home. We sit listening to the peaceful sounds of the lake, rocking with the water, the hum of the engine still ringing in my ear, and I find that I don't even care about Hari's nearness. In fact, I might actually . . . like it?

No. Not like. I don't like it. It's just the nostalgia and peacefulness of the water making me less tense. It has nothing to do with Hari's smile or his eyes or the laugh that used to be annoying but that for some reason I don't mind as much right now. But it's still *Hari*. For all I know, this is when he's going to take his chance to push me off and desert me in the middle of the lake. If he does, then I'll *know* this little truce is bogus.

As if wanting to tempt him to take the bait and prove me right, I scooch to perch on the edge of the seat and dangle my feet over the footwell, making his attempt to throw me into the water that much easier.

"I'm not sure how I'll compete with your driving, though," Hari admits, hands resting on his knees and apparently not yet itching to shove me off. "If I'm honest, I wasn't even expecting you to do that."

"Expecting me to do what?"

He laughs, and somehow I know he doesn't mean it in a bad way when he says, "I don't know exactly. I guess I wasn't expecting you to just jump on and . . ."

"Be an adrenaline junkie?"

"Yeah, if you want to put it like that." He laughs, and it's a warm sound. "I hope I can stack up against your talents."

I wave him off. "Liv and I used to come up every weekend and race these. We've put so much time in on these things that we're practically professionals." We'd spend all day out on the water, only coming in when we needed to refill the gas tanks. She loves it, and I'm secretly glad Alessio isn't here right now. This is her last chance to be out on them, and she always lets him drive, but I want her to have fun, not acquiesce to whatever her stupid boyfriend wants.

I make a mental note to take some time to go out on the water, just me and Olivia like old times, before this week is over. Hari asks, "Your parents took you up here a lot, then?"

The mention of my parents instantly sours my mood. We *did* come here a lot, and now I'll never get to come here again. I must forget I'm not alone for a moment, because Hari pushes, "You're making a face. Tell me what you're thinking."

"I'm not making a face," I say automatically, internally scolding myself for always letting my guard down with him. Why is it that I let my emotions show so clearly around him? "I'm just thinking about the hole in the wall. My dad is going to kill me, especially after the damage from the last party. He was very clear about how screwed I'd be if I made a mess here." Kind of a lie but also kind of the truth to cover up for my facial slip.

Hari studies me, and I try my hardest to hide what I'm thinking. I don't know how he does it, but he always seems to know exactly how I'm feeling. No one else can, even my friends who've known me the longest, but Hari slices right through my defenses, whether it's by annoying me so hard I slip up or noticing something that's my own damn fault.

"I can help fix it," he finally says.

"Fix what?"

He stares at me like I just admitted to forgetting my own name. "The hole in the wall. I can fix it."

"You?"

"Yes."

"Can fix a man-sized hole in the wall?"

"Yes."

I arch a skeptical eyebrow. "You know it needs to *actually* be fixed, right? We can't just put a painting over it and call it a day."

"I wasn't talking about hiding it with a painting or a large piece of furniture, which would work equally well, by the way."

I roll my eyes at him to hide my smile, and he continues, "I meant I can fix it with sheets of drywall, drywall tape, and joint compound. And paint. And a few other things I'd have to grab from the hardware store."

Those sound like the technical terms of a man who actually knows what he's doing. Is it possible Hari really knows how to fix this? Properly? He seems completely genuine and doesn't have that little scheming twist of a smirk he normally has.

"How?" I ask.

"Well, first you cut the current drywall to clean up the edges, then you—"

"No," I interrupt, glaring when I realize he knew exactly what I was asking and was only screwing with me. I ask aloud anyway, "I meant how do you know how to fix it?"

He shrugs like it's no big deal. "I guess I'm technically a carpenter, and it's kind of a part of it. I took woodworking in high school, but I spent all my free time at my part-time job, a small custom furniture shop run by a great man named Arthur who took an unskilled, lonely kid whose parents deserted him at boarding school and taught him everything he knows."

Now that he mentions it, I remember he said something this morning during our impromptu lake swim about turning a piece of oak into a dining table.

"Carpentry, huh? That's not something I ever pictured you doing."

"It sounds silly, but there's something beautiful about starting with nothing but some wood and ending up with an ornate chair or table or showpiece dresser or anything you can imagine and knowing that *you* made it, that it wouldn't exist if not for your time and energy. And the process itself is really calming, when it's not incredibly frustrating." He laughs like it's an inside joke. "But it either gives you time to think or takes your mind off everything for a while."

The way he describes it, with awe and respect, *does* make it sound beautiful. Like he genuinely enjoys doing it, like it's given him a sense of purpose.

"Can I see some stuff you've made?"

He raises his eyebrows slightly, surprised, but he recovers quickly, plucking his phone from the pocket of his swim shorts. "Sure, anything in particular you'd like to see? A gazebo? A deck? A chest of drawers?"

My jaw drops. "Really, Hari? You brought your *phone* on the Sea-Doo?"

"What? The rice worked perfectly, no water damage at all. Besides, after this morning, I figure it's practically indestructible. It's not like I'm going *in* the water."

I shake my head at him, but he only unlocks his phone and adds, "You're only worried about my shirtless pictures, aren't you? Don't fret, darling, I can create a special album to send you so you can gaze upon my gloriousness whenever you choose."

He is so ridiculous. Why am I laughing? "Just for that, I hope your phone flies out of your pocket and you don't even notice."

He uses his phone to point at me. "Now that's evil. Do you want to see my work or not?"

I shouldn't care, because it's Hari and I don't care about him or anything he does. But I *am* curious, although I tell myself it's only professional curiosity to verify his work before letting him touch the wall in the living room.

"Show me your favorite," I tell him.

Excitement lights up his eyes, and for a moment, I'm jealous. There's nothing I can think of that gives me that look.

"Hmm, my favorite?" He uses his thumb to scroll through pictures, the angle making it impossible for me to get a sneak peek. "They're all my favorite, but here's one I think you'd really like."

He passes me the phone so I can see the photo. It's a gorgeous, antique-style, one-armed chaise longue; the detailed carvings and intricate patterns in the wood are ornate and extravagant, the upholstery a lush, deep red velvet. It looks like it's waiting for a rich Victorian-era princess to collapse over it, wailing about unrequited love. I immediately wish I had one, then remember I'd have nowhere to put it in my tiny, lonely dorm room.

"Wow. It's gorgeous."

"All right, all right. No need for the sarcasm." He tries to take the phone away, but I hold onto it firmly.

"That wasn't sarcasm, and quite frankly, I'm offended you can't differentiate my sarcastic tone from my genuine one, since I use the sarcastic one on you so often. You must not be paying enough attention."

His eyes bore deep into mine as he says, "Believe me, I pay plenty of attention."

The intensity behind his gaze becomes too much, and I dip a foot in the water as if that will help me cool off. "Well, quit trying to grab the phone and let me see again."

He considers me for a moment, then finally relents, and I let out a breath once his attention is off me.

I stare at the picture again, at the detail. "It really is gorgeous. You *made* that?"

"With my own two hands and some solid birch." He holds up his hands as if to punctuate his point, and like always, my eyes are drawn to them. They're manly—rough and calloused, probably from all the woodwork—and I tear my gaze away from them when he speaks again. "I had help with the upholstery, though, since I don't have too much experience with it."

I pass his phone back. "You're really talented. That chaise belongs on the set of a movie."

His smile becomes shy. "Funny you should say that." Hari skims through his phone and holds it up to show a new photo. It's another chaise longue, but it's simpler than the first and looks like something my dad's designer would put in a staged house, more modern yet still elegant with some carvings and white upholstery. "I made this for a rich woman from Kensington, and a few days later, her friend came inquiring. Turns out she was a set designer for some famous historical drama series on television and wanted to furnish the set. I made her the red chaise and a bunch of other furniture too."

My jaw drops as I stare at him. "Are you joking? Which show! Has it aired? If it was a romance, I bet I've seen it since Olivia always picks those on our movie nights."

A small blush colors his cheeks, one I've never seen on Hari before. "It's not a big deal."

"Tell me," I demand, but he shakes his head.

"Bossy as ever," he says before quietly admitting the show's name, which is an insanely popular romantic historical drama that Olivia *has* forced me to watch, and I even make him show me some stills taken from the show where his furniture is in the shot. There are actresses, fully made up with fancy updos and corseted dresses, lounging on the red velvet chaise he made. Other pictures show more furniture in the background: the fancy coffee tables the actors set their tea on, the chairs they perch on, the dining room table they eat at. It all comes together perfectly to make the scene believable. I've never thought about the work that goes into the set before. But Hari's talents helped bring the show to life, and it's clear from the way he talks about it that he's incredibly proud of his work, even though he's uncharacteristically shy about it.

"That is seriously the coolest thing I've ever seen," I tell him, and I have a fleeting thought of how cute his blush is before I shake it from my head. "And you know I'm telling the truth because I'd never willingly admit that to you unless it was incredibly true."

"It's not that cool." He tucks his phone back in his pocket. "You're only saying that because you're hoping I'll send you my shirt-less pictures."

It's weird that with everything else in his life, he's overly con-fident, cocky, and so self-assured that no one can tell him shit, but talking about this, something that he *does* deserve to be cocky and confident about, he's shy and unsure.

"For the love of all that is good, please do not send me your shirtless pictures."

"You're right," he says, pointing to the life jacket covering his torso. "Why bother with the pictures when you have the masterpiece right in front of you?"

"Quit trying to change the subject," I say rather than letting my eyes wander. "You're clearly—and this hurts to say—talented. So why not stay in England and work with Arthur full time? You've already got a great portfolio to show off your past work; I bet with the right marketing you'd have client orders stacking up." My dad's designer would definitely order custom pieces for her clients' homes, especially the modern ones he showed me between the photos of the vintage-style ones, and she's not the only one who'd like an original Hari piece.

He lifts a shoulder. "I was born and raised in England before we moved here when I was seven and I got my Canadian citizenship. I spent every single summer after that there, but even after doing high school there, it never really felt like home, you know?"

I do know, more than I can say. "Just because you live somewhere doesn't make it feel like home."

"Exactly." He nods, shoving his hands through his drying hair to push it off his face. "I considered going back after this summer for . . . I don't know. Familiarity? Family obligation? My parents are there. But then again, they shipped me off to boarding school for four years and rarely saw me, so they don't really care if I decide to stay here or not. And they cut me off financially when I turned eighteen, so where I stay is up to me."

I rub a water droplet dripping down my thigh as I think about how my dad doesn't care if we stay together or not, either, but I'm ignoring my own problems, so I say, "Really? I always remember one or the other of your parents being so involved in school. Volunteering for field trips and bringing in cake on your birthday."

I remember it distinctly, because his mom was a blond-haired, blue-eyed white woman, and kids and teachers alike would never believe they were related because he didn't look like her.

He frowns down at the seat. "That was when we were younger, before they decided to become entrepreneurs and spend more time on their company than with me."

"I had no idea."

His lip tilts up in the corner. "Really? Looking back, I felt like it was obvious to everyone, especially in seventh and eighth grade."

Was it? It was around that time Hari went from just another classmate to someone who was focused on torturing me every chance he got. "You *were* extra annoying then."

He laughs, but it's humorless. "I was so angry, so bitter. My parents split their time between London and here, and even when they *were* here, I never saw them. I spent most of my time with chefs and chauffeurs and maids, and they just punched in and out for their shifts and left me to my own devices."

It sounds lonely, almost as lonely as I felt around that time. I had no idea that Hari was going home to a cold, empty house just like I was. The realization makes my stomach hurt. He clearly doesn't want to think about it, and because I can sympathize with that, I don't push it like I normally would with him.

"Then what's next for you?" I ask, changing the subject. "Everyone here is starting university next week, but it sounds like that's not the case for you."

"Nah, no more school for me. If anything, I'd get an actual apprenticeship for carpentry, maybe go to trade school and get certified." He says it like it's a relief not to have to go back.

"I never realized that not going to university was an option. We were all told that's what we were doing and to pick a subject." My confession is unplanned, but it feels normal, talking with Hari. The sun is high in the sky, the heat kissing my skin, and rocking with the waves on the Sea-Doo, staring out at the lake together, feels like the most natural thing in the world, like we've been doing it forever.

"University is great, but it's not the path for everyone," he says. "If I had to sit in class and write essays and do readings for one more semester, I would rip my hair out."

No, he wouldn't have. His hair is dark and thick and flowy and curls around the bottom of his ears. It's beautiful, and he knows it.

"What's stopping you from starting your own business?" I ask, gesturing to the phone he was reckless enough to bring out on the water. "You clearly have the talent."

His shy little smile, the one that keeps popping up every time I compliment his work, is back, and an urge to hug him flits through my mind before I shake it away.

"Hmm, I guess I wouldn't know where to start. I don't have a proper shop right now, so this summer I've been purchasing shitty, run-down furniture pieces from secondhand sellers and fixing them up—sanding, filling in the cracks, staining, giving them new designs and hardware. You'd never recognize the piece if I showed you the before picture. I've been selling those and slowly investing in new equipment, but it will take forever until I can buy enough to make a proper shop. Plus, I still have a lot to learn, and Arthur isn't here, hovering nearby, to give me advice."

"Maybe you could find an apprenticeship with someone who wouldn't mind if you used their equipment after hours for your own personal projects. That way, you could keep making your own stuff and building a clientele but also get your hours in to get certified and keep learning."

Hari purses his lips. "I never thought about that. I'd love to be my own boss, but I don't have the proper equipment yet, so that's an interesting alternative." He pauses like he's embarrassed to admit the next part. "My parents think it's stupid. They think I should go back to school for business or finance or accounting. They think this should just be a hobby, so it's kind of weird that *you're* the one who believes in me."

He means it. His eyes seem to peer right into my soul, as if to make sure I understand the genuineness of his statement. Suddenly, the sun isn't the only the reason I'm warm all over, and I tuck my hair behind my ear just to have something to do with my hands other than reach out and trace the curve of his smile.

"You're right. That *is* weird," I say, adding, "I take it back. You suck. Go be a douchey finance bro, that's more your speed."

He laughs at my joke. "Well, now I want to take a chance on my carpentry even more, just to spite you, even though I have no idea where to start."

"Well, if I were to help you, which I *wouldn't* because you're the worst, I'd suggest social media. At least an Instagram page. You could post your pieces, the ones made from scratch and the ones you flip. You could even film videos of the process with a voiceover." Hari, so lean and handsome, being all manly and skilled would definitely get attention from the algorithm. "It'll be easy. I can help—I mean, I *would* help, if I were actually giving you advice and not just talking out loud, and if you were actually staying in Canada."

For some reason, the thought of his leaving doesn't bring me as much joy as it should. Which is weird, completely and totally uncalled for by my nervous system.

"What's your plan then, Miss I Have All My Shit Together? What are you going to school for?"

"Criminology, then hopefully law school." It's always been the automatic answer, the path I decided on when I was little and stuck with.

"Wow, a lawyer, huh? Why did you land on that?"

I consider it for a moment, and the truth slips out. "My mom was a lawyer, and I want to be like her. She was strong and assertive and decisive; she always got things done. I'd be good in emotionally distressing and complex situations, too, because I'm good at controlling my emotions and focusing on what needs to get done—I have been since she died." As soon as the words slip from my mouth, I realize how open I just was with Hari, and I want to jump in the lake and swim away from the understanding in his eyes. Instead, I divert his attention with a joke. "And I'm shit at math and good at writing essays, so it seemed to be the natural path."

Hari seems to want to say something, something deep and personal that will dig into my skin and crack my defenses wide open, so I speak again before he gets the chance. "I've decided you can fix the hole in the drywall."

His eyebrows rise. "How generous of you to allow me the honor."

"Isn't it? As long as you're sure you can do it."

He shrugs like it's no big deal. "It's technically a part of carpentry. Arthur set me up with a friend who does house renos, and I worked with him every Sunday when Arthur was closed. I've patched, taped, sanded, and painted more walls than I can count throughout my high school career. The one in your wall is completely fixable. It'll probably take us two days, and we'll need some materials. Do you happen to know what color paint was on the wall?" A huge weight lifts off my chest, and I take my first proper breath since watching the guy go through the wall last night.

Before I can think about it, I throw my arms around him and hold him close. He's warm and smells like nature, and my body heats up everywhere my skin touches his. But then I realize what

I'm doing, that I'm *hugging Hari*, and shock replaces my elation. He's just as shocked as I am, his body stiff under mine, and I rip myself away from him. His eyes are wide as they travel my face, and I instantly school my emotions into place, feeling secure under my emotionless mask. "Hari, I am never going to say this again, so make sure you're listening, but you're not totally the worst. Thank you."

He clears his throat, adjusting his life jacket as he says, "You're, uh . . . you're welcome."

"Can we do it the last two days? So we don't have the smell of paint ruining the week? We keep extra cans of paint in the garage, so we have the color." Dad's interior designer recently repainted the walls anyway, a tactic they often employ to give the house a new, fresh look. *A fresh coat of lipstick on a house can make all the difference*, Dad always says.

"Sure, whatever you want." His smile is gentle, and I have the sudden urge to press my lips against his before I force the thought away.

What the hell is wrong with me? Just because we're in a truce and he's being kind of likable right now doesn't mean he's not Hari. I shouldn't be having these thoughts no matter how soft and kissable his lips look, no matter how much the butterflies in my stomach tell me to lean in and taste him, no matter how beautiful he looks sitting there rocking with the waves, no matter how natural it feels to talk with him, no matter how he seems to always dig under my shield. Besides, even if I decide we can be friends, he doesn't know if he's coming or going, and I already have enough abandonment issues. I can't add Hari into the mix.

I rip my gaze away from him and force myself to remember why we stopped riding in the first place. Clearing my throat and hoping my voice doesn't give me away, I say, "Okay, let's switch. Put your leg like that and I'll lean this way to get around so you can scoot up."

"Always so bossy," he says with a laugh, but he follows my instructions anyway.

We begin maneuvering so Hari can drive, and I properly tune into my surroundings. I was so caught up in our little bubble I didn't even notice another Sea-Doo in our vicinity. There's an odd feeling in my chest telling me something's wrong, and I stand to get a better look.

"Is that Olivia and Fletcher in the water? And is that . . . is that my Sea-Doo upside down? Oh my God! My Sea-Doo is *sinking*!"

ELEVEN

Day 2 of Muskoka

Olivia

I never asked, but I'm secretly thrilled Fletcher offered to switch so I can drive the Sea-Doo. As soon as we're clear of the dock and the others, I take off, shooting down the lake like we're being chased. It's such a thrill, being out here on the water with the wind whipping in my hair and water spraying us, nothing to think about except the next wave—not Alessio, not my relationship, not my future. My mind is solely occupied by having fun in the moment, and I chase the feeling all over the lake.

"My goodness, woman!" Fletcher calls from behind me, and I ease up on the accelerator to hear him better.

"You okay?" I ask. "Am I being too aggressive? Want me to slow down?"

"No, you're fine," he says, shaking his head, the water making his hair look more brown than red. "I just didn't know you had *that* in you! I've never seen you drive one of these before."

"Alessio likes driving," I say with a shrug, like that explains it all. I've never minded, since I wanted him to have fun, and he liked it when I rode behind him. But now that I'm here, *single*, I don't have to feel guilty about taking a turn driving, don't have to worry about making anyone upset for taking their spot in the driver's seat.

"So? He can like driving, and you can like driving. I like driving, and here I am playing passenger, although playing passenger to you might be more fun than driving."

I keep my speed slow as we pass other people on their own watercraft, and we wave at our fellow cottagers. More people are coming this way, so I maintain the pace, which gives Fletcher time to continue the conversation I so desperately want to move on from.

"Where is he, anyway?"

I can't even pretend I can't hear him, because the engine's not as loud at this speed. "He's sick. Flu."

"That sucks. For him, not you, because you get to be out on the water with me instead of glued to his side the whole time. I swear, sometimes we'd be here a whole week and I'd only get two words in with you."

He says it lightheartedly, but there's truth to his words. If Alessio were here, I'd be doing whatever he wanted, whenever he wanted. I'd be focused on making sure he's happy.

I wave to a group of people who pass us on a small boat instead of answering, and once they clear, Fletcher taps my shoulder.

"All right, little thrill-seeker, let's punch it."

I glance back, relieved he's letting it go. I don't want to think about Alessio. I want to be happy and have fun, like I was earlier. I was having fun during the mud fight last night, or even this morning with Dylan, when we bickered over the proper way to make pancakes from scratch. It was *my* way, of course, and he graciously accepted defeat, declaring me the superior pancake maker.

"Less giggling, more flying!" Fletcher demands jokingly, and I gesture at him to grab the straps.

"You asked for it!" I remind him right before I squeeze the throttle to send us speeding up the lake. We run into Jenna and Hari, as well as Dylan and Elena, and we wordlessly play around with one another, riding in circles and making waves for the others to jump off like a well-choreographed routine.

Eventually, Jenna takes off in a straight shot down the lake, and Dylan waves at me before he turns to weave through the islands.

A weird feeling settles in my chest as I watch Elena and Dylan. She has her arms wrapped around his torso instead of holding onto the straps, and my stomach knots at the way they're pressed against each other.

Elena's indisputably beautiful, and she's kind too. Dylan's the type of handsome that turns heads, and he's sweet and thoughtful and has a way of making people feel seen and heard all while putting a smile on their face. It would make sense if they got together; they'd be a power couple to end all power couples. But even though it's true, I can't help the way my heart sinks at the thought as the weird feeling in my chest intensifies.

I slow us to a crawl and turn back to Fletcher. "Want to switch again?"

"Have I got freckles and an irresistible charm that'll get Martina to fall in love with me before the week is over?"

I pause for a moment. "Um, is that a yes?"

"That's a *hell* yes."

You can say a lot about Fletcher: that he's loud, large, and incredibly persistent when it comes to getting what he wants even when no one else believes in him, but you can't say he lacks confidence. He goes for what he wants without reservation, and it's kind of inspiring.

We maneuver around each other to switch, and it's a miracle

neither of us tumbles off the seat into the water, but eventually I get into place behind him, he ties the key to his life vest, and we take off.

It's a beautiful Saturday, so there are tons of boats and people out on the water, which, combined with the rain from last night, makes the waves bigger than normal and the water extra choppy. He's a more reckless driver than I am, so I hold onto the straps tightly. We're bouncing extra hard, and it's getting more difficult for me to hang on and stay in place.

"Fletcher, slow dow—"

It happens before I have time to process it. We hit a wave too fast at the wrong angle. I'm ripped from the seat, flying through the air and hitting the water with such force it's like I've slammed into a brick wall. I'm disoriented under the water for a moment, instinct kicking me toward the surface.

I gasp for air, treading water as I shake off the pain. My head pounds, and my side is throbbing, but I push through the haze. Fletcher emerges from the water about ten feet behind me with a monstrous splash.

"Shit." He rolls out his neck, rocking with the waves. "You okay, Liv? I should've been more careful. Sorry."

It's not the first time I've been thrown off a watercraft, and it won't be the last. "I'm all right. Where's the Sea-Doo?"

We circle in the water and spot a flash of red. The key was attached to Fletcher's life jacket, so it shut off when we were flung from it, but that's not the problem. The problem is that it's far away and upside down, and it looks like the waves from surrounding boats are pushing it not only farther away but also downward.

Crap. "Fletcher, help me!" I call, already swimming toward it. We have to flip it over right away or we won't be able to at all. I hope there's no damage and the hull hasn't taken on any water, or we're really in trouble.

I hear another engine closer than the rest out on the lake but don't stop swimming until I reach my destination. It's Hari and Jenna, and they're speeding right toward us.

Fletcher reaches me, and together we jump to try to grab onto one side and flip it back over, but it's hard. Waves keep hitting us, and I keep swallowing water, and the Sea-Doo is sliding lower and lower into the water.

Hari shuts off his engine before he gets too close to not make more waves, and Jenna yells, "Liv! I'm coming!" She dives into the water and makes it to us before I can blink.

"We have to flip this!" she exclaims, panicked hands trying to get a proper grip somewhere on the hull.

Large hands land on my waist under the life vest, and then I'm lifted from the water, landing flat over the hull to grab the other side of the Sea-Doo. I grip hard, letting Fletcher and gravity pull me back down, and when it's close enough, Jenna and Fletcher grab on too. Together, we manage to flip it back over.

Jenna's frantically examining the Sea-Doo, swimming around it to check everything as it drains out the water it took on. "Is it all right? Is it broken? Oh god, if the engine doesn't start, I'm screwed."

I take the key from Fletcher and climb up onto the vehicle, slotting the key in and twisting. It takes a few moments, like it's trying to decide whether it wants to turn over or not, then finally gives way.

Jenna's sigh of relief is so impactful, her whole body loses its rigidity. "Thank goodness," she breathes, but she's still shaky and seems like she's two seconds away from a panic attack. It's odd, because we've flipped the Sea-Doos plenty of times—we even stole her dad's speedboat for a joyride when we were eleven and crashed it onto a random deserted island, and even then she was never this distraught. She has no reason to be: her dad always replaces anything that's been damaged without question.

"You okay?" I ask Jenna, who's still staring at the watercraft like the engine might fail at any second.

"Yeah, I just . . ." She takes a moment to compose herself, and when her eyes open again, any signs of panic are gone. I could've imagined the whole thing. "It's fine. Let's just be more careful with the Sea-Doos."

"Sorry, Jenna," Fletcher says, scrubbing the back of his neck. "It was my fault, I hit the wave wrong."

Another engine joins us, and Dylan and Elena pull up beside Hari. Dylan takes in the scene, but his eyes land on mine before he asks, "Everything okay?"

"Yes," I say, ignoring the way my face heats up. My eyes flick to Jenna, who's as unreadable as ever, but the memory of her distress has me suggesting, "Why don't we all call it and head back? We should start dinner soon and get ready before people start showing up."

"Great idea," Jenna announces, swimming back to Hari. "And let's all be a bit more careful with the water toys, please."

Dylan gives me another once-over before seemingly deciding I'm fine, and once Fletcher is back on behind me, we ease back to the cottage. Jenna and Hari stick close, as if wanting to monitor that our Sea-Doo is fine, and it is. We make it back to the cottage and dock all three machines without any problem, covering them with their color-coded tarps before grabbing our stuff and heading inside.

Robbie and Kyle are already in the kitchen prepping for dinner, chuckling as they take turns throwing cherry tomatoes into one another's mouths from a distance.

"Hey," Robbie greets the group of us as a timer goes off. "Just in time, we threw some frozen pizzas in the oven while marinating the steaks." He stuffs his hands in oven mitts, and as soon as he pulls open the door to the oven, the mouthwatering scent of pizza fills the space, making my stomach grumble. A quick glance at the clock has me raising my eyebrows. We haven't had anything to eat since breakfast, and it's nearly 4:00 p.m. now. I must have lost track of time out there. Usually around noon I'm in here making sandwiches for everyone and bringing them out on the dock, the grateful smiles and moans thanks enough. Alessio always gets hungry when out on the water, and it seemed rude to make just him something to eat, so I'd be in here preparing food for everyone, watching them enjoying themselves through the wall of windows.

I glance at Dylan, who smiles at me as he picks at some cucumber slices in the huge bowl of undressed salad before heading outside to help Jenna and Hari put away the canoes and kayaks.

I *used* to sacrifice my lake time by making lunches. But not today. Today, I wasn't Alessio's doting girlfriend, I was Olivia. And Olivia had fun.

While they set the pizzas on the counter and everyone lunges for them, I run to the bathroom really quickly, since we've been out there all day. When I get back, not even a few minutes later, the pizzas have disappeared, and so has everyone else.

I survey the crumb-scattered trays, spotting a singular slice of pineapple pizza, my favorite, as Kyle exits the walk-in pantry.

"Sweet, one slice left!" he exclaims, eyeing the pizza before catching me standing there. "Oh, you didn't want that, right, Liv?" It's a considerate question, but his hand is already reaching for the slice, as if he knows what my answer will be.

My stomach protests as I say, "No, it's all right." Instead, I grab a blueberry muffin to hold me over until dinner, finishing it as I head up the stairs to my room.

It smells like Dylan in here, which is odd because he didn't spray any cologne today, but the scent of him still lingers—warm and smoky and instantly putting my nerves at ease. It's almost overwhelming how much I like it, so I open the balcony doors to let in some fresh air and help clear my head of the sudden dizziness.

Dylan's still outside. I see him down by the water's edge with Jenna and Hari, and I glance at the couch he slept on last night. He didn't complain once, not even this morning when he told me he got a great night's sleep and hid the way he rolled out the crick in his neck.

Discarding the muffin's wrapper, I tiptoe toward my phone sitting on the nightstand and stare at it. I haven't looked at it since this morning, after I called my mom and filled her in on what happened. But now I'm hesitant to turn it on. I'm not sure what scares me more, turning on the phone and seeing a ton of messages from Alessio or turning it on and seeing none.

The longer I stare at it, the faster my heart beats and the shallower my breathing becomes.

"Grab the turtle, Liv," I whisper to myself before switching the phone on. Floods of messages and voice mail notifications come in, most from Alessio and a few from my sisters and my mom, checking in on me.

It's been more than twenty-four hours since I've talked to Alessio. Before he left for Cuba, not speaking for that long would have been unthinkable. But it's almost like his ignoring me for over a month since he got back has softened the blow for me a bit. I miss him, sure, but it doesn't hurt as much as I thought it would, especially when I remember *why* we're not currently talking.

Listening to the voice mails will be too much, but morbid curiosity has me scrolling through his texts. They're all along the same lines.

I miss you.

I'm sorry.

She meant nothing to me.

I'd take it back if I could.

Please give me another chance.

I was miserable the entire trip in Cuba, so wracked with guilt for what I'd done. Please believe me, Liv.

The last one has me gripping the phone so hard my knuckles turn white. Am I supposed to feel *bad* that he was miserable in Cuba? He did it to himself! And now he's trying to guilt me into taking him back?

I shouldn't have looked at the phone. I was having fun today, and now I'm pissed.

A knock on the bedroom door has me dropping the phone like it burned me, like I was doing something wrong when I've just been standing here.

"You changing in there, Livy, or can I come in?" Dylan calls, and his friendly voice helps ease some of the tension in my shoulders.

"You can come in."

The door swings open, revealing Dylan in all his bare-chested, muscular glory, the tattooed arm stark against the rest of his smooth torso.

"I'm just grabbing a dry change of clothes. I'm on barbecue duty with Hari, so I'll shower after dinner. It's all yours now," he says, and I swear as the words leave his mouth, his eyes widen slightly, like he's said something he wishes he hadn't, although I can't pinpoint what.

He swiftly crosses the room to shuffle through the drawer where he's stored his clothes, and I shift from foot to foot, suddenly not knowing what to do with my arms or where to look without giving away the fact that I was thinking about Alessio when I promised I wouldn't this week.

He shrugs on a T-shirt before turning to me, and I realize I'm awkwardly standing here in my bikini. This morning, I scurried into the bathroom in my lingerie with a change of clothes before he saw me, but now that I'm facing him in a little purple string bikini that reveals more than my lingerie pajamas did, that seems kind of silly. But there's something more intimate about being in lingerie in a bedroom at night with someone, even if it's conservative lingerie, compared to a bikini in broad daylight.

He scans my face, and his eyebrows immediately draw together. "What's wrong?"

I nibble on my lip, contemplating my next words carefully. I don't want to know, but the part of me that likes organizing and filing away facts *needs* to know. "Can you be honest with me?"

"Always."

He says it without an ounce of hesitation, which makes me wonder if I really want the answer or not. But I forge ahead with the question anyway. "Did Alessio . . . did he seem sad in Cuba? Like he was wracked with so much guilt he couldn't have any fun?"

Dylan's face blanks, and even though he stares at me in silence, he might as well have yelled the answer through a megaphone in front of the entire cottage. But still, I need the verbal confirmation. "Dylan?"

A muscle in his jaw works as his eyes roam my face. "Liv . . ."

"Tell me, Dylan. Please."

I can see his mental conflict. Is his loyalty to his friend warring with his instinct to be honest? Or is his need to be honest warring with the desire to not hurt me?

After a moment, his eyes go hard, and I realize his internal battle was the second option when he says, "You can't unhear it, Liv. Are you sure you want to know?"

No. Yes. I don't know.

"You said you'd be honest."

This time, he doesn't hold back. "I had absolutely no idea any-thing was going on until his cheating was outed in front of everyone. He acted the same as he always did, no signs of guilt, no way that anyone would've known something was up. You know he slept with her multiple times already, so he was sleeping with her for days and not planning on telling anyone. The only time he was miserable was after we all found out, when we all railed on him." He says it all firmly, like he's stating a fact that makes him angry, but his voice softens the tiniest bit when he adds, "He wasn't thinking about you, Liv, and he only felt bad about getting caught."

I had my suspicions, but hearing it out loud is like a kick to the stomach. I wait for the sadness to overtake me, but instead, the heated anger in my chest only intensifies. I'm feeling guilty for hav-ing fun when he's not here, yet he was cheating on me and having the best time ever in Cuba, planning on living it up and coming back to me like nothing happened. I'm so stupid for wasting my time at the party last night feeling depressed when I should be focusing on *me*, just like he focused on himself.

Something inside me changes with this last bit of information. I can feel it all tightening and hardening, locking my resolve into place and, with it, sealing away any last bit of grief I felt for this situation. Alessio's girlfriend Olivia is well and truly dead.

"Thank you for telling me."

He reaches out to me as if he's about to say something more, but Jenna waltzes in, a small travel bag in her hand. "Can I shower in here? The other two showers are occupied, and I need to start getting ready for the party tonight."

Dylan steps back, whatever he was about to say lost, the tick in his jaw returning as he says, "I should get started on barbecue duty."

Then he's gone, and it's just me and my cousin.

"Yeah, sure, I'll go after you," I tell her. I need to answer some emails and set up some more last-minute promotions for my app's launch next week anyway.

"Great, I won't be long," she says, and then I remember how she acted earlier when the Sea-Doo flipped, how she got up even before I did this morning and started cleaning. I didn't think Jenna even knew *how* to clean. When it's just the two of us up here, she sits at the kitchen island sharing gossip and drama while I clean up after dinner.

I stop her before she enters the bathroom. "Hey, is everything okay? You've kind of been acting . . . I don't know. . ." I don't want to say *weird*, so I settle on, "out of character. I would've helped you clean this morning if you had waited for me."

Jenna's guard goes up. I can see it slide into place, clearing her face of any emotions. "Everything's fine, I just don't want to destroy the cottage. Is that so hard to believe?"

"No, but—"

"Speaking of 'out of character,' what the hell's going on with you? If anyone's acting weird, it's you."

She clearly doesn't care about holding back, but then again, Jenna's never had a problem telling me the truth, even if it's hard to hear. I may be the only person on Earth that Jenna doesn't have to put up a front with, and the fact that she is doing it right now when it's just the two of us only tells me something *is* wrong. But when she gets like this, there's no way of pushing her until she's ready.

"I don't know what you mean—"

"Don't lie to me, Liv. I've been a bit . . . preoccupied lately, so I haven't been able to properly call you out on it. But we're here now. What's going on?"

"Nothing's going on."

"Bullshit," she accuses, her icy blue eyes piercing through me. "You're sharing a bed with a man—an incredibly hot and tempting man—who's *not* your boyfriend and acting totally chill about it. I bet Alessio's losing his shit, and you, what? Just don't care? You never *don't care* about Alessio. Don't lie to me."

She's right, and we both know it. But still, I evade by mumbling, "We're not sharing a bed, he's on the couch."

"*Liv.*"

"Okay, fine," I sigh, the fight leaving me. "Alessio and I are on a break."

The toiletry bag slips from Jenna's hand, landing on the floor with a clunk. "Holy shit. Seriously? I thought you were going to marry the guy."

Me too.

"Are you all right? What happened?" Her eyes shift to the couch where Dylan's blanket still lies in a rumpled heap, then she looks back at me. "Does it have to do with Dylan?"

"What? No. Why would you say that?"

Jenna gives me a pointed look, and it has my defenses rising instantly. "What?"

"If you don't already know, then I'm not going to tell you."

Don't already know *what*? Why am I always oblivious to things everyone else knows? "Just tell me. I hate not knowing when everyone else does." Just like everyone else knew Alessio cheated on me six weeks before I did.

Jenna must see the desperation on my face because she relents. "It's clear the dude is in love with you. I have no idea if Alessio just ignored it or if he never noticed, because anyone with eyes can see how he feels. Just the way Dylan looks at you gives it away. No one has ever looked at me like that, not even any of my exes."

My stomach flips, and I can't decipher the emotions causing it. My throat is dry when I ask, "How does he look at me?"

"Like you could kick him in the face and rip out his heart and he'd thank you and ask how he could help."

He does *not* look at me like that. No one looks at me like that; no one looks at *anyone* like that. Right? That's just Jenna being Jenna. I would have noticed if that were true . . . right?

I push down all the emotions tangling within me and in my calmest voice say, "You're being dramatic."

She shrugs like it doesn't matter either way. "Fine. Don't believe me. Now tell me what happened with Alessio."

I tell her how he cheated on me in Cuba multiple times, how he avoided me for weeks afterward to put off telling me, how I broke up with him to give me time to think, and how he's been messaging me nonstop since, and her rage grows more evident with each word out of my mouth.

When I'm finished, she looks ready to hop in a car and speed right to Alessio's house to punch him herself.

"That fucking . . . *fuckface!*" she exclaims. "I can't *believe* him! If I ever see him again, I'll make him eat his own di—" She cuts herself off when she looks at me, taking a calming breath before closing the space between us and placing her hands on my shoulders. More composed this time, she lowers her head to look into my eyes and says, "You're too good for Alessio, and you always have been. He knows it, everyone knows it, and deep down, even you know it. Breaking up with him was for the best, even if it doesn't feel like it right now."

Her soft tone breaks the last little bit of strength I had, and my voice cracks when I admit, "He was all I knew for years, Jenna. Basically my only friend. I . . . who am I without him?"

Any kindness on Jenna's face evaporates with those words, and pissed Jenna is back in her place. "That's bullshit, Liv. I'm not going to sit here and give you a pep talk, because you don't need it. You're Olivia Rossi, the smartest girl I know, the girl who can take any idea, like a whole-ass *app*, and make it a reality, the girl who sees the good in people, even assholes like Alessio, the girl who decides what she wants and makes it a reality even when no one else believes in her. So screw Alessio. He doesn't know who *he* is without *you*, not the other way around. You're going places, and you don't need him holding you back. Never forget that."

I sniffle as a few tears escape, swiping at my face. "You sure are good at pep talks for someone who just said they weren't going to give one."

My phone rings, and we glance at it on the dresser, the name on the caller ID instantly making both of us tense.

Jenna grabs it first, turning it off and shoving it in the nightstand drawer. "Screw Alessio. Have fun tonight. You're always so concerned with Alessio, but tonight, I want you to do something *you* want to do. You're your own person, Olivia, not Alessio's girlfriend, you get me?"

I do. It's what I've been telling myself I wanted to do on this trip. Now that both Dylan *and* Jenna have essentially said the same thing, it makes me feel like I'm on the right path.

"Yes."

"Good. At least now I know why you were more interested in staring at the wall than stopping those assholes from going through it." Jenna picks up her dropped toiletry bag and points at me. "Have fun tonight. I know everything just happened yesterday and Alessio's an asshole, but this is the last ti—" She cuts herself off with a frown before continuing. "This is the last week of summer. Enjoy it. You've been so dependent on him that you feel like you don't know yourself anymore. So tonight, talk to people, have fun, hell, maybe even get a little wild and have a beer."

I'll try. I really, really want to try. "I will. And please don't tell anyone. Only Dylan, Mom, and the twins know."

"I won't, if you promise to enjoy yourself."

"Jenna!" a deep voice yells from downstairs. "Which oven do we use for the potatoes? The one in the wall or the big one?"

Jenna sighs, mumbling, "I can't believe Kyle talked us into letting only the guys cook today if he's asking me that kind of question."

"Jenna!" he calls again, and she yells back, "I'm coming!"

She sets her toiletry bag beside my suitcase on the bench in front of the bed. "Go shower. It's my turn after." And then she's striding to the door, but just before leaving, she stops, turning back and throwing her arms around me. She pulls me in close, and I let myself sink into her comfort.

There's none of her normal harshness in her tone when she says, "I'm proud of you for not locking yourself in your room to cry like I know you wanted to. I'm glad you came, Liv. I . . . I needed you here." She hugs me tighter for just a second before pulling away. She adjusts her bikini top and fixes her hair, which has already dried perfectly straight, and it's like the moment never happened. Then she's gone, and I'm left staring after her, trying to make sense of what just happened.

Jenna's not really a touchy-feely, hugging and talking through feelings kind of person. She once told me big emotional scenes in rom-coms make her skin crawl, which is why she always chooses horror or action films for her turn on movie night. In fact, her breakup with Adam was only a five-minute conversation, so she must really love me to want to comfort me in that way, and I appreciate it.

I'm gathering some clothes for after my shower when my eyes land on the drawer beside the bed. Sheer curiosity has me turning the phone back on, and I click on the voice mail notification, playing the latest one.

"Liv, babe, please call me back. I don't know what I can do to prove that she meant nothing to me. I was so miserable in Cuba because I knew how badly I screwed up. Please call me back."

It hurts to hear his voice, but not as much as it hurts to realize that he's lying through his teeth. I believe Dylan when he said Alessio was only miserable after he got caught. Dylan wouldn't lie to me, especially not after how big a deal I made about him lying to me at Elena's birthday when I asked if something had happened. I know he's telling the truth now; I feel it in my gut.

I power off the phone and drop it back in the drawer without looking at any of the other messages or voice mails. He had fun in Cuba while he had a girlfriend, but I'm single now.

The steel spine that started forming after my conversation with Dylan now fully forms with the realization that Jenna and Dylan are right. I'm going to have fun, maybe even make a few of my own mistakes, and nothing, not Alessio or my own damn guilt, is going to stop me.

TWELVE

Night 2 of Muskoka

Jenna

It probably wasn't the smartest move to throw another party after what happened yesterday, but it's been over an hour since the party started, and it's remained small and controlled. Only the people explicitly invited are here, so it's lively enough to make it a party without anyone standing around awkwardly but not so crowded that things are getting crazy and out of control. I can actually relax, sitting on a chair outside with a group of people from school I haven't gotten the chance to catch up with this summer, instead of frantically running around in chaos-control mode like last night.

It's a beautiful night, too, not raining and muddy like yesterday, so lots of people are enjoying the back patio and the yard instead of huddling around inside, which is better for me, since fewer people inside means fewer things to dirty or break. Robbie's still playing music, and someone even brought a keg and set it up on the grass, but for the most part, it's a chill party, and the anxiety in my chest remains at a low simmer in the background instead of reaching that uncomfortable level I hate.

Since it's an impromptu party, there's no huge theme or photo sets. It's just a regular, low-key high school party, and I actually start enjoying myself as the night goes on. I almost forget that I'm not supposed to be throwing a party at all, not supposed to be *here* at all. At least I relax until my phone rings, and the name flashing on my caller ID has me crashing back to reality.

Shit.

I scramble away from the group, off the landscaped path and through the trees to get away from the noise. It's a faint hum in the background by the time I answer the call.

"Hey, Dad." I'm breathing like I've been running through a forest, so I try to calm my racing heart to pull off the just-lounging-on-the-couch vibe I'm going for.

"Where are you?"

My heart pounds. "At Western, why?"

"Is that really the story you're sticking with?" he deadpans. Is he on to me? What's with the doubt? I frantically glance around like he's somehow teleported from Vancouver and appeared here to bust me.

Even though this might be a test, I still double down. "Yes."

He sighs, like he's over waiting for me to come clean on my own. "I explicitly told you *not* to go to the cottage, Jenna. Multiple times. Almost once a day."

My heart drops to my stomach. I couldn't speak even if I tried. He knows. I'm dead. I'm so, so dead.

He doesn't wait for my response. "You're supposed to be at your dorm! You *told me* that's where you were."

This is it. The week is over. The last memory my friends will ever have of me is my dad coming and shutting down our week before grounding me for eternity.

"Dammit, Jenna!" he exclaims, and I can picture him tugging at his tie. "This isn't a good time for you and your irresponsible, property-damaging friends to be throwing a party at the cottage I'm trying to *sell*. It's already hard enough to unload a multimillion-dollar property, never mind a *lake house*, and now when I've got people lined up to come view it, you and your friends are going to destroy the place. Not to mention that all my cards are already maxed from the move and the new company, and I can't afford to fix the inevitable damage." Dad sighs, his voice going scarily even. "I never ask anything of you, Jenna. Never bother you, let you do whatever you want whenever you want. You've been so independent since your mother died that you've never needed any type of policing from me. But I ask you this *one thing*, this one thing, and you can't even give me the respect of listening?"

I've never felt disapproval this sharp, this overpowering. I lean against the trunk of a sturdy tree. Despite how upset and hurt I am at him picking up and leaving me, I still can't help but yearn for my father; I need him to love me, to not believe that I'm more trouble than I'm worth.

"No, that's not what's going on," I rush to interject because I don't want him to keep using that disappointed tone with me.

"Really? Because I was talking to your aunt, and she said Olivia is with you. At the cottage."

Shit.

Dad *rarely* talks to my aunt, and I know it's because she reminds him too much of Mom, even if he won't ever admit it. I never thought that of all times, *now* is when they'd decide to have a little chitchat, when I needed this trip to go smoothly and for him to stay in the dark for at least this week, if not forever. I should've told Olivia *not* to say anything, but then again, Olivia wouldn't lie to her mom for me, and I can't ask that of her.

He takes my silence as admission, letting out a frustrated groan. "You couldn't have picked a worse time to blatantly disregard me, Jenna. When did you get there? Yesterday? I bet your friends have already caused thousands of dollars' worth of damage."

It takes everything in my power not to think about the giant hole in the drywall in the living room, as if it's possible for him to sense it over the phone. My brain scrambles, and the lie is out before I've even thought it through. "No, it's just me and Olivia here! None of my friends. There won't be any damage, I promise!"

"You shouldn't be there in the *first place*."

"Okay, yes, fine. I know. But Olivia needed a break. She and Alessio are having a rough time, so we spontaneously decided to come up, just the two of us."

"You're *still* lying to me?"

I am, but I don't waver. "I'm not throwing a party. Only Olivia and I are here."

"Really?" he questions, completely unconvinced.

"Don't believe me? You know Olivia. If I was really throwing a party with all my friends here, would she come without Alessio? Ask Aunt Eloise if Alessio's here. He's not. It's just me and Olivia doing some bonding and girl talk and eating pints of ice cream while discussing every way Alessio sucks. She needed a getaway after what happened . . ."

I'm a shitty person for using Olivia's breakup to make my lie believable, but I'm desperate, and if Dad talked to Aunt Eloise for the first time in forever, then it was a big catching-up phone call, and he has to know about what happened.

Dad's silent for a moment, and it's confirmation that I'm right about him hearing about the breakup. Finally, he relents. "Fine. I'm still incredibly upset you went to Muskoka when I explicitly told you not to and that you aren't where you're supposed to be, but since it's just the two of you—and it *better* be just the two of you and none of your inconsiderate, house-destroying friends—and Olivia is having a rough time, you can stay." *Yes!* This is a win. *Technically* only a half win, because it's all complete lies, but I'll deal with one problem at a time. "And the cottage needs to be in pristine condition, and all the money for damages is coming out of your pocket. We do not have the money to replace the hot tub or broken windows or a broken refrigerator door or all the other things your friends have destroyed at your parties in the past."

"You're being dramatic; my parties aren't that bad." He's not being dramatic. My parties *are* that bad, and I never realized it until I had to start cleaning up after them myself and confronting the damage done. Even if I had a house to keep throwing parties, I don't think I'd invite those same people again, at least not if they're going to be disrespectful to my property.

"I'm serious, Jenna." His voice is stern, and I can picture him pinning me with his eyes in that intense way he does. "You can't just close your eyes and continue doing whatever you want because you don't like the alternative. I'm trying to teach you some responsibility here. You're going to be on your own in Ontario for years, so you're going to have to learn to take care of yourself. I haven't even been gone for seventy-two hours, and you've already gone and proved you can't handle being left alone."

The reminder that I'm alone is a punch in the chest, and I have to bite back the retort that I *already* know how to take care of myself because he's never home anyway.

"Everything will be fine," I promise, a hard certainty in my voice. It *will* be fine.

"Don't make me regret trusting you." The sharp edge in his voice unnerves me, and at that exact moment, there's a loud bang. I wince, trying to smother the phone so he won't hear whatever commotion is going on at the party he's explicitly outlined I was under no circumstances to throw.

I peek out, trying to see what the hell is going on while keeping my voice calm. "Everything will be fine. I promise. You know how Olivia is."

My jaw drops as my eyes land on Olivia, my responsible, party-mom cousin. She's being held upside down over the keg, chugging beer up the hose like she's dying of dehydration.

What the hell is going on?

"Fine, all right. At least Olivia is there to be the responsible one."

"Mm-hmm." I sound my agreement as I watch Dylan release Olivia's feet to help her back to the ground, and they high-five each other in victory.

Dad sighs, and I know he's rubbing the bridge of his nose. "I don't mean to be so harsh. But I'm under a lot of stress uprooting my life and starting this new venture. It's risky. It's an all-hands-on-deck situation, so I'm counting on you here."

Before I can answer, Dad adds, "Oh, I've got to go, I have potential buyers on the other line. We'll talk later, but don't forget what I said. It's time for you to be responsible, so I'm not bailing you out this time. Make sure you clean up properly when you and Olivia leave and keep the noise down. You know the neighbors live there in the summer and like to complain and call the cops for noise complaints."

The ache in my stomach I've been trying so hard to ignore is back and at an all-time high. Maybe we shouldn't have come here. Maybe the risk wasn't worth it. Maybe I can come clean right now and call this whole thing off. I'll kick everyone out, and Hari can help me fix the hole in the drywall, and it'll be like we were never even here. I won't have to deal with the pit of anxiety in my chest for the rest of the week.

"We'll clean up," I reassure him, my heart pounding with what I'm about to do. I start pacing, failing to talk myself out of it. My breathing turns shallow, and I might literally puke all over my dress, but I push forward anyway. "Hey, Dad? Actually, I wasn't being completely honest before. I'm not here with just Olivia, I—"

"Jenna? Hello? Can you hear me?"

I stop pacing, and my heart feels like it stops beating entirely. "Hello?"

"Oh, there you are. Are you outside? You know the connection is spotty near the trees."

I look up at the hundred-year-old pine tree I'm standing under. "Did you hear what I said? I was saying—"

"Hello? I keep losing you. You said you'll clean up. Are you asking for instructions? All the products are in the garage or under the counters in the bathroom cabinets or in the laundry room. Make sure you read the labels."

"That's not what I—"

"Jenna, I have to go, it's an important client on the other line. But remember what I said about actions and consequences," he threatens. Before he hangs up, like it's an afterthought, he says, "Oh, and Jenna? Happy birthday."

Then he ends the call, and I stare at my phone with a lump in my throat. My birthday was *yesterday*.

I was going to come clean. In fact, I *did* come clean. But like divine intervention, I was stopped. The *cottage itself* stopped me.

I place a palm on the thick trunk of the tree, like I can absorb its calming, sturdy energy, and look up at its expansive branches. Mom's face pops into my mind. Her smile, her steadiness, her *presence*. Maybe it *was* divine intervention that stopped my confession.

I glance at my friends down by the fire pit. Elena and Hari are laughing at something Kyle is saying to a group of people, and

Martina is dragging a grinning Fletcher away to a private seating area.

Maybe the fact that Dad didn't hear my confession was a sign that I should see the rest of the week through. I'll just be on my very best behavior, doing everything I can to make sure we have a chill, relaxed, disaster-free week. And then I'll make sure everything is put back the way it was when we got here, making sure the house is perfect and staged for when Dad comes back to do showings, and no one will ever know we were here. But for now, I've been given a chance to enjoy this last week before everyone truly leaves me, and I'm going to grab it with both hands.

But in order to do that, I need to take care of one last thing.

Instead of running over to join my friends, I find Olivia. She's in the kitchen instead of near the keg. She's holding a bag of giant marshmallows.

"Hey, can I borrow your phone?" I ask her, ignoring the niggling guilt rising up my spine.

"I haven't touched it since you turned it off and left it in the drawer upstairs. Want me to get it for you?"

"No!" I say a little too quickly. "No, that's good. Ignore it for the night, ignore *him* for the night, and have fun."

I don't need to specify who "him" is. "That's exactly what I'm doing," she says with a coy smile like she's holding onto a secret.

"Good, very good." I nod just as I spot a group of girls I *didn't* invite dancing on a table and rush off to deal with them. This party is supposed to be small and calm, and that means no party crashers.

"Hey!" I yell, running over to them. "Get off of that! Who even are you?"

"Sorry, Jenna," Salma, a girl I *did* invite, says. She pulls the other girls off the table. "These are my cousins; they were at the cottage with us and wanted to come. I didn't think you'd mind."

Maybe before I wouldn't have, but today I do. "It's invite only, and this is a nondestructive party, which means no dancing on tables." I pin the cousins with a glare, and they step behind Salma.

"Can they stay, please?" Salma begs. "I promise we'll be on our best behavior. I'm designated driver, I'll watch them all night."

It's only a few more people, and Salma *is* the one who told me that Faye had written my number on a gas station bathroom door with the promise of a good time and that's why I was getting so many disturbing messages and calls last year. "Fine. But I'm serious. No more dancing on tables."

The four girls nod their heads so vigorously they might damage the vertebrae in their necks. "Yes! Swear!"

"And your party last night was *amazing*," Salma adds. "My older sister is getting married, and when I showed her the pictures, she asked what you'd charge for engagement parties and bridal showers. Her other friend asked if you would do her twenty-fifth birthday."

My mind is already so preoccupied with everything going on, I barely understand what she's saying. "Asked what I'd charge?"

"Yeah, to plan it. Your parties always look amazing."

Someone wants to pay me to throw a party?

"Um, that's not . . ." I shake my head. I don't have time for this. "I'll talk to you later." Before she has time to reply, I turn to head upstairs and finish my mission, but then Elena appears, hooking her arm through mine.

"There you are! I've been so busy tonight we didn't even get to hang out. But we're about to play flip cup and need you on our team!"

"Actually, I—"

"It's starting in a minute. Come on!" She drags me in the opposite direction of the stairs. She's surprisingly strong when she's dead set on a goal, and I let her pull me along.

All my friends are standing there, along with friends who aren't part of my core group. They're laughing and setting up the plastic cups on the outdoor table for the game, and the ball in my chest loosens. This *is* why I'm here this week, to have some fun. I'll deal with Olivia's phone later.

I lose track of time. I'm having so much fun playing and enjoying being at a party without running around, it's like I forgot all about my dad and our phone call. But then I hear someone else answer a call with *Hey, Dad*, and it's like the realization is slammed into me all at once.

I need to keep this going, and to do that, I need to tell a few more lies.

Sneaking away from the group and tiptoeing up the path back to the house, I check to make sure the coast is clear before sprinting up the stairs and slipping into the primary bedroom. I don't turn on any lights, but both the standing floor lamp and the bedside lamp are on, and the blinds are open, letting in some of the muted atmospheric light from the party below.

Ignoring how messed up what I'm about to do is, I slide open the nightstand drawer, and Olivia's phone is right where she said it was, right where I left it earlier when I came to shower and ended up in a mini heart-to-heart.

I can't believe Alessio; I wish I could kick him in the dick. How incredibly fucked up do you have to be to cheat on *Olivia*? But then again, he's best friends with my ex, who also wasn't the most considerate or attentive boyfriend. His sister hated my guts and went out of her way to be extra cruel to me, and Adam never said anything. *Plus*, he made heart eyes at her best friend, Lori, right in front of me and then told me I was *overthinking* and being *dramatic* when I asked if he had a thing for her and told him to break it off with me if he did. He even asked if I pushed her into the pool at prom! As if I care enough about *anyone* to push them into a pool. If he felt something for her, then good for them, I wasn't forcing him to stay with me. I may be a lot of things, but I won't be someone's second choice.

I power on her phone and am greeted with a picture of Olivia and Alessio, one that I took of them while on a double date with Adam, and I'm pissed off all over again. Olivia deserves better than Alessio, and he knows it. He took advantage of her caring and eager-to-please nature, and I sincerely hope Olivia never ever ever takes him back, no matter how many voice mails and messages he leaves her, which, judging by what I see on her phone, is a lot.

I meant what I told Olivia earlier. I'm glad she's here. She's hiding it pretty well, considering, but I know she's crushed. Alessio was her whole world, and finding out *yesterday* that her boyfriend is a major dickwad would've given her all the reason in the world to hide in bed and ignore the world. But she came anyway, she's *here*, and she gets to be here *with me* one last time. She's been my built-in best friend since we were born, and if she weren't here this week, I would've spent the whole time wishing we could've made a few more memories together. She came, though, and now we do get to make those memories.

But first, I have to make sure our week doesn't come to a fiery end.

I pull out my own phone and dial my aunt's number.

"Jenna?" she answers, her voice groggy. "Is everything okay? Did something happen?"

I pull back the phone to check the time. Shit. It's way past midnight. I didn't think this through. Well, I didn't think it through *more* than I already haven't thought it through.

"Everything's fine. I'm sorry, I didn't realize how late it was."

She breathes out a sigh of relief, and I hear a lamp click on.

"Well, what's going on? I haven't heard much from Liv. Are you girls having fun? Is she doing okay with . . . you know . . . the breakup?"

The guilt gnaws at me, but I push forward. "She's doing all right. It helps that we're here, just the two of us, trying to be as relaxed as possible. You know, meditating, taking in nature, having a little spa day, all that stuff."

"Oh, I thought other people were there with you?"

"Nope! After what happened with Alessio, we figured it would be good to have girl time. She has a lot on her mind, so I'm trying my best to cheer her up." My throat tightens, and it's suddenly too hot in here, so I open the balcony doors to try to get some air.

"Good, that's good," she says, and I can hear the worry in her voice. It only makes the tightness in my throat worse. She cares about her daughters and their well-being. She'd never pick up and move to another province. In fact, when Olivia started university last year and chose to live in the dorms, Aunt Eloise cried for two months straight, even though Olivia was only a forty-minute drive away, sometimes less if traffic is good. "I know she must be having a hard time juggling so many emotions right now."

"That's actually why I called you," I say, remembering why exactly I'm doing this. *It's for the greater good.* "I feel like Olivia is having a hard time processing with Alessio always calling and texting and with her seeing old pictures and social media and stuff, so I'm going to do some tough love and take her phone away from her. It's only hurting her more to see his name and face popping up everywhere. She needs time to process." Technically true. Olivia doesn't need to see that scumbag's face, and the last thing she needs is for him to somehow convince her to take him back.

"You know, that's probably a good idea," Aunt Eloise agrees. "She's so dependent on Alessio, sometimes it feels like she's muted a part of herself to make him shine. It would be good for her to think things through without him influencing her."

Looks like Aunt Eloise is team *fuck Alessio*, but being the classy, elegant woman she is, she's not going to say it in so many words. I wonder if Olivia told her mom Alessio cheated on her or just that they just broke up. If she knew he cheated on her, she might have some stronger words, elegant woman or not.

"That's the plan," I say, thinking on my feet when I add, "Actually, we're both going to unplug, you know, in solidarity. So you probably won't hear anything from either one of us until we're back. If there's an emergency, just text me, I'll check my messages every once in a while. But definitely let Olivia unplug." The less Olivia talks to her mom, the less likely it is that she'll tell her there are other people here. Once she gets home and tells her mom there were other people, it won't matter. Dad can know other people were here after he sees there's no damage and everything is in pristine shape for buyers.

"No, don't worry, I won't bother you girls. Enjoy your time together before school starts."

"Thanks, Aunt Eloise. I'll let you get back to sleep; sorry for calling so late!"

"No problem, call anytime," she says, and just before I'm about to end the call, she adds, "Oh, and Jenna?" There's a hesitancy in her voice, like she's thinking how to gently approach the subject. "I know you know, but I want to remind you my door is always open for you. My home is your home."

My heart skips a beat. "Um, okay."

"Your dad will be far away, but you're not alone here. You can come by anytime, no invitation needed."

Her words make my eyes water, and I instantly swipe at them, pissed they're betraying me. *I'm fine. Everything is fine.*

"Thanks, Aunt Eloise." I clear my throat, trying to rid myself of the overwhelming mix of emotions threatening to bubble up. "I should go now, though, the movie's starting. Talk to you later."

When we hang up, I blow out a huge breath. I'm a terrible person for lying to her and manipulating Olivia's breakup to work in my favor, but I do what needs to be done, and it's in all our best interests, Olivia's included, to finish our week here.

And what was that with the whole *my home is your home, you're not alone here* thing? It's like she snuck into my brain and read my deepest fears. I've never told her anything, and she's never mentioned it before, but somehow, it's like she knew I needed to hear it.

Still shaken, I stuff both my phone and Olivia's in my bra for safekeeping, since this dress has no pockets, and cross the room to close the balcony doors to make it look like I was never here. Just as I grab the handle, the bedroom door bursts open.

I open my mouth to bullshit my way through a plausible explanation for why I'm in here but freeze at the sight.

It's Olivia, but she's not alone. She's with Dylan, and they're *kissing*.

THIRTEEN

Night 2 of Muskoka

Olivia

I make an effort for tonight's party, not only socially but with my appearance too. I figure if I look good, I'll feel good. So when Elena and Martina are getting ready together at the double sink in the hall bathroom, I walk by a few times, trying to build up the courage to ask for help. They must notice me and take pity, because after my fourth pass, Elena calls out, "Hey, you want to get ready with us?" and I immediately join them with my tiny makeup bag in hand. They somehow know tonight is important to me, even though they don't know it's symbolically the first night I'm actually accepting my singleness, and help me get ready like I'm one of them. Without even asking, Elena curls my hair, and Martina does eyeshadow and eyeliner on me that make my brown eyes look just as sultry as hers. When Jenna joins us with a mini speaker for music, she hands me a natural pink lip gloss and, in that calm, neutral Jenna way of hers, tells me it would look good on me.

It's nice, getting ready with the girls and feeling like I'm part of the group. I've never done that before. Usually, I'd hang out with Alessio until he decided it was time to join the party. I didn't realize what I was missing out on, and I force myself not to get teary-eyed and mess up my makeup.

When the party starts, I sit at one of the tables outside with Jenna and a few other people I don't really know, and I even contribute a comment every now and again. Jenna, because she knows me, keeps pulling me into the conversation and keeps me involved, saying things like *Liv, tell them about the time you convinced me to go bungee jumping* or *Once Liv and I went into a haunted house attraction, and the first guy who popped out at her, she punched right in the nose! It was so hilarious, tell them, Liv!* I appreciate it more than she knows, but then she gets a call and excuses herself, and I'm back to awkwardly sitting with a group of people I barely know who break off into their own smaller conversations while I try and fail to think of interesting things to say.

"Look at you, coming out and joining the party," Dylan says, sliding into Jenna's empty seat. He does a double take when he realizes I'm all done up, taking in the thick black eyeliner, my contoured cheekbones, the loose curls cascading down my back. He even dips his eyes briefly to the push-up halter top Jenna squeezed me into before ripping his gaze away to the can of beer in front of him on the table. He clears his throat before continuing, "But part of that includes, you know, mingling and actually *talking* to people."

I may not be talking, but I'm sitting with a group of people. That counts for something. "I'm doing better than yesterday's party."

Dylan gives me a pointed look. "*Anything* is better than sitting on the couch staring mindlessly at the wall, though."

Okay, fine. That's a valid point. "I'm not used to this."

"Why? You've been to parties."

"Yeah, but they were always with . . ." I trail off, refusing to say his name, but Dylan knows exactly who I'm referring to. "He was social enough for the two of us, and I was part of the party because I was by his side without actually having to contribute or actively participate. I'm not used to being on my own."

Dylan's smile is sad, and it feels like a punch in the chest. It makes me want to justify myself. "Jenna said I always let Alessio make the decisions." And it's true. I let him decide where to eat or whose parties we attended or how we'd spend our weekends. "And I never minded because I wanted to make him happy. But since we're broken up and he's not here . . ."

Dylan seems to pick up what I'm saying, that not having Alessio around to make my decisions like he's been doing for the last five years is contributing to my identity crisis. "Well, we *are* at a party where anything can happen, where tons of decisions need to be made. So let's make the most of it. I declare tonight Livy's Night of Decisions, where anything you decide goes."

He's deadly serious, in that lighthearted Dylan way of his, and I can't help but laugh at the suggestion. "I don't even know what that means."

"It's literally in the name, Liv. Livy's Night of Decisions."

"I *know* that," I shoot back. "I just don't know how . . ." How to *decide* to have fun at a party, how to fully enjoy a party instead of standing back on the sidelines, how to do it right.

Even though I've said nothing out loud, Dylan seems to know what I'm thinking. "There's no right or wrong decision here, Liv. This isn't school, you don't need to research or do homework before every decision. We're here to have fun."

I bite my lip, still not sold. Dylan leans in and whispers, "Come on, grab the turtle, Livy."

Be brave when I don't feel like it. Take a risk when I'm scared. Be bold. Be courageous. Stop being a coward.

"All right, fine. I'm in."

Dylan cheers and claps his hands once, rubbing his palms together. "Atta girl, Livy. So tell me, what's your first decision?"

"Umm . . ." I haven't thought that far ahead. I glance around the party. It's almost completely outside, and there are fewer people than yesterday, though more have been showing up as the night goes on. There are groups of people clustered in different sections. Some people are dancing, some are playing drinking games, some are making out, and some are just chatting. What would I normally do at one of Jenna's parties if Alessio and I got separated?

"Um, I don't know. I guess we can refill the cooler with drinks from inside?"

"*No.* You're doing it wrong."

"I'm deciding wrong? That's great to hear if it's supposed to symbolically be my first decision without Alessio."

"Exactly! This is your first night of symbolism."

I narrow my eyes at him, trying to make sense of his words. Is he drunk? He doesn't look or smell drunk. "Are you aware you aren't making any sense?"

He laughs me off, and it's carefree and light and infectious. "Don't make boring decisions. Let's have some fun. Do something you normally wouldn't do. Don't decide on things based on what you think will make other people happy. What is something fun *you* want to do, solely for *you*?"

It takes me an embarrassingly long time to think about something fun I want to do. We're at a party, surrounded by people having fun, and my first thoughts are to make sure the girl in the corner stops trying to get up to dance on the glass table and to make sure no one slips on the liquid spilled on the paved steps. My eyes drift further off onto the grass, where a group of people are counting out loud like a chant while a guy is held upside down over the beer keg.

"I guess I've always wanted to do a keg stand?" It comes out timid, like a question, but Dylan's face lights up nonetheless.

"Hell yeah! That's what I'm talking about." Dylan pulls me to my feet, keeping his hand in mine as he leads me over to where the keg is set up. "Now remember, Livy, just because we're at a party doesn't mean all your decisions have to be alcohol based. You can do anything you want. The sky is your limit! The oyster is your, uh . . . some other motivating saying!"

I can't help but laugh at his ridiculousness, already feeling more at ease. It helps that the group of guys and girls at the keg greet us like we're longtime friends, even though both Dylan and I barely know them. They were in Jenna's grade, so we only know them from the few times we've interacted at Jenna's parties, but they chat with us, and we join in the cheering as someone helps a girl turn upside down on the keg for her turn.

We clap for her as she dismounts and does a curtsy, burping and laughing it off as one of the guys jokingly shoves her.

"Hey, can Olivia go next?" Dylan asks the group, and they nod and cheer encouragingly as I approach the stainless steel barrel. To me, he asks, "You ready?"

"What do I do?"

"You've got to use your arms to hold yourself up, then just chug until you can't or don't want to anymore. Bend your knee and I'll know to let you down." Dylan puts his hand on my shoulder and adds in a low tone close to my ear, "You don't need to do it if you don't want to."

I've always watched as Alessio and Dylan and their friends like Adam and Kellan—and even Adam's sister, Faye—have done this, but I've never actually done one myself despite my curiosity. Alessio would've told me not to, that I couldn't handle it or that I don't like beer so it would be a waste, but I think it would be fun to try just to say I did. I place my hands where the other girl did and nod to the guy holding the tap to signal that I'm ready. Dylan and another big guy grab my legs, and on the count of three, they lift me so I'm doing a handstand over the keg. Beer flows into my mouth, and I do my best to chug down as much of the bitter liquid as I can, but it's only four seconds later that I give the signal and am lowered right side up on the ground.

I stumble a moment, trying to get my bearings, but Dylan's right beside me, steadying me.

"You were amazing, Livy!" Dylan exclaims as he high-fives me before pulling me into a hug. He's being generous, because I clearly was not amazing, but his energy is contagious nonetheless. "Did you have fun?"

Everyone's cheering and patting me on the back, and I realize I *did* have fun. It was gross—I really do hate the taste of beer and lasted an embarrassingly short time—but I *did it.*

"You know what? I did have fun," I confirm, then I point at him. "Now it's your turn to show me how it's actually done."

He laughs and saunters over to the keg, joking with the other guys who instantly fall for Dylan's effortless charm. Dylan's able to hoist himself up with barely any help, and I cheer with everyone else as he chugs much more impressively than I did. He could probably go for longer—I've *seen* him go for longer—but I don't think his goal tonight is to get drunk, so he elegantly releases back to the ground, his wide smile ready for our cheers.

"You made me look like a total amateur," I joke when he rejoins me, but he waves the statement away.

"What matters is that you did something fun you never would've done before when you were . . . not single," he amends quickly, and I appreciate that he avoids any mention of his best friend. He throws a heavy arm over my shoulders as we walk back toward the house. "So that's one decision down, an endless night of possibilities to go. What's next, Livy?"

We pass the bonfire area, where a few people are snuggled up in front of the fire despite the weather still being quite warm. Fletcher's there, sprawled out on a Muskoka chair with Martina in his lap. I'm pretty sure she has her tongue down his throat. She lifts her head and meets our eyes, sending us a wink before returning her attention to the boy she's draped all over.

Dylan and I break into a fit of laughter, knowing she'll deny it in the morning, but the fire gives me an idea. "Let's roast marshmallows over the fire. I haven't had those in *forever*."

"Great decision, Livy! Good thing we brought jumbo marshmallows."

In the kitchen, I find the bag while Dylan hunts for the steel marshmallow roasting sticks. Jenna runs in briefly to make sure I'm staying off my phone and away from any temptation to be sad about Alessio but disappears before I have a chance to talk to her.

"Found 'em!" Dylan exclaims, returning from his search, proudly holding up a few steel rods with wooden handles that we can stick our marshmallows on to hold over the fire. He crosses the kitchen and stuffs a few jumbo marshmallows in his mouth, his cheeks puffing out, which makes me laugh.

I can't help but think about how cute he looks, in a charming kind of way. Dylan's hot, everyone knows that. Hell, every girl at this party has been not-so-subtly staring at him or trying to get his attention all night. But in this moment, despite his obvious hotness and muscles and jawline and tattoos, he's so boyishly cute that a weird sensation stirs in my stomach, one I haven't felt for anyone in a really long time. It makes me want to get closer to him but simultaneously to put as much distance between us as possible.

"Everything okay?" Dylan asks, swallowing his marshmallows. "Your face is all red."

I'm blushing? Why am I blushing?

"Yeah. I guess it's hot in here," I deflect, grabbing the supplies and turning away from him as quickly as I can. "Let's get going before the fire burns out."

"It won't burn out," Dylan says, joining me with two drinks he must have grabbed from the fridge. "Fletcher will come up for air eventually and throw another log on."

"I don't think he's untangling himself from Martina anytime soon." I laugh as we exit the house and join everyone on the large back patio. There are drinking games set up on some of the tables, and Robbie's in the corner with his DJ equipment, talking with a bunch of people. He waves at us and points at Dylan before clicking a button on his equipment, changing the song to a remix of AC/DC.

Dylan shoots Robbie a smile and a salute, which Robbie returns with a wink. "He knows I like AC/DC," Dylan explains. "We bonded over it today."

"Really?" I ask. "And he remembered? Robbie barely remembers my name." Dylan, Alessio, and I were all a grade above Robbie, but I'm the only one he doesn't know. Maybe it's me. Maybe I'm forgettable. Robbie forgets my name, Alessio forgets our relationship while in Cuba . . .

I shake my head, forcing the negative thoughts away. *I'm at a party. I'm having fun.*

"He knows your name," Dylan says, placing a hand on my lower back to help me swerve around a group of rowdy boys. "I bet you've just always been referred to as Jenna's cousin or A—" He promptly shuts his mouth before finishing the statement. "Fuck, I'm sorry. I've had a few drinks; I'm talking without thinking. I'm sure that's not true either."

But it is true. I'm always *Jenna's cousin* or *Alessio's girlfriend*. But not anymore.

"It's all right, I—"

"Hey, Dylan!" a guy who graduated with Jenna calls from one side of the beer pong table. He twists his Toronto Blue Jays baseball hat backward on his head and points to the guy beside him. "We defeated every other pair here. You in for next?"

I look at Dylan expectantly, but he's already looking at me. "What do you say, Livy? Feel like beating the reigning champs at beer pong?"

"Do you want to play?"

Dylan shoots me a look. "It's Livy's Night of Decisions. I'm happy doing whatever you decide to do. You want to play?"

Beer pong is another thing I've never really done at a party. I've played before, but Alessio hated being my partner because I'm not very good at it, so I started hanging back, and he's never insisted I play with him. I've become very good at cheering from the sidelines, and it's time to put a stop to that.

The reigning champs and the small crowd of people around them watch us expectantly as they reset the table, and I set the bag of marshmallows down. "You guys are going down."

Cheers go up around us over the music as they finish setting up in earnest, getting new beers to drink from. Dylan cracks open the mango vodka cooler he grabbed for me and sets it aside before opening his own beer. "Let's kick some ass." He grins, picking up the Ping-Pong ball.

We do not kick ass. We lose, because of me. Dylan pulls all the weight, sinking the ball into the red plastic cups almost every shot, and I waste my turn every single time. Our opponents win by two cups, and they jump to chest-bump each other in celebration.

"Still the reigning champs!" the guy in the Jays hat cheers, prancing with a little happy dance. "You'll never beat us! You all *suck*! *Losers!*"

"I'm so sorry, Dylan." I wince, waiting for him to tell me I'm the reason we lost, that he would've done better alone, but he throws an arm around my shoulder and laughs.

"What do you say we try again? That was just a warm-up."

He wants to be my partner? Again?

"I'll only hold you back."

Dylan's brows draw together, and he looks like I've offended him somehow. "Livy, there's literally *nothing* you could *ever* do that I'd consider holding me back. I'm the lucky one who's getting to spend time with you. Whether we win or lose a stupid game doesn't matter." He ducks his head to look directly in my eyes, like he's making sure I'm paying attention. "The only thing that matters to me is that you smile like you did last night when we were having a mud fight, like you did when you were racing around on that Sea-Doo, like you do when you drop all your worries and fears and just be *Olivia*."

He says every word with such conviction it's almost hard to breathe. "You don't care if we play again and lose?"

"Hell no. It's almost more fun if we lose." He holds up another can of beer that someone handed him and wiggles it to punctuate his point. "If you want to try again, we try again."

The tension in my shoulders loosens. I spent that first round so nervous Dylan would be upset with me for sucking that I barely even remember what happened. But I believe he only wants me to have fun, and I want to try again this round without the pressure of needing to win for him.

"All right. Let's go again."

His wide smile is my answer as he turns to the current champions and demands a rematch. They reset the game and grab new drinks, and this time, when we play, I focus on the way Dylan laughs, on the jokes our competition tell, on the way the girls watching boo extra hard when the men take a turn but cheer for me. Dylan and I still lose, but we have fun, and I even manage to sink two balls. We concede to the reigning champions and say quick goodbyes to everyone at the table, wishing the new challengers better luck than us.

"Best beer pong partner I've ever had," Dylan proclaims, draping his arm over my shoulders as I collect the marshmallows and sticks.

"You are such a liar," I accuse him lightheartedly. He could've beat them without me wasting turns, but he only cared about us having fun together, and that makes me feel warm and light.

"I never lie to you, Livy," he says, steering me down the path to the bonfire. He grabs the bag of marshmallows from my hand, somehow managing to remove the elastic and stuff his mouth with the jumbo sugar confection without removing his arm from my shoulder.

"Hey, guys!" Dylan calls when we near the bonfire. Fletcher and Martina immediately yank themselves apart, Martina sliding off Fletcher's lap and into a seat beside him. She seems sheepish even though this is the second time we've caught her; meanwhile, Fletcher's eyes are glazed over in a love-induced haze, his grin so big it practically takes up the majority of his face.

"H-hey," Martina stutters, attempting to smooth out her curly hair and adjust the straps of her dress.

My steps falter for a moment, and I'm only guided forward by Dylan's gentle steering. I feel bad interrupting their private time together, even if Martina's pretending she doesn't like Fletcher and neither one is glaring at us for interrupting. Dylan seems to know where my thoughts are heading, because under his breath he tells me, "You decided we're roasting marshmallows, so we're roasting marshmallows." He drops his arm from my shoulders and takes the sticks from me, turning to our friends and cheerfully announcing,

"We're going to roast some marshmallows, but don't let us stop you from"—he thinks for a beat before settling on—"whatever it is you were doing. We'd leave you to it, but you're hogging the fire, so . . ." Dylan holds out the extra sticks to them like a peace offering.

Fletcher takes them, handing one to Martina. "I can go for a marshmallow break. How about you, *mi corazón*?"

She rolls her eyes at his Spanish but takes the stick anyway. "As long as I can do my own. You always set them on fire."

"They taste better that way!" he defends himself, earning a chorus of disagreement from the three of us. Dylan and I sit in our own chairs across from them, and we all launch into a debate on the best marshmallow roasting technique as we pass the bag around. Soon Elena wanders over from wherever she was, and so do a few other guys, and we share our marshmallows and sticks with them.

My fingers are all gooey from the melted marshmallow, and I laugh when the marshmallow on Fletcher's stick stretches and falls off into the fire, earning loud grumbles of complaint from him.

"Livy, you've got marshmallow all over your face," Dylan says, laughing, and I try to lick my lips.

"Did I get it?" I ask, touching my face with my hand before realizing there's stringy marshmallow all over it, and I probably made it worse.

"No." Dylan grins, setting his stick down. "Guess we should've brought napkins."

He holds up his hands, and despite having had three roasted marshmallows, they're perfectly clean. Who knew eating a melted campfire marshmallow and keeping clean was a skill Dylan possessed?

"Here, let me help." He laughs then brings his hand to my face. His thumb brushes the corner of my lip, and my breath hitches. Here in the dark, illuminated by the gentle glow of the fire, with his warm hand on my skin, it's so painfully obvious just how beautiful

Dylan is. His smile is welcoming, his jaw is sharp, and I have to fight the most intrusive thought telling me to run my fingers over his cheekbones. Suddenly, the lighthearted, joking atmosphere between us shifts into something heavier and more intense, something that makes my stomach tighten with anticipation and nerves. Without realizing it, I find myself leaning closer to him, and his eyes dip to my lips for the briefest of moments.

"Hey, is that Olivia?" a new voice calls out, breaking whatever trance Dylan and I were in. I jump back from him, and his hand falls from my face, making a fist in his lap.

The new voice is Kenji, a guy who graduated in our year. He's someone I've always been cool with. He's walking toward us with a girl from Jenna's graduating class whom I've heard that he's dating.

"And is that Dylan?" he asks as he gets closer to the light of the fire. "It is! How the hell are you, man?" He and Dylan do that bro handshake and back-slapping thing before Kenji sits beside Dylan, his girlfriend perching in his lap. "You add more to that sleeve? I swear there was a blank spot on your forearm last time I saw you. I contacted that artist you sent me and booked an appointment for next week. I'm stoked."

"It's good to see you, Kenji," Dylan replies, slipping back into his easygoing persona while my mind is still racing from whatever it is that came over me a few moments ago. "What are you doing here? Last I heard, you and Fernanda were living it up in Miami."

Kenji playfully shakes his girlfriend in his lap. "Yeah, Fernanda's parents have a place on the beach, so we've been staying there for a while, but we just got back." He turns his dark eyes on me. "But if you're here, Olivia, that means Alessio must be close by. Where is the pretty boy? I'd love to show him some pictures of these classic cars I spotted the other day."

The mention of Alessio makes my skin crawl, and the way it's brought up is like a punch in the stomach. Dylan gets asked about his tattoos. I get asked where Alessio is. No matter how hard I try, I'm still being reminded that I'm nothing *more* than Alessio's girlfriend.

"He's, um . . ." Kenji doesn't know we're broken up—pretty much no one does—and being reminded of that makes me nauseous. I don't want to have to explain myself; I don't want to have to play Alessio's keeper anymore.

"He's sick. Nasty flu," Dylan interjects smoothly, and I send him a grateful look even though he's had to lie for me.

"Oh shit, that sucks," Kenji replies. To me, he says, "Tell him I say hi and to answer a goddamn phone call every once in a while." He laughs at his comment, and I force myself to smile back. It's stiff and probably unconvincing, and Dylan takes the opportunity to jump in and ask Fernanda how Miami was, effectively switching the topic.

I don't blame Kenji, he's just making conversation, but my stomach still sinks and my heart still turns heavy. I'm more than Alessio's girlfriend. I know I am. Why doesn't anyone else see that?

The three of them talk, and I'm so in my head all I can do is smile politely and nod. But then I realize that my behavior is exactly what I would've done while dating Alessio—smile and nod and be content at Alessio's side instead of part of the conversation—and it only makes me more pissed off, which causes me to be more in my head. I've trapped myself in a cycle, and not even crossing the campfire to join Martina and Fletcher will help, because they've gone back to making out, this time not even caring that we're all witnessing it.

I pick up the empty marshmallow bag, my fingers still feeling sticky, and collect the used steel sticks while the small groups around me continue their conversations.

"Oh, hey! You guys roasted marshmallows?" Fernanda exclaims. "Are there any left?"

I hold up the plastic bag. "No, sorry."

She pouts, and Kenji pats her thigh reassuringly. "This is a cottage. I'm sure there are more marshmallows somewhere. Are you going back to the house, Liv? Think you can grab us a bag?"

It's posed as a question, but it's actually an expectation, because he knows I'll agree like I always do. "Oh, um . . ." My automatic impulse is to say yes, to be helpful, to do what I normally would. But Dylan's head swings to me so fast, and the look he shoots me is so intense, it makes me pause.

He mouths something to me, and I just make out *Livy's Night of Decisions*.

He's trying to remind me of the rules of the night. Make decisions based on what I want, not what will make other people happy.

The three of them are looking at me expectantly, and I stand. "Actually, I think I'm going to turn in for the night, so I won't be coming back out. It was nice seeing you again." Before anyone can say anything, or I feel bad for being standoffish instead of agreeable, I scramble up the path and into the house. No one is inside as the party is mostly in the backyard, but the music still seeps in from open windows and screen doors, making it feel just as loud in here.

I throw out the garbage and wash my hands and the roasting sticks, wiping down the counter just as Dylan steps into the kitchen.

"Hey, you okay? What happened back there?" he asks as he crosses the open space.

I shrug, neatly hanging up the dishcloth. "Was I supposed to get them a new bag of marshmallows?"

"No. I'm glad you didn't." He sits on the bar stool at the kitchen island, resting his forearms on it like he's trying to lean in closer to analyze me. "But you were having a great time tonight, then it's like a switch flipped and you were back to the Livy who stares at nothing all sad and contemplative. Was it because they mentioned his name?"

I appreciate that he doesn't repeat the name. Thinking about him hurts but also pisses me off.

"He cheated on me. I've lost all trust in him, and he's no longer the person I built him up to be in my head," I tell Dylan, resting my own forearms on the island in front of him. "I'm realizing that I lost myself in our relationship, and I'm beginning to notice the small things like how I'd sacrifice what I wanted in order to please him."

"But?" Dylan prompts, somehow knowing that's coming.

"But sometimes I still miss him. How messed up am I?" I let out a sad laugh, shaking my head because it angers me to acknowledge the truth out loud. "Is it fucked up that I still care about him?"

Dylan's quiet for a minute, frowning as he considers his words carefully. At first, I think he's going to tell me that while Alessio's his best friend, he screwed up and I deserve better, like he has before, but he surprises me by quietly asking, "Do you remember when my granny died?"

I do. We were in seventh grade, and he missed a full two weeks of school before returning and telling us why he was absent. He was devastated; he loved his grandma. She was a vibrant Jamaican woman who always wore a colorful headscarf and hung out the window of Dylan's dad's car to wave at Dylan when they picked him up from school. Sometimes she'd leave notes in Dylan's lunch box, and the boys would tease him if they noticed, but Dylan's smile never faltered.

"Yes, I remember."

"I was sitting alone at recess one day—remember the hill on the back of the field? I just wanted some space, and everyone else went off to play soccer or whatever it was. But you came and sat near me. Didn't talk or anything. Just sat about five feet away and pulled out what looked like a college book about quantum physics or some other insanely smart subject. When the bell rang, you looked at me and said, in that sweet, quiet voice of yours, 'I'll be sitting here again next recess, if you want to talk about it.'"

We weren't the closest of friends, but in a school with a total of fifty students in your grade, you get to know a person, even if it's not super in-depth. And that day, he seemed so sad, so different from the vibrant classmate I knew.

I move around the kitchen island to sit beside him on a stool, and he continues, "And you were there at the next recess, and we talked about my granny. I told you about how she'd come over every Saturday morning and wake me up by banging a spoon on a pot and singing out of tune. I told you how she'd scare the shit out of me with tales of Ol' Higue or the Rolling Calf, and she'd laugh when my dad told her to knock it off. And I cried when I told you that I'd never get to experience the small things with her again, like how I'd never get to taste her rum cake again, and that the recipe wasn't written anywhere, so my dad couldn't recreate it for me."

He pauses for a moment, looking at me earnestly as he collects his thoughts.

"You remember what you did, don't you?" he asks, and I'm so enraptured with him and his voice and his memories that all I can do is nod. He continues, telling me anyway, "You came the next week with a slice of rum cake you'd made for me. You said you would've had it sooner, but the recipe said to let the fruit soak for a week, and you were on a mission to find a recipe similar to, if not just like, my granny's. And then you came, week after week, with different slices of rum cake for us to try." He laughs and shakes his head. "Imagine that. You, a seventh grader, at what, twelve? Eleven years old? Spending her free time making rum cake to try to cheer me up, to give me a piece of my granny back."

I went through so many recipes, and my mom was kind enough to help me out even though she'd never baked a rum cake in her life.

But I was determined to do it for him. I couldn't bring his granny back, but I could do something for him to give him back a piece of her so that he'd be able to have that cake and remember her.

He seems sad, thinking about her, so I try to lighten the mood by joking, "My parents wondered where all the rum kept going."

He laughs but then grows serious again, and the intense way he's looking into my eyes makes heat rush through my body. "I got to experience what it was like to be cared about by Olivia Rossi. When you care about people, you care about them so deeply, so truly and genuinely, that you make them feel like they matter, like they're important. And week after week, as you showed up so hopeful with a little slice of rum cake you'd baked specifically for me, you made me feel like I was someone worth giving a damn about. Like I mattered, but more importantly, like I mattered to *you*. And *fuck* if that wasn't the best damn feeling in the whole world."

I'm speechless, staring at him with a tightness in my stomach and a pounding in my chest. No one's ever said something like that to me before, especially not with so much conviction, so much authority. He says it like he believes every word, like he wants *me* to believe every word.

"You have a big heart, Livy. You care about people, and that's what makes you you. So no, I don't think it's fucked up that you still care about Alessio because that's who you are, and you're a good fucking person, even if you care about someone who doesn't deserve it." He leans closer to me, and I'm held captive by the way he peers right into my soul. "So don't confuse caring deeply for people with being weak. Because you're not weak. In fact, I'd argue that your thoughtfulness and compassion is your biggest strength, as long as you don't let it overtake you. Don't let your desire to help others consume who you are. Because you're Olivia Rossi, and Olivia Rossi is the most amazing, beautiful, brilliant woman I know."

My breath catches in my throat as I stare at him and take in the most beautiful words anyone has ever said about me. My heart beats extra hard when I realize he's not exaggerating or saying this just to make me feel better—he genuinely means every single one of those words. He really believes I'm kind and caring and brilliant and beautiful. He really thinks being cared about by me is the best feeling in the world, that it's important to be someone who matters to me. It's almost too much to process. Here's Dylan, this wonderful, funny, sweet, caring boy who's gone out of his way to make me comfortable this week and make sure I don't spend all my time sobbing into a pint of ice cream, and *he* thinks this about *me*? He doesn't think of me as a burden or a pushover or someone's girlfriend or the smart girl or Jenna's cousin. He sees me as me, for who I truly am.

I don't think about it, I just act. One moment I'm staring at him, and the next I lean in and press my lips to his.

Dylan's still for a moment, like I've shocked him with my kiss, or maybe he's thinking of a way to politely turn me down, and mortification washes over me. I pull away, apology at the ready, but Dylan quickly grasps my jaw and pulls me back to him, kissing me hard.

My heart pounds, and fire spreads through my veins as he seizes control of the kiss. He's not holding anything back, and I gasp when he grabs my waist and yanks me off the stool, pulling me closer to settle in between his legs. His lips are so soft yet so demanding, and he holds me tightly, possessively, as he deepens the kiss. It's rough and punishing. He's taking from me like he's been waiting for this moment forever, like he's showing me just how much he wants me, and I'm loving every moment of it.

He tastes smoky and sweet, and he feels so solid and strong, it's utterly addictive. I sink further into him, into his touch, into his warmth, wrapping my arms over his shoulders and letting his scent envelop me. His fingers dig almost harshly into my sides, like he's trying to keep them from wandering. But I need him to wander. I need him to touch me and make me feel like this everywhere. Never before has a kiss felt so passionate, so right, so full of every single unsaid desire.

He stands, the suddenness of it causing our kiss to end abruptly. But he doesn't pull away, and neither do I. We stay there, holding each other, our chests heaving and breaths mingling in the minuscule amount of space between our lips.

His eyes search my face, like he's drinking me in, and I know my cheeks are flushed. Dylan's still just as heart-stoppingly handsome as he always is, even more so with the burning fire in his eyes. I glance at his lips, and I can still taste them on mine, still feel the way they made my whole body come alive, and I need more.

"Dylan . . ." I plead. It comes out as a breathy whisper, but it seems to snap any semblance of self-restraint out of Dylan, because his eyes flash, and then his mouth crashes back to mine.

The tingles from his touch light up right away, and I'm pulling at him, trying to get closer. He lets me, his kiss more frantic this time, more desperate.

I'm right up against him, soaking in his heat and strength, and yet it still doesn't seem close enough. Dylan must feel the same way, because he growls then picks me up, my legs wrapping around his hips, and he starts walking, all without breaking our connection. I don't know where he's taking me, and I don't care. All I care about is the way he feels against me, the way my heart feels so full and whole it might burst.

Distantly, I realize that we're moving up the stairs, and then I'm standing, but he never breaks the kiss. I'm up against what feels like the hard surface of a door, and then it opens, and we're stumbling in together. I hear the door slam shut, then the backs of my legs hit the bed, and we tumble together.

Dylan catches himself, keeping all his weight off me, and then he pulls away.

"Don't move," he whispers, half a demand, half a plea. I'm so breathless I can't tell him I have no desire to be anywhere other than here in his arms, so all I can do is nod.

He kisses me quickly, chastely, before tearing himself off the bed and walking over to the open balcony door, closing and locking it. Then he plucks the remote from the nightstand and presses the button to lower the blinds before throwing it over his shoulder haphazardly and turning his hungry gaze back to me.

FOURTEEN

Night 2 of Muskoka

Jenna

Olivia and Dylan are all over each other, and it's so frantic, so passionate, that they don't even notice I'm frozen here when Dylan kicks the bedroom door shut and they fumble to the bed.

With a silent gasp, I rush out to the balcony, desperately surveying the space as if an exit will suddenly present itself. I hear rushed steps and duck behind one of the chairs just in time for the door to swing shut and the blinds to lower.

I'm locked out here, effectively trapped on this balcony. There's no amount of money on Earth that could get me to knock on the door and interrupt whatever the hell is going on in that bedroom, and there are no stairs leading down to the ground.

In the distance, the party goes on. It's stayed small, and everyone's partying outside now like I hoped, so at least that's taken care of. But I can't stand around on this balcony all night. What would I do, anyway? Wait for Dylan and Olivia to open the blinds bright and early in the morning and find me passed out sideways on their balcony's Muskoka chair? I don't think so.

I peer down over the railing, estimating the distance to the ground. It's just over a story drop. I might get lucky and land on my feet, or I might break a limb.

I glance back at the door and *swear* I hear a moan, and my decision is made for me.

Chucking my wedge heels to the ground, I step over the railing, crouching to grab onto the lowest part of it to minimize the distance of the fall, and then I let my feet go. There's nothing but air and space beneath me now as I dangle off the balcony, my grip tightening on the slats of the railing.

I glance down at the distance, and my breath catches in my throat. It's *much* further now that I'm only one slip away from bashing my head open. My heart pounds so fast I can feel my pulse in my palms against the metal.

Nope. Nope nope nope. This was a mistake. I'll wait it out on the chair or even knock on the door, anything but fall what now seems like a hundred feet to the ground.

Using all the muscle I have, I attempt to pull myself up, straining and grunting and cursing myself for always skipping arm day at the gym. With a sigh, I let myself fully dangle again. It's no use. I can't do it. My palms begin to sweat, a terrible inconvenience given I'm dangling a story above the hard, rock-laden ground, and now I can't climb up again even if I wanted to.

This was stupid. *So* stupid. Of all the stupid things I've done this weekend, this has to be near the top of the list. I peek down again and tighten my grip so much my fingers begin to burn.

"Hey! You okay up there?" a voice calls, and I'm torn between annoyance he's caught me *again* and relief he's here.

Hari's staring up at me, an eyebrow quirked as he takes in the scene. There's no way I can explain this, no plausible reason I can give as to why I'm dangling from the primary bedroom's balcony without seeming like a lunatic—or like *more* of one.

"Oh, yeah, you know, just working on my upper-body strength," I reply, adjusting my grip.

He plays along. "I can see that. You must be very dedicated to your workout regimen to raise the stakes by doing pull-ups almost ten feet above the ground. At night. In the dark. During a party."

"Yup, that's me. Super dedicated. I love fitness," I say, unable to hide the strain in my voice.

"You need help getting down?" he asks, and I can't even risk any energy to spare him a glance, all my focus on holding on for dear life.

Even though we're in a truce and I kind of sort of don't hate him anymore, something in my DNA refuses to admit to Hari I need help. "Nope. I'm doing great."

"You sure? You always were shit at gym class. I don't think you made it a foot off the ground climbing the rope."

I ignore the pain in my hands. "Climbing a rope is a stupid and unrealistic activity that will never be used in real life."

I hear his shoes scuffle against the dirt. "Bet you're wishing you were better at that stupid and unrealistic activity right about now."

"If you didn't notice, I'm not dangling from a rope. I'm dangling from a balcony."

"I can see that," he says, pausing as my hand slips, and I quickly readjust it, gripping harder. He continues, "If it's all right with you, I'm going to help you down from there before you hurt yourself."

It's all right with me. It's more than all right with me.

"That would be acceptable."

Of *course* it had to be him who caught me here. He always catches me at my lowest, so why wouldn't it be him witnessing me dangling over the ground during a party without a reasonable explanation. I feel so dumb. Dumb and vulnerable. And I'm sure I look even dumber than I feel.

He moves, and I sense him directly underneath me.

"Are you looking up my dress?" I ask, trying to distract myself.

His reply is quick. "No."

"Why not? I'm wearing cute panties today."

He laughs, and the sound is warm and makes my heart pound for an entirely different reason. "I know you're only flirting with me to distract yourself." I am, and it's annoying that he knows it. I hear him shift again, and his voice turns serious. "Okay, whenever you're ready."

"Whenever I'm ready, *what*?"

"Drop."

My hands tighten again in protest as I glance down. He's standing under me with his arms outstretched and legs braced. He really wants me to release my grip and fall all those scary feet to the ground. The grassy, *rocky* ground. Granted, that *was* the plan when I climbed over the railing, but now that I'm actually here, the idea is laughable. Laughably *scary*. Laughably *stupid*.

"But I'll crush you."

"I'll catch you."

My fingers are slipping, and my arms are burning. I might not have a choice in the matter. "Are you sure?"

"Scout's honor."

My pinky fingers come loose from the metal slats. "I bet you weren't even in the Scouts. Isn't that an American thing?"

"Stop stalling, you'll be fine. Drop on three. One—"

My fingers slip, and there's a terrifying rush of air around me. My stomach jumps to my throat, and then the wind is knocked out of me as I land on something hard but soft at the same time. Hari catches me—mostly—and we go tumbling to the ground together.

"I meant to let me *count* to three," Hari groans from underneath me, "not when I *said* three."

"You know me, I prefer to be in control," I joke as I slide off him and sit up, rolling my neck out. It's not sore, and all my fingers and toes and limbs are where they're supposed to be. "Thanks for catching me . . . or, I guess, thanks for breaking my fall would be more accurate."

I help him up, and though he stretches his arm, everything on his annoyingly glorious body seems to be intact as well. "I've been told I'm an excellent breaker of falls."

"Then it's a good thing you were here." I pause. "Wow, that must be the first time anyone's ever said that to you."

He laughs at my dig as we dust ourselves off. It's almost enough to make me forget about the pit of anxiety in my chest and the conversation with my father.

"People are delighted with my company, and you know it." I do know it. He's annoyingly charming with everyone but me. "What were you doing up there, anyway?" he asks, gesturing to the balcony, which, now that I'm firmly on the ground, doesn't look so menacingly high after all.

"Oh, it's a funny story," I say, buying myself time to make up said funny story. Sticking as close to the truth as possible, I say, "I went to grab something in Liv's room and got . . . distracted by something." I still cannot believe Olivia and *Dylan*! I totally called it. "I ended up on the balcony and got locked out. Jumping down seemed like the best option at the time. Good thing you showed up. What are you doing over here, anyway?"

He picks up smushed bags of pre-popped popcorn. We must have landed on them. "I volunteered to go in for snacks, then I thought I heard a noise and came to investigate."

The crumpled bags remind me that I also had sensitive things on my person, and I pat the side of my bra to make sure both my phone and Olivia's are in one piece. They are, but now I'm thinking about why I needed her phone in the first place, and the belated, offhand birthday wish from my father. He's only been apart from me for a few days, and he's already forgetting about me. What's going to happen after a few weeks? Months? Years? Will we even talk? Will he even remember he has a daughter? Will he start a new family and forget all about me?

Hari's eyes scan my face. "Want to take a walk with me?"

I'm not really in a party mood after those phone calls, and he must know it in the same way that makes it so easy for him to read me.

"Don't you need to get back? What about the snacks?" I ask, but he waves me off, holding up the crushed bags of popcorn with a cheeky grin.

"I think we've officially claimed these as ours. Come on." He shifts both bags to one hand and uses his free hand to intertwine his fingers with mine. It's an odd action, but the butterflies in my stomach stop me from protesting. His hand is large, rough, and warm, and giddiness bubbles in my chest. I force myself not to think too deeply about it, instead allowing him to lead me through the trees deeper into the forest. The music is only a faint hum in the background now, with the tranquil babbling of the water becoming louder with every step we take. Hari picks our path by moonlight and the faint lights from the house, which are diffused by the thick trees. I'm glad I forgot to put my shoes back on because this is probably easier to do barefoot compared to my tall wedges.

There's something so calming about being surrounded by trees and moonlight with Hari, his hand in mine, walking in comfortable silence, that I take the lead, tugging him left down a path when he wanted to go right.

"Where are you taking me?" he asks, allowing me to lead.

"A secret spot," I answer, picking my way down the path with ease.

"I like secrets."

"Good. Then you'll love this. No one's been there, not even Olivia." And I have no idea why I have the sudden urge to share it with Hari, but here I am, leading him to my secret place anyway.

I pull us to a halt, and Hari looks around, confused. We're in the middle of the forest, with no discernible landmarks or notable features.

"Should I be noticing something, or is this one of those things where you ditch me in the middle of nowhere and force me to find my way back?" Hari asks, scanning the property. "Because I have great directional skills and could totally do it. The house is *that* way." He confidently points in the opposite direction of the house.

I push his arm to point in the correct direction. "It's actually that way. And no, that's more something you would do to me." I glare at him for extra measure, but he only smiles innocently at me, not even bothering denying it.

"We're here for this," I continue, gesturing to the tree behind him.

He drops my hand and circles the thick trunk, probably hundreds of years old, finding the ladder and looking up. "Okay, this is awesome." He disappears behind the tree, leaving me to trace my fingers over the bark, circling the tree to its northernmost side, the side facing the water. The blood rushes straight to my stomach at the sight of my, Mom's, and Dad's initials roughly carved into it, and I trace my fingers over Mom's.

"Are you coming or what?" Hari calls from somewhere above me. I crane my neck and see my treehouse sitting high up, Hari peering over the edge of it expectantly.

I round the tree and climb the wooden ladder quickly, like I've done hundreds of times—barefoot, in flip-flops, holding snacks, in the pouring rain. Hari helps me when I get to the top, grabbing my arms and guiding me to my feet.

I do a small circle at the top, taking it all in again. I haven't been here in years, and yet it looks like it hasn't aged one bit. It came with the property and was definitely professionally made, and Mom and I stumbled upon it one day as we hiked through the woods. We showed Dad, who admitted forgetting about it when finalizing the sale, and we made it our own. It's less of a traditional treehouse and more of a tree platform. There's no roof or walls, just a sturdy, deep-brown wooden platform below us with wooden rails running along the sides for safety. It's just big enough for Hari to lie on if he wanted without his feet dangling off, the perfect size to be small and cozy but still spacious. We're high up off the ground, higher than I was while on the balcony, but everything feels safe and secure—the floor doesn't even creak or groan at our weight as we walk across it to take in the view.

I follow Hari's lead and sit on the edge of the platform, my feet dangling, and rest my arms on the second, lower layer of the railing, which was built just for this activity. Once I get settled, I look out at the scenery, and like always, it takes my breath away. We have a clear view over the trees to the lake, which seems to go on forever, the houses on the other side of the water tiny specks of light in the distance. Above me are twinkling stars, so bright and clear it's unfathomable that I'm looking at the same sky I gaze up at from home.

For a moment, neither Hari nor I say anything to break the peaceful silence. It's beautiful here, sitting up in the trees, looking at the sky and the lake, breathing in the soothing scent of pine and nature, listening to the cicadas, the gentle rustling of the trees, and the occasional hoot of an owl. If it weren't for the way the entire left side of my body is warm, I'd even forget Hari is here.

"Wow," Hari whispers, like talking any louder will disturb the peace. "I can see why you kept this place a secret."

"Mom and I used to wrap ourselves in blankets, getting comfy up here as we read stories to each other before bed." I close my eyes and breathe in the forest, getting lost in the memories. "If I lay back and stared up at the sky right now, I'd probably hear Mom's reading voice, smell the sweet honey scent of her shampoo mixed with the pine of the forest as she lay beside me."

"Do you miss her?" Hari asks, voice surprisingly gentle.

"Every day, even when I try not to think about her." My mouth snaps shut after the admission slips out, like I didn't even realize I'd been sharing memories I try to keep hidden away. It's an automatic reaction when her name comes up, especially with my dad. But if I'm honest, talking about Mom with Hari—talking about Mom in general—feels kind of . . . nice. Regardless, I steer the conversation back to our surroundings.

"I'm really going to miss this place," I say, thinking about all the memories that were made here.

"Why? Are you selling it?"

"Oh . . . no . . . I mean in general. Like when I go to school." I don't want Hari to know we're selling it. I don't want anyone to know we're selling it. I don't even want to know we're selling it.

Hari nods, opening a popcorn bag and passing it to me. "For sure. Thanks for sharing this little hidden gem with me. This is really high-quality lumber, and someone did a great job constructing it."

I laugh at his comment, which he so obviously didn't mean as a joke. The cute little hint of excited nerdiness only makes me like him more. "Of course the carpenter is looking at the wood. I meant the *view*. The *vibe*. The *atmosphere*."

His face, illuminated by the almost full moon, burns a shade deeper. "Yeah, I meant that, too, of course."

He's so achingly beautiful in this moment, with the dim lighting and the soundtrack of nature and that familiar smirk that doesn't seem to bother me as much anymore. I can't even blame the nostalgia of my treehouse for the thought, because I've known he's beautiful since the first moment he spotted me at the mall. But now that we've talked and, beyond all doubt, connected, somehow that pull to him is even stronger.

He shifts to get more comfortable, bumping my bare shoulder with his and letting it linger there for longer than necessary. We're so close, and he's so warm, it's hard to focus when all I can feel and smell and hear is him.

Maybe it's the way the cicadas are singing or the way the only light comes from the moon and stars or the way it feels like we're alone out here and completely untouchable, or maybe it's just the way Hari breaks through my defenses, but something compels me to shift even closer to him, his leg and shoulder pressed completely against mine. He turns his attention from the water to me, and I suddenly have the urge to lean in and kiss him.

His eyes flicker to my lips, like he's having the same thought, and the action jars me into remembering where I am and who I'm with.

Breaking away, I stuff my face with a handful of popcorn as if I can't trust my own lips to keep to themselves and not act on my intrusive thoughts. "I guess it's a good thing you didn't bring these back to the party," I say, shaking another handful out. They're mostly small pieces and crumbs, not a single fully popped kernel in sight.

He tips his head back and pours the kernels from his bag directly into his mouth, and I laugh at the absurdity of it.

"Oh, I found a whole one!" I exclaim, and when I hold it up, Hari must instinctively know what I'm about to do because as soon as I throw it, he maneuvers a bit to catch it in his mouth. "Yes!" I exclaim, doing it a few more times with the biggest pieces of popcorn I can find. He catches every one, even the ones I throw over my shoulder as trick shots or three at a time. Each one he throws at me bounces off my nose or hits my cheek.

"You're aiming badly on purpose, admit it," I say, but he laughs off the accusation.

"You have incredibly bad hand-eye coordination." He throws a piece that bounces off my forehead as if to punctuate his point, but instead of getting mad, I only laugh.

"Did you suddenly become cooler or something after graduation? Because if you were this cool in elementary school, we would've been friends."

His smirk is both cute and annoyingly self-righteous. "I know it must have pained you to admit that."

"Deeply so."

"Then no, I have always been this cool. You just refused to acknowledge it."

My spine straightens, and I shift to face him. "The only thing I acknowledged was how much of an ass you were. You always pushed my buttons, always poked and prodded and tried to piss me off or embarrass me or make me look stupid in front of everyone. It was a weird game that only you wanted to play. *How can I piss off Jenna today? What's the best way to get a rise out of Jenna? Oh, one point to me for making Jenna look stupid.*"

"My accent is posher than that."

I swat the popcorn he throws up in the air away before he can catch it in his mouth. "I'm being serious. What the hell was your deal?"

Turning serious, he sets the bag down. His eyes scan my face as if he can read me so easily even though I'm trying my hardest to remain stoic. My face heats and my heart pounds and I *know*, I just know, that he's seeing something deeper than I want him to, than I want anyone to.

"How do you do that?" I ask, dropping the facade. It's only been two days plus that day at the mall, and already he's called me out or caught me vulnerable more times than my friends have throughout all four years of high school.

"Do what?"

My hand circles the air in the general area of his face. "That. Do *that*. Intrinsically know what I'm thinking and catch my vulnerabilities when no one else can." He's the only one who ever notices when something's not right with me and jumps into action to be there for me. Like helping me remove the breakable objects or cleaning with me or taking me out on the Sea-Doo when he noticed I was tense, or even right now, catching me as I dropped from the balcony and asking me to go for a walk when he realized I was upset about something. He hasn't even pushed me to talk about it. "How can you read me so well?"

He's quiet for a moment, like he's deciding what to say, then he settles on, "You're not as hard to read as you think you are."

"That's bullshit. No one else sees through me like you do, not even my own father."

"Maybe they're not looking hard enough." His eyes become intense again, like he's peeling back my defenses layer by layer, and the rawness makes me squirm.

Needing control of the conversation again, I steer it back to our past. "You're avoiding the question. Why were you such an ass in grade school? To me specifically."

He sighs, looks down at his knees like he's contemplating just how honest to be, then looks back at me, eyes determined.

"I've been around people who have lost someone important to them: parents, siblings—hell, when I lost my dada I was a mess for weeks, my dad an even bigger one for longer. But there you were, eleven-year-old Jenna, coming back to school a week after your mom's sudden passing, and you were . . . completely okay. Well, not okay, but *unfazed* would be a better word. From then on, you were always cool and detached. You had your emotions shut down, no matter what happened in school, and it intrigued me."

Part of me wasn't expecting him to be so honest, but the mention of my mom's death has my guard instantly up. "Intrigued you?"

"Yeah, it did. You were like a robot, and I guess it did almost became a game to see what it would take to get you to crack, how far I'd have to push you to get you to reveal the real side of you, the human side, not the side you use as a front to make everyone think you have it all under control. You're still doing it, and it makes me want to provoke you, push you, get under your skin like I used to." He leans in closer to me, like he's sharing a secret. "No one has everything under control one hundred percent of the time, and I always liked seeing what you were hiding under your perfectly curated shell—the messy, human side of you."

I'm not sure how he thinks I'll react to that, but he's caught off guard when I shove him away from me.

"So it *was* a game to you. *I'm* just a game to you?"

"Well, not in the traditional sense—"

"You *just said* it was a game to you," I interrupt, heat rushing through my body. "That my life, my emotions, were a game to you. That you enjoyed seeing me broken down and pissed off and annoyed and all that other shit I tried so hard to keep in. All the stuff I don't want to deal with, that no one needs to deal with. You went out of your way to prove to yourself and to everyone how weak and sad and messed up I really am. And for what? Sheer curiosity? Just to prove you can? For *fun*?"

"Well, you've got to admit, sometimes it *is* fun when we—"

"This is my *life*, Hari!" I slide away from him, suddenly feeling suffocated by his presence. "And you take *joy* from seeing me become an emotional mess, seeing me humiliated and vulnerable in front of everyone!"

"I didn't humiliate you."

"You 'spilled' soda all over me on picture day and not only ruined my photo but had me smelling like a broken vending machine all day! And that's only one of many instances!"

"Okay, I admit that one went a little too far—"

"They *all* went too far, Hari. You pranked me and humiliated me to see what it would take for me to cry, to yell, to be weak. And you're still doing it! Only now, instead of stupid pranks, you're being nice and cool and understanding, being patient and playing the long game to get me to be vulnerable—a new tactic to an old game." I let out a humorless laugh as the realization dawns on me. He admitted that it was fun to see me crack, that he still likes it, that I'm a game to him. "I bet this way is even more fun for you, huh? Getting me to like you and willfully open up instead of throwing eggs at me or whatever other juvenile prank you had lined up. This way, you get to feel superior because I let you in all on my own." I stand up, needing to put even more distance between us. I can't believe I fell for him, can't believe I let him in, told him about my mom, shared my treehouse, my special spot, and all this time it's been a game to him. All this time he's never really cared, even though he did a damn good job of making me feel like he did.

Hari jumps to his feet. "It's not a bad thing to let people in, to let them see how you're feeling. Every time I catch glimpses of the girl beneath the cool and composed mask, it only makes me want to know more. All this is only a front for your insecurities, and I want you to let me in."

Of course it's a front for insecurities, for weakness. It's no one's business how sad and lonely I am, and letting people know only pushes them away. Hell, every time I tried to have a deeper conversation with my ex-boyfriend, to open up and make our relationship less superficial, he'd completely freeze over and get that panicked look in his eyes before finding an excuse to bail. Whenever I tried talking to my dad about anything that needed a semblance of emotional maturity, like grieving Mom or how much I missed him when he sent me to summer sleepaway camps, he'd get that same panicked look and throw his credit card at me. It only reaffirmed my belief that not locking your negative emotions and problems in a little mental box drives people away and that being in control of your shit is the only way to get things done.

"I don't have to let you in." I repeat his words, except mine sound more venomous. "I don't have to do anything. My insecurities are none of your business."

He takes a step closer to me, approaching like he's stalking a skittish, injured animal. "Talking through them will help you feel better. You don't have to be on guard all the time, Jenna. It's okay to ask for help; it's okay to be vulnerable."

I back away from him, anger making me shake. "Yeah? Well, what about you? What are your insecurities? What are you keeping hidden away?"

"I don't have any. I'm an open book."

"No, you're not. You're in Canada, you're in England, you don't know what you're doing. Why can't you just make a decision? Because you're insecure about something. Don't pretend like you're the only person who has their shit together and everyone else is a mess." Like he's always thought I am, like he went out of his way to prove. "So what, maybe I don't like processing complex emotions. Maybe I have abandonment issues. Maybe I'm using this stupid cottage trip to distract myself from the fact that everyone is leaving and everything I ever knew is changing and I'm starting over with nothing and no one, not even a proper place to call home. At least I don't walk around making games out of other people's emotions and forcing them to deal with their issues before they're ready while pretending to be superior." I point at him, anger pumping through my veins and my heart pounding. "You're not better than me, Hari. Just because seeing me weak makes you feel better about yourself doesn't make it true." I can't believe I told him he was cool, can't believe I actually *liked* him, can't believe I wanted him to *kiss* me. He's the same boy who made it a game to prove how weak and sad I truly am, and that's who he'll always be.

"Come on, Jenna. That's not what I meant."

I snatch up the popcorn bags to prevent littering on my property, then cross to the ladder. "The extent of the truce is now as follows: you stay as far away from me as possible, and I'll do the same. Do not talk to me, do not look at me, do not even *think* about me. You are back to being nothing and no one to me, Hari, and that's the way it's always going to be."

He calls after me, but I climb down the ladder and storm all the way back to the cottage without looking back once. He should know the way back, but he can sleep in that treehouse for all I care. I'm not going to be a weird psychological experiment. I'm not going to let Hari trick me into liking him. I've already let him in more than I should've, more than he had any right to, and he's demanding I let him in *more*, all for his own entertainment? No. I will not do that. And since I can't kick him out of this trip without everyone asking questions, I'm going to keep my promise to him and to myself.

Hari Virani is dead to me.

FIFTEEN

Night 2 of Muskoka

Olivia

After shutting the balcony door, Dylan kicks off his shoes. I pull off my own sandals before he rejoins me on the bed. The king-sized mattress feels infinitely smaller with him on it, but also like it was made just for the two of us.

He's hovering over me, resting his weight on his forearms, kissing a delicious trail up my neck. I can't believe we made out, can't believe we're *still* making out, can't believe how *incredible* it is.

"Fuck, *Livy*. You're driving me crazy."

It's the nickname that does it. Livy. It sounds so good coming from his mouth. The only one who calls me by that nickname is Dylan. My Dylan. My *friend* Dylan. Alessio's *best friend*, Dylan. A Dylan that I should *not* be kissing, no matter how good it feels or how much I want to.

"Wait, Dylan, stop."

He rips his lips from my skin right away, and I regret it almost instantly, then feel guilty for regretting it.

He hovers over me, so close but not touching me anywhere, eyes scanning my face. "What's wrong?"

"What's wrong? What do you mean *what's wrong*?" I'm kissing the best friend of my ex-boyfriend of two days, and I liked it! That's what's wrong!

Dylan rolls off me, sitting up and scrubbing his hands over the sides of his head.

The haze of whatever spell overcame me clears, and I sit up, sliding my hands down my face like that can erase the mortification that's slithering its way over my skin.

I kissed Dylan. Dylan kissed me. We might have gone further if I hadn't put a stop to it when I was slapped in the face with reality. We seemingly both *wanted* it to go further. It's been nice playing pretend with Dylan these last few days—pretending everything is normal, pretending that nothing outside this cottage exists and we don't have lives with consequences to return to in five days, pretending that a kiss between us can mean anything more.

"Why did you kiss me?" I demand, shifting so that there's more space between us, so I can breathe easier when all I can still smell is him. His face falls at the action, but he hides it immediately.

"You kissed me," he points out.

"Well, why did you kiss me back?"

"Why did *you* kiss *me* back?"

"Stop repeating my questions back to me!"

The intense look on Dylan's face returns when he states, "It's Livy's Night of Decisions, rules be damned, and you *wanted* to kiss me. *Me*, Livy." He leans closer to me, eyes scorching and face more determined than I've ever seen. "And you liked it. Maybe even loved it."

Oh God, he's right. I did. Even now, I'm thinking about the taste of his lips, the feel of his tongue, the sparks that came alive under his touch. I haven't felt this way in a long, long time. I haven't been touched like that in a long time, either, especially since I haven't seen my ex-boyfriend in six weeks, and we weren't exactly getting along before that. But even I know that the way it felt when I was with Alessio was never as intense, as passionate, as all-consuming as that kiss with Dylan.

Or was it? Am I lying to myself? Is my mind playing tricks on me? Even though I haven't been kissed in weeks, it hasn't even been forty-eight hours since I officially became single, and I'm already falling into another man's arms—my ex-boyfriend's best friend's arms, the strong and bold and comforting arms of my *friend*. Am I so pathetic that I can't be without a guy? Am I so desperate to be liked, so lonely, that I jump at the first decent guy to pay me any attention? I'm supposed to be working on myself, figuring out who *I* am and what *I* want, not jumping from being Alessio's girlfriend to being Dylan's girlfriend. I'm supposed to be figuring out who Olivia is, and I can't believe I threw myself at Dylan, even if he's hot and fun and considerate and makes me feel whole like I've never felt before. That kiss shouldn't have happened, and he should have stopped me.

I tell him so. "You should've stopped me from kissing you!"

His face turns blank. "Why would I have done that?"

"B-because . . ." I stumble to find the proper words and fail. "Because you should have!"

I jump off the bed, suddenly feeling too antsy to be sitting beside him, especially since he seems so calm.

"Are you drunk?" Dylan asks, standing but keeping his distance.

"What? No. I only had one cooler and four seconds' worth of beer from the keg."

"And were you consenting?"

"Yes."

"Then why should I have stopped you? You wanted to kiss me,

we're two consenting people, so we kissed, and it was fun. Don't overthink this, Livy."

I freeze, my stomach dropping and my heart clenching. His words should comfort me, but they somehow make everything worse. "Wait. Did you . . . did you feel anything from the kiss? Were you just having fun to have fun?"

He's silent for a moment, tension thick in the air between us. He studies my face, suddenly seeming uncertain, which is unusual for Dylan. "Is that what you want it to be?" he asks.

Oh my God. I'm such an idiot. I feel like I might throw up. I kissed Dylan, felt all these emotions between us, and all the while he was just having fun. Yes, I decided to kiss him, yes, I wanted it with such an overwhelming force that I wasn't thinking logically, but then the kiss was more than I ever thought it would be. And he didn't feel any of what I did. He didn't feel the heat and connection like I did. And on top of that, of all the people I could've chosen to kiss, I had to go and kiss my ex's best friend. Alessio will be *crushed* when he finds out. Will he think I did it just to get back at him for what happened in Cuba? *Did* I do it as some type of revenge? I don't think so, and the sparks I felt during the kiss speak volumes. But I don't want anyone—Dylan, Alessio, or otherwise—to think I'm throwing myself at Alessio's best friend in some twisted act of revenge. I have too much respect for myself and Dylan to participate in that narrative.

"You shouldn't have kissed me back," I tell him, crossing my arms and looking down at my toes so he can't see the embarrassed blush crawling up my neck. "And I'm sorry for kissing you and putting you in that position."

"You're sorry?" he repeats, his voice hard.

"Yes. You're Alessio's best friend. You're *my* friend. I shouldn't have kissed you."

I glance up just enough to see his jaw clench as he says, "You regret it."

It's a statement, not a question, because he already knows how stupid I feel for throwing myself at him when he clearly didn't feel anything during that kiss like I did.

I want to save myself from at least some humiliation, so instead of answering, I say, "I'm going to get ready for bed. If you don't mind, I'm going to use the bathroom first."

I can feel Dylan's eyes drilling holes in the back of my head as I grab my toiletry bag and the sorry excuse for pajamas I'm using before he finally answers, "Yeah. Sure."

He's still standing in the same place when I slip into the bathroom and close the door, leaning against it with my heart pounding in my chest. Tonight was Livy's Night of Decisions, but it turned into Livy's Night of *Bad* Decisions. Dylan asked if I regret the kiss, and for all the reasons I shouldn't have kissed him, I do. I don't regret the way I felt during the kiss, but knowing what I know now, feeling the way I do now, I don't know how I'm supposed to face Dylan for the rest of the trip. Because of me, we're sharing a room, so there's no way I can avoid him.

I finish my pre-bedtime routine and change into my makeshift pajamas, peeking out the door. The room is awash in the soft glow of the bedside lamp, but it's empty. I stuff my bag and clothes in my suitcase then slip into bed.

When I shut off the lamp, the room is shrouded in darkness, and I lie there, staring up at the ceiling as the muffled music from the party outside breaks up the heavy silence. I don't know where Dylan went, and I'm not sure what I'll say when he gets back. I wonder if he regrets the kiss or if it wasn't as big of a deal to him as it was to me.

Jenna's voice from earlier pops into my mind, telling me that Dylan's in love with me, which causes more uncertainty. But that can't be true. Dylan isn't in love with me: he practically said that he just kissed me back because it was Livy's Night of Decisions and he had fun. I'm the one who threw myself at him, and now I'll have to deal with the awkwardness and aftermath.

I stay up almost the entire night, but Dylan never returns.

SIXTEEN

Day 3 of Muskoka

Jenna

We may be sharing a room and sleeping five feet from each other, but I do an impeccable job of ignoring Hari's presence for the rest of the night and the morning. He tries to talk to me before bed, but I go so far as to lie with my back to him all night, even though I like to switch sides while sleeping, just in case I catch his eye and he tries to goad me into a conversation. I'm done being manipulated by Hari, done letting him provoke me into arguments or attempt to convince me to open up about my insecurities.

I wake up still pissed off, so much so that I almost accidentally plow over Martina on my way to the bathroom. It's the wake-up call I need to lock away the anger I feel toward Hari and act like everything's fine, like I'm completely unaffected by him and his words and his longing glances. I told him he's nothing to me, and I'm keeping up my end of that promise.

I make an extra effort to be happy and smile through breakfast, all while ignoring Hari at the other end of the table. I must be doing a good job because Elena mentions that perhaps my daily horoscope was wrong, since it said I would have a stressful day. The statement makes my smile tighten, and I make a silent vow to have the most *fun* today. And that's what I do.

Elena, Martina, and I take the kayaks out on the lake in the morning before the sun gets too hot. Dylan, Robbie, and Kyle make us the best-tasting hamburgers from scratch that I've ever had for lunch, and I genuinely laugh when Fletcher has a giant bouquet of flowers delivered to the house for Martina, which she promptly thrusts at Olivia and tells her to keep. We settle for leaving them on the center of the huge kitchen table so we can all admire them, and they'll be out of the way since we're eating outside. Olivia's been hiding in her room for most of the morning, claiming she's catching up on work and preparing for her app launch, only popping out for lunch. I know her mind is probably running a mile a minute trying to process whatever happened last night with Dylan, and even though I'm dying to find out exactly what happened, I'm not supposed to know, so I can't exactly barge into her room and demand a full rundown. Besides, Olivia will tell me eventually, she always does, and I don't want to pressure her when she's already got so much going on. But if she doesn't come out by tonight, I'll have to kick the door down. I can't properly celebrate this last week of summer and this place without Olivia.

It's mid-afternoon when I'm alone for the first time all day, slicing lemons in the kitchen for a pitcher of water. Everyone's relaxing out on the dock, playing cards with low music streaming from the speakers in the background. I can even spot Fletcher floating on the lake in the giant swan floaty he loves so much. I'm on my second lemon when Olivia comes down the stairs, stopping at the counter and sitting on the stool in front of me.

"You've finally emerged from your work-induced haze," I

comment as I continue slicing, glad I won't have to drag her down here. "You know the point of this week is to relax and have fun, not to do work, right?"

"I know, I know. I just . . . felt overwhelmed and needed something to focus on. Plus my course syllabi were all posted, so I had to go over what we'll be doing next week, then I started some readings to get ahead, and before I knew it, it was two thirty."

Syllabi, readings, all new things specific to university life that I haven't even thought about yet. It was just yesterday that I was graduating twelfth grade and attending prom, and now I'll be in school and living in a city I've never spent time in before, doing coursework I don't really care about and being all alone.

As I pluck the lemon seeds from the fruit, I say, "You have plenty of time to be a girl genius. This week is for you to have fun and not think about a certain dickwad who never deserved you."

She squirms in her seat. "On a completely unrelated note, have you seen my phone? I thought it was in the bedside drawer, but it's not there."

Yes, it's in *my* bedroom drawer, where she can't be sending pictures to her mom that may get back to my dad, who will kill me. But instead of saying any of that, I only glare, silently accusing her of wanting her phone to talk to her shitty ex.

She holds up her hands defensively. "I said on an unrelated note!"

"Then yes, I have seen it. I decided to employ tough love—which was clearly warranted—and confiscate it in case you crack and let a certain cheating scumbag weasel his way back into your life. I would've confiscated your laptop, too, if it were connected to your phone or if I knew you'd be doing work. But don't worry, I talked to your mom and messaged the twins, and they're all on board. They'll contact me if there's an emergency."

She nods. "Okay, fine. The only people who message me are you, my parents, the twins, and Alessio anyway, so it's not like I need my phone."

The statement makes her sad, and I set my knife down to study her. "Hey, why don't you and I take the Sea-Doos out on the water later? It'll be just like old times. Maybe we'll find another turtle to save or island to crash into."

"Yeah, sure," she says, but there's no real enthusiasm in her voice. She's pouting and has that little line between her brows that she gets when she's thinking really hard about something.

"What's going on? What are you stressing about?" *Other than Alessio* goes unsaid, because that's a given.

Olivia chews on her lip for a moment, deciding what to tell me. She lands on a question. "Remember when you said Dylan's in love with me? Why do you think that?"

"Um, because I have eyes? Why? Did something happen with you two sharing that comfy bed?" I waggle my eyebrows at her, and Olivia's face turns bright red. I *know* something happened between them last night, but I can't let her know that I witnessed it.

"We're not sharing the bed! I told you he's sleeping on the couch!"

"Well, if you *were* sharing the bed—"

"Which we're not!" she interrupts.

"But if you *were*, I wouldn't judge you if something happened."

Olivia opens her mouth to rebut my claim then pauses, pursing her lips in thought. "Even though I've only been single for like three days?"

A humorless laugh escapes as I say, "Olivia, please. You've been single for a lot longer than that, even if it wasn't official."

"What do you mean?"

"I mean that you may have labeled it a relationship, but you've been emotionally single for at least the last six weeks while he's blown you off, and probably for a few months before that. When was the last time you guys went on a real date? When was the last time he did something for you that made you feel special just because? When was the last time you looked at him and felt the butterflies everyone in those romance movies you force me to watch keeps going on about?" I can't even count how many Friday and Saturday nights Olivia's spent at my house because Alessio was out at the bar or club with his friends, or how many special occasions of Olivia's he's missed, or how many times he's blown off something that was important to her, making her feel dumb about something she was excited about, like single-handedly winning trivia night seven times in a row.

Olivia frowns. "That's why he cheated on me? Because we haven't had that emotional connection in a while?"

"No. He cheated because he's a dick and a shitty person who doesn't deserve you and can't recognize a good thing even when it slaps him in the face."

"But you said—"

"I'm not condoning cheating, Liv. Cheating is always wrong. If you're not feeling it with a person, save everyone's time and just break up with them. What I'm saying is that you're single, and *if* something happened between you and Dylan, or you and someone else, then you have no reason to feel guilty." Her frantic, passionate make-out session with Dylan might have gone further than what I saw, but she doesn't seem ready to admit anything, and as someone who hates being pushed to open up, I won't hound her for answers. She'll tell me when she's ready.

"You think?"

"I think if you really look inward, you'll see that you've been ready to move on for a while. You were just too stubborn and loyal to notice."

I have no idea if what I'm saying is helping or not, but her lip pulls up at the corner. "You're just saying that because you've never really liked Alessio."

"No. I'm saying that because I'm brilliant and wise beyond my years." She looks at me expectantly, and I don't disappoint. "But also, yes, I never liked Alessio. He took advantage of you and made you dim your light to get down on his level. A person who truly loved you wouldn't do that; they would lift you up and be proud while the world appreciates your shine."

It's ironic that I'm giving Olivia all this great advice about boys and relationships when my own track record isn't exactly stellar. Adam was always cold and detached, almost like he was too cool to care about anything. I often wondered if he even cared about me or if I was just the pretty girl on his arm. In the years we were dating, we never had a single deep conversation. Maybe that's why I stayed with him so long, why I liked him so much at the beginning. He was hot, we had fun together, and we kept things light. We didn't have to get into the things that bothered us, the problems we had at home, the worries we had about our future. With Adam, I could ignore my problems because he never cared enough to ask, never noticed if I was quieter than normal one day or if my eyes were red-rimmed from crying on another. I could pretend that everything was fine. But with Hari, it's different. He sees right through my facade, past my walls, and somehow knows exactly how to get under my skin. It's annoying.

Olivia fiddles with the hair elastic on her wrist. "So you don't think it's too early to move on?"

"Hell no."

"And you don't think that, if I *did* happen to move on with someone so soon, it would be out of some deep-seated need to get back at Alessio? Like I was only getting with someone because I know it would hurt him?"

I study her conflicted face. "You don't have a spiteful bone in your body. You could screw his brother and everyone would know it was because you had feelings for him, not because you were trying to hurt Alessio."

She considers it for a moment, and I lean over the counter to punctuate my point. "You are not with Alessio anymore. You don't have to live your life according to what you think will make *him* happy. You don't have to make choices based on *his* happiness. It's time you started putting yourself and your happiness first, Liv. If it happens to hurt Alessio, oh well, but we all know that's just a by-product of you living your authentic life, not the intended result. You don't owe him anything, especially not after what he did."

Olivia nods, the wheels in her brilliant brain spinning. "Yeah," she says, then, like it finally clicks, her tone turns confident. "Yeah. You're right." She stands from the stool, grabbing one of the lemon slices and eating it like an orange, because she's ridiculous like that. "Thanks, Jenna. Want some help?"

"Absolutely not. Go outside and enjoy the day."

I shoo her out of the kitchen and finish up with the lemons while thinking about how much I hate Alessio for making Olivia doubt herself. Just as I'm washing the cutting board, my phone rings. It's Dad.

My heart rate speeds up, and I take a deep breath to control it when I answer. "Hey, Dad."

"I had an event last night that required me to turn off my phone," he starts immediately with no preamble. "And when I turned it back on this morning, I had thirty-seven missed calls from Diane next door, complaining about the noise. What the hell are you and Olivia doing? That's a *lot* of calls, even by Diane's standards."

Shit. I should've known Diane would be up here this weekend.

There are about two acres separating our properties, but she's so cranky she calls my dad over *everything*, especially when there's music.

"You know how Diane is," I reply, using the neighbor's reputation to my advantage. "We were playing music out on the dock late, and it must have been louder than we realized."

"But I even got a text from the neighbor on the other side, and we rarely hear from them. They said to keep the party down. *Party*, Jenna? What were they talking about?"

Shit. Shit shit shit. My mind races, thinking about what that neighbor could reasonably see from their property. They're a few acres of forest away, so they wouldn't be able to actually *see* that I was throwing a party, just hear it.

"It wasn't a party, Dad," I say, keeping my voice even. He's not going to believe it was only Olivia and me eliciting such a strong response from the neighbors, so I think on the spot. "I did have Martina and Elena over for the day. But it wasn't a party! We had a barbecue and must have left the music on the dock for longer and louder than normal."

Dad sighs heavily, annoyed. "I told you *no parties*, Jenna! You're lucky I'm even allowing you and Olivia to stay. It needs to be in pristine condition. I've got potential buyers lined up to come see it soon, and I'm supposed to be selling *luxury*, not *frat house*."

The sting of someone else potentially owning this cottage is swift and sharp. I push past the nausea arising at that image to force out, "It wasn't a party! It was just the girls, and Elena and Martina didn't even sleep here. The neighbors always think a group of more than three people is a party, especially Diane. She lives for anything to complain about, you know that."

Another long-suffering sigh. "I don't appreciate you lying to me, Jenna. I'm living very far away from you for the next four to seven years, and I already have a lot to worry about. For this to work, I'm going to need you to act like a responsible adult and be real with me."

Another punch in the stomach, another wave of nausea. He doesn't want me to be *real* with him, because if I was, it would make him so uncomfortable he'd throw his credit card at me and never speak of it again. He'll never acknowledge just how shitty it was for him to pick up and desert me, not even waiting to see me off to my college dorm like the other parents—like Mom would've.

"You're right," I admit, my voice hardening, and with it, my resolve. "Elena and Martina didn't leave last night, they left this morning."

There's a muffled "Thank you" on his side, like he covered the phone to talk to someone, and for the first time I realize Dad's not at home; it sounds like he's at a restaurant, maybe on a patio. Clear now, he says, "I don't appreciate you having people over when I said not to. Did you clean their rooms when they left? I actually called you because I have someone coming to—" He cuts himself off as he greets someone named Esme in a much friendlier way than when he addressed what I assume was a waiter. She must be a client he's really familiar with because he even calls her *sweetheart*. To me, he says, "I've got to go, Jenna. Don't have any more people over!"

Then the call drops, and I hold my phone to my ear for a few more seconds, processing that he hung up on me without even saying goodbye.

It's at that moment, while I'm standing at the kitchen island staring at nothing in complete disbelief while holding a silent phone to my ear, that Hari decides to enter the room.

He takes one look at my face and seems to *know*. "What's wrong? You okay?"

I drop my phone and fix my face into place, making a show of drying the dishes I washed and putting them away rather than answering him.

"Silent treatment? Really? That's mature."

I'm tempted to stick out my tongue or stick up the really imma-ture finger on my right hand, but that would mean acknowledging his presence, which I refuse to do.

He trails after me around the kitchen as I continue cleaning. "You can't freeze me out, Jenna. It hasn't even been twenty-four hours, and I already miss our banter. If you're not going to talk to me about what's going on, you've got to at least give me something here."

I'm proud of myself for not faltering at his words, even though there's a part of me that misses our banter too. But then I remember that none of it was even real and he was only trying to see me weak, and I ignore him even harder.

The doorbell rings, giving me a welcome distraction. I glance at the back, and everyone minus Hari is either lounging around a table on the dock, playing cards, or in the lake. Did Fletcher order *another* bouquet of flowers for Martina?

Hanging up the dishcloth, I head to the huge wooden door, Hari on my heels the whole time.

"At least tell me who was on the phone that made you look like someone socked you right in the stomach."

I continue ignoring him, and he continues following me. He's annoying me, and I want nothing to do with him, and to prove it, when I open the door, I do so in a way that shoves Hari away from me and behind the reinforced wood. Hidden from sight, where he belongs.

A polished woman with straight black hair wearing a navy skirt suit over a crisp white blouse is standing on the front steps, looking at me expectantly.

"Um . . . can I help you?" I ask. She doesn't look like a flower delivery person, and she's holding a designer purse.

"Yes, I'm Christine Zhao?" The statement ends in an uptick, like a question, like I'm supposed to know who she is.

"Okay?"

Her brow furrows; she seems annoyed by my confusion.

"I spoke with Alexander McAndrews on the phone yesterday? My clients are interested in viewing this house, and I'm here to tour it on their behalf and video chat with them to see if it meets their criteria. Alexander said you could show me around. Aren't you Jenna? He said he'd tell you to expect me today."

The blood drains from my face.

This is a real estate agent. For clients who want to buy this house. Which is currently in various states of disaster—complete with a hole in the living room wall—and full of friends who aren't supposed to be here. She wants to come in and see it. Then report back to Dad.

Shit shit shit shit.

This must have been what he was saying he called me for before whoever it was showed up and became more important than speaking with me.

Hari attempts to peer around the door at Christine, but I shove him back.

"Oh, right. Christine. Of course," I say, masking my emotions despite my internal panic. Hari tries to step into view again, and I wave my arm at him behind the door, hoping he'll get the hint and stay hidden. Before he can make another attempt, I step outside, closing the door behind me. This way, he can't give me away, and she can't see right through the open-concept space and floor-to-ceiling windows to the backyard where my friends are hanging out. "He did mention something, but we must have gotten our days mixed up. I was told you were coming tomorrow."

Her confusion clears, and a pleasant smile takes its place. "Nope. I'm here today. My clients are very excited to see if this property fits all their criteria." She tries to peer around me, like she's ready to head inside, and I casually sidestep to block her view.

How can I get rid of her without giving myself away? My dad is expecting her to head in and tour the place, and I obviously can't let her do that right now.

"I'm really sorry, but you can't come in."

"What do you mean I can't come in? I drove all this way to be here."

"I understand that. It's just, um . . ." *Think, Jenna.* What *possible* reason can I have for her to not only not come in but also not tell my dad I denied her access? They usually say to stick as *close* to the truth as possible when you're lying, but I don't think that's applicable here. "I, um . . . I screwed up! The house is a mess!" I blurt out, then I quickly hide my own shock. I was supposed to stick close to the truth, not tell it!

Her eyes narrow. "You ruined your house?"

"No. I, um . . ." Why can't I be faster on my feet with lies? Why would a multimillion-dollar property lined up for viewings not be in perfect condition? "I'm trying to prove to my dad that I'm responsible enough to be hired as his intern, and I guess I bit off more than I could chew trying to impress him. He asked me to prep the house, but there's way more stuff than I expected, then a bunch of boxes broke and spilled stuff everywhere, and I dropped a wine bottle I was moving all over the carpet. I'm still in the middle of cleaning. I can't possibly show you the house in this condition, and you can't show your clients any videos of the house looking like this. You're a real estate agent, so you know people like to see the fantasy of the house in the perfect staged condition. I can't let my dad know how badly I screwed up; I really need this job, so I really need to prove that I can handle this. Can you come back in three hours to see the house? I promise it will be in perfect condition."

I'm almost impressed with how logical the lie is, since I made it up as the words left my mouth, but I stay in character, sending her pleading eyes and repeating the words *say yes say yes say yes* in my head like it can somehow influence her decision.

She studies me for a moment. "You seem like a nice girl, and I remember how tough it was for me when I first started in this business. I messed up more than a handful of times." *Yes!* The sympathy route worked! "I do want the clients to like this house; it would be a great commission for me . . ." And so did the staged house comment.

Quickly, to help sway her opinion, I add, "They'll love it! Just not in its current condition. Come back and I'll give you the best tour ever."

The potential commission on a $14 million sale must be what sways her, because she finally relents. "All right. I have another property in the area they're interested in seeing as well, so I'll do that one first." It takes everything in me not to jump up and down and pump my fist in the air, but then she adds, "But I won't be three hours, maybe one and a half, if you're lucky."

My mind races to see how I can make that work, but at this point, I'll take anything. "Okay, thank you! Every angle of that video chat will be perfect, I promise."

"Let's hope it is." She descends the front steps in her designer heels to the most beautiful Maserati I've ever seen. It looks even more extravagant next to Robbie's used sedan. Thank *goodness* we moved all the cars except Robbie's into the garage to make room on the driveway before the party yesterday, or she'd wonder why so many people were here.

"Oh, and Christine?" I call out, praying for this last-ditch effort. "Could you please not tell my dad about this? I'm trying really hard to prove I can handle this, and he's already being so hard on me because I'm his daughter; he'll fire me to prove a point. If you keep this secret, I'll do better from here on out, I swear." I feel bad lying to her and attempting to manipulate her emotions, but she can single-handedly ruin this week—and my life—with one phone call.

She tilts her head, and my heart stops. She's going to call Dad, I know it. But then she nods, and I have to stop myself from throwing my arms around her and squeezing her so hard I permanently wrinkle her pretty blazer. "If you're ready by the time I get back, I'll keep your secret."

"Thank you!" I call out as she gets in her car, starting it and turning around in the driveway. I stay in place, smiling and waving like I'm not antsy to run back inside until she's completely out of view. Once I'm certain she won't turn back and catch me in the lie, I sprint inside, almost bashing Hari as I throw the door open. Instead of being mad that he eavesdropped with his ear up against the door, I'm actually *grateful* that he resisted every instinct inside to barge outside and shove his nose in my business.

"What was that all about?" he asks me as I rush into the house, frantically surveying the mess and the very obvious signs that people are living here. I've only got an hour to hide all this evidence and somehow get everyone out without telling them why. While I think, I start stuffing snacks and items from the counter into random cabinets, washing and putting away the remaining dishes to make the kitchen look unused again. Hari follows me, peppering me with questions.

"Tell me what's going on. Who was that? Why did she say she was here to tour the house? Why did you lie to her? And what's with all that business about interning for your dad?"

I continue ignoring him, shoving things into random drawers.

"Jenna? Come on. You're clearly freaking out. Let me help. Talk to me."

When I don't stop to answer, Hari crosses his arms and leans against the kitchen island. "Fine. If you're not going to tell me, I'll just go ask everyone on the dock why we're not supposed to be here."

I set the package of cookies down on the counter harder than I was expecting, the unmistakable crunch of its contents blaringly loud in the silence that follows his statement. "You're a dick, you know that?"

His lip twitches. "Fitting those are the first words you use to break your silent treatment."

Why did it have to be *Hari* who witnessed that conversation and connected the dots? Now he'll definitely blackmail me for the rest of the week, maybe even the rest of eternity. But on the bright side, at least it's Hari who caught on and not any of my friends, since I don't actually care about *his* opinion of me.

He ignores my heated glare. "Listen, you're clearly panicking right now. I don't know what's going on since you refuse to open up, but if you need help, you can always ask for it. You'd be surprised how agreeable I can be."

I hate asking for help, and he knows it. I hate asking for *his* help specifically, which is why his eyes are glittering in anticipation.

It takes tamping down all my pride to spit out the words, "Please don't tell anyone about this."

He purses his lips. "I don't know, that didn't sound very nice to me."

I shove past him, my patience having run out.

"I was joking! I was trying to lighten the mood!" He hurries after me. "If you're not going to explain anything to me, at least tell me how to help."

Screw him. It was better when I was ignoring him and didn't have to deal with his stupid, handsome face or quick comebacks or soul-searching gaze.

"Jenna, come on. I push things too far, you know that. Talk to me again."

I do not. Instead, I grab a rag and begin wiping down the table, trying not to let the hurt show on my face. I actually *like* Hari and miss talking to him, and that may be the most messed-up part about all of this.

"If you're not going to tell me how to help," Hari starts, "I'm going to stand here and stare at you until you do. Even if you tell me to take a hike, I won't. You—"

"Hari, that's it!" I exclaim, dropping the rag and pulling my phone from my pocket. "I cannot believe you actually helped."

He straightens up, confused but taking credit regardless. "I am a genius. A beautiful one at that."

"Grab everyone and get them in here right now," I tell him, still scrolling on my phone.

"Does this mean you're calling off the silent treatment?"

I study him as I consider my options. Hari seems determined to stay, and he knows something is going on. Even if he hadn't witnessed Christine, the man can read me better than anyone. A quick glance at the clock tells me I don't have time to stand here and argue, and four hands are better and faster than two.

With a sigh, I relent. "I don't have a lot of time, and you can't ask me any questions or tell the others, but I need it to look like no one was staying here, and I need it done in the next thirty minutes."

"What? Did we break into this place or something?" Hari jokes, and because he's so frustratingly good at reading me, realization dawns on his face. "Shit, *did we* break into this place?!"

"No! It's obviously my lake house!"

"Then tell me what's going on."

I stand my ground, him demanding answers, me refusing to give them.

"What part of *no questions* do you not understand?" I ask, cutting him off when he opens his mouth to answer my clearly rhetorical question. "I'm asking you for help, Hari. Please help me."

His eyes widen before he masks it, and I know he's seeing something on my face I'd rather not think too hard about, because after a quick scan, his jaw clenches, and he gives a single nod before marching outside.

I blow out a breath once he's gone, and some of the tightness in my chest actually eases now that he's agreed to help me. Who would've thought? I actually feel *better* now that *Hari* is helping. What it will cost me later, I don't know, but I have to focus on one thing at a time.

I'm looking at Maps on my phone when everyone is ushered into the kitchen. Fletcher sets a sweating can on the counter I just cleaned, and my eye twitches.

Elena sidles up beside me. "What's going on? Hari said there was an emergency and to come inside right now." She sends him an unsure glance. "He said you fell into the toilet and needed everyone's help immediately."

Hari gives me an innocent shrug and a look that says, *Hey, you said you needed everyone inside.*

"I clearly *did not* fall into the toilet. And I wouldn't need *every-one's* help with that even if for some reason I ever did." I aim that last part at Hari, unsubtly telling him that was a stupid excuse. His smirk says he knows it and doesn't care. To all my friends, I say, "But I had a great idea. Know what would be fun? A hike! We haven't gone on one yet this trip, and I feel like we're missing out on Muskoka's great trails and amazing views. There's one we've never done before that goes right by not one, not two, but *three* waterfalls, and a cliff's edge too! And it's only a fifteen-minute drive from here! Everyone go get changed, we're going right now!"

"Like, *now* now?" Robbie asks, holding a half-empty beer bottle.

"Yes, right now! We've been sitting and drinking and eating and partying for three days straight. It'll be good to get out in nature and hit some trails. Great exercise, and great pictures too!"

My friends exchange uncertain looks, all in no state to pick up and go on a hike.

Hari claps once, drawing everyone's attention. "You heard the woman. Let's get changed and hike!"

"I am so down!" Kyle exclaims, and I could kiss him. "There's only so many laps in the lake I can do. A hike will be a great change for me."

"And I would like to get some great pictures for my Instagram feed," Martina says, and I know I've won her over too.

"That's the spirit!" I cheer, ushering them all toward the stairs. "Liv should know the one I'm talking about, but I'm sending a link to the trail and a map in the group chat. Now come on, everybody go get ready, we're burning daylight here!"

"Can I have a snack first?" Fletcher asks, trying to reach around me, but I slap his hand away. "I'll pack water bottles and protein bars. Now, I want everyone back down here and loaded up in cars in the next ten minutes. Whoever didn't drink alcohol yet today will drive." Which works for me because Christine would wonder where my—aka *Robbie's*—car went if he drives.

They all seem to know I mean business, because they go up the stairs and to their rooms. Elena and Olivia send me questioning looks, but I wave them off and go back to frantically tidying up the space to make it look the way it did when Dad staged it. Good thing we all cleaned up the yard this morning or Christine and her clients would witness the aftermath of last night's party.

Fifteen minutes later, everyone's standing outside, packing themselves into Dylan and Kyle's cars.

"Wait, you're not coming, Jenna?" Elena asks me when I don't get in after her.

"No, I don't feel good. My horoscope was totally right, I'm not having a good day. I'm going to hang back, and I'll see your pictures after!"

"I can stay with you," she offers, but I wave her off, already heading back to the door. "No need, the quiet time will do me some good. Have fun, bye!" I wave then run back into the house, shutting the door and leaning against it. I've only got forty-five minutes or so, and there's still a lot to be done. *And* that's not even counting the hole in the drywall, which I can't possibly fix now.

"What can I do?" a voice asks, making me jump and bang my head against the wall.

Hari is standing there, and a cursory glance shows that he's alone. "What are you doing here? Why aren't you going on the hike?"

His eyebrows draw together. "Because I can't help you pretend that we were never here from a random Muskoka hiking trail?"

I stare at him, lost for words. For some reason, I didn't expect him to stay past corralling everyone inside. But I should've known he'd want to stay and see it through, whether it's for his own sinister reasons or for another more honorable motivation I don't want to think about right now.

He steps closer to me. "Come on, silent treatment again? You're killing me here, Jenna." I believe him. He really does seem to genuinely hate when I'm not talking to him.

I clear my throat, trying not to think too hard about why that makes the butterflies in my stomach start up. "Grab the vacuum from that closet and do the quickest job possible; it doesn't have to be thorough."

His smile is bright and makes my chest tighten. "Right. And then?"

"Then we need to do whatever it takes to get this house looking like a show home, and you need to disappear as soon as possible."

For a moment, I fear he's going to harass me with questions, hold me hostage until I *open up* and tell him everything that's going on, like he wanted me to last night. But he doesn't. He only nods and opens the closet door to grab the vacuum. But of course, he wouldn't be Hari without prodding and remarking, "This would be a lot easier if you just told everyone what was going on. We could all help, and it would go much faster."

I stop throwing discarded shoes into a closet I'm sure Christine won't open. "If I wanted your advice, I'd ask for it."

"No, you wouldn't." He's right, I wouldn't.

"Just vacuum as quickly as possible," I say, adding after a pause, "please."

He wants to push me for answers, I know he does, but because he knows me so well that he realizes this isn't the time, he gets to work. Meanwhile, I sprint to the garage, gathering the breakable things I moved there before and placing them back where Dad's designer originally put them. I finish tidying up the main floor, and Hari makes quick work with the vacuum. Then we head outside to quickly fix all the pillows and collect any life jackets and snacks and drinks that were left out. That's quick, since we did the bulk of it this morning, and then we spend time upstairs.

My friends will undoubtedly notice that I've moved their stuff, but I don't have any other options right now. Any clothes left out are thrown in drawers, and all suitcases are zipped up and moved into the very backs of the closets. If Christine opens them, I'll just say the suitcases held all the things used to stage the house, like bedding and whatnot. Hari helps me make all the beds, and we take out all the garbage from the bathrooms and kitchen. It's a rush job, and it's definitely not up to the standard I know Dad would've wanted, but the house is clean and neat and still looks like a $14 million lake house. Hopefully the clients are preoccupied with the views and the beautiful space and don't notice that the faucets aren't shiny or the mirrors aren't perfectly streak-free, and in certain lighting footprints are noticeable on the hardwood.

There's nothing I can do about the stain on the carpet from the first party, and the hole in the drywall is an even more difficult situation. Hari and I end up rearranging the living room, pushing a large bookcase that holds knickknacks instead of actual books in front of it. It's not a permanent solution and throws off the harmony of the room, but there's no visible hole in the wall, and it will have to do for now.

I have to begrudgingly admit that Hari is amazing through it all, acting with the same urgency as I am and never once questioning anything I ask of him. It only makes it that much harder to remember why I'm pissed at him, to remember that he thinks playing with my emotions is a game.

In record time, the house is in shape, and it's as close to perfect as it can get. Standing there, viewing our work, I could break out in tears.

I hear a car pulling up on the driveway, and a quick peek through the window reveals Christine's Maserati.

"You need to get out of here right now." I push him toward the garage while shoving my keys in his hand. The only thing worse than Dad finding out I lied about being here with only Olivia is him finding out I'm here alone with a boy. "When she's in the house, open the garage door and drive off. Don't worry about closing the garage door."

He wants to argue with me, and if there was ever a time to blackmail me into sharing what's going on, it would be right now while Christine is walking up the driveway. He could do it, force me to spill my guts to him and get exactly what he came here for.

His eyes flick to the door as Christine shuffles around on the porch, and it kills me to know he's debating taking advantage of this situation. It would be the ultimate win for him.

I grab his hands in mine, not even caring that he can read every single emotion I'm feeling right now. "Please, Hari."

His jaw tightens as he scans my face, and it's like an eternity passes between us as he decides whether to let this go or crack me wide open. The doorbell rings, and he drops my hands.

"No more silent treatment," he demands, backing toward the garage door. "That's all I ask. You don't even have to tell me what's going on. Just don't shut me out anymore."

My knees practically buckle as I blow out a relieved breath. I'm still upset with him, but I can keep things civil. Say hi and bye and pretend like I wasn't having fun when we were together. "Thank you, Hari." He opens the door leading to the garage as the doorbell rings again.

"Wait two minutes before driving off," I instruct him. It'll give me enough time to get her away from the front entrance and distract her with the view. "And remember, don't tell anyone. And also if you could keep them from coming back until I text you, that would be amazing." I know we're running short on time, but I pull my phone from my pocket. "Quick, give me your number."

He rattles it off, and I add his contact information. A distant part of my brain realizes that thirteen-year-old me would've been horrified that I've willingly entered Hari's contact information into my phone, but there's another part of me that becomes giddy with excitement.

An impatient knock rattles the door. I can't leave Christine waiting any longer.

Hari helped me pull this off, and he did it all without pestering me for answers. An overwhelming feeling consumes me, and unable to help myself, I throw my arms around Hari, holding him tight, before I remember I'm mad at him and release him. "Thank you again," I say, stepping back. "Text Kyle for the trail address. Okay, bye!"

The door closes behind him, and I race to the front door, stopping just in front of it to compose myself and pretend my heart isn't going a million beats per second. Smoothing out my hair, I open the front door with a pasted-on smile.

"Hi, Christine!" This time I hold the door wide open for her, inviting her in. "Thank you so much for agreeing to come back!"

"You're welcome. Shall we begin?"

I smile warmly at her as we enter the house. There haven't been any angry calls from Dad, so she must not have called him, and it raises my confidence.

"As promised, the house is in perfect shape for your clients to see. And just look at that view! No one in their right mind could pass that up. We've got all this custom marble and engineered hardwood, creating the perfect luxury lake house while still giving that cozy feeling." I don't know where the real estate agent voice and charm come from, but I must have more of my dad's abilities in me than I realized. I don't think I've ever sounded so much like him before, but it helps that I genuinely love this place. I try not to think about how much I hate the fact that *I* need to be the one giving a tour when it kills me to think about selling it, but I need to get Christine away from hearing the garage open. So I channel everything I think Dad would do and usher her into the main section of the house, gushing about the floor-to-ceiling wall of windows and how the light hits just right at sunset.

We talk a bit more, and when I'm sure Hari has left, I tell her I'll wait outside while she videos her clients, reminding her that my cousin and I are staying here, so it's not perfect, but I cleaned it up for her.

I sit on the front steps while she tours the property, my stomach in my throat and my phone clutched in my hand, trying and failing not to let the guilt eat at me. Guilt for lying to Dad, guilt for pushing Hari out, guilt for knowing this would be so much easier if I told my friends what's going on, and guilt for being complicit in the selling of the one place where I still feel a connection to my mom. The pressure in my stomach is a tangled web of all the things I feel guilty about, and yet addressing any of them is something I'm not sure I'm ready to face.

SEVENTEEN

Day 3 of Muskoka

Olivia

Dylan slept on the couch in the living room. I don't know if he was giving me space or avoiding me, but when I come downstairs for breakfast, he's still passed out on it.

Robbie and Kyle are a bit louder than normal with their breakfast banter, which wakes Dylan up. He looks in our direction, and I quickly glance down just before I overpour my cereal. My stomach pitches, and I count to twenty before sneaking a peek to find Dylan sitting up, stretching. I force myself not to look as his shirt rises up on his stomach and the muscles on his arms bulge. He gives everyone in the kitchen a generic wave, then he goes up to the room, I'm assuming to change and brush his teeth.

As soon as he's gone, I blow out a breath. He didn't say anything or even look directly at me, and I still felt every emotion from last night rise to the surface. A few hours of restless sleep can't wipe the memory of Dylan's touch and kiss from my mind. I can still remember the way his fingers left a trail of fire on my skin, the way his lips dominated mine, the way he held me so tightly I felt cherished and desired. I'm not even sure if the mouthwatering scent of smoky firewood and something that's distinctly Dylan is a memory or if it's lingering in this open space from where he slept, but it's so good it's almost overwhelming. Regardless, a few minutes of Dylan just being in the same room as me without even looking at or talking to me is already corrupting my mind and senses, and that is *not* a good thing, especially when it's so clear he doesn't feel the same way, *and* he's technically off-limits.

When he returns, he sits at the kitchen island at the only open space, which happens to be right beside me. He gives me a small smile, which I return, then we sit there in awkward silence with a thick tension between us that I ignore by staring into my bowl of soggy cereal. I wouldn't even know where to begin a conversation with him. *Morning, Dylan! I haven't stopped thinking about the way we shoved our tongues down each other's throats even though you made it clear you were just having some consensual fun. Pass the toast?* No, not happening. I'd rather sit here and pretend my heart isn't pounding and my stomach isn't in knots than figure out what to say.

Thankfully, Fletcher, Robbie, Kyle, and Martina do most of the talking, especially since Martina and Fletcher start getting teased for their campfire make-out session, which Martina claims meant nothing, but Fletcher insists is a milestone on their journey to falling in love. All the talk of kissing only makes me feel more guilty and awkward, especially since I can feel Dylan's presence burning my entire right side.

Standing, I dump what's left of my cereal and wash my bowl before slinking up the stairs. I can feel Dylan's eyes on me the whole time, but I keep my head down until I'm around the corner, where I finally breathe a sigh of relief.

We have the rest of the week together, so I'm going to have to face him eventually, but I'm not sure I can right now when all this is so fresh. Are we going to pretend nothing happened? Are we going to tell anyone?

Are we going to tell Alessio?

I don't owe Alessio anything, but Dylan is his best friend, and it'll kill him to learn about it. He'll probably think I'm being vindictive and trying to maliciously hurt him. But that wasn't my intention at all. Has Dylan already said something? Is Alessio calling and messaging me freaking out?

A voice in my head—which sounds suspiciously like Jenna—says, *Who cares if Alessio's freaking out? He's not your boyfriend, you don't owe him anything.*

She—or I guess my subconscious—is right. Yet a small part of me is curious to see how he'd react, to see if he'd even care.

Before I can overthink it, I pull open the bedside drawer where I stashed my phone, but it's empty. I feel around as if it could be hiding underneath the zero other things in there, but my hand meets only the smooth surface of the wooden bottom. I check in the bathroom, between my bedsheets, and under the pillows, but it's not there. I didn't bother unpacking, so I have to dump my entire suitcase out on the bed to sort through it, but it's not there either. It has to be somewhere in this room, but by the time I finish repacking my stuff in the suitcase, I decide it was fate intervening, making sure I have a clean break from Alessio like I intended.

Since I'm being a coward, I don't rejoin everyone downstairs, even though I can hear them all. Instead, I set up on the bed with my laptop, sorting through emails and getting to work, promising myself I'll go down for lunch. Hopefully by then I'll figure out how I'm supposed to face Dylan and what to do with my arms when they itch to touch him.

I send out a few emails for ad partnerships to some businesses near Canadian universities for the app, then I check my school email for course updates. I have a full course load this year, and I even took a few electives like advanced coding and marketing for businesses because I thought they'd help me with my app. I have so many ideas, and I know if I just had the time and energy I could really make a difference in the lives of university students. During my scroll, I notice a course on my list that makes me pause. It's a medieval history course that Alessio took to fulfill his general election credit, and I took it, too, despite not needing it because we thought it would be nice to have a class together.

I stare at the little Drop Course button. School doesn't start for just over a week, so I can still drop it without all the hassle and paperwork. I can even fill its slot with another coding course, which would be more helpful to me than medieval history ever could be, and it would set me up for pursuing a minor in coding. Dropping this course feels like shutting the door on Alessio. I told him I need this break to think things over, but it might have only taken the first few days to come to a decision.

Before I can take any action, the doorbell rings, and I realize I wasn't imagining the smell of burgers because I'm hungry; they're actually making lunch downstairs. I leave my den of safety but stay as far away from Dylan as possible while I help set the table outside. He doesn't make any effort to come closer or talk to me, and I can't help but be irritated at the pang in my stomach. Fletcher and Martina help take any attention off me during lunch, since he repeatedly insists she keep the giant bouquet of flowers he ordered for her, and their arguing and the group's amused reactions keep us entertained. It isn't until after Martina attempts to palm the flowers off on me and Jenna declares they now belong on the kitchen table that I sneak back upstairs undetected.

I can't hide up here forever, but I don't know how to be near

Dylan. Jenna would tell me to grab the turtle, to be brave and face my worries head-on, but how can I do that when those worries confuse, anger, and scare me at the same time?

When I look at the time again, it's mid-afternoon, and I've wasted the good hours of the day inside. I told myself I would stop letting Alessio ruin this week for me, and yet today I indirectly let him. It's that thought that has me closing my laptop and heading downstairs, where a brief but insightful conversation with Jenna has me feeling a bit better. She claims Alessio and I have been over for a while and that it's not a crime to move on. But though she may be onto something, it still doesn't help the guilt, or the fact that it was *Dylan* my brain and body decided to move on to.

After leaving Jenna in the kitchen and joining everyone at the dock, I get roped into a conversation about food macros and protein calculations with Kyle, which I don't mind. It's easier to talk with him than acknowledge the burning at my back where Dylan sits, playing cards with Elena and Robbie.

Ignoring him forever isn't the solution, so maybe I'll just pretend nothing happened instead. That way I don't have to figure out the churning in my stomach or the pressure in my chest, and neither of us has to feel awkward about what we may or may not have felt during the kiss that shouldn't have happened.

Yes. That's what I'll do. Pretend it never happened.

And that's exactly what I do when Jenna wrangles us into going on a hike. I *have* been inside all day, and constantly moving instead of being trapped in one location sounds like a better way to ignore Dyl—I mean, pretend it never happened. So I'm ready to go and sitting in Kyle's car before everyone else, staring straight ahead, pretending I don't notice that Dylan's the other driver and that I normally would have driven with him.

The drive takes us about fifteen minutes through the secluded

Muskoka wilderness and into a free conservation area. Even though there's plenty of nature and trees by the cottage, the air feels clearer here, filled with the scent of pine and earth.

"All right, everyone," Kyle announces, clapping his hands to gather us from where we're grouped around the cars. I guess as the fitness buff, he's decided to take charge of this outing even though Jenna and I have walked similar trails a few times before. "This map shows the blue trail is the one that runs along the cliff and the waterfalls. It says it's intermediate, but that couple that looks older than my grandparents just came from it, so I have full confidence in us." He stuffs his phone in his pocket and examines the large sign with the map printed on it in front of the trail opening, running his finger along the path. "Let's get to it!"

"I'm too out of shape for this," Robbie grumbles even though we haven't started yet, but Kyle only grabs his hand and urges him forward. The rest of us follow behind them, even though the trail is wide enough for us to walk four in a line if we really wanted to. I hang near the back with Elena, nodding as she tells me about the marine biology program she's starting next week and the list of touristy things she wants to do in Newfoundland before the coursework gets too hard.

I'm listening, but every once in a while, my eyes drift a few paces in front of us to Dylan's broad shoulders. He's laughing at something Fletcher said, and it's a velvety smooth sound. It makes me miss him, miss our friendship.

No one knows about last night. Neither Dylan nor I has said anything, so maybe he's also planning on pretending it never happened.

I'm not sure if that makes me feel better or worse.

I hate how indecisive I'm being. I hate how I'm scared to decide one way or the other about everything. Now that the future I had mapped out for myself with Alessio has come crumbling down, it's like I'm incapable of knowing how to act or what to do in any situation. I'm always second-guessing myself. I hate it.

"How did you decide to go to Newfoundland?" I ask Elena as we pick our way along the rocky trail. I didn't pack proper running shoes, so my white tennis shoes have quickly gotten dusty. "Jenna told me it was a last-minute decision, and it's so far away and such a different program than what you originally applied for here. How did you decide to just . . . do it?"

I need to know how she was so decisive. The way she's talking about it with me sounds like there was never any doubt in her mind that this is what she wants to do, even though she's going to be far away from everything she knows and starting over alone in a place she's not used to. There has to be some secret, and I *really* hope she doesn't say something about the moon being in Saturn or her horoscope told her to do it or some other whimsical thing that doesn't help me. For so long, I've tied what I want and who I am to Alessio's happiness, and I need to figure out how to stand strong on my own.

She thinks for a moment then shrugs. "I don't know. I just knew going there would make me happy and decided based on that."

"Didn't that upset people?"

Elena carefully picks her way over a fallen tree branch. "Well, yes. But at the end of the day, it's my life and my decision. People who truly care about me will support me no matter what."

I'm still pondering her statement when we stop at the first waterfall. It's a small thing, no taller than Fletcher, but the stream is beautiful nonetheless, and the group pauses to take pictures.

Kyle corrals us when he gets antsy to continue, and then we're back on the trail, with me bringing up the rear again. Except this time, it's not Elena who joins me.

"Hey," Dylan says, falling into step with me. It's the first thing he's said to me all day.

"Hi."

I keep my gaze on the trail, which is getting progressively more uneven and unkempt the further we travel along it. But Dylan's presence is hard to ignore, and as embarrassed and awkward as I feel, I still miss my friend.

"Are you going to ignore me forever?" he asks, and I stumble on the uneven terrain. His hand wraps around my bicep to steady me, but he quickly pulls it away. Last night, he held me so tightly, so possessively, and now it's like he can't bear to touch me at all.

"I'm not ignoring you."

I don't have to look at him to know he's sending me a disbelieving look, challenging the statement.

"Okay," he says. "Are you going to not look at, talk to, acknowledge, or be near me forever?"

He doesn't intend it to be funny, but it's such a Dylan comment it makes me miss him more. "Is that what you want me to do?" I ask, trying to keep levelheaded and calm, like his answer won't affect me either way even though it definitely will.

"What?" He pulls me to a stop. "No, Livy, of course not."

"You didn't come back to the room last night," I point out, like this awkwardness is all his fault and not mine for kissing him in the first place.

"Hey," Kyle calls from the front of the group. They're a lot farther ahead of us now, all looking back at us expectantly. "You guys need a break? Want us to stop?"

"You guys go on without us," Dylan instructs, "we'll catch up."

None of them miss the obvious tension in the air between Dylan and me, and they must now be realizing we haven't spoken to each other all day—well, apparently everyone except Fletcher. "Are you sure? We should stay together and take a break. I've been dying for those protein bars Jenna said she packed, and Kyle keeps running away with the backpack."

Martina discreetly elbows him and mutters something in Spanish that I think means he's oblivious. The group leaves, and she drags him away, ignoring his protests. Soon they round a corner and disappear into the forest, leaving me and Dylan surrounded by trees and the sounds of nature with nowhere to run.

With no audience or distractions now, Dylan pins his gaze on me. It's so heated and serious I almost have trouble meeting it.

"I didn't come back to the room because I was giving you space," he starts. "I figured you wouldn't want me there after what happened."

I did want him there, but I also didn't.

"You regretted the kiss, Livy. I wasn't going to force myself in your space and make you uncomfortable."

I did regret it; how could I not? He's Alessio's best friend, and he said himself that it didn't mean anything to him. But I also don't regret it because it was *so good*, because it made me feel things I didn't think I ever would. I'm so full of contradictions, and it's definitely contributing to this mini life crisis I'm having.

I look away from him, wrapping my arms around myself like I can hide my emotions from him.

"What? We're just not going to talk about it? We *kissed*, Livy. It happened. Me and you."

And it was good. So, so good. And he felt nothing.

"Did you tell Alessio?"

He goes still, and I peek up at him. His jaw is clenched, and he's studying me hard. "That's really the first thing you're worried about?"

I'm worried about a lot of things. My mind hasn't stopped racing since last night. I can't stop thinking about the story he told me about his granny, about the words he said about me.

You made me feel like I was someone worth giving a damn about. Like I mattered, but more importantly, like I mattered to you. And fuck if that wasn't the best damn feeling in the whole world.

That's what he said, and staring up at him now makes realization dawn on me. *That's how he made me feel last night with that kiss.*

But then he said it was just for fun and not to overthink it or make it into something it's not. I have to remember that Dylan is my friend. I can't project all my emotions onto my ex's best friend, can't make this out to be more than it really is because I'm desperate to not be lonely and don't know what it's like to be single.

After a while passes without me answering, Dylan shakes his head, letting out a disbelieving scoff. "Even after everything Alessio did to you, you're still loyal to him."

"That's not what this is."

"What else is there? We kissed, and you're still only thinking of him."

"This isn't about Alessio!"

"Then what's it about, Olivia?" he exclaims, spreading his arms. "You regret kissing me because you want him back, even after he cheated on you, even after he treats you like shit."

He's angry. He's never been angry with me like this. He even called me *Olivia*, and I feel a pang in my chest.

Quietly, like the mere mention of my full name has ripped all the indignation from me, I say, "You don't know what you're saying."

Dylan's eyes are ablaze as he watches me, and it's almost a demand when he asks, "Did you like the kiss?"

That's a dumb question. "It doesn't matter."

Dylan looks like he's trying really hard not to tear his hair out. "Of course it matters! Your thoughts and feelings *matter*. Stop trying to make everyone else happy or trying to put them first when the only person who matters is *you*. So be honest with yourself—me, Alessio, and everyone else be damned. Did. You. Like. It?"

I've gone years without putting my feelings and desires first, ever since that very first day I skipped a grade and started with the older kids. I could've skipped a few more, but my parents were worried about my social development, not considering the fact that kids of any age hated the weird younger girl who always had her hand obnoxiously raised and reminded teachers to assign home-work. It was already so hard to fit in—it still *is* hard for me to fit in—but doing what I could to make other people happy helped; it's what made people like me. It's not something I can turn off. But Dylan's asking for it, *demanding* it, even if it means my honesty pushes him away. But something about his demanding tone or his proximity or the way we haven't talked all day or his plea for me to be honest breaks the dam inside of me, and everything comes pouring out.

"Yes, I liked it!" I practically yell, tears welling up in my eyes. "I liked it so much it fucking scares me! I liked the way you held me. I liked the words you said. I liked the way you kissed me. I liked the way my entire fucking body was practically singing for you."

He stands there, stunned that I'm bold enough—or maybe delu-sional enough—to admit this out loud.

"And yes, I regret it," I continue, angrily wiping away the tears that fall freely now. "I regret it because I felt everything, and you felt nothing. I regret it because I've been broken up for a few days and already all I can think about is my ex's best friend. I'm a shitty fucking person—I put you in a bad spot, and now I screwed up one of my most meaningful friendships."

I can't believe I admitted all that out loud, and I snap my mouth shut in case I reveal anything else.

Dylan's mouth opens and closes, trying and failing to find the right words. Finally, he steps closer to me, putting his hand on my arm. "You're not a shitty person, Liv. *I'm* the shitty person."

Great. Now I've made him feel guilty for being my friend.

"No, you're not, Dylan."

He steps closer. "Yes, I am. You don't even understand how shitty a person I am."

I shake my head, unable to even be this close to him without feeling the spark between us. He's my *friend*, who's *still* just being nice, and yet I can't shake these thoughts toward him.

"No, you're not," I say, stepping away from him so his hand falls off my arm. "You're a good person who's spending the last week of summer with a bunch of people who aren't even your friends because you're making sure I don't spend it crying alone in my room. You've been going out of your way to cheer me up the entire time we've been here and probably didn't even get any time to enjoy yourself. You've been nothing but a good friend to me, and now I've put you in an awkward situation with your best friend by kissing you."

I was supposed to stop word-vomiting and making him feel uncomfortable, but from the way he's frozen, staring at me with wide eyes, it's clear I'm doing the opposite. Face burning, I back away from him as quickly as possible, as if I can outrun all the words I've said. "You know what? Forget it. Pretend I never said anything. Pretend the kiss never happened. Let's just go back to normal—"

"*Livy!*" Dylan yells, reaching out for me. But it's too late. I'm backing away from him so fast, it's a shock when my foot gets caught on something, sending me crashing to the ground.

I land hard and awkwardly, crying out as an intense fire rips through my ankle.

Dylan's kneeling at my side in an instant, eyes frantically scanning my body. "Are you all right? What hurts?" His hands hover over me, and I try to shift, but it only makes the pain deepen.

"Olivia," he commands, voice stern. "Tell me what's wrong."

"My ankle." I try not to think about it. But it hurts.

I'm still lying on my side in the dirt, so I start to shift, only for Dylan to grab my shoulders and stop me. "What are you doing? Don't move."

"I'm lying in mud, Dylan."

"Wait a second. Let me make sure you won't make something worse by moving."

I don't even want to think about the implications, so I ignore him and sit up. He tsks and grumbles but helps guide me up. My ankle throbs at the movement, forcing me to blink back tears.

"Okay, *now* don't move," he instructs, taking a closer look at my left ankle. I hold my breath even though he doesn't touch it.

"It doesn't look broken," he says, and I sigh in relief. I didn't think it was, because I'm sure I'd be in much more pain if it was broken, but having it confirmed helps ease the psychological anxiety.

"I'm going to touch you, okay?" Dylan looks in my eyes, calm and steady, which makes me feel calmer too. I bite my lip but nod, and gently, like he doesn't want to apply any pressure at all, he adjusts my foot, slipping my tennis shoe and sock off. I wince, but overall the pain remains the same.

"Wiggle your toes," he commands. It's sore, but I do.

"No, it's not broken," he confirms, "but it's already swelling. What's your pain level at?"

I truly think about it. Now that the initial shock has worn off, the pain radiating from my ankle isn't as intense as it was before. "Maybe a four?"

"Okay, good," he says, nodding to himself. "Think you can stand?"

I don't know. "Yes."

Dylan's arm wraps around me, and on the count of three, he lifts me to standing. I try putting my foot down, and it's like my ankle is stabbed with a hot knife. I immediately pull my foot back up with a cry. "No. No, I can't do that."

"Stop moving," Dylan demands. Keeping a hand on me, he bends to retrieve my sock and shoe, flattening them and stuffing them in his back pocket. Then, before I even realize what he's doing, he braces one arm behind my back and the other behind my knees, carefully sweeping me off my feet.

My arms automatically go around his neck. "What are you doing?"

With me in his arms, Dylan walks back toward where we came from, carefully picking his way down the trail. "We're going to get your ankle checked."

I stare at him, dumbfounded, as he continues down the path, unbothered that he's carrying me. "We're pretty far up the trail, Dylan. You can't carry me the whole time!"

His eyes narrow. "Watch me."

The determined set of his jaw and the effortless way he holds me makes butterflies erupt in my stomach. He's deadly serious about carrying me the entire way back to the car, even though we've been on this trail for an hour.

"Dylan, you're being ridiculous. Let's call the group back, they can help."

He doesn't slow. "They've got at least ten minutes on us, Livy. That means we'd have to wait another ten minutes for them to come back, and I'm not wasting any time. And that's assuming they have signal, because last I checked, I didn't have any bars."

He's being stubborn. So annoyingly, charmingly stubborn.

"Then put me down and I can hop back. I'll lean on you."

He sends me a look, like my suggestion is too absurd to even consider. "If we do that, it'll be sunset by the time we get to the car, and I want to get you looked at as soon as possible." His grip tightens, holding me closer even though I'm already entirely pressed up against him. "So no, I won't be putting you down."

He's really going to carry me for an hour, and because he's Dylan, he won't complain once, no matter how heavy I am or how tired he gets.

"Can you at least text everyone and tell them not to wait for us?" I suggest.

"Pull my phone out of my front pocket."

"Can't you put me down for a second?"

The look he shoots me says no, he can't, in fact, put me down for a second. "Just grab the phone and text Kyle."

Sensing I'll lose the argument, I reach down and grab his phone, texting Kyle that we're leaving and to go on without us. The message doesn't seem to be delivering, but I'm sure it'll go through once we get signal. After I put the phone back and stop wiggling around, Dylan's pace picks up, and I resist the urge to point out that it might have been faster if he'd stopped for a second to text them himself. But he presses on with steady strides, easily maneuvering over the terrain even with me in his arms, and even though I'm in pain and we just had that awkward blowup, I can't stop thinking about how attractive he is. He's *literally* playing knight in shining armor to my damsel in distress, making carrying me look effortless. It's enough to make any girl swoon, especially a girl who knows what it feels like to be held by him, to be kissed by him.

He still smells like the outdoors and that addictive scent that's all him, and it's strong now that my face is practically right in his neck. He's warm and solid against me, heart pounding in his chest just as fast as mine, except I'm not even doing any strenuous exercise.

He can't possibly keep this up forever, no matter how much he insists. I'm not exactly light, and this isn't exactly a stroll in the park.

"Will you at least put me down every once in a while to take a break?" I ask, but the way his fingers tighten gives away his answer.

"Won't need one."

"Dylan—"

"I *won't need one*, Livy," he asserts, meeting my eyes, and it steals my breath away. His eyes are resolute, so unyielding that I can't possibly look away. They make all the sparks from last night come back stronger than ever, so much so that I even forget about the pain in my ankle for a moment. I'm reminded of the possessive way he held me, kissed me, made me feel like I was his. It brings all the memories rushing back, and I look away because I know I'm blushing, and then I feel guilty.

Here I am again, feeling things for my friend who's only being nice. *Get it together, Olivia!*

But we had that big blowup, and nothing has actually been fixed between the two of us. He may be carrying me bridal style in his arms, but that doesn't negate all this unresolved tension, even if he's put it aside to stubbornly carry me down this trail.

"Dylan, about before—" I start, but he shushes me.

"Let's get your ankle taken care of first. We'll talk about everything later."

But I don't want to talk about it later. Everything is still sitting heavy in my chest. He might know how I'm feeling, but I can't even guess what he's thinking about all of this.

He must notice me frowning because he says, "You and I are good, Livy. Always."

I don't really know what that means, so I don't know how to feel about his statement. I practically poured my heart out to him, and all he can say is we're good? What does that even mean? *What's* good?

Dylan dodges a squirrel that darts across the path, and the quick action jostles me, causing pain to flare up my foot and ankle. He curses at my groan.

"Sorry, Livy. You all right? I'll be more careful. Just focus on breathing."

So that's what I do as we head down the trail. I push aside thoughts of what happened before I fell and the argument we had. Instead, I concentrate on breathing, then breathing in Dylan's scent, then the rhythm of Dylan's breaths. He's sweating from the August heat and must be exhausted, but he doesn't slow his pace or take me up on my offer to set me down for a while. Not once do his arms shake, and not once does he complain. He keeps his eyes forward with the single-minded goal of getting to the car, and it makes me think of that cliché *actions speak louder than words*. Sure, he didn't say anything other than *we're good*, but isn't this proof enough that we actually *are*? A shiver runs down my spine, at least until I remember Dylan's an incredible guy and would probably do this for anyone, not just me.

"I didn't tell Alessio, by the way," Dylan admits quietly. It's almost a shock to hear his voice. He's been so quiet this whole time, I thought he was focusing on getting us there.

"Why not?" I ask.

He shrugs, even with me in his arms. "Do you want me to?"

"I don't know," I answer honestly. The thought that he might have told Alessio doesn't bother me for the reason I thought it might. I was worried before about people thinking I kissed Dylan out of spite, but I no longer care if they do. What I'm really worried about is Dylan. "I don't want you to ruin your friendship with him." Especially if the kiss meant nothing to Dylan.

His eyes flick down to me briefly before returning to the trail. "Our friendship has been strained ever since Cuba anyway."

"Really? Why?"

Dylan sends me a look that says I'm being oblivious, and my heart races.

"Because he cheated on me?"

His jaw clenches, and he gives a stiff nod. "I lost a lot of respect for him when I found out what happened."

Dylan and Alessio, along with Kellan and Adam, have been best friends for a long time. It must be hard for him to have that strain on their friendship. "I'm sorry."

He gives a humorless laugh, shaking his head in disbelief. "Why the hell are you apologizing? He's the asshole."

"He was an asshole to me, not you."

"Being an asshole to you *is* being an asshole to me," he declares, and my breath hitches. "Besides," he adds, "he was an asshole in general, and I don't put up with that. So I'm not afraid to tell him about our kiss, Livy. Let him be pissed, let him realize what he's lost, let him see how it feels to have the best thing that's ever happened to him slip right through his wandering little fingers. He deserves far worse."

Every word he says makes my heart pound even harder. He's genuinely angry at his best friend in solidarity with *me*. I don't know why I'm so shocked. He's been telling me to move on this whole time, that I deserve better, that I shouldn't waste any tears over Alessio, that I shouldn't take him back. But hearing him say out loud that he lost respect for Alessio for cheating on me that whole week in Cuba makes me like Dylan even more. "Why didn't you tell him then?"

"Out of respect for you."

My throat turns dry, and I force a swallow. That's such a Dylan answer, I don't even have a reply. He doesn't seem to mind as we both get lost in our own thoughts until we emerge from the trail onto the gravel lot where we parked.

"Dylan?" a voice asks. It's Hari, and he straightens up from where he was leaning against a parked car, tucking the phone he was playing with in his pocket. He meets us at the trail entrance. "Is everything all right?"

"Olivia fell and hurt her ankle," Dylan explains. "We're going back to the house to grab her ID and health card then get it looked at."

Dylan tries to move around Hari, but he sidesteps to block his path. "Are you all right, Olivia? I'm trained in first aid. Let me take a look."

Dylan tries to step around Hari again, but Hari moves closer to inspect my ankle. Dylan huffs. "We don't have time for this; it's already pretty swollen."

"I can see that," Hari says. "Why don't you put her down so I can get a better look?"

Dylan clutches me closer to him, like the very suggestion of putting me down offends him. "I'm getting her to the car, and then we're going to get it looked at by a professional."

"As you should. But let me see if it needs to be wrapped. I'm sure Jenna has a first aid kit in her car."

Dylan tries to move around Hari, but the latter is still so concerned about my ankle he unintentionally blocks us again.

Dylan steps back, his eyes narrowing. "Dude, what's your problem? We want to get going."

"I'm just trying to help," Hari replies.

"It's all right, Hari," I interject. "Let us get back to the house and sort it there."

"But I—"

"Hari, you and I have been cool," Dylan starts, "but if you don't get out of my face, I'm going to deck you."

The threat is clear, and Hari recognizes it immediately, stepping back with his hands raised in the air. "All right, I'm sorry." He moves out of the way and pulls his phone from his pocket. "I'm just going to give Jenna a heads-up that you're on your way back."

"Do whatever you want, man," Dylan says over his shoulder, fed up with the entire interaction. He gently sets me down for the first time in almost an hour, and I balance on my uninjured leg beside his car while he digs for his keys.

"How are you doing, Livy? It won't be much longer."

My ankle throbs, and when I look at it for the first time since I fell, my eyes bulge. It's grown four times its regular size. That can't be good.

Dylan must see the panic rising to the surface, because he calmly says, "You're all right. Let's get you in the car." He opens the door and helps me in, putting my seat belt on for me even though nothing is wrong with my hands, and helping get me settled before closing the door.

My ankle is throbbing, and I try not to think about it as Dylan makes the trip back to the cottage even faster than the drive here. I wait in the car as he runs up and grabs my purse from Jenna, and then he takes me to the closest hospital, sitting with me half the night as we wait our turn and get sent to different rooms for different tests, and he never once complains.

By the time we return to the cottage, the moon and the mosquitoes are out in full force. Jenna opens the door in her pajamas before Dylan even hands me my new crutches, taking in the chunky removable ankle boot on my foot with disdain.

"I wish you would've let me come to the hospital," she tells me once I hobble over to the door. The cottage is dimly lit behind her; everyone else has already gone to bed.

"It's enough that Dylan was with me, no need for you to sit there for hours too," I tell her as I sit on the little seat in the entryway, resting my crutches against the wall as we wait for Dylan to park the car and join us. "Besides, it's only a grade-two sprain. I'll be fine in a few weeks, and there's nothing you could've done to help."

"Can I at least tell your mom now?" she asks, helping me remove the shoe caked in dried mud from my non-sprained foot.

"No!" I exclaim, almost kicking her. "There's nothing she can do from home except worry, and she's already worried about me after the breakup. I don't want to stress her out more. I'll tell my parents and sisters when I get home."

Jenna grumbles a bit more about wishing she could help and then fusses over how I'm feeling before Dylan enters the house and locks the door for the night. He's tired and slightly sunburned and covered in dried mud that transferred to him when he carried me, and yet he still smiles when he sees me.

"Doing okay, Livy?" he asks, and my face heats at being caught staring.

"Yes. I just want to shower and get in bed."

His eyes widen for a second before he nods and closes the space between us. "Then let's get you to the room." Before I realize what's happening, he scoops me into his arms and carries me up the stairs despite me protesting that I can do it myself.

"Quicker this way," he rationalizes before gently setting me down in the en suite bathroom of our room. Jenna's behind him, setting my crutches down and shooing Dylan away so I can shower. He leaves, and once Jenna sets me up, she waits in the bedroom for me to finish. She helps me get settled in bed even though I swear I'm capable of doing it all on my own, but I think she secretly likes fussing over me, so I don't fight her too hard. Once she's gone, Dylan showers, too, and even though I'm exhausted from the day and the room is shrouded in darkness, I can't fall asleep.

I'm staring straight up at the ceiling with the covers tucked to my chin like normal when Dylan tiptoes from the bathroom and lies down on the little decorative couch he's sleeping on. He moves around, trying to get comfortable on the couch, which is an impossible feat. Even though he's never complained, I know he didn't get a good night's sleep on Friday and woke up sore and stiff, despite wanting me to think otherwise. He did so much for me today, and it's unfair of me to monopolize the whole bed when there's plenty of room for the both of us.

"Dylan?" I call out into the dark. The shifting on the couch halts.

"Livy? You all right? Is it your ankle?"

"No, my ankle is fine." The boot is heavy and awkward, and my calf already itches, but I'm supposed to sleep with it on. "I just—" I take a breath, trying to steady the nerves. "Why don't we share the bed?"

Dylan's so quiet and still, if I didn't hear his quick inhale of breath, I'd think he'd fallen asleep. His voice is unsteady as he asks, "Are you sure?"

My eyes haven't adjusted to the dark yet, but I can make out his silhouette on the couch. "Don't worry, the bed is big enough for both of us, and I promise not to touch you. We can build a pillow wall between us if it makes you more comfortable." It's a joke, and I feel lighter when he laughs.

"Are you sure?"

"You carried me down a trail for almost an hour, and your reward is waking up with a messed-up back from sleeping on the world's most uncomfortable couch? Not on my watch. We can share tonight."

"It's not *that* uncomfortable."

"Are you lying to me?"

"I don't lie to you."

His feet literally hang off the end if he stretches out all the way; he is definitely lying. "Then tell me you'd rather stay there on that little contraption—basically wood with a sheet over it—than be in this bed with me." He says nothing, silence descending over us until I break it. "Exactly. Get over here, I'm tired."

Dylan rolls off the couch and crosses the room, not even hiding the way he rolls his shoulder out. My heart pounds harder the closer he gets to the bed, and I have to remind myself we're just friends sharing a sleeping arrangement, nothing more.

Dylan stands on the side opposite me, holding up the covers to prepare to slide in, but he pauses. "Only if you're sure."

It's cute that he's so concerned about me and how I feel. But I *am* tired, and I don't want the guilt of knowing Dylan's suffering on the sofa when I could've easily done something about it. "Hurry up and get in, I'm getting cold with the covers like that."

"You sound like Jenna when you get bossy." He chuckles, finally slipping in. He gets settled much faster than he did on the couch, and I can smell his shampoo and feel the warmth radiating from him even though we're two feet apart in this bed, which suddenly feels much smaller.

We lie in silence, both staring up at the dark ceiling. There's an awkward tension in the air between us.

"Bet that feels way better than that sorry excuse for a couch, huh?" I ask, trying to break the tension. "Let's hear it: *You were right, Livy.*"

He laughs, and the knot in my chest loosens. "My back and neck will definitely thank me. You were right, Livy."

I giggle at his imitation of my imitation voice, and it helps us break the awkwardness of lying in bed together. I settle in properly, getting as comfortable as I can with the boot on my leg, but it's really hard to calm down when all I can sense and smell and hear beside me is the handsome man who's spent all weekend empowering me to be my own person.

Quietly, almost scared to break the new peace we've made, I say, "Hey, Dylan?"

He's still wide awake. "Yeah, Livy?"

"Thanks for today. Thanks for this weekend in general."

His voice sounds thick when he replies, "Anything for you, Livy."

EIGHTEEN

Day 3 of Muskoka

Jenna

Hari messages me about Olivia and Dylan returning to the house right as Christine, the real estate agent, is leaving. Apparently, her clients loved the place, because Christine is in a good mood and promises not to tell Dad about my sending her away. She's long gone before Dylan runs up to grab Olivia's purse, which I'm outside waiting with when they pull in. He peels out of the driveway before I have a chance to talk to Olivia or even try to hop in the car to come along with them.

With nothing to do but wait for updates from Olivia and the return of my friends, I go through the house and put everyone's suitcases back out and try to make the bedrooms, the bathrooms, and the furniture in the living room look the way they did before Hari and I went through and tidied everyone's stuff. We did it so frantically I don't remember exactly how everything was, but I'm hoping no one will notice the little variations.

After my friends get back from their hike, we're all in a somber mood, barbecuing for dinner and relaxing out by the fire before call-ing it an early night. No one is in the mood to party because we're worried about Olivia, and we're all partied out from the last two days anyway.

I get a text around 11:00 p.m. that Olivia's ankle is sprained and that she's coming home, and I help her get ready for bed before crawling into my own.

Hari hasn't harassed me once all night for answers about why we needed to make the house look like no one was here, and he's already sleeping by the time I get into bed. I'm grateful for the reprieve, but I think he knew he'd be pushing his luck looking for answers while I was already worried about Olivia. Now that she's home and all right, I'm not sure anything will stop him from pressing me even though he said he wouldn't. That's why I sneak out early in the morning while everyone else is still sleeping, sitting on the dock in my favorite Muskoka chair, sipping a coffee while watching the sun rise.

The sky is swathed in pinks, oranges, and blues, and the lake glimmers under the light. The splashing of ducks in the water, paired with the chirping of insects, is the only noise. It's so peaceful out here, and I allow myself to take a deep, calming breath.

I tug my sweater sleeves over my hands to ward off the early-morning chill but otherwise don't move as the sun rises higher and higher in the sky. I can't believe that I'll never get to be here again, and if Christine's clients really love the property, it'll be theirs before I can even clear out our belongings. Where will I put the hammock Mom and I got at a garage sale we found by accident when we took a wrong turn coming up here one year? What will I do with the paintings of the Muskoka scenery currently decorating the bedrooms, which we bought from local artists at street fairs? All of the things that still connect me to Mom will be gone, and my memories of her are already fading. How long will it take for me to forget about how we'd roast s'mores at 2:00 a.m.? Or how we snuck onto the neighbor's property to use the slide on her dock, giggling the entire time we swam back here? When I come here, I remember, and now on top of everything that's changing and all I'm losing, I'm losing the chance to remember her too.

A sharp trill draws me out of my memories, and I fish my phone from my pocket, my stomach dropping as I read Dad's name. It's 9:00 a.m. here, making it 6:00 a.m. there; it must be important for him to call me this early in the morning. Did Christine's clients love it so much they've already put an offer in? I almost want to ignore the call so I can live in ignorant bliss in case that's what's happened, but morbid curiosity wins, and I accept the call.

"Hey, D—"

"Christine left me a message last night." Straight to the point, as always. "Her clients loved the house and want to see it in person. I'm thinking since you're there, they can come tour it before you leave for school so I don't have to fly back. Show them around and really sell the house and the amenities. Make sure you point out the marble and the custom touches. And open the garage door in the boathouse to let in the extra light, it helps it look bigger. They're thinking of coming tomorrow at—"

"Dad!" I interrupt, and he finally stops to take a breath. This is business-mode Dad, fixated on selling a luxury property. He would've kept going then hung up before I could even get a word in. "I am not showing the house," I say, keeping my tone even despite the rapidly increasing beat of my heart. "They cannot come while I am here."

"Of course they can. You're there anyway, Jenna, and it's a miracle it's garnered interest this quickly. A property listed for that much can sit on the market for months, if not years."

"That's great. They can come when I'm not here."

Dad gives me his infamous sigh, and I hear him put down what sounds like a coffee mug on a glass surface. "I know you're trying to enjoy your time with your cousin, but showing the clients around won't take all day."

"That's not the point."

"Jenna, you're being very immature right now, and you're supposed to be an adult capable of living on her own. If you don't show it, I'll have to send Carlos up, and he's got other things to do than to drop everything and drive three hours up north to open the house when you're already there."

"Then send him. He's your business partner, the one who gets to stay here while you start over in Vancouver, right? That's what he's for." I'm being bitter, but I don't care. I'm holding my ground this time.

"Jenna Penelope McAndrews, you're sounding like a spoiled brat and not the mature eighteen-year-old I know you are."

It's my middle name that does it—*Mom's* name. The anger I've kept close to my chest finally unleashes, and I don't hold anything back the way I've trained myself to do for years. "I want *nothing* to do with selling off Mom's property. It's *Mom's*. She bought it. She loved it. She would've never let you even *consider* listing it. Just letting Christine in and showing her the view from the kitchen made me want to puke—I'm still nauseous thinking about it. So no, Dad. I'm not going to show this place to some people who will probably come up one weekend a year and change everything great about it. They won't appreciate it or the memories, and I don't care how bratty that makes me sound. If you want this place and everything to do with me and Mom officially out of your life, then you come here and do it yourself."

I'm breathing hard, chest rising and falling as I stare at the lake, not even realizing that I have jumped up from my seat and stopped at the edge of the dock. Dad is silent on the other end of the line, neither of us saying anything. That might have been the most I've ever said about Mom to him in the years since she's passed.

We're both so silent that it's clear as glass when a woman on his side of the line asks, "Is that Jenna you're on the phone with?"

I recognize the voice. "Is that Esme?" The woman I thought was his client from the last time we spoke. What is she doing at his house at 6:00 a.m.?

"No, it's not Esme."

Because it's so quiet on both our ends, I hear the woman say, "Oh, she knows about Esme? I thought you were going to wait to tell her about us? When can we meet her? Esme keeps asking about meeting her new sister."

Nausea rises up my throat as that one sentence confirms my deepest, most secret fears. "What is she talking about, Dad? Who is *Esme* and what does she mean, *sister?*"

Dad sighs again, except this time, it's long and defeated, not exasperated. "I don't think now is the best time to explain—"

"*Tell me,*" I demand, blood pumping so fast I'm dizzy.

Dad clears his throat, and for a moment I wonder if he's going to claim he has to go and hang up rather than have this conversation with me, but he must feel like he can't in front of that woman, so he says, "That was Rebecca. My girlfriend."

"Girlfriend?" I repeat, the word tasting sour. "For how long?"

"Just over a year. We're living together now."

He's had a girlfriend for a whole year and never thought to tell me? A girlfriend who lives in a different province. A girlfriend whom he's clearly picked up and *moved* for. No wonder he's visited Vancouver for work more often than usual in the last year and decided to expand his firm there. He's doing it all for her. He's choosing her.

When I offer nothing but silence, Dad continues, "And Esme is her daughter. She's seven."

He could've told me he had a girlfriend—I would've been fine with that. I don't expect him to remain single and lonely, pining after Mom until he dies at a ripe old age. I would've encouraged a girlfriend, maybe even grown to like her. But *this*, this is something I was not expecting, something that shakes me right to my core.

Not only did he pick up and leave me to be with his new girlfriend, but he picked up and left me to be with his new *family*. He's starting a new life, a new family, one that doesn't include *me*. No wonder he keeps harping on me to be responsible and ensuring I can live alone, because he's planning on washing his hands of me and never looking back. I'm eighteen, legally an adult, as he keeps reminding me, meaning he's free. He gets to start over with a new family while I get nothing and no one.

"I can't believe you," I finally choke out. "You just couldn't *wait* for me to turn eighteen so you could replace me and Mom."

"This is why I was hesitant about telling you, Jenna. I knew you'd think that, but that's not what's happening."

"Isn't it?" I ask, gripping my phone so hard my fingers hurt. Now that the lid to my emotions is off, there's nothing either one of us can say or do to stuff them back in their little container where I can pretend to have control over them. "You *left*, Dad. You sold everything attaching you to here, shipped me off to school for years, content with the fact you'll never see me again, and now you're starting over with a new partner and a new daughter. You've barely been there for five days and I'm already an afterthought, a vessel to help rid you of the last property tying you here."

"You're not an afterthought—"

"My birthday was *Friday*, and you didn't even call!"

"I wished you a happy birthday."

"The next day! As an afterthought!"

"Jenna, sweetheart, I . . ." He groans, sounding completely exasperated. "I'm screwing this all up."

My blood runs cold. *Sweetheart.* It's what he calls me, what he's *always* called me. It's also what he called Esme. He really is replacing me. I really am being abandoned, and not just by distance.

My vision tunnels, and my legs are so weak it's a miracle I don't tip over and fall into the lake. I lost Mom all those years ago, my friends are moving on to bigger and better things, and now I've lost Dad.

This is why he wants to sell the cottage so badly, why he's been all over me about keeping it clean and presentable for viewings. It's the last thing he needs to rid himself of to be free of anything connecting him to his past, connecting him to *me*.

I don't want to be alone. I *hate* being alone. And yet, I am.

Dad's been talking, and I finally tune into what he's saying. ". . . a lot at once. We're settling in, I'm still setting up the office, and I'm booked up with clients on top of that. I must have lost track of the days. Maybe once we're settled and you've had time to process, you can fly out to visit us over Christmas break. Or maybe summer break would be better for you."

Maybe. He said *maybe.* Like it doesn't matter if he spends Christmas with me or not.

"This is me announcing myself, so you don't get startled and fall in like last time!" a deep voice behind me says, and I turn to find Hari setting two mugs of steaming coffee on the picnic table. He doesn't realize I'm holding the phone to my ear. "Although at this point it's your own fault for always standing at the edge of the dock like that."

"Who is that?" Dad asks, his somber tone quickly turning angry. "Is that a boy? You said it's just you and Olivia. Are you throwing parties, Jenna? The neighbors weren't exaggerating, were they? I *told you* the house needs to be in perfect condition! Especially with these buyers interested."

He doesn't wait for me to reply before continuing. "If I send Christine and her clients tomorrow, they can't show up to a wrecked house! Bubbles in the hot tub, the refrigerator door hanging off its hinges, dented hardwood floors, and holes in the walls. That's not what clients want to see in a luxury vacation home." A new voice says something in the background where he is, a young, sleepy one. Dad pauses his ranting to say, "Good morning, sweetheart," and it's the last thing to push me over the edge.

"Don't worry, Dad," I say. "Wreck or not, they'll love the place. How could they not? Then you'll be free of me forever."

"Jenna, I—oh, hold on. Of course I'll put chocolate chips in your pancakes, sweetheart."

I whip my phone as hard and far as I can into the lake. It plunks into the water, and I stare at the place it disappears, blackness edging into my vision as my stomach churns.

"And you scolded me about my phone last time," Hari says as he joins me. I completely forgot he was here. "At least when my phone went in the lake, it was in my pocket."

I'm not in the mood for Hari and his remarks right now. All I feel like doing is curling up in bed and crying, or marching into the forest and punching something, or jumping into the lake and swimming until I'm so exhausted I can't use my brain. There are so many thoughts swirling around in my head I don't know *what* to do. I should probably get away from everyone for a while; I can't control my feelings or filter my thoughts right now even if I channeled all my energy into it, and there's no telling what I'll say or who I'll say it to.

"But seriously," Hari says beside me, tone turning somber, "what's wrong?"

I storm past Hari without a word, and he lets me.

"We should talk about it!" he calls out, but I don't turn around to acknowledge him, don't even slow my stride. I may be an emotional wreck right now, but even I know the last thing I need is to bare my soul to the one guy who's admitted that seeing me weak gives him joy.

Maybe I should've kept my composure on the phone with Dad. Maybe I should have been *robot Jenna*, as Hari called me. All I accomplished was working myself up and pushing Dad away, and now I've all but confirmed he made the right decision. Martina and Elena are getting a fresh start at a school and program they genuinely love where they'll make new friends, Dad gets a fresh start in Vancouver with a new family, and I'm going to be alone at Western doing a program I don't even think I want to do.

At least I always have Olivia, the only family that's always there for me. She even came this week right after finding out that Alessio cheated on her. I should spend time with her today. Maybe that's what I need to clear my head: good quality time with the most stable and reliable person I know. Even with a sprained ankle, which is the last thing she needed on top of everything, she's still here for me. Maybe we can sit in the shade and play one of those strategy board games she loves so much; I have some in the basement she brought years ago. That might be what I need to help rein in these nauseating feelings, to help me feel back in control.

I'm not even halfway up the path to the house when, like my thoughts summoned her, Olivia appears. She's working her way down the path on her crutches with Dylan hovering behind her as if worried she'll slip on the uneven ground. Just the sight of her helps calm some of my inner turmoil. It's good to have family, *real* family, here with me.

"Hey," I call, crossing the distance between us much faster than she can. Her hair falls down her back in unkept waves, and the freckles on her nose have become more pronounced from the sun, but the chunky gray medical boot is the first thing that draws attention. "How are you feeling?"

She rests her weight on her uninjured foot, using the crutches for balance rather than support. "I'm all right, the pain level is manageable right now. This thing is just really annoying." She gestures to the boot. "I spent twenty minutes putting it on and taking it off multiple times this morning because I had an itch from last night that was bothering me so much I had to scratch it three times. *Three times*. I'm itchy right now just thinking about it."

I'm glad to see her spirit hasn't dimmed despite everything, and it helps level my temper a bit.

"We can always find you a good stick you can shove in through the top," I joke, the knot in my chest loosening when she laughs. "Why don't we go inside and get you set up on the couch in the sunroom? I'll dig up all those board games you keep forgetting here and not even complain when you inevitably kick my ass." I take a backward step toward the house, slowly so she can keep pace, but she doesn't follow.

"That would be fun. But I . . ." She trails off, looking back at Dylan, who nods encouragingly. "I think I might have to leave."

My step falters. "What do you mean you have to leave?"

"I don't know. My ankle is sprained, maybe it's better if I go home."

She can't go home. If she leaves right now, I'm not sure when we'll see each other again. I'll be at Western, and Olivia's at U of T. They may only be a few hours away from each other, but I don't have a house to come home to visit whenever I want like Olivia does so we can see each other, and I can't just show up at her house without feeling like a sad, abandoned burden. But I still don't want her to leave. She's my cousin, the closest thing to a sister I'll ever have—a real sister, not whatever kind of sister Rebecca told Esme I'd be.

Thinking about Rebecca and Esme gets my blood boiling again after I finally managed to calm it a bit. "You can't leave. Why would you even do that? You're going home to sit in bed and cry about Alessio? Or you're going home to take him back? Is that it? Because he's been blowing up your phone like crazy since I confiscated it."

Olivia's eyes widen. "I'm not going to take him back. Dylan just thinks that I—"

"Ohhh. *Dylan* thinks you should go home? So because Dylan tells you to do it, you *have* to do it? Can't you make *any* decisions for yourself?"

She stiffens. "What does that mean?"

"Come on, Liv. Alessio wanted you to grow out your hair, you grew it out. He wanted to go to U of T, you went there despite getting full rides to every other university. You're single now, and you're having fun. I saw you doing a *keg stand* the other day, something you never would've done with Alessio. Why are you turning back into the Olivia who does nothing without her boyfriend's approval? You're going from clinging to one boyfriend to another."

"Dylan is not my boyfriend," she states, spine rigid.

"Even if he was, you don't need to depend on him. Make your own decisions. Be your own person. Just because he says you should go home and be miserable alone rather than spend time here with us doesn't mean you have to."

Dylan, who watched this all quietly, finally steps in. "I wasn't telling anyone what to do, I was only suggesting that maybe she'd be more comfortable at home."

I turn my glare on him, the one that can make a grown man shrink into himself. It works. "Yeah, knowing that by you suggesting it, Olivia would agree. She always goes along with people's suggestions to make them happy, and you know that."

"That wasn't what I was—"

"It's fine," Olivia interjects, looking at Dylan. "I want to stay. And *not* because Jenna is telling me to."

She says it with such determination I want to cheer. "Atta girl, Liv! Nothing is going to stop us from spending this last week together."

Dylan places his hand on the small of Olivia's back, voice laced with concern as he asks, "Are you sure? What about your ankle?"

Olivia moves, ripping Dylan's hand off her. "You're not my boyfriend."

"And even if you were, Olivia can make her own decisions, right, Liv?" I add.

"Yes . . . *yes* . . . I can. Jenna's right. I've let Alessio tell me what to do for our entire relationship. I dropped everything to cater to him, to make him happy, and I lost myself in the process. I've been trying to figure out who I am this week because it's the first time in forever that I don't have to base all my decisions on what someone else wants, and sometimes I feel so lost, it's easy to turn to others to make decisions for me. But I *know* I can't just jump to the first guy who pays attention to me, and that realization was one of the reasons I stopped our kiss." Olivia stands straighter, adjusting herself on her crutches, so lost in her revelation she doesn't realize she just admitted to kissing him in front of me. She sets her crutches up again. "I told myself I'd spend the week away from Alessio and try to have fun, and that's what I'm going to do." And then she turns and walks away as quickly and confidently as her crutches let her.

Dylan and I are stunned for a moment, until he looks at me incredulously. "I'm not trying to control Olivia or tell her what to do, I'm just worried about her ankle."

"What would she do at home that she can't do here? She's on crutches and in a walking boot. There's no reason her vacation—the last free time she gets before she goes back to reality where she over-loads on courses and has no fun—needs to be cut short."

"Maybe you're right, and maybe you're not," Dylan says, backing away from me. "But even I know that wasn't so much your concern about Olivia as it was about whatever it is you're dealing with." He turns to leave, then pauses to say, "You know, you sure are quick to call people out on their issues when you clearly have trouble dealing with your own."

Then he leaves to chase after Olivia, and I'm left just the way I was earlier: alone, mind reeling, and with too many emotions to know how to deal with them.

NINETEEN

Night 4 of Muskoka

Olivia

After my realization with Jenna, I avoid Dylan for the rest of the day, even though he keeps asking me to talk. It helps that I stick close to other people, even playing referee to Fletcher and Martina's mix between fighting and flirting rather than being alone with him. I keep replaying Jenna's words in my head, thinking about how accurately she called me out. I had the same thoughts when my mind cleared after kissing Dylan, and it's an insecurity I've been stuck on. Am I so lonely and desperate to be with someone that I moved onto Dylan? Am I so unused to being single that I'm looking at Dylan to fill that void? I don't really have any friends, and Jenna always tells it like it is with me, so there must be some truth to her words.

I woke up this morning cuddled up with Dylan, with no recollection of how I crossed the unofficial middle border of the bed to be wrapped up in his arms, but it was so warm, so perfect, being there with him. Then I remembered where I was, *who* I was being held against, and awkwardly untangled myself before hobbling away to the bathroom, yelling at him to keep his eyes closed without telling him why because I would be mortified if he saw me in my makeshift pajamas. After I emerged, fully dressed because Jenna had moved my suitcase into the bathroom, Dylan suggested that if I want to recover at home, he's happy to drive me whenever I want to go. And although I hadn't considered it before, he had a point that I might be more comfortable resting at home. The doctor told me to stay off my foot, and it might be easier to do that at home versus this huge lake house with all these people around. But when I told Jenna, she was really upset at the thought of me leaving and pointed out, very accurately, that I might have agreed just because Dylan suggested it.

But Dylan feels different than Alessio. With Alessio, I always knew what he wanted and went out of my way to make it happen for him. Dylan never makes me feel like I *have* to do anything. In fact, he went out of his way to help me make my own decisions. He even deemed a whole night Livy's Night of Decisions to do just that. He's never forced an opinion on me. Even when I asked him directly if I should get back together with Alessio or end it, he never tried to influence me one way or another until I prodded him for an answer.

But maybe I'm seeing things I want to see? I felt things so quickly with Dylan, fell for him so hard and fast as soon as we kissed. Were the emotions always there under the surface, waiting for a chance to explore them with him? Or am I feeling things that aren't there because I'm desperate not to be lonely?

I successfully avoid Dylan until after dinner, when the sun is going down and everyone is around the bonfire. Even though we're on cottage time and weekdays versus weekends don't apply, it *is* still a Monday, and we're keeping the night chill instead of forcing another party. Fletcher and Martina are still bickering, Jenna and Hari have been gone for a while, so they've probably killed each other, and Robbie, Elena, and Kyle are trading stories of the intense science teacher they had who snapped her pointer stick by hitting a desk with it when Kyle pissed her off. Dylan's sitting across from me, nursing what's probably a warm can of beer, watching me intently.

We have always been friends, *always*. Even after high school when most friendships fade, we'd meet for coffee between classes, and he'd let me go on forever about what we were learning even though it didn't pertain to him, or he'd be the only one to show up to trivia night at the all-ages bar to support me even when Alessio wouldn't. We've always talked, always known where we stood with each other, and now that everything is getting muddled between us, I don't know what to make of it. Just looking at him across the bonfire has my throat closing up and my mind reeling.

It suddenly becomes too much, and I excuse myself to use the restroom in the house, opting to use the one in my room so I can freshen up. After washing my hands, I splash some cold water on my face in hopes it'll help me sort things out. It doesn't. And now my face is cold, and my leg is *still* itchy.

That's it. I can't be going through an emotional crisis *and* constantly wanting to shove a branch down my hard boot like Jenna suggested, so I give myself a break and remove the boot, sighing when I finally get that spot just above my ankle that's been driving me crazy. I leave it off as I exit the room and hop down the stairs on my uninjured leg. A few hours of freedom won't cause any harm, especially since I'm sitting the whole time anyway.

I only make it halfway down the landscaped path to the bonfire before Dylan intercepts me. He looks so handsome in the ambient lighting of the string lights decorating the yard, like a fairytale prince with a sleeve tattoo.

"You've been avoiding me," he states, crossing his arms like he's settling in for a while. "And why aren't you wearing the boot?"

"I'm giving my foot a break from it."

He raises an eyebrow like he's waiting for me to address the first part of his question, which I purposely ignored. I give in. "I'm not avoiding you."

"Yes, you are. I've been trying to talk to you all day about what happened this morning."

I adjust myself on my crutches. "I don't really want to talk about it."

Dylan's jaw clenches, and his eyes are blazing. "Are you really going to go back to avoiding me like you did after our kiss? Because it really fucking kills me to not talk to you. You don't have to be my best friend or anything, but at least tell me what's wrong and why you're so upset with me. I wasn't trying to control you."

Logically, I know he wasn't. Of course he wasn't, it's *Dylan*. My conflicting emotions aren't his fault, and yet, because I can't sort out how I feel about him, all I'm doing is hurting him. It's unfair to him, but I can't unload on him again, especially not since the last time I did he called himself a shitty person, then I sprained my ankle.

"Talk to me, Livy," he prompts gently. "Tell me what you're thinking."

I gesture to my ankle. "Last time I tried that, it didn't go well."

He glares at my ankle like it personally offends him. But now that we're standing so close to each other that I can smell him and watch the way his forehead creases when he frowns, I don't want to go back to avoiding him. I've always been honest with him and never held anything back, so why start now?

"Not just the ankle," I add. "I told you how I can't stop thinking about you and the kiss, and you never answered me. So there's no need to keep talking about it."

Dylan stands there, dumbfounded. "I never had the chance. Yesterday you retreated, then you sprained your ankle, then it was so late, and then you avoided me all day today. When was I supposed to talk to you about it?"

He has a point, and I ignore the heat creeping up my neck. "Well, we're here now. Might as well get it over with and let me down gently."

"What are you talking about?"

I take a deep breath, trying to summon my courage. This is going to suck, *again*, but it's not fair to either of us to pretend nothing happened. *Grab the turtle, Liv.* "I don't want you to think I kissed you as some fucked-up, roundabout way of getting Alessio back for what he did. I kissed you because I wanted to, because I felt like I'd die in that moment if I didn't."

His eyes widen, but I push through before he answers. "I told you how much I liked the kiss, how much I felt from it, how I couldn't stop thinking about you, and you replied by saying you're a shitty person for kissing me in the first place. You don't have to feel the same way about the kiss, it's totally cool. We can go back to being friends. So actually, now that I think about it, I don't know how much more we really have to talk about." Maybe I was wrong. Maybe it's better not to talk about this and keep my mortification to a minimum. I try to maneuver around him, but suddenly Dylan is right there, right in front of me, forcing all of my attention solely on him.

His face is determined, and his eyes are fiery as he says, "You've got it all wrong."

I purse my lips, trying to keep my breathing even with him over-loading all my senses. "No, I think that about sums it up."

"No, it doesn't, not even close."

I shift on my crutches. His eyes are so intense I have to look away. "Stop lying to make me feel better."

"I don't lie to you; I never lie to you."

"You lied when I asked you if something happened in Cuba."

He shakes his head. "I didn't even lie then. I never said nothing happened, and I owed it to you to have you hear it from Alessio, not me."

"Then it's a lie by omission." But he does have a point. It should've been Alessio who told me, not him.

Dylan sighs, running his hand over his forehead. "I guess you're right. We'll add it as reason number seventy-eight why I'm a shitty person."

"You're not a shitty person."

"No, I really am."

"No, you're—"

"I am, Livy." He cuts me off, his voice final. He drops his hand from his forehead, blowing out a breath. "I'm a shitty person because I *have* lied to you. I've been lying to you for years, lying to *myself* for years." He steps forward, looking deep in my eyes to ensure that I can't possibly look anywhere else, like he wants to make sure I hear what he's about to say. "Because I've been in love with you forever—I *am* in love with you, Livy—but I could never do anything about it. I'm a shitty person because I've been in love with my best friend's girlfriend, convincing myself that I'm happy for the two of you but actually being miserable deep down."

All I can do is stare at him with wide eyes, mind reeling. He's *in love* with me?

Dylan doesn't need me to say anything, getting more and more passionate as he continues. "I never wanted to get between you and Alessio, and I've never acted maliciously about your relationship, so I've been lying, hiding my feelings about you even though every time I talk to you I fall more and more in love with you. I'm a shitty person because I knew my feelings before Alessio asked you out, but I never told you how I felt because I was scared of being rejected by the one girl who matters, the one girl I really want. And I'm a shitty fucking person because you two *just* broke up, and I'm already dreaming of all the ways I can make you mine, all the ways I can be the man you want, the man you need."

He—I—we—*what*? He's been in love with me this whole time? Did I hear all that right? I must have, because all the butterflies in my stomach have turned it upside down.

I realize belatedly that I'm staring at Dylan without replying, and he shakes his head. "Screw it. Where I fucked up was never telling you how I feel, so I'm going to leave everything out in the open. You said in the forest that I felt nothing during the kiss. You're wrong. You've never *been* more wrong. That kiss was without a doubt the best kiss I've ever had. It was the best thing I've ever *felt*. It's a miracle I've been able to talk about anything other than how much I enjoyed it, how much I want to do it again. In fact, it's a miracle I've been able to function when all I want to do is grab you and do it again and again and again."

His words heat me from the inside out, and my eyes are drawn to his lips, remembering what they tasted like, how he used them. He lets out an unamused laugh. "Jenna thinks I'm trying to replace Alessio? That couldn't be further from the truth. I don't want to be *anything* like Alessio; I don't want to treat you anything like how he treated you. He took advantage of you, he didn't appreciate you, and he took you for granted. I don't want to hold you back, Livy. I want to be the person you can lean on, the one you can talk through ideas and decisions with, not the one who makes them for you. You've always been this amazingly brilliant and passionate girl who goes after what she wants, and I'd never hold you back. I'd be there to cheer you on, to be proud of you. And it would be an honor to be by your side as you did it."

Dylan's breathing hard from getting that all off his chest, and my heart is beating fast like I've run a marathon even though I haven't moved or said anything this whole time.

I believe him. I believe every single word coming out of his mouth. He's really in love with me. He really *has* been in love with me but has been trying to move on without sabotaging me and Alessio. He really isn't trying to make decisions for me, but I should've known that because I know Dylan. And I *wasn't* imagining the connection between us when we kissed. What we felt *was* real, and not fabricated from my loneliness or a subconscious attempt at revenge, because you can't imagine that kind of connection. And now here we are, both single, both feeling things for one another, both unable to hold back.

He's still so close to me, still so warm and large and overwhelmingly *good*. "Dylan," I breathe, and that's all it takes.

He closes the distance between us and finally, *finally* kisses me. His hands land on my waist, and I drop my crutches to wrap my arms around him and pull him closer. It doesn't even matter that I'm balancing on one leg, because Dylan lifts me up, wrapping my legs around his waist so I don't risk setting my foot down. It works for me, because it eliminates all the empty space between us, sealing my body flush against his.

His kiss is just as hungry, just as harsh as it was the first time we kissed, his lips taking like he's wanted this forever, and I gladly let him. My body is alight as fire spreads down my spine, all the turmoil lifting as it realizes this is exactly where it's meant to be.

"Olivia?" someone asks, and Dylan and I break apart to find the source of the voice.

It's Alessio. He's standing a few feet away on the path from the house, looking bewildered and heartbroken at the same time, holding a sad-looking bouquet of red roses.

"Alessio?" I ask, hardly believing that he not only showed up but let himself into the house and out through the back to find us. Dylan sets me down but doesn't release me, since I don't have my crutches and have to balance on one foot. "What are you doing here?"

Alessio looks back and forth between me and his best friend. "I've been trying to reach you all weekend, and I haven't heard anything, so I came to talk to you in person. But I get here and see *this*? You and *Dylan*?" He says it like he's just realized that it was *Dylan* I was kissing, not some random guy, and the heartbreak morphs into something stronger. "What the fuck, man? That's *my* girlfriend you're kissing!"

Dylan's grip tightens on my waist, and he pulls me closer into his side. "You two are broken up."

"Not forever!" Alessio exclaims, using the bouquet to point at us. "That's my girl! And you're my best friend!"

He's practically yelling, and we've definitely gotten the attention of everyone at the bonfire; they must all be incredibly confused as to what's happening. "Alessio," I start, "why don't we go inside where we can talk."

"Oh, now you want to talk?" he asks, the petals of the roses falling off as he gestures with them. "I had to drive three hours and leave dozens of voice mails only to walk in on my best friend and my girlfriend all over each other before you finally want to talk?!" He throws the bouquet on the ground, storming over to us. "And you don't even have the decency to stop touching each other? Let go of her, man."

"Wait, Ales—"

He shoves Dylan, and he loses his grip on me. I stumble to stay upright, automatically putting my foot down for balance and immediately shrieking when pain radiates up my leg.

"Livy!" Dylan exclaims, reaching for me, but Alessio slides between us, shoving Dylan away.

"Stop trying to touch her! She's not yours to touch! She's my girlfriend. Of five years! And you're trying to weasel your way in only days after we broke up? You're supposed to be my best friend!" He pushes Dylan with every statement he makes, and Dylan only holds his hands up and asks him to calm down.

"Alessio, stop it!" I demand, putting my hand on his shoulder to get his attention. But he's too focused on Dylan, and when he moves, I lose my balance, falling to the ground with a shout.

"Olivia!" Dylan pushes Alessio aside and runs to me, crouching down and inspecting me. He puts his hand under my knee to lift my injured leg, checking my ankle. "Are you all right? Did you land on your ankle? We should get the boot back on."

"You really can't keep your hands off my girl for a whole five seconds, can you?" Alessio rages, his nostrils flared. I've never seen this side of Alessio before; he's always been smiley and charismatic. I know this must be hard for him, but he has no right to come here and start pushing us around.

"Alessio, stop," I say as Dylan helps me up, keeping his arm around me since my crutches have somehow migrated several feet from us.

"But you—"

"*No,*" I interrupt forcefully, more forcefully than I've ever talked to him before. "You're being a giant, hypocritical jerk." I push away from Dylan, wanting to stand on my own for this, and he quickly scrambles to hand me my crutches. "You cheated on me; we are *over*. You don't get to come here and act like a caveman, freaking out at Dylan and deciding who can and can't touch me. You're the one who threw away a five-year relationship and our future, not me. And maybe you thought I was so needy and lost without you that I'd eventually take you back, but that's *never* going to happen. Not only have you betrayed my trust, but I've realized how messed up and one-sided our relationship really was, and I ignored the signs because I was so desperate to be loved and give love."

Alessio looks like I've slapped him. "That's not true, we were great together—we can still be great together. Give me a chance to prove it."

"You've had plenty of chances over the years. I told you we were broken up the day I found out you cheated on me, and I meant it. We're over."

Alessio's taken aback, like this really wasn't a part of whatever scenario he envisioned on the drive up here. He really thought a dying bouquet of supermarket roses and a half-assed apology would be all it took to get me to jump back in his arms.

His eyes turn to steel. "This is because of Dylan, isn't it? You're just going to go from me to my best friend? Like he can ever recreate what we had?"

Dylan, who I appreciate has been letting me handle this, takes a warning step forward. "Hey, calm down, man."

I don't need Dylan's help. When I first found out about Alessio's cheating, I was too shocked and hurt to actually say anything. But now that I've had some time to digest it and made some realizations about how our relationship might not have been as perfect as I made it out to be in my head, I can actually get my feelings off my chest. And it feels *so* good. "This has nothing to do with Dylan," I tell Alessio.

"Really? Wasn't it his tongue down your throat five minutes ago?"

"Wasn't it your dick in another girl a few weeks ago?"

Alessio's mouth snaps shut, and it makes me feel vindicated. I hold my head high, no longer worried about who I'll be with or without Alessio. I don't need a boyfriend to tell me who I am, and I don't need to frame my existence around someone else. I know who I am. I'm Olivia Rossi, and I'm pretty damn cool.

"Who I choose to kiss or not is none of your concern. Not now, not ever. We are no longer together. I'm too good for you, Alessio, and I deserve better. Whether it's with someone else or all by myself, I know my worth, and it's not being with someone who doesn't appreciate everything that I am or who makes me dull myself down. I'm great just the way I am, and it's time I realized it."

In my head, there's cheering and clapping and someone shouting *You go, girl!* But that's not what actually happens. Alessio looks hard at me, really hard, like he's seeing me for the first time, before looking at Dylan, who's watching me with a proud smile. Then, without warning, Alessio swings at Dylan's face.

TWENTY

Night 4 of Muskoka

Jenna

I'm so upset about my conversation with my dad, and the fact that I impulsively threw my phone in the lake, that I'm not the best company all day. I try to act like everything is fine, but that's getting harder every time my mind wanders to how I'm being abandoned and how Dad wasn't planning on telling me about his new family. I can't even join Elena when she asks to take the kayaks out on the lake because it reminds me of my phone at the bottom of it, which brings up the conversation with my dad, and I get upset all over again. It doesn't help that every single time I'm alone with Hari, he asks what upset me so much and if it had anything to do with our cleaning the house yesterday. I deal with it by brushing past him, and he calls after me, saying, "You can't be a robot forever!"

I make it through the day in a haze, cycling between forcing myself not to be upset and being reminded why I'm upset in the first place. Part of me wants to call my dad for more answers, but then

I remember how well that conversation went the first time and I'm glad I threw my phone in the lake. As everyone gathers around the bonfire at sunset, I sneak away to the dock. Someone left a red plastic cup on the picnic table, so I dump out the stale beer and fill the cup with smooth, flat rocks I pick on the shore. Back on the dock, I methodically palm the rocks before skipping them on the lake, trying to beat my old record of fourteen.

Ironically, this is the one activity I didn't do with Mom; I did it with Dad. We've never been big on communication, and this was a way we could hang out together without actually having to talk. When something was bothering either of us, we didn't talk it through, we handed each other the best skipping stones we could find, then stood out on the dock trying to outthrow each other. I don't know why I'm drawn to it now when I don't want anything to do with Dad, but I was so deep in thought, my body brought me here before I even realized what I was doing.

It's already night four, meaning I've only got two more nights before I never get to see this place again—the lake, the dock, the treehouse, all gone. It's also only two more nights before I move into the dorms. My stomach twists at the thought. I was using this week to distract myself from the fact that I'm going to be alone, and yet I spent this whole week thinking about just that.

I pick up a pebble from the cup and skip it over the lake, counting four bounces before it sinks. Even that makes me sad. Dad always got at least five.

"So you've run out of phones to throw into the lake and have resorted to stones, have you?"

I groan audibly, making sure Hari knows I don't think he's funny.

"Maybe I can call it, and we can hear the ring to find it."

I throw another stone, counting six skips. "Those jokes are getting really old."

I feel him sidle up beside me. "Ah, so she does speak to me. You promised to stop giving me the silent treatment if I helped you yesterday."

"I'm not giving you the silent treatment."

"Yes you are."

I throw another stone. Six again. "I'm talking to you right now."

"But it's not the same as before. And you won't even look at me."

I sigh, setting the cup down. "What do you want from me, Hari? I'm clearly not in the right headspace to trade insults with you right now. But if it makes you feel better, fine." I take a step back to scan him from head to toe. "You look like you got dressed in the dark, your voice is so irritating I get a headache every time you open your mouth, and you're in desperate need of a haircut."

He's unfazed. "You're lying."

I am. He looks spectacular, and I love his voice, but I hate that I think that.

"Well, I've given you your obligatory conversation," I say, turning back to the lake, "so I'm going back to skipping stones now."

"All right, that's it," Hari declares, pulling his phone from his pocket and tossing it onto the dock. "Do you have anything in your pockets? Keys? Another phone? A secret note professing your love for me?"

"What? I don't even have pockets."

"Good," he says, and without warning, he speeds toward me, not stopping as he wraps his arms around me and throws us both in the lake.

The water is a shock of cold, and I swallow a mouthful as I kick away from Hari. I break the surface with a gasp, sputtering lake water and pushing my now-drenched, tangled hair off my face.

"What the fuck was that for?" I yell at Hari, wiping water from my face. The sun is setting on the horizon, bathing us in deep oranges

and purples, and the water has already cooled down. If I wasn't so shocked and pissed off, my teeth would be chattering.

Hari pushes his hair off his face. "I'm sorry, Jenna, but it needed to be done."

"Why?!" I yell, splashing him. "Why could it *possibly* have been needed?!"

He holds his hands out wide. "Clearly the only time we communicate is when we're in this lake—either in it or on it like when we went out on the Sea-Doo—so I figured if we were going to get anything done, we needed to be back here."

"We *were* on it, you dick. We were on the dock, which is *on the lake*!" I splash him again, anger squeezing my throat shut. I cannot *believe* he threw me in the lake to *talk* to me. After everything I learned today and everything going on, the last thing I need is to be plunged fully clothed into the lake after the sun has gone down, all because Hari feels entitled to my inner thoughts and secrets. "And I have nothing else to say to you."

I turn and swim to the ladder on the dock, but Hari's not ready to drop it.

"Fine, don't say anything to me. Let me say this to you," he calls out, and I pause with my hand on the ladder instead of climbing up only out of morbid curiosity. "I may look stupid, but I can put two and two together. Your dad is selling this place, he asked you not to come here, and you did anyway because you said it yourself, you have abandonment issues and everyone is going in different directions in a few days, and you're using this week as a distraction to not think about how lonely you'll be." Not only is he throwing my words back at me from the other night, but he's accurately put everything together. He swims closer to me. "But newsflash, Jenna, *everyone* feels lonely. People feel lonely even when they're surrounded by a room full of people. But the trick to combating that? They *let people in*, not shut them out. They don't walk around suppressing their feelings and pretending like nothing ever affects them. You can't keep ignoring how you feel, especially when you're clearly going through something right now. So *tell me*. Let me help!"

He's breathing hard, eyes determined as he stares me down, daring me to say everything is fine. It's not fine, and he knows it. He's known it since he first spotted me at the mall; he knows it because, for some reason, he *sees* me, sees more than everyone else.

He already knows everything that's going on, and he's already caught me vulnerable when I was trying not to be more times than I can count. The week is basically over anyway, and then he'll go back to England and I'll never see him again, so at this point, what do I have to lose? I'm too tired to hold it all in, and there's something about Hari that cracks me wide open.

"You want to know, Hari? You want to see the real, raw, messy side of me?" That's what he said in the treehouse, and I'm going to give it to him. Maybe then he'll leave me alone. "Fine. You're completely right. My dad *is* selling this place, and we're *not* supposed to be here. My friends are all leaving me, and I'm terrified to be all alone in a new place knowing nothing and no one. But it's more than that. My dad picked up and sold everything and moved to Vancouver to be with his secret new girlfriend and her daughter that he never told me about. He doesn't *care* if I visit for Christmas, doesn't even care if he doesn't see me for the next seven years I'll be in school. I've already lost my mom, and I'm losing my friends to distance, and now I'm losing my dad to a new family. And to make matters worse, I'm losing *this place*. The only place that's ever felt like home, the only place I can look around and see and smell and hear and feel my mom everywhere."

I don't know when I start crying, but by the time I finish getting everything off my chest, tears are streaming down my face, mixing with the lake water. It did feel good to finally admit everything I've been pushing down, but it doesn't make me feel better. It doesn't change anything. I'm still going to be alone, and I'm still losing my last attachment to Mom.

Hari's staring at me with wide eyes. Maybe he wasn't expecting me to actually open up or thought I'd fight back more, or maybe he's always wondered what I'd look like crying but never expected to actually see it.

"Change is scary, Jenna," he says gently. "And everything is happening all at once. Starting school alone, your dad moving, selling this property. I get why you feel the way you do, but everyone is only a phone call away."

I angrily swipe at my face. "I can't just call up the new owners of this place and ask them to describe the sunset in the morning from where I'd sit with Mom or ask them to recreate the way she would chide us for coming in the house soaked but then make a bigger mess herself. I'm not ready to say goodbye to this place, Hari," I admit, my voice breaking when I add, "I'm not ready to say goodbye to my mom."

And maybe that's what this is really all about. The small details about Mom are already fading. If I don't come here and feel her everywhere, will I lose her completely?

"And you don't need to say goodbye to her," Hari says, closing the distance between us and grabbing onto the ladder. Neither one of us has to tread anymore, but now he's so close to me I can see the droplets of water in his thick eyelashes. "She's always with you, whether you're at this specific location or not. Take it from someone who moves countries twice a year—this property, while beautiful, doesn't keep your mom around. *You* do. She lives on in you, in your memories, and you'll always have those. You can be living in a huge lake house like this or a shitty shoebox dorm at Western and you'll still have those memories. You'll still have your mom."

Maybe, maybe not. But I don't want to risk it. I'm already doing a degree for a career I don't think I even care about to feel closer to her, and that's a poor substitute for being here and being surrounded by memories. But my eyes sting, and my hands are shaking, and I'm tired of having to talk about it, especially with Hari.

I take a deep breath, willing myself to stop crying. "Well, you wanted to know what I was thinking, and that was it. I hope seeing me weak and vulnerable was everything you ever imagined and more." I climb up the ladder, not waiting for him to push further. "You win the weird game you created way back when to try to crack me. It took you a while, but you got there."

"Come on, Jenna, it's not about that," Hari says, quickly climbing the ladder and standing before me on the dock. We're both soaked, shivering messes. The moonlight, little solar lights lining the dock, and house lights in the distance are the only sources of illumination now that the sun has completely dipped beyond the horizon.

"Then what's it about, Hari? You admitted to getting joy out of seeing me break down. Well, you got what you wanted!" I hold my arms out to the side, putting myself on display. "Here I am! Broken and flawed and just as vulnerable as the next person!"

"No, you're not, Jenna!" he exclaims, just as fired up as I am. "You're beautiful and strong and witty and so fucking stubborn it somehow becomes a good thing."

His words catch me so off guard it almost dims some of the fire burning in my chest.

He steps forward, determined. "All the stupid pranks I pulled in grade school? All the times I tried to force you to show us the real you? I was jealous. Jealous and curious as to how you hid it so damn well."

Hari? Jealous of *me?*

We stare at each other, breathing hard even though we're no

longer treading water, neither of us making a move to get a towel even though we're both freezing.

When I don't prompt him, Hari continues, "My parents' net worth was twenty million dollars and steadily growing by the time I was eleven, and that's when they made it known they wanted nothing to do with me. They shipped me off to summer boarding school in England so I wouldn't be around when school was out for the summer, and when I was here during the school year, I had nameless staff pick me up from school and cook for me. I was lonely. Lonely and sad and angry. And there you were, the girl whose mom just died in a car accident, who had all the more reason to be a mess than I did, and yet you still had it together. You stuffed all the messy emotions behind this unbothered, robotic mask, and no matter what happened, no matter how many reasons you had to lose your shit, you still had it all under control. It pissed me off. It made me jealous. I needed to prove that you were just as flawed and human as me, that if I pushed you hard enough, you'd crack."

I never knew Hari felt like that back then, and it's almost ironic that we both felt sad and lonely while feeling like we were two worlds apart.

All of the fire has burned out now, leaving me feeling hollow. "Well, it's been proven. Happy now?"

"Yes, but not for the reason you think." He steps closer to me, like he's worried I'm going to run away from him before he's ready to let me go. "When I saw you losing your shit in the parking lot that day and I realized who you were, it didn't bring me joy like I'd thought it would. Then I got up close, and you were so fucking beautiful, the most stunning girl I ever saw, it's a wonder I kept it together. I couldn't get you out of my head, and when Kyle told me about this trip, I got him to invite me without him realizing that's what I wanted. I needed to see you again, needed to know you."

He's directly in front of me now, the heat from his body practically steaming off him, puncturing through the cold. "So I *am* happy when you're real with me, not because seeing you sad brings me joy but because I don't want you to hide how you're feeling from me. I want to be the one person you feel like you can be yourself with. You've opened up with me even when you didn't realize it, and you liked it, I know you did. And I like who you are, like who I am when I'm with you. You shutting me out fucking killed me, Jenna. And I know all of this is quick, and sure, we barely know each other, but at the same time, we may know more about each other than anyone else. It feels good talking to you, teasing you, hanging out with you. It's like the most natural thing in the world. When we're with each other, we can just *be*."

I can't believe what he's saying. Even more, I can't believe that I *agree* with him. He's right in saying I enjoy my time with him, that I always end up being myself since he somehow gets me to lower my guard without realizing. He's right that it's quick, but it feels natural between us. He knows more about what's going on in my head than anyone else, even more than my best friends or Dad or even Olivia, and I know he feels discarded by his parents, that he feels like his carpentry isn't good enough, and like he doesn't truly have a place to call home.

I almost let out a humorless laugh. We're just two lonely, abandoned people, finding peace in each other—because I do find peace in Hari, and that realization *does* make me laugh.

"Tell me what you're thinking," Hari demands; it's so very like him to want to be in my head.

I wrap my arms around myself, trying not to let my lips pull up in the corner as I say, "I'm thinking how annoying it is that you still look beautiful soaking wet in jeans and tangled hair, and I probably look like a sewer rat."

Hari laughs, a beautiful, light sound that sends tingles down my spine. He places his hands on my waist, drawing me closer, and I go willingly. "You don't. You look like a regular rat, not the sewer kind."

I shove him with a laugh, but he only pulls me closer. My body is pressed right up against him, feeling every deep line and contour since we're soaking wet, and I wrap my arms over his shoulders.

He smirks at me, but I don't find it annoying like I once did. "You didn't let me finish. I meant a *beautiful* rat—"

"Hari!"

"Fine!" He laughs, running his nose up the length of my neck, the action sending electricity down my spine. "You look beautiful, period. Beautiful like always. So fucking beautiful I'm terrified you actually drowned me in the lake after I threw us in, and this is an oxygen-deprived induced hallucination. So beautiful that if I don't kiss you this instant, I may die on the spot."

Hari admitting he wants to kiss me sends the butterflies in my stomach into a frenzy. I very much want to kiss Hari. I wanted it the other night, I want it now, I even wanted it when I was pissed at him.

I draw up on my tiptoes, our lips barely touching in a whisper of a kiss. "Well, we can't have that now, can we?"

Hari's fingers tighten on my waist, and finally he presses his lips against mine. Everything around me vanishes, all the worries and anxieties swirling around my brain melting away. All that's left is Hari—the way he tastes, the way he smells, the way his hands, rough and strong, pull me harder against him.

His tongue runs along the seam of my lips, and I open for him immediately, sinking into him as he deepens the kiss. His lips are warm and soft yet controlling and demanding, exactly how I would've imagined a kiss with Hari would be. My hands tangle in his thick hair that's somehow still soft even when it's soaking wet, pulling him closer to me.

He chuckles as I attempt to take control of the kiss, his lips skimming mine as he murmurs, "Always so demanding." But he doesn't mind, not one bit, because he lets me take control, lets me set the pace, happily lets me take what I want, giving back just as much.

Part of me wonders if we shouldn't have wasted the last few days arguing when we could've been doing *this* the whole time, but then the thought is quickly brushed away. I like how Hari teases me, like how we argue-flirt back and forth, like how I don't have to filter myself around him. I could get used to being around him all the time.

The thought has me pausing, remembering something important, and I pull away from him, ending our kiss.

"Wait," I say, narrowing my eyes to scan his face. "Are you going back to England?"

"Why the hell would I ever go back to England?" Hari asks, eyes hazy as he tries to draw my lips back to his.

I pull back. "I'm serious, Hari. I don't know what *this* is," I say, gesturing between the two of us, "but you know I have abandonment issues, and I can't get attached to someone who's only going to leave me in the end." I should be embarrassed admitting that out loud or feel some type of urge to hide the truth, but I don't. Hari already knows everything, and I suddenly don't feel the need to censor my feelings around him.

Hari tugs me back to him, wrapping his arms around my waist. "I'm serious too. I have no desire to go back to England, ever. Nothing is there for me, and I've always known that. I'm going to stay here and find a carpentry apprenticeship like you said, while trying to do some work on the side. Maybe a certain beautiful girl can even help me set up a social media account to promote my work like she said I should."

His words have me melting back into him. I never thought I'd actually get upset at the thought of Hari leaving me. "Said beautiful girl might be persuaded to help, with the right incentive."

He tugs a strand of hair behind my ear, his finger leaving sparks against my skin in its wake. "Ah, incentives. I know exactly what you're asking for. Don't worry, darling, I'll transfer the whole file of my shirtless selfies to you once you get a new phone."

I playfully shove his shoulder as he laughs, though he doesn't budge from where he's pressed against me, and I'm not actually mad.

"All right, fine," he says, the playful smirk turning serious. "How about I visit you the second you're all set up in school, and I take you on a date. A real date. One where I can impress you with my outstanding charm and wit, and all the other kids at Western can be amazed at how handsome and posh your boyfriend is."

"Boyfriend, huh?"

His eyes widen, but the confidence never falters. "If you think you'll find someone hotter, funnier, and with better hair than me, good luck. But if you want to take it slow, then we can go on a few dates and see if we get sick of each other or not before committing to the official label."

Never in a million years did I think I'd be excited by, never mind *open to*, the idea of Hari being my boyfriend, but here I am. Just thinking about seeing his annoying smile every day and wondering what he'll say to inevitably piss me off but make me laugh at the same time causes giddiness to course through my body. But something makes me pause, and uncertainty creeps up.

Hari likes being in my head, and I like keeping people out of it. Will he always be pushing me? Always trying to force me to be vulnerable and tell him what I'm thinking even when I'm not ready to or don't want to?

I smooth the fabric of his wrinkled, wet shirt against his chest. "It won't work if you're always trying to get me to open up. There will be times I don't want to talk about things, and you can't be pushing me."

Hari tilts his head to the side, considering it. "As long as you don't shut me out."

Fine. I can do that. Talking to Hari, whether I'm happy or sad or pissed, already comes easy. "We'll have to work on the communication thing."

"Deal. Now say you'll date me. I'll even sweeten the deal by saying I won't throw you in the lake anymore . . . this week."

I laugh, thinking about how he calls *me* the bossy one. Am I really going to do this? Am I really going to date *Hari*? "Then I guess that will be . . . acceptable."

"I knew it. You're so obsessed with me," he says, laughing as I push away from him and spray him with water droplets from my hair, my chest feeling lighter than it's felt in a while. Nothing is fixed, and everything is still falling apart around me, but I feel better with Hari, even if we're bickering. I don't feel so alone, not because we've decided to give dating a try but because I feel like I have someone I can talk to about anything, someone who *wants* me to talk to them about everything.

He grabs me again, and just as his lips are about to touch mine, a voice calls out, "Jenna?"

We pull apart to find Elena looking over at us, standing at the edge of the dock where it meets the land. "Oh, sorry! I didn't realize you were . . ." She trails off, and even in this lighting I can tell her cheeks heat. "I wanted to talk to you, but I didn't realize you were busy. I'll go."

"No, it's all right," I say as Hari and I join her. She takes in our soaked, disheveled appearances. Compared to her cute pink sweater and jeans, we must really look a mess. "I'm freezing anyway. We should probably get inside and change."

"You stay and talk," Hari says, giving my hip a pat. "I'll grab towels."

He leaves without waiting for a response, and Elena looks back and forth between me and his retreating body. When her back is turned, Hari walks backward, exaggeratedly mouthing *Talk to her*. I realize what he's doing, but I've already had too many heart-to-hearts.

"I know, it's all unexpected and new," I tell her, wringing out my shirt as best I can. "And he is so annoying but also so—"

"You hate me, don't you!" she interrupts, eyes widening like she didn't mean to blurt that out.

My hands freeze on my shirt. "What?"

Her lip quivers. "It's so hard to read your face sometimes, but I know you're pissed at me. If you hate me, just tell me! You've been distant since I broke the news and you have been avoiding me this whole trip. You didn't spend any time with us at the parties, and I always have to pull you to hang out with us, and yesterday you sent us out of the house to hike and didn't even come! And normally you're so good at hiding your emotions I can never read you, but even I know something's wrong, like you don't even want to be here. I'm sorry I'm going to Newfoundland instead of Western like we planned, but you're my best friend, please don't hate me. I don't want to lose you over this!"

Both of us are stunned into silence. She doesn't seem like she expected to admit all of that, and I didn't expect her to think it.

She's been worried this whole time about losing me as a friend, and I've been worried about losing *her* as a friend. I spent the last four days running around trying to cover for us since we're not supposed to be here, or taking a break from reality with Hari, or stewing because of unresolved issues with my dad, but I haven't spent any quality time with Elena, and that's what I wanted for this week. I was supposed to make my last memories here with my friends, and now all Elena is going to remember is how I spent the week avoiding her.

"You've got it all wrong," I tell her, shaking my head. "I don't hate you, Elena."

"But you're mad at me! I'll decline Memorial University and try to get Western to take me back so we can be together like we planned."

She means it too. She's got her shoulders back and a determined look on her face, and while I appreciate the sentiment, the thought of Elena dropping her dream program just for me only pisses me off.

"Absolutely not," I tell her. "I'm happy you're bold enough to follow your dreams. If anyone deserves to get into that competitive program, it's you, and I'm proud of you. It's a once-in-a-lifetime opportunity, so under no circumstances are you to give it up just to make someone else happy, especially not *me*."

Her eyebrows draw together. "But I thought that's what you wanted?"

I take a deep breath, mentally preparing myself to get vulnerable once again. "Maybe it's what I thought I wanted, but I realize now it's not. I can't hold you back from your dream just because I'm scared to lose you. Hell, part of the reason I planned this trip even though we're not supposed to be here is because I thought if I gave you and everyone else the best end-of-summer trip ever, you'd remember how awesome I am and never even think of forgetting about me. It's sad, but it's true."

Elena's eyes widen, and it makes her look even younger. "You're my best friend. I'd never forget about you just because I'm going to school somewhere else, awesome cottage trip or not."

Deep down, I knew that, but hearing her say it out loud fills me with the comfort and reassurance I didn't know I needed. "I know, it's stupid. This whole thing was stupid."

She settles her hand on my arm, uncaring that it's soaked and freezing. "No, it's not. It's been a great week. I only wish we had talked about this sooner, especially since we were both feeling the same way."

She's right. Opening up and exposing myself like this physically makes my skin crawl, but now that we each know where we stand, I do feel much better, like I did after talking with Hari. I don't think I'll ever go around telling everyone how I feel all day, but if something is really bothering me, maybe I'll start sharing.

"I know." I agree with her. "Forgive me for making you feel ignored?"

"Forgive me for making you think I'd abandon you once school starts?"

"Forgiven," we say at the same time, smiling stupidly at one another. She holds her arms out, approaching me slowly like she's giving me time to back away, but I think in this instance, a mushy, making-up hug is permitted. I hold my arms out and pull her in. We hold each other close for a few moments, taking solace in the fact that we're best friends and always will be no matter where we are.

"You're freezing," Elena whispers, adding, "and you smell like the lake." We laugh as we pull apart. There's now a dark, wet spot on Elena's pink sweater, but she's smiling regardless.

"I know. Let's go inside and get changed. Hari clearly forgot about bringing me a towel. Minus points for him on the should-he-be-my-boyfriend scale." He was never planning on coming back, but I'm not actually mad about it.

We fall into step beside each other as we head up the path to the house. "You and Hari, huh?" she asks, waggling her eyebrows at me. "And did you say we're not even supposed to be here? You're going to have to tell me . . ." She trails off when we get closer to the house and hear shouting. After sharing a glance, we race up the path, past the now deserted bonfire, just in time to see Alessio, haggard and fuming, punch Dylan right in the face.

And my dad pull them apart.

TWENTY-ONE

Night 4 of Muskoka

Jenna

"What the hell is going on here?" Dad exclaims, gripping Alessio's arm and yanking him away from Dylan.

Alessio raises his free arm. "It was self-defense, I swear!"

"Was not!" Martina exclaims, standing with all my friends a small distance away from Alessio, like they were trying not to make it obvious that they were watching whatever was going on, but they totally were.

Dad looks around at the group of us, then his eyes land on me, and my stomach sinks. "I said no parties."

"It's not a party!" Elena, trying to be helpful, rushes to say. "It's just us, no one else."

He doesn't care; there wasn't supposed to be an *us*.

My legs get heavier and heavier with each step I take closer to him, like they're slowly filling with cement. I'm in trouble for lying and having everyone over, but I'm not the only one keeping secrets in this family, and I could argue his are way bigger than mine. That little fact fuels the courage that keeps me going, stopping only when I reach him.

Olivia is murmuring something to Dylan, fussing over his face where Alessio nailed him right in the cheekbone. Dad releases Alessio, making sure he keeps his distance from Dylan, and says, "I'm disappointed in you, young man. You cheated on Olivia, and you have no right to come here, fists swinging like you're the one who was wronged. You're a grown man, act like it."

Alessio hangs his head. I'm shocked Dad had a deep enough conversation with Aunt Eloise to know the specific reason Olivia and Alessio broke up. He doesn't even know why I broke up with my last boyfriend.

"I'm going to take Dylan in to get some ice," Olivia announces, glaring at Alessio like there are some swear words she'd love to say but can't because her uncle is here.

"Good idea, Olivia," Dad says, putting on the authoritative voice that he uses when trying to negotiate bids between clients. "You two"—he points to Fletcher and Kyle—"make sure the bonfire is completely out; I can see it flickering from here. You"—he points to Robbie—"go with them, then the three of you pick up any litter and dispose of it properly. You . . ." He points to Hari then realizes he's soaking wet. He looks back at me, his eyes narrowing. "Get my daughter a towel, then go shower."

Hari nods his head up and down so fast even I get dizzy. He takes off without another word.

"I want the rest of you inside and in bed by the time I finish talking with my daughter."

"Dad," I exclaim, heat rising to my cheeks. He's never cared like this before, never made a scene in front of all my friends.

"Don't *Dad* me. You're lucky it's late and I'm not sending every-one home right now. But it's almost midnight, and I'm sure you've all been drinking." He turns to Alessio, who looks down at the ground and sheepishly kicks a rock. "It's too late and you're too emotional to drive home. If I let you sleep on the couch, I want your word that you won't cause any problems."

Alessio and my dad have always gotten along, talking about market trends and stock prices or whatever it is they discuss at family events, and I know Alessio respects him. For that reason, I believe Alessio when he says, "Yes, sir," and follows the group into the house.

Elena hesitates. "Do you want me to . . ." Her loyalty is heart-warming, but this conversation with Dad is something I have to do on my own.

"No, it's all right. I'll catch up with you inside."

She nods, passing Hari as she goes. He hands me a towel but doesn't stick around, instead mouthing *Be honest with him!* before retreating. Then it's just me and Dad, standing a few feet apart, staring at each other under the moonlight.

I'm the first one to break the silence. "What are you doing here?"

He shakes his head incredulously. "What do you mean? I've gotten countless calls and texts from neighbors complaining about parties, I hear a boy in the background of our call, you hang up on me in the middle of an important conversation, then you don't answer any of my calls or texts following that, and neither does your cousin. I was on the first plane out. I was worried about you."

I wrap the towel around my shoulders, hugging the ends tight. He got on a plane and drove all the way here to check up on me? I suddenly feel small under his scrutinizing gaze. It's not a look I'm used to from Dad. "I didn't hang up on you," I finally mutter. "I threw my phone in the lake."

He blinks at me. "You threw your . . ." He lets out a surprised laugh. "Really, Jenna? My god, we suck at communication, don't we?"

We do. We really do.

Dad blows out a breath, putting a hand on my back and guiding me down the path to a seating area with a view of the lake. Little lights planted in the ground and charged by mini solar panels illuminate the area, and now I can see the dark circles under his eyes, the unkemptness of his hair in which usually no strand ever dares to be out of place.

"Sit," he orders, and I sink into the chair opposite him. He looks out at the glittering lake, beautiful in the moonlight, and I pull the thick towel tighter around myself, trying and failing to figure out what he's going to say. He's never been a yeller, never really had to *parent* me beyond advising me not to drive drunk or get in a car with a stranger, but we've also never had such an explosive fight before.

He surprises me when he starts with, "Your mom really did love this place." He watches as loons gracefully land on the water, gently floating on the ripples. "I told her, as a real estate agent, there would be better places to invest in, but she didn't care. She loved it. She loved that you loved it. And she proved me wrong, since this place has exponentially increased in value."

I think of the listing price, and my stomach churns.

"I don't come up here as often as we used to. I didn't even pack up our stuff; the crew did." Dad looks around the property, eyes turning sad. "There are just too many memories here."

"That's what makes it great," I tell him. I point to a big tree in the distance with a huge branch that arches over the lake. "That's where Grandpa built that rope swing for us to jump into the lake, and me, Olivia, and the twins broke it when we all tried to go at the same time." I point to another spot. "That's where Mom originally wanted to put the bonfire before we found the burrow of baby rabbits, and we'd go check on them every day. Right here, where we're sitting, is where you and Mom would have drinks before bed while I pretended to be sleeping but was watching movies."

Dad runs a hand through his hair, making it messier. "I had no idea how much you loved those memories, and I . . ." He sighs, gesturing around us. "I didn't know you came here to remember her."

My eyes sting, and my nose tingles, but I refuse to cry. My voice cracks anyway when I say, "I can feel her here, Dad."

"I get that now." He nods, resting his elbows on his knees as he faces me. "I'm not selling this place to get rid of you, sweetheart. It tore me apart to hear you say I'm replacing you or that you thought I was trying to be free of you."

My spine turns rigid. "Then what do you call selling all our possessions and moving to Vancouver with your new secret family?"

Dad scratches his chin and clears his throat, and I know what follows is usually him throwing his credit card at me and running away as fast as his legs can take him. But he seems to be fighting his natural instincts, staying planted in his seat as he says, "I love your mom, Jenna, and no one can or ever will replace her, just like no one can or ever will replace *you*."

I bite my lip, but the words come out anyway. "Then what about Rebecca and Esme? If it's not some big conspiracy, why didn't you tell me about them? You've hidden it for a *year*, Dad."

"I know how it looks, sweetheart. I may be the adult here, but I'm still figuring it out as we go, just like you." Dad shakes his head, and he looks genuinely remorseful as he says, "I thought I was protecting you by not telling you about Rebecca yet. She was my first *serious* partner since your mother, and I was so worried about you thinking I was replacing you and Mom, I never told you about Rebecca and Esme, which I guess screwed it all up in the end anyway." He grabs my hand, and I stare at where we're connected. "I'm sorry for not telling you, but I'm *not* replacing you. I—I can get someone else to run Vancouver so I can move back here. I can make long distance work with Rebecca; we've been doing it this whole time anyway."

My gaze flicks up to Dad so fast my hair sends water droplets flying. He's watching me intently, and I know he means it, know he'd move back to Ontario for me, and my chest tightens, the feeling becoming almost overwhelming.

"You've been so independent and strong, I didn't think it would matter much to you if I moved to Vancouver, but I should've talked to you about it. *You're* what matters most to me, Jenna. I'll stay here with you to prove it."

I'm being handed what I thought I wanted, but it's not easing the pressure in my chest or untangling the knots in my stomach. Just like with Elena, I'm forcing someone I love to choose between their future and staying here for me.

"No, that's not what I want," I tell Dad, and his eyebrows jump up his forehead.

"But I thought—"

"I know." Dad must really like Rebecca to make this kind of move, and he *has* seemed happier this past year, even if I didn't realize why. If I make him move here, he'll be alone while I'm away at school, and I'll have made him desert his new business and Rebecca just so I can avoid feeling lonely. "I thought I wanted you and everyone to stay here and for nothing to change, but that's not fair. I got so caught up in feeling abandoned, I didn't stop to think about how you felt."

Dad squeezes my hands. "I'm not *abandoning* you. No matter where we are or how many time zones are between us, you're my daughter." He sighs, and I pull my hands away to stop the towel from dropping off my shoulder. "I should've talked to you about all of this earlier. We could've sat down and properly hashed this out."

If I had known about Rebecca—and even Esme—I probably

wouldn't have spun out as badly as I did. I might have even welcomed the thought of having a potential new little sister—she seems excited to meet me, so that's a good sign at least. But all of this could have been avoided with some good old-fashioned communication on both our ends. When Hari pesters me for details later, I can't tell him that. He'll only be all smug and annoying and *I told you so*. Even though he *was* right, and I feel better after talking with my dad, I can't *tell* Hari that.

"So are you going to stay in Vancouver?" I ask, and it doesn't come out sounding bitter.

"Only if that's all right with you."

As much as I'd like everything to stay the same, I can't let my fears hold everyone back. "Will I meet Rebecca and Esme?"

He smiles, relieved, and I feel a pang in my heart. "They'd really love that, sweetheart. For the record, they hound me all the time to meet you; it was me who was too scared to tell you. They know all about you, and Esme tells people her sister is a model. She asks me to show her pictures all the time."

That gets a laugh out of me, and points for Esme. It also makes me feel a bit better. People who want to kick you out of their lives and replace you don't want to meet you, so I take that as another good sign. I'm not going to be okay with it overnight, but I'll try. "Then I guess you'll have to send me a plane ticket over reading week. That's in October, by the way."

Dad's face instantly changes, and it's like thirty years instantly lifts. I didn't realize this was weighing just as heavily on him as it has been on me. "I've got a better idea. Why don't Rebecca, Esme, and I get on a plane and have everyone spend reading week here?"

"I thought you were selling it?"

Dad looks out at the lake again, like he's mesmerized by its beauty. "Maybe I should take it off the market. It *is* beautiful, and you can come up here for most of the summer and almost every weekend in the winter that you can spare."

I look down at my hands, at my chipping nail polish that I need to fix immediately. "Hari thinks I don't need this place to keep the memories of Mom alive."

"Hari, huh?" Dad fidgets in his seat, clearing his throat. "That the boy who took a midnight swim with you?"

"That's the one."

"You guys . . . uh . . . together?" It kills him to ask, but I appreciate that he's trying.

"Kind of, I guess. It's new."

He nods, rubbing the back of his neck, and the fact that he's fighting his instincts to avoid this conversation warms my heart. "Right. You want me to talk to him?"

"No! Please, no." Dad has never given any boy the threatening *hurt my daughter and I'll hurt you* talk, and I don't need him to start now. I can give that speech for myself.

"Good, good." Dad doesn't even bother to hide his relief. "Well, I think Hari is right. I carry your mother in my heart, not in this place. But I didn't realize how much it means to you. Maybe we'll hold onto it for a bit, at least until you're old enough to make your own decision about keeping it or moving on."

I'd like that. I'd like that very much. As much as I want to believe I don't need this place to remember Mom, I'm still not ready to lose it, especially at the same time I'm going to university and starting a new chapter in my life. It will be nice to have one thing remain consistent, a place to come to and *breathe* when everything around me is changing.

"Does that mean I'm not in trouble for coming here this week?" I ask hopefully, putting on my most angelic-looking face.

"Oh no, you're in trouble. I'm going to subject you to daily video calls to make sure you are where you say you are and with whom you say you're with. You're going to get so sick of my name popping up on your phone screen everyone will ask why you're constantly groaning at your phone."

I try and fail to hide the way my lips pull up at the corners. Daily video calls with my dad? I think I can live with that. "That's a cruel and unusual punishment, Dad."

"It's a punishment befitting the crime."

"There's just one tiny problem with that," I say, turning sheepish. "My phone is sitting somewhere at the bottom of the lake."

Dad groans, but he's not as upset as he would've been before this talk. "Well then, it's a two-part punishment. The first part is you'll have to do a bunch of boring paperwork for me to earn a new phone. The second part will be my annoying calls."

"Fine. Only if my friends and I can finish out the rest of the week here."

He lets out a disbelieving laugh. "Are you haggling with me right now?"

"Come on, Dad. We brought a week's worth of food, and I think everyone needs this time together just as much as I do."

He debates it, but I know the answer before he says it. "Fine. But no more lying to me. We're going to need to be honest with each other if we're going to make this new living situation work." He pauses before gently adding, "I didn't know how to raise a daughter; I never expected to be in this position. I know there are things I could've and should've done better, and I promise to try to do better for you, but I need you to promise you'll reach out and tell me what you need. I can't become the perfect father overnight, and I most likely never will, but if you're honest with me, if we . . . if we talk more openly about stuff, then that's a great first step."

I didn't know how much I needed to hear those words until heat pricks at my eyes. It means a lot to me that he's trying, despite the fact that his teenage daughter coming to him about her problems freaks him out just as much as it does me. Neither of us has ever attempted to sit down and have an open conversation, but now the invitation has been formally shared. I can't promise we'll be perfect or that I'll always want to share my feelings—or even know how to—but I can promise to try.

"I won't lie to you if you won't hide things from me."

"Deal," he says. We stand at the same time, and when he opens his arms, I go into them willingly.

I *may* be growing up, and I may be more independent than most people, but I'll always need my dad. Moving away to Western is going to be hard, but at least I'll have my daily punishment to look forward to now.

We walk back to the house, and he keeps his arm around my back.

"Is there anything I should know about before I step in there?" he asks as we get closer to the house. "There's not a bunch of giant, inflatable, flailing-arm men wearing bras for some reason again, are there?"

I laugh, remembering the shock on his face before growing sheepish. "There may be a human-sized hole in the drywall in the living room."

"What?!"

"But don't worry! I know a great carpenter who can fix it, no charge."

TWENTY-TWO

Day 5 of Muskoka

Olivia

I don't get to talk to Dylan once we get inside. I barely get a bag of ice for him before everyone else comes piling in, harassing me with questions about Alessio. Then Alessio himself comes in, and an awkward silence falls over the house.

"I—uh," he starts awkwardly. "Jenna's dad said it's too late to drive home and to leave in the morning, so . . ."

We all look at him, no one volunteering to speak first. I certainly have nothing else to say to him, and I don't care if he stays or goes as long as he doesn't try to talk to me or Dylan or start any more problems. In the years we've been together, I've never seen Alessio get in a fight. He hates confrontation, sometimes even refusing to tell a waitress she got his order wrong, so I'm still unsure where that punch came from. Everyone else saw it, too, heard the whole confrontation go down, and now everyone knows we've been broken up this whole time. But instead of feeling mortified like I thought I would, I feel another weight lift from my chest, especially since no one is looking at me with pity. They're too busy sending daggers with their eyes at Alessio, probably trying to decide whether to kick him out or let him stay for the night.

Fletcher sets an armful of beer cans down. "We're going to make sure the bonfire is out like Mr. McAndrews said. You guys . . . uh . . ." He looks between me, Dylan, and Alessio. "Bye."

Then he's gone, taking Robbie and Kyle with him.

Thankfully, Elena, ever the polite host, steps up. "I'll find you a spare blanket and pillow for the couch. We'll have to shift sleeping arrangements for Jenna's dad first, so I'll get to it." She turns to look at me. "And let's get your boot back on before you make the sprain worse."

With an excuse to leave, I follow Elena to the stairs, pausing to send Dylan a questioning look. He nods his head, telling me it's okay to leave him alone with Alessio, and I figure he wants a chance to talk to him alone. Martina sends Alessio a death glare that has his eyes widening before she follows us.

We're only halfway up the stairs before Elena pauses and gently tells me, "You were always too good for him anyway."

"Thanks, Elena." I'm starting to realize that too.

By the time everyone gets inside and we get settled, it's past 1:00 a.m. and I don't get to talk to Dylan. Elena managed the sleeping arrangements so Uncle Alex can have the primary room to himself. Jenna gives Dylan her bed, and she and I sleep with Elena and Martina in the queen beds. I sleep with Elena, who seemed like a safer bet than Martina the sleep kicker, especially since my ankle is fragile right now. But Elena really *does* talk in her sleep, and I wake up multiple times thinking she's asking me something when she's really just sleep-talking.

Alessio is already gone in the morning by the time I come downstairs, and I'm grateful. There's nothing left to be said between us, especially not in front of a huge group of people and my uncle.

I'm sitting at a table outside under the canopy in the back while everyone is either waking up or rummaging through the kitchen for breakfast.

Footsteps approach, and two cups of coffee are set onto the table. "Hey," Jenna greets me, pulling out the chair beside me before sinking into it. "How are you feeling?"

I take the coffee, letting the mug warm my hands even though it's already a beautiful morning. "All right. My ankle is itchy." I gesture in the distance to the dock, where Uncle Alex is sitting with a coffee, watching the glittering lake. "Why is your dad here?"

He almost never comes up with us, not even when my mom and sisters come up too. And he seemed upset last night.

"He's leaving in a bit." Jenna stirs her coffee. "But we weren't really allowed to come this weekend or throw any parties, and I did both. He listed this place for sale."

I almost spit out my drink. "What? He's going to sell?"

"Well, not anymore. We talked it all out, and it's been sorted. He sold the house, though, and he's kind of moving to Vancouver, so I don't really have anywhere to go on breaks now . . ."

She doesn't offer any more information, and she's making that face that tells me she doesn't want to talk about it, so I don't push her. But her actions this week finally start making sense. Jenna's *never* liked being alone since her mom died; anytime her dad went on business trips, she'd stay at my house or have me come over for the weekend if she didn't stay with a friend. All of the transitions happening this summer must've really been messing with her, and I feel bad for not realizing it sooner. Now with her dad in Vancouver and her house sold, she must be feeling even more alone than usual. But Jenna always has my back, and she should know I always have hers. She would've never added that last part to her statement if she didn't already know that.

Casually, to avoid scaring her into running away from an intense heart-to-heart, I say, "Well, since my name was the only one on the lease and I don't have a roommate you despise anymore, there's nothing stopping you from coming to stay with me every once in a while when your classes are lighter."

Her smile is slow, like a realization dawns on her. "I guess you're right. Nothing's stopping me from showing up at your place when I'm bored."

Now that I don't have Alessio to occupy my free time, I wonder if I'll feel lonely, but at least I'll have Jenna's visits to look forward to. "Well, you better come now while you're in undergrad. When you start law school, you'll be too busy and cool for me."

She shakes her head. "I'm already too cool for you and we still hang out."

I fake indignation at her joke, putting my hand on my heart with an outraged gasp and everything.

"No, but seriously," she continues, "I'm not sure I want to go to law school. I was doing it because I thought it would make me . . ." She takes a deep breath, like she's finding the courage to finish her sentence. "Make me feel closer to Mom." She swallows like she's pushing the moment away, and then it's like she never said anything at all. "But I think I'm going to take a few different courses. I might switch to a business degree, maybe even take some hospitality and event planning courses. I hear there are people who would really love me to organize engagement parties and stuff for them. I could totally plan a wedding if I put my mind to it."

Jenna loves throwing parties and bossing people around; she'd be a great event planner. "That's definitely something you could do."

"Right?" she agrees, not bothering to be humble. "And Hari's a carpenter, so I can totally get him to build elaborate setups and champagne walls and stuff." She smiles like she's already imagining the differently themed backdrops before adding, "By the way, when I asked how you were feeling, I meant about the whole Alessio situation."

"I know," I tell her, watching a bird land on a tree branch. "I'm feeling . . . all right." And it's true. I feel fine about everything. Holding onto the hurt and anger was draining, and I already wasted so much of my energy over the last five years thinking about Alessio, I don't want to give him any more of it.

"I'm proud of you for making a firm decision about not taking Alessio back, even though it must have been hard." She pauses, taking a deep breath. "And I'm sorry for claiming you were using Dylan as a replacement boyfriend and for saying you don't make your own decisions. I was going through my own shit and was too hard on you."

"It got me thinking. I don't want to be that person anymore. I don't want to be *someone's girlfriend*. I want to be my own person and *also* have a boyfriend." Two separate things that can be true at the same time. I don't want to lose myself in a relationship or worry about making someone else happy, especially at my own expense. I don't regret my time with Alessio because it's helped me realize who I do and don't want to be, but I don't want to stay stuck in the past either.

Jenna raises a perfect eyebrow. "Do you think you're ready for a boyfriend right now?"

"Hey," a deep voice interrupts, Dylan hesitating between coming closer or leaving us to our conversation.

Jenna abruptly stands and, not subtly at all, announces, "I hear Fletcher and Martina bicker-flirt again. See you later."

"I got one for you," Dylan says as he sits in the chair Jenna vacated. "Who's got two thumbs and is really sorry about how last night played out?"

Like always, I know the answer. But instead I say, "That's not a trivia question."

He finishes anyway, pointing at himself with his thumbs. "This guy."

He's the one who has the red-and-purple bruise blooming on his handsome face, and he's apologizing to me? "You have nothing to be sorry about. I'm sorry for putting you in that position in the first place."

He shakes his head. "Don't apologize. You didn't put me in any position. I was right where I wanted to be . . . with you."

His eyes are deep and soulful, meaning every word. It makes my heart hammer, but still I hesitate. "Dylan . . ."

He jumps in before I have the chance to finish. "Nothing that happened last night changes how I feel about you. Nothing that happened with Alessio changes how I feel about you. I'm in love with you, Livy."

Like the first time I heard it, it steals the breath from my lungs. My voice comes out light and breathy as I ask, "You're going to throw away your friendship with Alessio for me?"

"Fuck Alessio," he says, taking me by surprise. "Our friendship crumbling has nothing to do with you. He's changed since I first knew him, and I'm not liking who he's becoming. Me loving you and my relationship with Alessio are two separate things. I don't want you to place any guilt on yourself when there's absolutely no reason."

I'm almost scared to know the answer, but I ask anyway. "And if I didn't feel anything for you? Would you still feel the same about your relationship with Alessio?"

"Whether you have any feelings for me or not doesn't change the fact that I don't respect Alessio. We talked it out, and I hold no ill will toward him besides the fact that he hurt you, but we're two different people with different values and goals, and we just don't work as friends anymore. People grow apart, it's a natural part of life."

Part of me was worrying that maybe he was choosing me over his friend, and I don't want to be responsible for breaking up a friendship, even if that friend is my ex. But Dylan never lies to me, and he explains himself with so much conviction I have no choice but to believe him.

Dylan sits up, grabbing my hand and intertwining our fingers. "But I know that isn't the case. I know you have feelings for me. Kissing doesn't feel like that between two people who don't have feelings for each other. *This*"—he squeezes my hand, which feels so warm and right at home in his—"doesn't feel this good between two people who don't have feelings for each other."

I open my mouth to interject and voice my fears, but he beats me to it. "And I know you weren't only kissing me to get back at Alessio. You're not like that, Livy."

I look at our hands, his larger one swallowing mine. I was so loyal and obsessed with Alessio, I never considered Dylan as anything more than my friend, and he never did anything to make me suspect his feelings for me. If I were still with Alessio, Dylan would never have told me how he felt, and we never would've explored anything deeper, but that's not the situation we're in right now, so I allow myself to think about Dylan as more than a friend.

He's sweet and supportive and *so* very handsome. He's made me feel seen and understood this whole trip; thinking back, he always has, even when his intentions were strictly friendly. He's always shown up for me, even when no one else did—even when Alessio didn't. I can always count on Dylan to support me, no matter how odd or outlandish my ideas are, like starting an app with no experience. And there's no denying how our kisses made me feel.

"You're right, I do have feelings for you," I admit, my nerves firing just thinking about it, "and they're so strong and real it almost scares me."

Dylan's smile is so big and genuinely happy that I feel guilty for pulling my hand away and adding, "But . . ."

Dylan's smile melts right off his face. "But what?"

I hate letting people down, hate giving them reasons to not like me. But it's time I stop thinking about other people and start making myself the priority. "I've only been single for five days. I don't want to jump right into another relationship. I like you, Dylan, and I have no doubt that you would be an incredible boyfriend and make me so happy, but it wouldn't be fair to either of us to start a relationship before I've had some time to heal and focus on myself."

Dylan's shoulders sink, but he says, "I understand. I just want you to be happy, Livy."

"But that doesn't mean I don't have the world's biggest crush on you, because I do!" I rush to add, because it's the truth and I need him to know it. "I can't ask you to wait for me, that wouldn't be fair, but if you give me some time, maybe a few months to figure myself out while we continue being friends, I'd really love to go on a date with you. Start slow, from the beginning."

I don't want to lose Dylan as my friend—don't want to lose Dylan at all, especially not when I know how good we can be together—but I will respect his decision either way.

Dylan's brilliant smile is back, and I'm filled with relief when he intertwines his fingers with mine again. "I've waited this long for you, what's a couple more months?"

I can't even hide how happy I am, and we stare at each other, smiling like two kids with huge crushes on each other, even though the word *crush* sounds too weak to describe what we have.

Jenna opens the sliding door, calling out, "Hey, we made some breakfast pizza. There's one slice of Hawaiian left, and Kyle is eyeing it."

"Don't you dare touch that last slice, Kyle!" I yell, watching through the window as Kyle snatches his hands back from the tray. "That one is mine."

"Let's go get it then." Dylan laughs, helping me up and handing me my crutches. We walk into the house together, and everyone is standing around the kitchen island, pizza slices in hand. It's a bit too early for pizza, but one of the great things about the cottage is that we can make our own rules about when is and isn't too early for pizza.

Jenna hands me a plate, and I pluck the last slice of still steaming Hawaiian from the tray. It's *delicious*, the best slice of pizza I've ever had.

"So are you two dating now or what?" Fletcher asks, pointing at me and Dylan, and I almost cough up my crust.

"*Fletcher,*" Martina scolds, "have a filter for goodness' sake."

"We will be soon. There's no rush," Dylan answers anyway, giving me a wink from across the kitchen, and my heart rate picks up as I smile at him.

"But you know who *is* dating?" Hari announces, slinging an arm around Jenna. "I know. You'd never believe someone as handsome as me would lower the bar so much for—*ow!*" He rubs his side where Jenna elbowed him, but she's smiling innocently.

"Why can't that be us?" Fletcher asks Martina, looking ridiculous as he pouts at her.

She swats him with the back of her hand.

He releases a pained groan as he rubs his side. "That's not the part I was referring to."

She laughs regardless, and so do we, picking at the remnants of pizza toppings still lying on the trays.

Everything is changing, but at the same time, it's not. We're exactly where we're meant to be, and as Jenna picks a chunk of pineapple off my pizza and throws it in the air directly into Hari's open mouth, creating a food-to-mouth tossing contest, contentedness settles over me.

We may all be going in different directions while tackling this next stage of our lives, but we're doing it together.

ACKNOWLEDGMENTS

Thank you to you—the reader. This Best Vacation Ever series has been so much fun to write and share with you, and I'm so appreciative that you picked up my work and came on this journey with me. I hope you had the *best time ever*.

Thank you to my wonderful editor, Fiona Simpson. This book was a frantic mess of arrows and point form notes with question marks before you came along with your calm insights and guidance. Thank you for putting up with my chaotic mess and helping make this book shine, I couldn't have done it without you. Thank you to my copy editor and proofreaders for making sure this book is perfect for print. Also, thank you to Deanna McFadden and the entire Wattpad Books team for championing me and my work and getting it out there in the world. Austin, thank you for everything you do, especially for putting up with my frantic emails and putting out the fires.

Thank you to my parents, Bruno and Carmela, for being the best parents ever. Thank you to my entire family and all my friends for being so incredible and supportive.

Thank you to Mario for being the most supportive fiancé in the history of fiancés. And thank you to his entire family for being so amazing.

SJ, Lauren, Ken, Mason, Van, Cayleigh, Deb—you're amazing. Thanks for sprinting with me and being awesome writerly friends who are always there for me. Special shout-out to Jordan Lynde for keeping me sane while I wrote, rewrote, then rewrote this book again. I wouldn't have gotten anything done if I didn't have you sprinting with me and helping me choose just the right words or distracting me with Astarion GIFs. I'm so grateful we're friends.

As always, I'm being that person and thanking Leo. You're my bestest pal.

ABOUT THE AUTHOR

Jessica Cunsolo's young adult series With Me has amassed over 140 million reads on Wattpad since she posted her first story, *She's With Me*, on the platform in 2015. It has won a Watty award, been published in multiple languages, and is in development with Wattpad WEBTOON Studios. Jessica lives just outside of Toronto, where she enjoys the outdoors and transforming her real-life awkward situations into plotlines for her viral stories. You can find her on Instagram @jesscunsolo, on Twitter @avaviolet17, or on Wattpad @avaviolet.

ONE

One Week to Cuba

Lori

That guy is staring at me, I'm sure of it. He follows my movements as I squat, the heavy bar resting on my shoulders. We're the only ones in this section of the gym, where the long barbells and squat racks are, and he's directly behind me. I can see him in the mirrors that cover the walls, not even trying to hide the fact that he's a creep.

Stop it! I want to yell, but my voice is caught in my throat.

His gaze roams freely over my legs and butt as I stand to set the bar back on the rack. His eyes meet mine in the mirror and hold them.

You're being a perv! is what I want to shout. My best friend Faye would, if she were here, but she hates the gym. Faye wouldn't stand rooted to the spot in horror, too timid to tell him off.

I take a sip of water, breaking eye contact first, and inwardly curse myself. Thankfully, he reracks his weights, and I exhale in relief. But as he passes me, his hand grazes my butt, so fast it's like it barely happened. I jerk my head to glare at him, but he smirks at me and continues walking to the free weights. As he lifts a dumbbell with the same hand that touched me, the large lion tattoo on his bicep flexes, taunting me.

I should say something to him. *I should say something, I should say something,* just say something, *Lori!*

Clutching my metal water bottle so tightly my knuckles turn white, I march over to him, my pulse beating louder and louder in my ears with every step I take.

"Hey!" I exclaim in a voice that doesn't sound like mine. "Quit staring at me!"

The guy faces me, his eyes dropping to check me out before a corner of his mouth lifts. "Not staring, just enjoying the view you're so generously providing."

My face burns and I sputter as I try to think of something to say. Faye would think of the comeback to end all comebacks, but I only stand there, my pulse racing with anger and embarrassment.

"If you're gonna stand there, at least make yourself useful and hand me that fifty-pounder over there." The guy gestures to the dumbbell rack, that smirk still in place. "Bend over while you do it though, you're so good at that."

My mouth opens and closes once before I spin on my heel and speed walk as far away from him as I can possibly get. His chuckle follows me like a taunt, burning in my brain even when I can't hear him anymore.

This is why I never say anything. I've just made it ten times worse than if I'd ignored him. What if he thinks it's okay to come up to me now that I spectacularly failed to stand up for myself? I wish I knew exactly what to say to put him in his place. I scrub the spot he touched with my own hand as if that can erase the memory.

Still fuming at myself and the stupid lion tattoo guy, I refill my bottle, staring at the faded, cracked Grant's Gym logo painted on the too-white wall above the water fountain. The light overhead is so bright, like a spotlight, and the air's stuffy and rank, permeated with the smell of sweat. The second my bottle is filled, I dart all the way to the front of the gym near the large windows, and as far from Pervy Guy as possible. A few regulars wave as they see me, but I keep my head down until I reach the leg machines. I know it's rude, but I'm afraid that if I talk, I might cry.

Taking a deep breath, I try to let go of what happened so I can focus on my workout. I adjust my headphones and change the playlist to a Spanish hits one before placing my water bottle on the floor. When I look up, I see Mr. Blue Eyes; his eyes are so bright they make the blue of my own seem dull in comparison. My pulse speeds up, and I force myself to stop gawking at him as he talks to some guys by the benches.

I've never had the nerve to start a conversation with him. Faye tells me I should, but I'm always lost for words when he's in my vicinity. I don't like staring at him because I don't want to act like the creepy guys that stare at me, but he's so . . . wow. He's not the model type of pretty like Faye's brother, Adam. Mr. Blue Eyes is a rugged, manly type of handsome. I like to imagine he uses his muscles for chopping wood, wrestling bears, leading his men into battle, or some other ridiculous romance novel stereotype.

I busy myself with adjusting the weights on the leg press, then peek over at the place I last saw him, in a totally nonstalkerish way. He's not there, and my heart sinks. That sucks. Maybe today would've been the day I got up the nerve to speak to him. I bend down to pick up my water bottle, and when I stand, I spot him. It's like he's moving in slow motion as he runs a hand through his thick black hair, pushing it off his forehead. He's like a walking shampoo commercial.

As I'm reminding myself not to gawk, his head shifts, and we're looking straight at each other, with eye contact and everything. There's a burning heat in my stomach when he smiles. Is he smiling at *me*? I peer behind me in case he's looking at someone else, but no one's there.

He's smiling at me.

I return the smile, and I hope he can't tell that I'm squealing inside. It must be all the encouragement he needs because he's in motion. His long legs striding. Right. Toward. Me.

Oh crap. Ohcrapohcrapohcrap. What should I do? What would Faye do? She's the master of flirting and can make guys fall to their knees begging for her to give them the time of day, and why isn't she here when I need her?

Because I spent all that time panicking about how I should act and what I should do with my arms, the result is that I stand there staring at him with my mouth open until he reaches me.

He stops right in front of me. Smiles. His lips move. He's saying something, but all I hear is Maluma singing in my ears. He looks down at the leg press and back at me, his lips moving again. He must be asking if I'm done with the machine.

I frantically rip out one earbud. "Yes," I say, flinching at my excessive volume.

His eyebrows draw together, as if confused why I'm still awkwardly standing in front of the machine he wants to use. This is the closest I've ever been to him, and I'm positively failing at my one chance to make him fall in love with me.

He opens his mouth to say something, probably to ask what my issue is, but before I can embarrass myself any further, I turn around while popping my earbud back in, and speed walk the hell away from him.

"Maybe today would've been the day I got up the nerve to speak to him," I mimic myself in my head and roll my eyes at my sheer

stupidity. Yeah, because talking to him went real well, *and* I gave him my leg press machine before I even used it.

Ugh. What is *up* with me? I should quit while I'm ahead and leave now, but I've had such a shitty workout today I've totally wasted the gas it took to get here, and that's not exactly cheap, at least not cheap enough that the money I get from lifeguarding can comfortably cover it all. Maybe just one more exercise to make the drive here worth it, then I'll head out. Back extensions always make me feel strong, and that's exactly what I need after failing to stand up for myself with one guy or flirt with the other.

The equipment is on a forty-five-degree angle, so I lean on it and adjust the pads on my hips. Then I bend down over it so my head is close to the floor and my bottom is in the air and bring myself up with a straight back. Even though I'm a little sore, I decide to hold extra weights to really ramp up the intensity.

On rep six, I lift back up to peek at Mr. Blue Eyes. As if he feels my gaze, he looks in my direction. I dip back down to do another rep, and when I pull myself back up, I realize that he's not looking *at* me, he's looking at something behind me. When I go back down, I check to see what he's looking at, and even upside-down, I recognize Pervy Gym Guy with the lion tattoo behind me. Then there's a flash.

Blood rushing in my ears, I straighten and stumble off the machine. The weights slip out of my hands and land on the padded floor with a muffled thud. Pervy Gym Guy is looking at his phone, which he just used to take a picture of my butt.

My heart sinks and my vision blurs. I don't know what to do; I feel so disgusted and violated. I want to cry or slap that pervert or run away and hide. I want to yell at him until his head explodes. Destroy his phone with a barbell. Instead, I stand here helplessly, staring daggers at him, without doing any of those things, without grabbing his phone and bashing him with it.

Before I can blink, Mr. Blue Eyes is in Pervy Gym Guy's face, and Mr. Blue Eyes's arms are gesturing wildly.

I rip my headphones out so I can hear what he's saying.

"—the fuck raised you? I've never seen something so disrespectful. Who the fuck do you think you are to treat a human being like she's only here for your disgusting lonely jerk-off session later tonight?" Rage radiates off Mr. Blue Eyes, I can feel it from all the way over here.

"Whoa, chill out, dude. She's hot—"

"Chill out?!" Mr. Blue Eyes is bigger than Pervy Gym Guy, and gets even closer to him, making Pervy Gym Guy shrink into himself.

I glance around the gym, and *everyone* is looking at us. Looking at *me*.

My breathing turns shallow, and my head spins. I *hate* being the center of attention. I hate causing a scene. I hate everyone staring at me.

I don't know what happens next, because I scramble out of there and into the changing room before more people come over to judge me, to get a look at the girl too weak to speak up for herself.

Why violate someone like that while they're in the gym? This is the second time in one day I've had an issue with that guy. I should've said something harsher the first time instead of floundering the moment he talked back and embarrassed me. I should report him to management. I should tell Faye so she can rip him a new one. I should *do something*.

Throwing all my things into my bag without bothering to zip it up, I grab my car keys, faltering as I exit the changing room. People are looking at me. A group of girls in the corner are whispering and gawking. A bunch of guys close to them are doing the same, and one points at me. My breath halts. I'll tell management another time. I need to *leave*. I need to get out of here right *now*.

Racing through the gym with my head down, I'm almost at the door when a voice behind me calls out, "Hey, wait up!"

Even though everything seems hazy, I spot Mr. Blue Eyes jogging toward me in the reflection of the glass door. I should've known it was him calling out to me. Even his voice is perfect. Deep and silky.

If I was too embarrassed to talk to him before, no way do I want to face him now, after he had to start a fight with a stranger because I froze, too worried about other people staring to demand Pervy Gym Guy be brought to justice.

The cool evening air hits me as I exit the gym, the setting sun turning the sky shades of pink and purple. I inhale the summer freshness, my heartbeat already steadier. It must be around eight, and the calmness of the night helps me clear my head. I don't think anyone followed me, so I relax my pace, strolling along the side of the redbrick exterior.

"Hey! Hold on a second!"

A quick glance behind me reveals Mr. Blue Eyes jogging my way. He doesn't have any of his belongings with him; it looks like he ran out when I did.

My stomach drops. I increase my pace, lengthening the distance between us, and right before I cross the street, the end of my mortification only seconds away, I stumble and drop my bag and keys. I sense him gaining on me, and I need to get to my car before that happens, so I hastily swoop down to pick up my stuff, not looking back but knowing he's close.

Please let me stop embarrassing myself in front of him!

I straighten and step off the curb to cross the street in a rush.

A few things happen simultaneously. That deep voice yells something much louder and more urgent than before. A horn blares, and I whip my head around. Headlights blind me. A force knocks into me, taking my breath away as I'm tackled to the ground. The car I stepped in front of continues harmlessly along, the driver not even stopping to see if it hit me or not.

I take a shaky breath. I almost got hit by a car! I'm such a coward that in my haste to run away from Mr. Blue Eyes, I walked right into the path of an oncoming car!

"Are you okay? Man, you gave me a scare," comes his voice from under my shaking body.

Wait. Under me?

I finally tune in to my surroundings. I'm lying on top of Mr. Blue Eyes on the grass, my face mere inches away from his. His arms are iron bands wrapped around my waist after pulling me out of danger, and our legs are tangled together. I'm pressed so close to him that despite everything, I notice that although his eyes are blue, there's a tiny ring of hazel around his pupils.

"You *are* okay, right?" he presses again.

Oh my goodness! I'm still lying on top of him staring at him like a total creeper.

I scramble off and sit up. My voice is thick, and I physically can't bring myself to make direct eye contact with him. "Yeah, I'm fine." I clear my throat as I assess my limbs. "Are you?"

He sits up beside me and dusts off his hands. "Yeah, but geez. Way to kill a guy's ego. You'd rather jump in front of a moving car than talk to me."

That makes me look right at him. He's still gorgeous, even with the ruffled hair. "That's—that's not what happened!"

He's smiling at me, and his teeth are so white and straight I'm 90 percent sure his dentist actively practices witchcraft.

"Of course it isn't." That smile never falters. "Not to lecture you or anything, but you should probably look both ways before crossing the street."

"Yes, thank you for refreshing me on first-grade skills. I promise

I don't make jumping in front of cars a habit." I pick up the things that have fallen out of my bag, and he helps. I die a little inside when he gathers a bunch of tampons and deposits them into my gym bag.

"Guess I'll have to take your word for it," he jokes, helping me up and holding my keys out.

I take them, and when our fingers brush, electricity zips all the way up my arm. "Yeah, well . . . thanks for saving my life, I guess. And for what happened in there with Pervy Gym Guy."

He lifts an eyebrow at the nickname, and I don't realize I said it out loud until it's too late.

"He deleted the pictures, and I don't think he'll be coming to Grant's anymore," he says.

Pictures? As in plural?

Something on my face must alert him because he quickly adds, "Some people are just disgusting."

I give him a small smile, genuinely grateful for his interference *twice* today, but still embarrassed, especially about jumping in front of a car. My face is so hot I'm sure it's beet red.

"Yeah, thanks for that." I back away toward my car. I need to escape so I can die of embarrassment alone, the way you're supposed to. "And thanks again for the whole car thing. I guess I'll see you around."

Before he can say another word, I whirl around and run all the way to my Honda.

There is no way in hell I can ever show my face around here again.

———

While the incident from the gym weighs heavily on my mind, I don't have time to dwell on it, because as soon as I get home, I'm summoned to dinner. While everything today *sucked*, I have bigger problems now because tonight, for the first time in seventeen years, I'm going to disobey my parents. I've had nightmares about this exact moment but here I am, sitting at the mahogany dinner table that's been in our family for generations, about to tell them I'm ending three generations of Robertson tradition. Mom watches me fidget as I tug at the collar of my shirt. The grandfather clock behind her ticks in time with each beat of my heart.

"Something wrong with your dragon roll, Lori?" she asks, placing more on one of the heirloom china plates handed down from her great-grandmother. In the center of each, there's a hand-painted bluebird in mid-flight. I never thought I'd be so envious of a plate.

"Nope, it's great," I say, stuffing a piece into my mouth to prove my point. It tastes like ash, and I take a sip of water to wash it down. We've had sushi three times this week because the Japanese restaurant is open late enough to cater to Mom's schedule, but that's not the issue.

"Have you gotten your summer work schedule yet?" Dad asks me, refilling my crystal glass.

"Yes. They sent it two weeks ago when school ended."

Since I turned fifteen, I've been a part-time lifeguard at the community center and occasionally teach swimming to local kids. It's not the most exciting job, but better than being forced to go to summer science camp.

"Email it to me," Dad says. "We can plan a day around it to tour the campus again. Plus, I've been eyeing some volunteer opportunities at the hospital I think you'd be great for. Nothing major, mostly in the office, but it's important for you to get some experience in a hospital setting."

This is it. The opening I've been waiting for. A bead of sweat drips down my forehead, and I wipe it away. "Actually . . . about that . . . I . . ." *Deep breaths, Lori.* "I don't think that's a good idea."

Creepily in sync, my parents' heads swing over to look at me, and I shrink into my seat.

My parents, Paul and Mary Robertson, are both heart surgeons at the top of their field, and all my life I've heard about how I'm going to follow in their footsteps and be an amazing surgeon like them. Like their parents. Like their parents' parents. We've watched educational television after dinner, had conversations about tricuspid valves and atrial fibrillations, and they've even made me practice suturing supermarket chicken. I've been told that I was going to be a surgeon since before I even knew what a surgeon *was*. So, for them, my life is going exactly as they planned, especially once they saw my early acceptance letter to Life Sciences, one of the hardest programs to get into at the University of Toronto. They even googled "surgeon family photoshoots" to get inspiration for all the cute photo Christmas cards we'd send out each year in matching scrubs, with stethoscopes dangling from our necks. The thought terrifies me.

"What were you thinking?" Mom asks, setting her chopsticks down to fix me with a stare. Her gaze is intimidating. Her eyes are the exact same shade of blue as mine, but they're surrounded with lines from years of stress.

I've rehearsed this speech many times in my head. "It's not a big deal, but before I become a doctor, I think I should have more real-world experience." I sip my water, peering at them over the edge of my glass. The fact that they're not smashing their spicy salmon rolls to bits or grounding me for eternity must mean I'm doing a good job, so I push ahead, a tiny bit more confident. "I want to defer my admission to next year, so I can take this year off to backpack through Europe."

Okay, maybe I wussed out on the whole *I don't think I want to be a surgeon* announcement, but baby steps.

The air thickens as their silence persists. All I hear is the throbbing of my pulse in my skull and the incessant ticking of the grandfather clock. Right before I crack from the overwhelming quiet, Mom and Dad glance at each other, then erupt into laughter.

"Yeah. Good one, Lori," Mom says, then sips her wine.

My voice is shaky when I say, "I'm not joking. That's what I want to do."

Mom sets her glass down, then brushes aside some nonexistent crumbs on the white tablecloth. Dad's face is unreadable. "I wouldn't be alone, obviously," I add, trying to convince them before they shut it down outright. "I've done a lot of research. There are lots of gap year programs online. Some of them even give college credit. Studies show that students who defer for a year end up being more successful at university. I've printed out some sample itineraries for you to look at. Here's the best part, I have more than enough money saved up to pay for it myself, *and* I'll earn more lifeguarding this summer."

Mom sighs as if praying for the patience to deal with me, and my breath catches in my throat. "That all sounds magical and wonderful, but you know most people who take a year off don't return to school," she says.

"That's not true—"

Dad tosses his linen napkin over his plate. "Look, Lor, getting an education is more important right now than traveling. You'll have plenty of time for that once you finish med school." He points to the picture of his mother, Lorraine Robertson, sitting on the fireplace mantel. It's in a heavy golden frame, and he touches it every time he passes by. "Your grandmother would be so proud of you. You know how hard she worked to become one of the first female surgeons in Canada, and now you're carrying on her legacy."

My stomach twists. I've always felt all this pressure to be like her.

I've been hearing about how hard she worked, and how accomplished, smart, and passionate she was since I was old enough to hold her heavy picture frame in my little toddler hands. She died before I was born, but she's been a constant part of my life, always around, always haunting me, her eyes following me as I walk by, accusing me. *Why don't you want to carry on my legacy? Why are you such a disappointment?* I try to avoid this room when I can, avoid a picture that should hold no power over me but somehow controls my fate. But since we eat all our meals here, that's virtually impossible unless I snag the seat facing away from the fireplace.

"Don't you think I deserve a little break before I hop into ten or more years of schooling?" I plead, confidence draining from my voice. It's a losing battle, and the room is closing in on me.

"You have been working hard," Mom says, "but you need to do well on the MCAT or you won't be accepted into medical school after your undergrad, and all of that hard work will have been for nothing. This is not the time to slack off, Lori, not even for a single summer. This is a time for working, volunteering, and studying."

I swallow hard and weave my hands together under the table to stop them from shaking. The rest of my life looms in front of me, so I make one last-ditch attempt. "But what if I don't want to go to med school?" I blurt, shocked as the words leave my mouth before I can stop them.

"Of course you're going to medical school! It's what you're good at. It's what the Robertsons are good at," Dad declares, his words settling on my chest like a weight, meaning my second attempt to stand up for myself today has gone just as terribly as the first one at the gym.

"Now, pass the avocado rolls," Mom says, ending the conversation about my future just like that.

TWO

Six Days to Cuba

Faye

I FaceTime Lori twice before she picks up.

"Finally!" I exclaim, even though her screen is dark and I can't see her. "I have *news* and it's *huge*! Can you come over?"

"Faye?" she groans. There's rustling on the other side of the phone, and then a light turns on. She's in bed. "It's late, I have work tomorrow. What's going on?"

"It's only like nine p.m., grandma. You need to come here. I have news!" Lori and I do everything together. We've been best friends since ninth grade, but sometimes her responsible nature gets in the way of my fun.

"Last time you said you had 'news,' it was that Jenna McAndrews got highlights that you thought 'washed her out.'"

"They totally did." That was when Jenna and Adam were dating, so Lori got to see them firsthand when she walked past the pair of them in my kitchen.

Lori rolls onto her side, her eyes half open. "Well, I can't come, so tell me the news."

I can barely hold in my excitement. My smile takes up almost my whole portion of the screen. "Ray's appendix burst today, and they rushed him to the hospital! Isn't that great?"

Now Lori sits up in bed and rubs her eyes. Even half asleep, she's gorgeous. Her brown hair doesn't even stick up in every direction like mine does in the mornings.

"That sounds awful," she says. "Why are you acting like we've won the lottery?"

I was going to ease her into it, but I just can't hold it back anymore. "Adam is letting us come to Cuba with him next week!" I blurt.

She's silent for a moment. "Are you saying we're invited to Cuba with your hot older brother and his friends? What does that have to do with Ray's appendix?"

I huff. I wish we could just speed up this whole explanation thing and get right to the jumping-up-and-down-with-excitement part, but Lori is practical.

"Okay, first, *ew*. Adam is not hot. His friends are, but he's an ogre."

In both the literal and figurative terms of the word. He's mean, on top of being the uglier of the two of us, at least in my opinion.

He's only fourteen months older than me, so he's only a grade ahead. But if you didn't know we're related, you'd never realize it since he barely blinks at me in the halls. Even so, all through high school, girls have come up to me to say that Adam is hot and ask me to put in a good word, which is annoying and useless since Adam pretends I don't exist.

Adam and his friends just finished their first year of university and are celebrating by going away on an all-inclusive tropical vacation. I've been wanting to go on vacation forever, but my parents wouldn't let me go without them unless Adam comes, too, and he would rather die than voluntarily go to Cuba with me. I'd pleaded with him to let me and Lori come, but he refused, adamant that it was a guys-only, no-little-sisters-allowed trip. Nothing's swayed him, and I haven't had high hopes because Adam's never done anything nice for me. Desperate, I was about to offer to do all his chores for the year, but thankfully I didn't go that far because it all worked out.

I prop my phone up against my pillows so she can still see me while I sort through the piles of clothes I've dumped onto my bed. The trip is in exactly six days, and I need to figure out what to wear.

To Lori, I say, "Since Ray can't go to Cuba, his brother Freddy felt guilty going and canceled. That completely screws over Adam and his friends since they were getting a group rate. It's so last-minute that no one else can come, and they already had to ask Dylan's cousin to come to cover Eli's cancelation. So now there are two free spots! Adam can either sit around with his dick in his hand or let us take their place!"

I shriek and do a little dance on the bed, and she holds the phone farther away to escape my excited sounds.

I find my laptop under the mess of clothes and wake it from sleep mode. "I'm emailing you the information now. I know how your parents are so they can totally call mine, and they'll answer all their questions. We have to buy the tickets quickly though, but *we're going to Cuba!*"

I'm so preoccupied with forwarding her all the information that I don't realize she's quiet until she clears her throat.

"Um, Faye? I don't think I can come."

"What?" I dive for my phone and hold it as close to my face as possible to see her better. "Why can't you come?"

Lori chews on her bottom lip. I know that look, and I clench the phone tighter in my hand.

"My parents just finished telling me how this summer is for studying, working, and volunteering only."

"So?" I exclaim. Lori's parents have such a tight hold on her, it makes me appreciate my mom and dad's relaxed take on parenting even more. Lori's lucky I'm around to force her to get out occasionally, or she'd be locked in a tower, wilting away, studying until she's thirty. "It's a *week*, not the whole summer!"

Lori frowns and looks away from the camera. "I don't know, Faye. I really want to come . . . I'll try to talk to them."

This can't be happening. The stars have aligned to allow us to go on this trip, and I cannot allow Lori's superstrict parents to ruin it!

"I'll come over and convince them. I'll get my dad to come as well. That worked last time when we went to Niagara for the weekend. You *have* to come, Lori. At least look at the emails I sent you."

She sets her phone on her bed and gets up, and I hear her shuffle around her room. Once she's back, she props her phone on what I assume is her computer screen so I can still see her. "Before I bring it up to my parents, are you sure Adam's letting us come? Or did he just say 'maybe' and you interpreted it as 'pack your bags'?"

"Lori. We're *G-O-I-N-G*." I spell the word out for her. "He had a bunch of conditions, but I have the confirmed itinerary in my hands as we speak." I flap the stapled pages in front of the camera before pressing it to my nose and audibly inhaling. I sigh in contentment. "Smells like suntan oil and the ocean."

She laughs, her mood lightening. "You're ridiculous. What were the conditions?"

"Oh, I wasn't really paying attention. I'm sure it was the usual 'don't embarrass me, I don't want to see you the whole trip' blah blah blah." I fall back to lie on my bed. "Kellan's coming."

It's an effort to not start daydreaming about Kellan Reyes.

"Obviously Kellan's going." She hesitates. "Does he know you're going?"

Kellan is Adam's best friend, who I'm always around since Adam's friends are always over. Though I've known Dylan the longest, Kellan is my favorite. Kellan and I even hang out without Adam all the time, and it's in a totally non-datey way even when it's just the two of us. But when Adam has his friends over and if he's in a good mood—which is rare—he lets me hang out with them. I'm naturally flirty and flirt with everyone, and so does Kellan, so Adam thinks he has nothing to worry about.

Key word: *thinks*.

Because a few weeks ago, I slept with Kellan.

Twice.

Adam doesn't know, and never will, since Kellan and I swore to never tell anyone. Well, anyone except Lori obviously. She's my best friend, so when I say, *I won't tell anyone*, what I really mean is *Lori and I won't tell anyone*.

I sigh and shake my head to rid myself of images of Kellan. "I don't know. He hasn't messaged me about it. Do you think it'll be awkward?"

Lori's full lips stretch into a thin smile, and I can tell she's trying not to laugh. "Faye. It's you. It's almost impossible to embarrass you; Do you even possess the gene for that emotion?"

"You're right. I'm going to have fun either way. Get me a hot vacation fling," I say.

"Geez, Faye, we're sharing a room, right? I don't want to hear any of your sex noises!"

"That means you're coming! *Yes!*"

"I'll talk to my parents," she says, lifting her phone properly up to her face as I hear her laptop click shut.

"Good," I say. "And don't worry about the sex noises. I'll put the 'do not disturb' sign on the door." I chuckle, leaving her to decide whether I'm joking or not.

"Great. Can't wait to sit on the floor in the hallway, waiting for your booty call to leave."

"You're such a team player."

Lori jumps and lowers the phone, leaving me with a perfect view of her ceiling.

"Lori, what are you doing up? I thought you said you had a headache and were going to sleep?" Her mom asks from what I'm assuming is the doorway to her room.

"I am," she replies before holding the phone up to her face. She's chewing her lip again. "I'll talk to you tomorrow, Faye."

"Okay, bye!" I say, keeping it simple in case her mom is still standing there.

As soon as I hang up, I immediately text her: *Make sure you're convincing! We need to go!*

I'm going to Cuba! With Kellan. He's going to be shirtless practically all week. We're going to be around each other on the beach, in the pool, at the club . . . All. Week.

I squeal into my pillow.

———

I don't hear any news from Lori that night or the whole next day, but the following day, when I leave my room with wet hair after my shower, a very distinct voice flows up to me. Cracking a smile, I comb my hair with my fingers and bound down the stairs. I almost miss a step when I hear the word *Jenna*.

My brother and his friend Dylan are on the couch, watching some game on television.

"What was that about Jenna?" I ask at the bottom of the stairs.

Neither boy moves his eyes from the television or bothers to acknowledge me.

My nostrils flare and I move to block their view. They shout protests right away.

"You're not getting back with Jenna, right, Adam?" I stare him down as Dylan tries to peer around me.

"What, Faye? Move," Adam says.

I don't move. "Adam!"

"Go to hell," he retorts.

"If you get back together with Jenna, I'm already there."

He exhales heavily and glares at me. "We're not getting back together. Happy?"

I grin at him, plopping down on the couch and squeezing in between him and Dylan. "Extremely."

Adam grunts in annoyance but makes room for me anyway. Dylan drops his tattoo-covered arm over my shoulders and licks my ear.

"Ew!" I shriek, pushing him off me and swiping away the saliva. He just laughs and turns back to the TV.

Besides Kellan, Dylan is Adam's other best friend, and one of my favorites. I've always been close to Dylan, probably because I've known him since I could walk, and sometimes I feel like he treats me more like a little sister than my actual brother does. Adam even once suspected me of wanting to date Dylan because of how close we are, and the mental image of me with a dude that's like my brother almost made me puke. He's never brought it up since, especially since I often announce that Dylan is my favorite "brother," even if we like to flirt because of our personalities.

"So, if you're not getting back together, why were you talking about her?" I ask Adam, not caring that he's actively trying to ignore me.

Adam had been dating Jenna for about two years, until two weeks ago, when she dumped him after we graduated. Like, literally. We had just thrown our caps in the air when my brother went to congratulate her, before he even congratulated me, and she was all, *Oh yeah. We're over.* Not that I care. She tried to make my life a living hell the whole time they were together.

Adam was cagey about the reason and never told me, not that he tells me anything normally, but according to Dylan, the only person Adam confided in, it's because she didn't want to do long distance. She must be using the term very loosely because Adam already goes to the University of Toronto, and she's going to Western U in September, and they're only two hours apart. Unless that was a total bullshit reason that Dylan gave me to stop me from hounding him.

For some reason, my brother was like the golden child at school—everyone loved him, which totally baffles me because he didn't even do anything. He wasn't on any teams or clubs or councils; he just kind of . . . existed. Apparently when he's not too busy being a complete dick, he actually has a sense of humor. Personally, I think he's just a giant, grumpy baby.

Jenna used to *love* that her boyfriend was Adam Murray. I don't know much about their relationship, since Jenna is basically my mortal enemy, but it seemed like Jenna was dating Adam's name, not Adam. She would strut around school wearing his sweaters and be all, *Oh, this old thing? It's just my* boyfriend's. *You know. My boyfriend,* Adam Murray? *Yeah, it's his. And I'm wearing it, because he's my boyfriend.*

Adam doesn't reply, so Dylan volunteers the answer. "She's going to drop off his stuff tonight."

My eyebrows rise to my hairline. "Wow, you actually got her to bring it back. How'd you manage that?"

Adam shrugs, already bored with the entire conversation. "Told her she wasn't getting her stuff until I got mine."

"Wow, ruthless." I yawn.

"Oh, shut up, Faye. I can still be civil."

"She's a bitch and you know it. You know it was her life's mission to make me and Lori miserable, right? I'm your sister! Shouldn't you be all protective and all *no one messes with my little sister but me*?"

"You bothered her just as much as she bothered you." Adam rolls his eyes and checks his phone. "Plus, you and I both know you're completely capable of taking care of yourself. You yell at me any time I say something."

I don't know what he's talking about because he never says anything. "Well, duh, I can take care of myself. But it would be nice if my own blood wasn't sleeping with the enemy!"

"If you were ever in any real trouble, I would've stepped in, even if you'd get mad at me for it."

"Bullshit!"

He would not have. He never has. His doing nothing basically encouraged her to keep being a bitch to me and Lori.

"She's never—"

"Prom," I state, silencing him immediately, because he knows I'm right.

It was no *Carrie* moment with pig's blood or anything, but she still ruined Lori's prom, and Adam was just there all *None of my business*. A girl from school invited a bunch of the girls in our grade over to her house for a pre-prom party, with pictures and appetizers and everything. Jenna was there, and she *literally* pushed Lori into the pool. My running theory is that Jenna saw how gorgeous Lori was and got jealous. She denied it to Adam and said it was an accident, and he believed her.

"It was an accident, they bumped into each other," Adam clarifies. "And it worked out. Lori looked great at prom."

She did, but that was because there were eighteen girls committed to fixing her hair and makeup, and someone even called their mom to deliver a backup dress for Lori to wear.

I scoff. "Well, duh. Lori could wear a paper sack and still be ten times prettier than Jenna."

Adam gets up, clearly sick of getting the third degree. "Jenna will be here in five. Make yourself scarce, Faye."

I jump up beside him. "What? I haven't gotten to say anything to her since the pool incident!" And I have some *very* colorful words to share with her. The only time I saw Jenna after that was at the actual prom, where I couldn't kick her ass because of all the teachers, and then at graduation where, again, there were way too many witnesses.

"Faye, you're—" Adam starts.

"Let's go to Tim's," Dylan interrupts, rising from where he was lounging on the couch and sliding between me and Adam. "I want an Iced Capp. Keep me company, Faye?"

I know exactly what he's doing, and my narrowed eyes tell him that, but he just smiles at me in the lazy way that's all Dylan.

I debate for a moment before relenting. "Fine. But you're buying. And I want a donut."

"Deal," Dylan says, and I don't miss the appreciative nod Adam sends his way when he thinks I'm not looking. Jerk.

I follow Dylan to his car and buckle in as he reverses out the driveway and heads down my quiet street. Before he can argue, I grab his aux cord and plug in my phone to play my music as punishment for siding with Adam.

He groans when a boy band fills the speakers of his car but doesn't protest since he knows I'm not letting him get his cord back.

I look over at Dylan. He's conventionally good-looking. He's half-white Canadian, half Jamaican, with black hair shaved in a fade and eyes just as dark, set against the light brown of his skin. His entire left arm is covered in black-and-white tattoos with the occasional pop of color, which, combined with his height, definitely gives him that badass vibe, even though he's a teddy bear. But I've never been attracted to Dylan. Every time I look at him, I remember the scrawny little kid that pushed my face into my birthday cake when I turned eight, and nine, and ten, *and* eleven. It took me longer than I'm proud to admit to realize he shouldn't be allowed anywhere near me when I blow out my candles.

We pass Jenna's BMW as we turn out of my subdivision, and I scowl.

"He *really* isn't getting back together with her, right?" I ask Dylan.

"Not that I know of," he says without taking his eyes off the road.

"Why did he date her?" I grumble, remembering all the shit she pulled on me over the years. "He knew she hated me. He knew I'd come home from school pissed off about how she started rumors about me or made Lori cry, and he just opened the door to our house and invited her into my safe space. Why would he do that, Dyl?"

"You handled her all right, all things considered," he says, signaling and pulling into the Tim Hortons parking lot. "And she's not terrible. You guys just always butt heads."

"You're supposed to be on my side! Remember when she spread that rumor that I was blowing the PE teacher and almost got him fired and me expelled?"

No one believed me when I said I wasn't, and even Adam and Dylan asked me if it was true. Kellan's the only one who undoubtedly believed me, who sat with me in the principal's office even though he wasn't supposed to be there, telling me stupid jokes to keep me from shaking.

Dylan's lips spread into a thin line. "I'll give you that one. But Adam didn't know it was her who started the rumors, *if* it even was her who started them."

I didn't talk to Adam for like three weeks after he refused to break up with or even reprimand my mortal enemy.

"Why does he hate me?" I ask quietly, more to myself than to Dylan.

Dylan opens his mouth, closes it, then replies, "He doesn't hate you, Faye." But his hesitation says it all.

I slump into my seat as he inches the car forward in the drive-thru line. "Why can't he like me? I'm his sister, but it's like he can't even tolerate being in the same room with me."

He hates hanging out with me, hates having to do anything with me at all. Even Lori's shocked anytime he shows his face when we hang out at my house.

"Is he . . . is he still mad about the Zach O'Sullivan incident?"

Dylan gives an uncomfortable laugh. "I think *incident* isn't a strong enough word for what happened, Faye."

"What happened wasn't my fault," I mumble for what seems to be the millionth time in the last year.

"I know. It takes two to make a relationship start and end. But he did *explicitly ask you* not to get involved with his friend."

"Adam has *lots* of friends! I can't be expected to not date all of them!"

Dylan snorts. "He just doesn't want you to date his *best* friends, in case it ends up like Zach . . . which it did."

I cross my arms and grumble, "Well, Zach was a self-absorbed asshole."

"Maybe," Dylan concedes, "but he was a self-absorbed asshole who was one of Adam's best friends, who now won't even look at him, never mind talk to him."

Zach and I dated for a whole three months before we started fighting more than kissing, and it was over before I knew it. After that, Zach ran the opposite direction from Adam whenever he saw him and stopped inviting him to hang out. He didn't even ask him to come to his nineteenth birthday but invited everyone else.

"Zach still talks to you, Alessio, and Kellan."

Dylan shoots me a look as the car inches forward. "He also didn't fuck our sisters."

I huff in reluctant agreement. "Fine, I'll give you that. But I'm not dating any of his friends right now—" barring secretly sleeping with Kellan twice "—so why does he still hate me?"

"Have you talked to him about it?"

"No. You think Adam and I can have a serious heart-to-heart? You're delusional."

All I've ever wanted was for us to be closer, or at least to be *friends*. Hell, I'd even take him simply stomaching my presence for longer than an hour.

"Well, we'll be in Cuba for an entire week. There's nowhere for him to run."

He's right. We're going to be at a resort in five days. Sure, it's a big resort, but not big enough for him to ignore my existence. Maybe we can connect there. Maybe we can take a step forward in our relationship. It would be better than nothing.

Dylan pulls up to the speaker and lowers his window.

"I'll have an Iced Capp and a jelly-filled donut," I tell him, looking out my window, wondering what Adam and Jenna are talking about.

They broke up. I graduated high school. Maybe Adam and I can have a fresh beginning, and Cuba can kick-start it for us.

DON'T MISS THE NEXT READ FROM
JESSICA CUNSOLO!

The
Blind Date
Agreement

COMING SOON FROM WATTPAD BOOKS!